Gabriel's Eye

Also by C.W. Smith

Fiction
Thin Men of Haddam
The Vestal Virgin Room
Buffalo Nickel
Letters From the Horse Latitudes
Hunter's Trap
Understanding Women

Non-Fiction
Uncle Dad

Gabriel's Eye

by

C.W. Smith

WINEDALE PUBLISHING
Houston

Published by Winedale Publishing Co.

Copyright © 2001 by C.W. Smith
All rights reserved under International and Pan-American Copyright
Conventions.
Published in the United States by Winedale Publishing Co., Houston
Distributed by the Texas A&M University Press Consortium

Library of Congress Cataloging-in-Publication Data

Smith, C.W. (Charles William), 1940-
Gabriel's eye : [a novel] / C.W. Smith.
p.   cm.
ISBN 0-9701525-0-7 (cloth : alk. paper) — ISBN 0-9701525-1-5 (pbk.)
1. Teacher-student relationships—Fiction. 2. High school teachers—Fiction.
3. Women teachers—Fiction. 4. Art teachers—Fiction. 5. Teenage
boys—Fiction. 6. Young women—Fiction. I. Title.
PS3569.M516 G34 2001
813'.54—dc21   00-068554   CIP

Manufactured in the United States of America
2 4 6 8 9 7 5 3
First Edition

Book design by Harriet Correll

Acknowledgments

To my friends and colleagues who read various drafts of this and gave me honest opinions and helpful suggestions, I say thanks.

To Babette, who took it out of the heap and dusted it off and discovered all the big and little things it was missing, I say many thanks.

Gabriel's Eye

1

We enter their story on a rainy Tuesday at the cusp of night-fall, in a Dallas high school classroom, a dozen students, a teacher. The students sit in gray metal desks, and under them in the foreground—seen from the teacher's perspective—are slashes of black Xs made by the crossed legs of girls in black stockings.

Someone makes a joke. A boy comes through the door while they're laughing; when they swing their heads to look, he blushes, and Susan, the teacher, says, "Can we help you?" He says, squeaking like a damp cloth on glass, "Art club?" then he coughs. She says, "Yes, take a seat," but a chair makes a basso squawk when his hip hits it, so he stands against the back wall, arms folded, buried to his thighs in a nest of empty desks.

Beside him tall windows scumbled by cleanings patina his cheek with northern light. He's handsome enough to model Calvin Klein underwear but looks too shy to show up for the casting call. Susan would like to draw how the boy folds his arms, it's so expressive of insecurity. They're not tightly knotted high on his chest like a surly football coach or someone skeptical of what he's hearing; nor are they laced low and loose with hands dangling from wrists like a woman letting a man know she's listening seriously. No, his elbows press his ribs and his arms cross at the wrists, like the elevator's crowded. Like his stomach hurts. She can tell he's out of place by what he's wearing, as well—rumpled khakis, a tails-out blue Oxford button-down with one cuff rolled to the elbow and the other hanging loose, unbuttoned. Here at this high school for the performing arts most students go for the grunge look, hiphop fashion, heavy metal; and though some dress like preppies, none of those are here tonight on this second meeting for the new semester and none were expected. Aside from this stunningly handsome lad, the roster comes from last year's bunch and pet students she's snagged from her classes. They're assorted misfits, but they know one another.

The boy interrupted their talk of future projects, and, with him mute but still a vaguely disquieting presence, Matt continues. "I say State Fair, Susan. All that great geeky art on the midway freak show. The Half-Woman, Half-Alligator Man." He's the class clown, the school's cartoonist. "We can take some Polaroids."

"They haven't had the freak show for years and years," says Becki, whose gaze darts toward the silent blushing boy. "Until you show up, Matthew." Susan ascribes this uncharacteristic put-down to Becki's desire to impress the new boy.

Cheryl says, "We did a car wash for art supplies last year, remember?"

"Yeah, you collected the money—Anthony and I did the washing," says Matt. "What about, uh, hey Susan! What about life studies?"

Becki says, with a sneer, "You mean nude modeling, right?"

"Hey!" Matt wails in earnest. "I'm serious. I want to be an artist. Why can't we do that?"

Becki snorts. She and Cheryl roll their eyes. A couple of sophomores are tittering and whispering to one another.

Cracking a wry grin, Susan says, "Well, Matt, it's for the same reason you can't vote yet. Or drink. Legally, I mean."

While they bat about more ideas, Susan glances at the new boy. Is there anything more heart-rending than a kid yearning to join a circle of other kids unknown to him? He's got a cowlick; Nathan had one like that.

From her desk she picks up a questionnaire the others completed at the meeting's outset and hip-swings her way through the broken files of desks to hand it to the standing boy, comes near enough to stretch across a hurdle of chair-backs, and he reaches to meet her, and takes it, eyes averted. She says, "You are?" leaving an inflected blank. He looks up and says, "Jeff," in a voice so richly baritone Susan believes he's been itching to use it again.

"Nice to meet you, Jeff. Why don't you sit up here—" she pats the back rest of a desk behind Cheryl and Becki, "and fill this out?"

She calls for a break so she can load her slide projector. Everyone leaves but the boy bent over the form. He's now seated in a desk that he slid into without moving his feet from where he stood. When her preparations are done, she sits on the bow of her desk, legs swinging, and pretends not to be watching him complete her questionnaire.

She's never seen him before. Transfer? He writes with a blue-capped Bic; that tells her he hasn't begun to think of tools the way the others do: Becki writes her name in green and dots her "i" with a red heart, favors the four-color switchable ballpoint; Matt the cartoonist collects Rapiographs—he's been at this since age three and nothing she will do one way or another can make much difference. But maybe that blue-capped Bic says this is the first day in his life the boy has considered doing this, and yes, this is exciting to her, forming the unformed, molding the malleable. He's got a tall, slender form, lean face, high cheekbones, long lashes, full mouth, just enough dark blonde stubble to undercut the feminine sensuality of those lips and eyes. He needs to be rendered in pencil so that the artist can bring something, a shading, to that unmarked face: age, interest, whatever makes a face look as if it belongs to a body that's been lived in. He doesn't look shallow or empty so much as virginal, as if he's gone this far without a scratch and may not even realize that this is rare, takes it for granted that everyone will give him what he needs when he shines his big blond light at them. Add a mole, a scar? A squint? Why, though? Why not just try to capture what's there? After all, innocence and perfection are rare.

But they also inspire resentment. That face has too much power to lure her gaze. Unearned power. Yet she can sympathize with that, how having that power also leaves you feeling that you do something to people without meaning to, draw them to you before you're ready to have them at you and on you, how you try to nullify the power by looking blank, empty of intent. Men leer at your breasts when you're fourteen and you only want to grow them so you look like your peers and nobody'll mistake you for a child.

So she and the boy share the burdens of beauty; looking at him, her gaze compelled to his face, she is both the viewer and the viewed.

Oops. He looks up, his hazel eyes snag hers even as she hastily glances to the windows and fakes a sudden interest in the traffic oozing along Woodall Rogers Freeway in the misty dusk. She thinks, *I will not blush!* the way you say *don't sneeze!* and it works about as well.

Once they're all back, she hits the overhead lights, flips on her projector, framing a square of white light on a beige wall peppered with tack holes.

"Just like I warned you last week," she says, "I've got a million slides from my trip to Italy."

They chuckle politely, indulgently, to let her know they want to please her.

"I spent part of the summer baby-sitting my brother," cracks Matt, "at least until he got arrested and sent to Gatesville."

"What for?" bites Cheryl.

"Associating with dorks," says Becki.

"Excuse me," says Susan.

"Sorry," says Matt.

She launches into her spiel and slide-show. It's forty-five minutes of Italy's Greatest Hits: the Trevi Fountain, Ghiberti's doors, the Sistine Chapel ceiling, that odd wooden sculpture by Donatello of Mary Magdelene emaciated by her exile in the desert, top hits by Botticelli and Titian, treasures of the Bargello and the Uffizi, and so forth.

She comments on all and good-naturedly endures wisecracks by Matt and the others, thumbnail caricatures, "Hey, check it out—Gabriel fu!" he says about Botticelli's *Annunciation* in which Gabriel and Mary do indeed look like wrestlers posturing in search of an advantage upon one another, and when David's large nude form billows on the wall, there's laughter and sighs and whistles from the girls as the dorsal view comes up—"What buns!" Becki yells, and they giggle until Susan shushes them. Instinctively, she peers through the shaft of projector light to the boy, Jeff. He watches attentively, smiling stiffly like someone who's not sure he gets the joke.

A snapshot of her and the Englishman Harvel blinks up into the lighted space. By accident, she mixed snapshots with her research slides and apparently missed culling this one, so she clicks it quickly off, but they all howl in protest: "Susan, go back!" because they've seen enough to know that it's personal. So much for Michelangelo!

She clicks back, but only to avoid making too much of it. In the slide, she's dancing with a short bald fellow with a handlebar mustache, apparently in a street, at night, in a crowd, and both she and the fellow have been zapped with canned confetti string so that it looks like they're wearing a multi-colored, tattered volleyball net over their heads and shoulders. The flash has cat-eyed her, a devil's red orbs burning over a loopy grin.

"This was in Nice," she says. "A wedding."

Matt laughs. "You look totally whacked! How come you never told us you were on the junk?" Cheryl and Billie and Becki grin as if the idea of her, their teacher, actually getting down is amusing to them. It amuses Susan to think that it amuses them.

"Is that your husband, Miz Hart?" asks Cheryl.

"Better be," says Matt.

"No, just a guy we met. My... Curt took the picture." They'd gone to dinner with the English couple they met in their *pensione* and had put away three bottles of wine before getting swooped up in someone's wedding while strolling home. Shortly after Curt snapped the photo, he vanished with Harvel's wife, Philippa, leaving Susan and the pleasant and disconcertingly unruffled Englishman to pretend Curt and the woman had only gotten lost. Pretending, that is, until the Englishman wriggled a wiry brow and astonished Susan by an outburst of stammering: *What's guh-guh-guh-good for the guh-goose? Shall we?* Susan told him she didn't believe Curt would cheat on her. To this day Curt denies he did. But she lied to the Englishman; she's sure Curt lies to her.

When the show's over, she dismisses the meeting. They all come up to hand in their questionnaires, and the boy keeps to the rear of the group, peering intently at their backs it seems, and then finally when the others are filing out of the room, he steps forward—he's even taller than she thought, taller than Curt—and holds his paper out for her to take.

"Thanks," she says.

He shrugs, turns reluctantly, and sort of moseys toward the door. She occupies her hands with unloading her slide carousel but watches him from the corner of her eye. Something about that lurching, gangly amble toward the exit—like there's an invisible bungee tugging him backward—lets her know he wants to be chatted up but lacks the grit to initiate it.

"Ah, Jeff?"

He stops, twists his torso to look back. "Yes, ma'am?"

"Are you new here?"

"Uh-huh."

Her hands have been dismantling the carousel without her attention; the screw ring pops off suddenly, and she drops the big angel-cake cylinder on the desk with a clatter. She holds up one finger to say *just a sec* and retrieves the errant plastic ring and a few spewed slides from the floor, and when she straightens she sees that he has bent over to brace himself with a palm on a desk top. He's gone white.

"Are you okay?"

He smiles weakly. "Guess I forgot to eat."

"Sit down."

He slides into the desk. "Umm, man, that's—whew!—that's not fun!" He wags his head, sticks out his tongue. "I was dizzy for a second."

Susan digs a Power Bar out of her purse and peels back the wrapper. She tears off a hunk and passes it to him.

"What's this? Looks like jerky or something. "

"Emergency rations." As if to prove it's safe to eat, she tears off a bite and nibbles at it with her front teeth. He sniffs his portion, bites into it.

"Umm. Not bad."

They chew in a companionable silence. The leathery texture requires considerable jaw work, and he rolls his eyes for comic effect. His irises are an ambiguous hue, too green to be hazel and too hazel to be green.

"It's like doing calisthenics!" he blurts out after he has swallowed.

She laughs and passes him another chunk.

"They also make them in peanut butter."

"Good idea!" As he's chewing, his gaze swings to the clock high on the wall behind the teacher's desk. He lumbers up, knees bumping the underside of the desk. "I feel better. Thanks."

"Here—in case you feel dizzy again." She holds out the remaining hunk of Power Bar.

When he seems reluctant to take it, she says, "Consider it a loan—you can pay me back next time."

"Well… okay. Thanks!"

"You're welcome. And you're welcome to the club, too."

When he's gone, she stretches, bra pinching under her breasts; it's hot, her feet hurt, she's suddenly thirsty, and hungry, too. That one bite of Power Bar helped but it's no substitute for dinner. Because of an after-school staff meeting, she only had time to scurry over to Wendy's and grab a salad. She'd wanted to go home and change into something more, well, more funky, but instead, she wound up in the same skirt-blouse-blazer and pumps that are in the authorized mode of dress for female teachers.

Thunder, then rain drums on the metal cover of the AC unit outside the window. She wants to leave the empty room, but she eases a haunch onto the desk, swings her legs, glances at the form on top. The boy's blue ink. Her eagerness to read his entries is unsettling, smacks of playing favorites, so she deals his form to the bottom of the deck to prove she's vitally interested in each and every one. Her stomach growls, but not getting a drink of water is fit penance. The others are no mystery to her, however, and skimming through their forms turns up few surprises, though Matt has embellished his questionnaire with singing gremlins and a cartoon Italian movie producer hailing her with a Ciao, baby!

Boy's name is "Jeffrey Robbins, Jr.", and he has written "Senior" where her forms asks for classification. What nights are you free? (Circle) Jeffrey Robbins, Jr. circles every choice. How many art classes have you had? Jeffrey Robbins, Jr. scribes another circle she guesses means a zero. Art history? Boy leaves a blank. Other extra-curricular activities? Jeffrey Robbins, Jr. is apparently unengaged at the moment. Do you work? Jeffrey Robbins, Jr. writes, "help mother." His handwriting looks grammar-schoolish, not the cursive of a kid who's been in love for years with the squiggles and arcs and didoes his very own hand can make with a pen. Help mother what? Clean the house? Operate a business? His khakis, un-ironed, the shirt rumpled, not an overly mothered kid, she'd say, but maybe he works hard to undo maternal efforts to make him look mothered. Other high schools attended, if any? Boy says "Lakeview Prep." She pre-sumes he's a new transfer from the private academy where the kids of downtown lawyers and Lakewood doctors are sent to avoid the terrors of the Dallas public schools, and so the khakis and blue but-ton-down are remnants of his prep-school outfit? They'd been get-ting more of these kids since oil sank to twelve bucks a barrel and the high-flying S & L execs were carted off to federal prison farms. His parents, like many, probably believe this to be the last bastion of white influence in the city system, a star of the "magnet" program devised to circumvent busing and stem white flight.

She doesn't ask students what "cluster" they belong to because she presumes only art students will show. To judge by prior course work, Jeff Robbins is apparently not in Visual Arts. Maybe he audi-tioned as a theater student. It might be useful to know. If he comes again, she'll ask, though it would be easy to peek at his file. Is curios-ity reason enough to pore over a kid's record? She wants to be scru-pulous about this. She could have put other, more personal, queries on the form but they would be intrusive or inappropriate. Though she's resisted the temptation, some colleagues would ask for parents' livelihood and income, whether they are married or divorced, and are you presently practicing birth control? "Practice," an odd way to put it. Something you get good at. *I'm unable to bear children*, Curt jokes.

The room goes bluer than blue, sadder than sad.

Why was this young man here tonight? (And many weeks later: Why, oh why?) She'd not wanted to ask directly on the form, but the last section was designed to draw out their motives: *What activities would you like for the club to be involved in? What would you like to gain from being in it?*

Jeffrey Robbins says, *Learn about art.*

The answer is a profound disappointment. Any empty-headed student would write precisely that to second-guess a teacher when he or she has no earthly idea what to say, though such an answer tugs at any teacher's heart. It is, after all, the right answer. You have to steel yourself against getting suckered, but you also have to beware of becoming jaded. You have to be a mentor without becoming an enabler; you have to take an interest without taking over.

Well, he probably doesn't know, really, why he's here. That's okay. You don't have to know why you do things when you're seventeen. Learning about art might have sounded vaguely appealing. A whim. Nothing better to do.

But his phrasing bothers her; the bumper-sticker bluntness undercuts his credibility. His answer is either nakedly candid or altogether insincere.

This young man is a choir boy or a total cynic.

☞ 2 ☜

When he comes out it's drizzling and clouds have clipped a wing from the neon Pegasus on the Magnolia building. Students released from rehearsals wheel by squealing and laughing, hoisting books over their heads as they scamper for cars. Under the overhang at the side door, he hooks his book bag over his shoulder and peers into the street, sees neither his Dad's Saab or his mother's Chevy. He was expecting his Mom, but the two adults often miscommunicate. Today, he didn't go home after school; he watched people ice-skating at the Plaza of the Americas—the girl teaching the kiddy class wore a tiny red skirt over tights that snugged her ass cheeks—then he worked in the city library on his report about *Their Eyes Were Watching God*, wound up at Wendy's where Tamara, an algebra classmate working there, slipped him free fries. That and the bits of Miss Hart's candy bar were all he'd had since eating a breakfast of Frosted Flakes.

He forgot to call home after school. His mother will be worried, but if she's so worried, then why isn't she here? Or why couldn't she call his Dad? He hopes she is only worrying. But if she's having one of her spells, then he'd have seen the signs this morning before he left.

People beside him under the canopy stick out their palms to catch the drip from the eaves. Matt stands ten feet out in the yard with his arms spread Christ-like, face canted to the sky.

"What's the matter with you guys?" he calls to Cheryl and Becki. The girls huddle hardly more than an arm's length from Jeff, though they've not even glanced at him. "'I like blue margaritas,'" Matt sings, "'Getting caught out in the rain…'"

Cheryl snorts. "You're weird, Matthew!" But Jeff can tell she appreciates that. Envy stings him to the core.

"Jeff! Hey, Jeff! Come on out here!"

His heart bounces off his ribcage, but hearing his name so suddenly zaps his brain numb.

"Well?"

The girls watch him. He's speechless.

"He'll melt!" Becki calls out to Matt.

"There's my Mom!" yelps Cheryl, and all three dash for the black Lincoln now gliding to the curb.

Melt? What does that mean?

He's surprised that Becki has any idea of him. She's in his Health class but she hasn't uttered a word to him there or here or even looked his way. Now out of nowhere she makes sure he overhears her saying that. And is it good or bad? Was she teasing or putting him down? Melt? The witch in "The Wizard of Oz" melts when they toss water onto her—does Becki think he's obnoxious? Ice cream melts, but from the heat. Sugar "melts" in water.

Sugar? Sweet?

His heart plummets. She thinks he's gay. What a thoughtless bitch! He's never said anything to her or even made himself conspicuous, and she cuts him like that! Todd would come back with, What's your problem, bitch, you need a new flea collar?

Fuck Becki. Fuck Cheryl. And Matt—what an asshole! Hey, Mom, I took you advice and joined a club—for losers and jerk-offs!

He won't come again, that's for sure.

He stands alone under the awning for a few moments clenching his teeth, heart-sore. He conjures retakes on the scene. Jeff stands in the rain singing, "'I like blue margaritas...'" and coaxing the girls to join him. Cheryl ventures out, Becki looks on enviously, says, He melts, and Cheryl answers, In your mouth. Becki says, He melts, and he answers You mean my dick when I look at you?

Dream on.

Maybe he could take Drawing from Miss Hart next semester, get an in that way. He could become her best student and Cheryl and Becki and Matt wouldn't even know it, and then one day they're in her classroom and she's showing something of his and raving on and on about how great it is and it slowly starts to dawn on them he's that kid who showed up once for an Art club meeting and they made snide cracks about him.

There was nobody at Lakeview quite like her, that's for sure. She couldn't be more than twenty-four, he guesses, and when he saw her walking in the hall his first day at Carver, he'd thought maybe she was a senior all dressed up for a job interview, and he trailed her, captivated, weaving in and out of the vapor trail of perfume. Black hair, light gray eyes, oh, killer eyes!

Then he heard she taught Art. She was cool; everybody liked Miss Hart. Looking at her was restful and exciting at the same time, so joining the Art club appealed to him.

But he didn't know you had to be Picasso to be there or that they'd already tightened their circle into such a tiny knot. Swinging those legs as she sat on her desk, skirt hem brushing her kneecap. There's this video Todd has, *Teacher's Pet.*

A gust spits rain in his face and mists the sleeves of his shirt. The day started out warm, and he was too fucking stupid to take a jacket, even though his mother said rain was forecast. Or because she did. She isn't even shrewd enough to say *Don't take a jacket with you today, Jeffie, you won't need it, you'll just put it down somewhere and forget it!*

A car shoves a wake of water over the curb as it pulls into the school bus lane. Not a Saab or a Chevy—some cheap riceburner. A beep. He looks about, but he's now alone. Maybe the driver thinks he's someone else, or expects him to go out there and answer a question? (Get serious!)

He ignores the second beep. Then the passenger window lowers. Maybe his mother came with a friend from church? Or something has happened to her...

"Jeff, do you need a ride?"

Miss Hart's oval face, her dark bangs. She's bent over from the driver's side, straining her neck.

He hesitates then leans beyond the overhang. "My Mom is supposed to come!" he yells back, megaphoning with his free hand. "I think, anyway."

"Okay." She raises up, disappears, and he expects the glass to go up, dreads the loneliness in advance, but then her face is there again, filling the void with light, and he's grateful she's somehow read his mind.

"Are you sure?"

"No ma'am."

"Come on, then. I'll take you."

She doesn't wait for his agreement; the window goes up like punctuation. He wishes Matt and Becki and Cheryl could witness this; having Miss Hart all to himself is an unexpected but delicious prize. He has a small, nagging guilt over leaving a tardy parent in the lurch, but it's fit punishment for one to sit here for several annoying minutes before deciding he's gone already.

He dashes for the car feeling a cold splash on his ankle as one foot plunges into a pothole. Once inside, he falls into the bucket seat and slams the door. Something crunches under his feet.

"I'm sorry, I've got a bunch of junk…" She leans over his left thigh, her hair brushing his arm as she strains to tug something out of the floorboard. Her scent seems to suck the air right out of his lungs.

"I'm sorry," he says. He lifts his feet, and the thing—a plastic bag full of angular lumps—swings up at the end of her arm; oofing and grunting from the weight, she heaves it into the back seat.

"There!" She smiles. "My gosh! You're all wet!"

"It got pretty windy." The AC blower is clearing the windows, and he shivers involuntarily.

"Here." She digs into her trenchcoat pocket, then when she hands over a scarf to wipe with, he remembers his handkerchief. But by then he's already taken the scarf and she's put the car in gear.

He gingerly pats his face and arms; the scarf is silk, so it's not worth much as a towel, but it's saturated with her cologne, and the urge to press it to his nose and inhale the fragrance is richly irresistible.

"Where to?"

"Oak Cliff. It's not far, though, just across the bridge. My Mom was supposed to pick me up, but she must have gotten her signals crossed with my Dad, or she might have gotten held up in traffic or something." After a moment, he adds, "My Dad lives in Lakewood. He's a lawyer."

"Should we stop and call them, you think?"

"Aw, no. They'll figure out I got a ride, if they come."

He thinks "if they come" sounds bitter, and he realizes he said it to get pity. Like that kid in the Charter hospital ads who waits with his date in the rain for his boozer Dad to pick them up.

"A lot of artists I know live in Oak Cliff," she says. He understands this is to let him know blue-collar Oak Cliff is as good a place to live as Yuppiefied Lakewood.

"Yeah, I guess so. Where do you live?"

"In Oak Lawn."

"You like that neighborhood?"

"Yeah. It's high-crime but high-energy, too. It seems like it's hard to have one without the other. I'm your typical liberal who'd rather die young in a fast-food shootout than live to a dead old age voting Republican in Plano."

He laughs, and she grins. She's got the neatest grin; it's cock-eyed, tilts to one side of her mouth and makes a dimple there, makes her seem to be saying *I've got a secret!* Or *Let's prank somebody!*

"I'm a liberal, too."

"Yeah?"

"I went to this school before I came here, Lakeview? All these kids there were rich, I had this one friend he got a Beamer for his sixteenth birthday, and it was incredible to hear them talking about their money and their maids. They all even had automatic teller cards? And they'd walk up to a machine in the mall and stick in the card and come out with two hundred dollars to spend. Man, they had their own American Express cards, and they'd go eat in restaurants and take their friends with them and just use the card. And you wouldn't believe how they talked about black people and Mexicans."

She doesn't respond, and he realizes that she wasn't prepared to hear so much from him. Since he never opened his mouth during the meeting, he's dying to tell her something that makes her respect him.

"So you didn't get along very well with people there?"

A cold stab in his gut: was what happened at Lakeview on his record, even though the headmaster assured his father it wouldn't be?

"Oh, well, they were okay, you know. Reason I had to leave was my parents got hard up for money."

It wasn't true, and once again he feels like a phony for trying to arouse her sympathy. But can you expect sympathy for having to leave a school where the students have values you claim to find disgusting?

"But I was glad, anyway. I like it at Carver."

"Have you made friends here?"

"Oh, sure."

She glances at him, and he adds, "I've still got friends from my old school, too."

"What cluster are you in, anyway?"

"Theater. I think."

"You think?"

"Well, I came in pretty late here because my Mom and Dad couldn't agree on where I ought to go. So I told the people here I wanted to be in Theater. I don't want to be an actor, though. I'll probably be a lawyer, like my Dad. For the money."

"You didn't have to audition for the Theater cluster?"

Her tone—like she's uncovered a crime she'll report first thing tomorrow morning.

"Oh, yeah. I read for Miss…uh, Miss Bakewell."

"And you're taking theater courses."

"Only one this semester. Stagecraft."

"Oh. Well." For some reason, this information sets her at ease. "I guess you'll soon be busy every night working on a play?"

"I guess. I don't want to have to give up Art club, though." He's dying to know what she really thinks of the brown-nosers who dissed him—maybe she thinks they're twits and she's been hoping someone new would show up. But it wouldn't be cool to ask.

"Well, I hope you don't have to, too."

"Me too. But, you know, if I did have to, I was thinking maybe I could take some drawing lessons." That makes him sound like a total dweeb, so he adds, "I used to take them."

"Really? Did you study with one of our teachers?"

"Uh, no. It was this guy. An artist. He's a professor at SMU."

"Oh? Maybe I know him, I know some artists who teach there. Is it Bill Summers? He's been there for years."

Sweat's running down his ribs. He's digging himself into a hole, here. "No, this guy's new, real new. I forget his name. I've got it written down in here." He taps his book bag. "I'm not so sure I like him personally, though. Maybe I need a new teacher. Do you know anybody?"

"Oh, sure. I imagine we could find somebody."

"Did you ever, like, do that?"

Her face glows in the dash light, and he imagines the stroke of good fortune that would have her sitting beside him and with his arm touching hers as they look at a tablet on a table.

The raincoat lapels are draped at her sides, and when she raises her chin to peer intently through the rain, her throat looks soft and white. Sleeves whistle when she moves her arms, and when she lifts her foot from brake to the gas and back, there's another, softer rustle. That motion of her hips in the darkness stirs him. Wet ends of hair cling to her jaw. A curve of ear, a delicate crescent. He fights an urge to raise his fist from his thigh and smell the scarf wadded in it.

Hadn't she heard his question? He can't bring himself to repeat it.

But she says, finally, "I haven't." Then she nods toward the windshield. They're passing the Kennedy assassination's famous Grassy Knoll and are approaching The Triple Underpass. "Where to?"

He directs her west on Commerce, and they cruise in silence by the mist-shrouded county jail and onto the bridge over the Trinity. He wants to ask if she would consider teaching him but can't force the question out. She didn't say, "No, I don't" or "I couldn't do that." She said she has never done it, so far. The possibility has come so swiftly that it's like being told you might win a contest you didn't even know you'd entered, and he's superstitious about pushing too hard too fast.

Her wipers squeak, the tires thrum on the bridge, and he looks out the window but can't see the river: usually it's only a sludgy stream meandering between the wide high levees of the barren flood plain, but rains upstream sometimes swell it levee to levee. A jag of lightning strobes the bottoms, and he peers down in case a corpse has been dumped there. One afternoon he and Chris and Todd and James drove into the bottoms to drink a bottle of Scotch and fly a remote-control jet fighter Chris had brought. Todd had bet that Chris couldn't fly the plane through the open windows of his mother's Cherokee, and it looked hilarious when the plane slammed into the flank of the car and they staggered around laughing. But when he walked off a way to piss and faced that lonely flood plain—so bare you'd think it'd been Agent Oranged—he realized how really spooky, how lunar, it was. Ghosts down there, the ghosts of a thousand mutilated murder victims, the ghost screams of raped and tortured women. Valley of the Shadow of Death: the idea of demons was a whole lot more real down in the flats of the Trinity than anywhere else the people in his mother's geek church might imagine.

Despite the splash of tires and the rain beating on the roof, he feels safely out of the weather, as if in a cave, with the dashboard glow a semblance of a fire. Taillights ahead are so many blurry red lanterns. She's concentrating, hands tight on the wheel. Once when he was traveling with his parents, a flash flood sweeping across the highway prevented their going on in the darkness, and they spent the night in the car. He slept in the back seat with his head on his mother's lap. Now that he's not a child, he can take care of a woman in an emergency. Say they come to an intersection and get out into it, and the rising water floods the car: he could swim for help or save his companion from drowning. Or say if they had to park and wait the night, he could keep someone warm. They could play the radio. Maybe their clothes would be wet but there'd be a blanket in the car.

He flicks the wadded scarf across his nose. He looks at the woman, aware they're both too quiet. The longer the silence lasts the more she seems cold or aloof. He either said something weird and freaked her out or else he isn't important enough to stay in her mind. He considers saying something about the club. During the slide show, he'd had an idea but had kept mute. Here, in the safety of her car, there'd be no snickers from too-cool Becki.

"You know that portrait of the duke you showed?"

"The Duke of Ferrera?"

"Yes, I guess. That was really something. The face is so real. Don't you think they used these paintings to preserve for each other what they looked like? I mean, they didn't have cameras."

Jesus! Once uttered, his idea sounds stupidly obvious, something everybody else understood years ago. He hangs suspended not knowing whether to escape by changing the subject or to embellish the stupidity in an effort to disguise it.

"Yeah, I think so, too," she says, too eagerly. She's patronizing him, he feels. She'd encourage him no matter what he says—her job.

"I went to a show at the Kimball in Fort Worth not long ago that you just reminded me of. There are some miniatures?" She glances at him. "Portraits on paper or metal or ceramics or ivory and most of them not much bigger than, well, have you ever seen old silver dollars?" With her thumb and index finger she sculpts a circle out of the air between them, a hole, made by her flesh, for him to imagine. "It was incredible how detailed these portraits were and how small. They used metal brushes to paint them. They gave them to one another like snapshots, you know, say if you were going to be off on a trip or off to war, then somebody you loved might have a miniature done and give it to you to keep. Some were worn around the neck, the way women of my grandmother's generation wore lockets with tiny photographs in them. The craftsmanship it takes to make a faithful likeness that size is really remarkable."

"I'd like to see some."

That she picked up his comment gives him heart. Another idea zips to mind. He'd been especially struck by one slide showing a married couple because their faces seemed both now and then. Well, that would sound dumb. What he means is that the skill of the drawing made the faces seem to belong to distinct individuals, somebody he might know, even though their clothes weren't modern. Despite the foreign aspect to their faces (because of where or how long ago they lived, he didn't know which), the artist had so skillfully captured the minute detail of their features that they came alive in his mind as actual humans who had walked upon this planet in another age. And he'd shivered: seeing them was like walking through a window of time; the drawing was an opening between when those people lived and when he is living, right now. When he thinks of actually touching the drawing and feeling the old artist's pencil lines, it would be like touching those old faces, and when you also consider that this artist himself had probably touched these people….

But he can't imagine the opening large enough to say all this without sounding really cheesy.

Their mutual silence snowballs on its own momentum, until even when he says, "You need to take the next left," it sounds loud even though he'd swear he's only whispering, and when he adds, after a moment, "Next left, then it's about a block down on the right," his voice does that squeaky-creaky thing.

He points a moment later. "Here."

She pulls to the curb. His mother has left the porch light on.

"Oh, I love these old two-story frame houses!" Miss Hart exclaims, surprising him with the burst of cheer. "Those great porches."

"We had a swing and some rockers there but they got ripped off."

His bedroom light is on. His mother has probably been snooping, but is now most likely waiting behind the front door to rag him about not calling. But how come no one came to get him?

"That's my room, up there."

She bends over him to peer through the window, and her bangs touch his shoulder. A muscle in his thigh twitches. He holds his breath. When she comes close like this he's paralyzed.

"You've got a good view."

"I guess."

She straightens up. "Well, goodnight, Jeff. And—" Her tone makes him turn. She's pushed her face into the space between them, her expression sorrowful. She pats the back of his hand with three fingertips. "I hope you come to the next club meeting—you'll feel more at ease when you get to know everybody. Believe me, I know how it is to be new."

His face feels like a lighted jack-o-lantern. "Thanks…," he mutters, yanking at the door handle, "Thanks for the ride, Miz Hart. See you later," and he clambers out in a hurry to escape because she's seen into him all too well.

He bounds up the steps and onto the porch but slows as he approaches the door. The hand that he might use to retrieve his key from his pocket contains, he discovers, Miss Hart's scarf. He turns back to the curb. Her car idles there. Maybe she's waiting for him to return it.

He turns his back to the street, unzips his book bag, plunges the red hand deep inside it, and fakes digging around for a key. When at last he hears her car whish away, he opens his fist to release the scarf the way you'd free a captured bird into a sack.

$≈3≈$

Rains often end the summer drought there in late September, and the downpour Susan Hart and Jeffrey Robbins have driven through will fall on the watershed to the northwest for several hours, until, by morning, the saturated Elm Fork of the Trinity will boil like a cocoa-colored soup and heave down through the channels of the flood plain.

On the I-30 bridge at 9:30 P.M. the rain slows traffic; cars and trucks accordion too close for safety, and drivers are blinded by on-coming lights that glare in starbursts on their wet windshields.

The teacher steers her Hyundai Sonata with both hands as she creeps back over the bridge after dropping off her prospective stu-dent. The wipers thunk like a metronome without clearing the win-dows. The rain is not even an annoyance at the moment; it's a white noise backdrop for her thoughts. She's on auto-pilot, if you will. If she were to rear-end the semi now six feet from her front bumper, her explanation would be, as preposterous as it sounds, "I'm sorry, officer—I was picturing Michelangelo's David in a red Speedo."

Actually she was following up Matt's plea for doing life studies and is just playing with the idea of proposing it to her Dean of Instruction, Randall Jeter. She knows the obvious objections and could make them herself, chief among which is that only about two of the club members are sufficiently mature even to utter the phrase "life studies" without sniggering, let alone engage in it.

But then there's *art,* doggone it! Reclining nude, nude on a staircase, nude bathers—*if you scanned a catalogue of global museum holdings, you'd have a sky-high stack of nude figures,* she might say. *No artist ever learned to draw without doing complete anatomical studies…*blah blah blah. *Yes, yes,* he'd argue, *but there's a time and place for everything, and I'm sure you can encourage these youngsters without stirring up such a hornet's nest with total nude modeling!*

She might sniff, say quietly, *Not nude modeling—that's what it's called on Industrial Boulevard. Artists call it life studies.* He might say, *I don't deny that this is a legitimate undertaking for serious art students. We don't see anything wrong with having a live model in a leotard or bathing suit. There, are you happy?*

That's a tough one. Nude In Bathing Trunks is not really a nude, of course, only a semi-nearly-almost nude. And it's not as if she'd use one of her students. There are professional models.

Why quibble over a few inches of hidden flesh?

Because they're the inches that matter; they define the difference between being clothed and being nude.

Mr. Jeter, can you imagine Michelangelo's David in a red Speedo? It makes what's under there too important. In a nude, you see that every part of the human form is worthy of equal attention, respect, even adoration.

Imagining such a conflict makes her hands grow slick on the Sonata's small black wheel. Even if the cause were not so dubious, she'd still not fight—temperamentally, she's not suited to be an activist, never liked being particularly visible, and her indignation toward Philistinism hasn't inspired her to any action before, save for showing up at the Dallas Museum of Art recently for a protest rally against Congressional efforts to kill the National Endowment for the Arts.

Of course it's a silly idea to consider life studies for someone under eighteen in a public school setting. But, then again, it's not unreasonable to ask where's the real harm? She wants to *make a difference* in these kids' lives! She feels sort of, well, *adversarial* these days. Maybe the galloping conservatism of the Reagan era has finally risen to the choking point, and maybe her restlessness comes from having experienced, this summer, that day-after-day immersion in works from the Italian Renaissance. Sure, she'd seen most of the slides a thousand times; paintings about the Annunciation are the subject of her thesis, for God's sake. But being there—it has left her feeling that her own times are bland as biscuit dough. Spiritless. And vulgar. As an undergraduate she liked the moderns, but as the years clipped by she's been drawn back to that stormy narrative art, the religious themes. That passion—where can it be seen these days?

Curt says, *Get a grip. Watch out or you'll wind up back in church, too.*

Get a grip? Easy to say when nothing bothers you! Well, there's little chance she'd go back to the church she bolted as a teenager. If he's afraid that she might, it's because "Church" could mean "wedding" as in "Curt and Susan get married." When they staggered out of the restaurant that night in Nice, the wine and the pleasant company and the beautiful night air made her oozy-woozy with love for Curt; she wrapped her arm around his waist and kept leaning up to kiss him on his cheek, then when they rounded the corner, they saw the wedding party had taken over the *terrasse* of a cafe and people were dancing in the streets. The groom kissed the bride to rousing cheers. Susan kneaded Curt's hand meaningfully. He danced with Philippa.

Not so easy to get a grip when you feel like you're coming apart. That trip has really cut her loose—that's the only phrase she has for it. But she can't tell if it has cut her loose like she's let go of the bank and is really swimming on her own or has cut her loose as in losing her moorings. When the slide of her and that repugnant Englishman popped up on the wall, she wanted to scream. Good thing that night was one of their last on the Continent because it ruined the rest of the trip for her.

Easing off the bridge, her pilot truck curves north onto I-35 and she follows doggedly behind it until she comes awake almost too late to exit—she makes a quick, honked-at cut across two lanes and onto the Oak Lawn access, then has to stop at the first light at Maple.

Life studies…The phrase has an interesting ambiguity. Because it wouldn't just be about the human form, would it? Yes, she'd want her students to cultivate an appreciation for fleshly beauty, but, beyond that—here, this is very important!—in a culture where women's bodies (men's too, don't forget!) are exploited by advertisers and pornographers as a means to vulgar ends, precious few opportunities exist for kids to develop any sense of the essential nobility of humanity. It's laughable that a teacher might be condemned for exposing students to nudity when so many spend hours watching X-rated movies or MTV music videos on cable.

Sure, she knows that there's an area where beauty is not just aesthetic but also sexual; last summer, seeing Michelangelo's David in person for the first time, she experienced an exquisitely refined lust and yearning that were tangible, visceral, a head-to-toe kind of deal that made her shiver deep inside, and Curt later reaped the benefit of it.

She wants her students to know there's a place in your being and body where your spiritual yearnings link up with your hormones. Especially the boys, they need to learn that. In particular a boy like

Jeff who's probably had no experience with aesthetic images of the human form.

But you can talk too frankly about that kind of thing to teenagers. Red flags go up. Somebody might claim she's got a prurient interest. She honestly doesn't think so. She has the usual component of exhibitionism in her fantasies a la *My Secret Garden* and a phantom rapist or two in her day-dreams (well-tailored aristocrats only, with good manners and kabillon-dollar yachts), and the usual unspeakable and unrecallable scenarios that her unconscious alone is responsible for unveiling while she sleeps. But she believes her psychological template would easily fit under the rubric of "normal to healthy," all the more so for her being self-aware and not particularly disturbed by the mild aberrations with which she intentionally or inadvertently titillates herself. After Nathan broke her heart, she did have a spell in college of quick and casual sex with partners she doesn't want to recall because it hurts to do so. But she's been faithful to Curt and believes that when her thoughts stray, her actual monogamy is a kind of penance.

The class where she met Curt: she can't recall all the models now—they had several—nor can she remember Curt saying anything (titters, giggles, snide remarks?) about any male or female model. She remembers the weather that summer: dozens of consecutive days above 100 degrees. The air-conditioning never worked right in the building, so the models were sheened in their sweat like engine-room monkeys. One boy, she remembers, had a tobacco-colored birthmark on his hip and his right ball hung lower than the left.

Women were sunbathing topless on the beach at Cannes. Curt kept nudging her and grinning. He wanted her to try it. She said, *Maybe if your friend Philippa with the veddy posh accent were here, she would.*

She watched Curt watching one particular Swedish-looking cow who sat nearby slathering her tits with lotion.

So what do you think, Curt? Does that turn you on? she asked loud enough to be overheard by anyone passing.

He shrugged. *Eh, it's okay.* He was embarrassed to be caught ogling, though he'd gone to great pains to hide it—his Yankees baseball cap, sunglasses, the International Herald-Tribune held between his hands like a serving tray, the top edge tilted just high enough to give the appearance he was reading but also just low enough to see over it.

Okay? What do you mean okay? How about on a scale of one to ten?

He said, *Don't get political on me. I'm just a tourist on the Riviera. A topless woman's the indigenous crop here, like the wine in Burgundy. What they celebrate.*

What'd you mean by okay?

I mean it doesn't move me one way or the other. I guess I catch myself wanting to look at her, but when I do, nothing happens.

You think her tits are too big? She's not your type? You've got a headache?

He laughed. After a moment, he said, *Something about the context. It's too public.*

"Context? You're concerned about context?!"

She's shouting at her windshield. That ghost driver who attends to motoring functions while we daydream has wheeled the Hyundai into the two-strip concrete drive beside their duplex, and she finds herself glaring through the windshield at the rain-blurred yellow rectangle of their bedroom window on the second floor. Where Curt better be, right this minute. Her heart is thundering and she's clenching her jaws. She releases the wheel, and her hands curl tight into their respective palms, gripping the nothing there. It's like she's been lost in a terrible movie the last half hour. Or a bad dream. Often lately she goes "off" brooding and has a fight with somebody, then when she's alert again she finds it was only in her head.

Curt.

Context? The word jumps a synapse, completes a circuit. She thinks she knows now why Curt took off that night with the English woman.

With the teacher's little car safely around the corner, Jeff can use the hand that freed the scarf to snag his key from his front pocket.

He slips it into the lock. He wonders Lady or the Tiger? That his mother didn't come to get him was a bad sign.

Sometimes she lurks behind the door and instantly starts ragging him. But tonight he discovers her lying on the couch in the dark living room. She's wearing her chenille bathrobe, and her arm is draped across her forehead. When he turns on a lamp, she lurches up like a comic corpse and stares with alarm, as if he were a stranger.

"Mom?"

She groans, then swings to plant her feet onto the carpet. She presses her fingertips against her eyes. "I was having dreams. I'll bet I forgot something."

Looking at her yearbook picture sinks him half in love with her, and when she feels good, she's still attractive. But too often she looks worn down like now or her eyes have that strange glitter he associates with what he calls her turbocharged moods. Life's never on an even keel with her. This weird black depression settles over her and for days she'll mope, hardly speaking. Then she's forgetful and getting her attention is like trying to talk through a foam-rubber wall. His Dad says she needs to see a doctor or take medication, but she acts like she's going to get a medal for wrestling this thing with just herself and the Lord Jesus in one corner and her demons in the other.

Having won a round or two she'll be vibrating with energy and will yammer at him incessantly, and when he goes to his room or to bed to escape her, he can still hear her moving about downstairs, cleaning the house. If he gets up to piss at 3 A.M., the kitchen light will still be on, and he knows that she's sitting at the table writing letters to movie stars whose immorality has offended her and to congressmen she hopes to browbeat into passing laws against breathing. On mornings after those nights, she'll still be charged up. She'll jabber at him as they drive to school, and he can picture her talking at the car radio all the way to the government services building on St. Francis where she clerks in the driver's license bureau.

Judging by the relative stillness of her limbs at this moment, she's hovering just this side of what she calls her blue funk. She seemed pretty upbeat when he left this morning, but the way she said "dreams" means they were populated by devils.

"It's okay," he says. "I got a ride home with a friend. I didn't know if it was you or Dad picking me up."

"I was worried." Her voice sounds flat. "When you didn't call I thought you'd probably had enough of staying with a crazy person and you'd gone to your Dad's to live. I asked the Lord to bring you back."

Not surprisingly, she doesn't sound too happy that her prayers were answered. It's as if hours ago this meant a great deal to her but not now. He sets his book bag down by the door.

"I went to the library to work on my English paper, then I went to art club, Mom."

"But did you eat? Where did you eat?"

"Wendy's."

"I was too tired to fix anything. I went in there thinking that you'd be home, and I just stood there because I couldn't think of anything to fix. I couldn't decide what you'd want."

"It's all right. I ate at Wendy's."

"I don't know what gets into me. I just stood there."

"It's okay."

"Then I laid down. I guess I forgot to come get you. Was I supposed to?"

"I don't know."

"How did you get home?"

"My teacher. It was on her way."

"I was worried. I prayed and prayed."

"I know. I'm sorry."

She smiles wanly. "I guess it was silly of me to think you'd gone to live with your Dad. All your things are still here."

"I'm still here."

"I'm glad you're home. Did you have a good day at school?"

Without waiting for his answer, she lies back down, and he knows that she'll be zonked in seconds. Probably she's been there most of the afternoon, probably slipped away from work early. When she suffers these spells of exhaustion, she can't keep up with her job and about every six weeks or so he has to help her with the typing.

He finds a Jack-In-the-Box sack on the dining table—her lunch. It smells like tacos. He snatches up the sack by its neck and crushes it between his palms as he strides into the kitchen. He kicks open the lid to the garbage can, flings the crushed white bag into it, but the wad bounces out again, so he boots it like a field goal against the back door, and when it bounces on the floor, he scoops it up and slams it into the trash can.

The sink holds the dark soil of coffee grounds, splats of taco sauce like movie blood. He yanks on the tap and rinses the sink into the garbage disposal, hits the switch, and while the disposal whines and roars, he grabs a sponge and wipes the counter clean of lettuce shreds, tomato bits and taco shards, shoving the refuse into the howling gullet. On the counter is a carton of cold refried beans with the cheddar globbed on top like candle wax.

He picks it up, slings it into the garbage can, and it hits with a solid clunk that rocks the container. Let her find it there.

He shuts off the disposal. He looks about the kitchen. There is nothing else to do, but he has to do something else, so he grabs the plastic bag in the garbage can and, though it's only half full and he meant for her to see the wasted refried beans, he jerks up the sack, hoists it by the neck, twirls it to make a rope and ties it off in a knot.

The rain has let up. Bushes glisten in the back porch light, and the pecan tree drips. On his way to the alley, he is met by a golden retriever who whines and tries to leap up on his thighs as he hurries down the flagstone walk.

"Shut up, Tawny! Get out of my way!"

He goes through the back gate and shuts it to keep the dog from following him, and when he opens it, the dog is upright on its haunches, waiting.

"What's your problem?"

The dog whimpers and trembles, longing to jump on him but knowing better.

"Okay, bark once for yes and twice for no, all right? Is your problem your parents won't let you call Party Line any more? Are you needing a date to the prom? Or is it something more basic like food?"

He bends close to the dog's face and takes its snout between his palms, not knowing if he's going to hug and kiss this creature or strangle it. The pungent odor of wet canine rises to his nostrils. The dog tolerates the muzzling for a moment, then breaks free and barks at him, leaping about.

At the side of the house, he discovers, as he suspected, that the dog's dish is empty. Beside it stands a plastic container with a lid; he opens it and scoops out a cupful of Purina Dog Chow and pours it into the dish, and the dog is wolfing it down with its snout shoved into the bowl even as Jeff scoops out three more. He secures the lid onto the can. The dog's water bowl is fouled with leaves, so he dumps it then refills it from the garden hose.

The dog is more or less oblivious to him as it eats, so he feels free to massage its ears and stroke its damp flanks for a minute.

"Sorry."

Back inside, he retrieves his book bag from the foyer, then looks into the dark living room. He steps toward the staircase, then hesitates.

"Mom?"

He goes to her side, cups her upturned shoulder and shakes her. "Mom!"

"Wha—"

"Mom, don't you want to get into bed?"

She might say yes, she might say no. He hopes no. He's tired, he has homework.

She flings out her arm to grip the back of the couch and levers herself upright. She's really out of it.

"My glasses."

He reaches to the end table, hands her the glasses, watches while she settles them onto her face—she's so slow it's like everything is happening under water.

"Have you seen my Bible?"

"Here." The Bible is also on the end table. He snatches it up and inserts it into her opened palm, closes her fingers over it.

"Okay. I'm ready."

He steers her toward her first-floor bedroom and has to wait shifting from one foot to the other while she laboriously reverses their activity: putting down the Bible on her night stand, taking off the glasses. When she wriggles out of the bathrobe like a drunk or a sleepy child, he turns away, stares at the phalanx of family photos on the top of her dresser—the three of them at a picnic table, little kid-Jeff in a bathing suit, hair water-plastered on his skull, grinning, missing a tooth. God he hates that photo! What a stupid fucking kid!

She crawls under the bedspread still in her slip and lies on her back.

"Come give me a kiss, sweetie."

He leans over the bed, and her sleepy arm goes up and around his nape, hot, heavy, dragging him closer, and she presses tight lips to his cheek. Her breath smells rank, copperish.

"You're all wet, hon."

"Good night, Mom."

"Good night, my sweet Prince. Thank you. Don't forget your prayers."

"I won't."

"Will you call for me?"

"Yes. Go to sleep."

He snaps off the bedside lamp, and, hoping she won't hear him leaving, tiptoes through the door and closes it behind him.

Going up the stairs, he chants under his breath in time with his steps: *godDAMN you! godDAMN you, godDAMN you!* In his room, he drops the book bag onto the bed and shimmies out of his damp clothes, picks up a t-shirt and pajama bottom off the throw rug and slips them on.

He sits at his desk. His Star Wars fighter lamp is on. Next to the phone his mother has left two messages: "Some girl called." The next one says, "Another girl called."

"Aw, fuck! Thanks, Mom!" What's he supposed to do, call information and ask can you give me the number of Some Girl and Another Girl? Maybe it was only Becki taking another opportunity to insult him, or Cheryl setting him up: *Jeff, how about a date? Yeah, you want one? Okay, how about two-thousand ten A.D.?*

He lifts his phone, dials, speaks when the voice-mail directs him. "Message for Lionel Washington." He deepens his voice. "This is Dr. Stanley. I've advised my patient Rose Robbins to miss work to see me tomorrow morning."

Washington's probably wise to these calls, but what else can he do?

He sits with his elbows in the pool of light and tries to recall the assignment for World History. After a moment, he gets up and carries the book bag to the desk chair. He's unzipping it when the phone on his desk chirrups. Some Girl?

"Hello?"

"Hey, you slimy faggot. Sucked any big dicks lately?"

He dumps the bag onto the floor, sits in the chair, leans back, lifts his legs and lays them across a corner of the desk.

"Only your Daddy's, and that wasn't until he paid me ten thousand dollars. How about yourself, still eating that cream-of-afterbirth soup and licking your grandmother's butthole?"

"Naw, she wanted me to stop so she could take a dump on your Daddy's face."

"Was that before or after your sister was giving him a blow-job?"

They laugh.

"So, dude, what's up?"

"I just got home."

"Yeah, I know. I called earlier. Your Mom sounded weird."

"She is weird, dude. She was probably just busy loaning your Dad some dresses."

"She tell you I called?"

"Yeah." He's not surprised that his mother didn't note that Todd had called. In his mother's eyes, everyone at his former school consorts with Satan. Attending Lakeview had been his father's idea, and the more his mother had balked, the more his father had fought for it. When he was kicked out, his mother didn't try very hard to hide her gloating.

"So what are you doing, jerking off?"

"History."

Todd snickers. "You're not going to tell me they give you homework at that school. Half the people there can't even speak English, dude, and the other half's not going to understand it unless it's in rap rhythm." He makes hotcha-putta-pit noises that pop in Jeff's ear. Yes, Lakeview is demanding—the teachers assign an hour of homework every night for every subject—but, on the other hand, Todd's been going there since sixth grade, and, while he has an enviable talent for numbers, he's almost flunked every year, and Jeff suspects that Todd's father's donations have kept Todd enrolled.

"You're not going to tell me you did any, are you?"

Todd laughs. "Are you kidding?" He means that's for geeks. "So have you found her yet?"

"Who?"

"The girl of my wet dreams. You were supposed to line me up. All those punked-out girls down there, they all put out, right? They're like radical on sex. I can't take any more of these bow-heads at Lakeview, they're driving me up the wall."

"It's your reputation." This is a complicated thing to say: on the surface it means you've got such a reputation as cocksman the girls are afraid they'll lose their virginity if they go out with you. But actually, Jeff meant Todd's reputation as a jerk.

"I guess," Todd says. He is, Jeff thinks, basking in the idea of having a reputation. "Tiffany Rawlings said to say hello to you, dude. I think she wants it. She's hot."

"Yeah?" Jeff says mildly. He knows Tiffany a hundred times better than Todd does. She was a friend until what he did to get kicked out embarrassed her. It's safe enough to send a hello from long distance through a third party. "Well, say hello back." And up yours.

"Chris is dicking Paige Berman. Like every night."

"No shit." He doesn't believe it for a minute. Chris couldn't find his ass with both hands.

"Yeah, dude, really."

"Lucky Paige."

Todd laughs. "She's lost fifty pounds, dude. She's hot."

"Really?" Something in this news about a near-stranger intrigues him. A fat girl, butt of the school jokes, loses weight and looks great, all the guys think she's hot. Great underdog drama. "Why Chris, then?"

"He says it's the size of his dick."

"Give me a break."

Todd says, "You wouldn't believe the money he spends on her. He bought her a life-size teddy-bear, you know, the ones from Austria?"

"That's like fifteen hundred dollars. Shit, no wonder."

"Yep. I told him he could buy a platoon of whores off Harry Hines for that much."

"What'd he say?"

Todd sniffs. "He was offended."

Jeff laughs.

"So you want to see her?"

"Who?"

"Paige, dumbass!"

"Shit, I don't know. What do you have in mind?"

"Chris's folks are going out of town this weekend. He says let's party. I'll get some X, maybe we'll go to Club Barren first."

"Chris and Paige and you and me?"

"No, dick-head! Chris and Paige and you and me and the two hottest bitches at that lame-ass school of yours."

"Sounds great. Who are you gonna bring for you?"

"Your mother, I guess. I hear she's good. So whata you say?"

The question is will you get me a date? He has a moment of panic, thinks he ought to claim he has other plans, but hears himself saying, "Sure. Why not."

They banter for a few moments, but Jeff holds up his end with only half his attention. Tough assignment. He supposes it wouldn't be impossible to get lined up for Saturday night, though the girl would be more or less a stranger, and it would be a first date. But getting a blind date for Todd would be dicey, since Jeff himself isn't known at Carver. He can tell some prospect that Todd's good-looking, rich and drives a Beamer. What he'll have to leave out is that Todd usually insults whatever waitress has the hard luck to get his table and pukes on his date's pumps or grabs their tits almost before learning their names.

After he sets the phone down, he mentally scans faces from his classes, then very deliberately put the subject out of his mind. He gets out his history book and opens it flat on the desk under the light. He left a sheet of notebook paper with the assigned page numbers on the right page as a bookmark. He stares at it for several minutes then doodles on the sheet.

History. His Story? Her story? Everybody-but-Jeff's story.

⟫5⟫

The teacher sighs, turns off the engine, and sits a moment, hands in her lap. *Ommm*, maybe, or something like it. Inhale. Exhale. A very long day. The rain still pours.

Is it too much to ask that Curt be watching or listening for her and be coming out on the porch with an umbrella?

She stretches over the headrest to tug her book bag from the rear floorboard, heaves it up and over and hugs it like a child as she yanks the door handle, then dashes through the rain for the porch. If she were a husband, she'd turn the porch light on, too.

In the dim foyer, she hears TV noise from the upstairs study. She treads through the darkened living room and into the dining area that Curt has appropriated for a model workshop (Red Baron biplane laid out on the table), then enters the kitchen. The burst of fluorescent light from her fingertip sends a roach acrobating to the underlip of the counter where it imagines it can't be seen, though the quivering antennae are still visible.

She lets the book bag slip from her shoulder and fall to the floor. She stands paralyzed by the prospect of fixing a snack. Curt has been home since six—wouldn't it be nice if he'd greeted her at the door, sat her down and served her supper? Her mother would have watched for her, would have stood at the door while she came down the walk, instantly noticed the weariness and waxed solicitous. But, then, you had to live with your mother to get that.

A magnetic carrot pinning paper to the refrigerator door falls to the floor, and—oof!—she bends to retrieve both. Notice about a model plane meet.

There's brie in the fridge from Marty's—Curt must have bought it today—and she unwraps it on the counter. Why didn't he leave it out? God, don't men know anything? She digs a saltine from a canister, unceremoniously whacks a chunk of brie, smashes it rind and all on the cracker, stuffs it into her mouth.

She puts the cheese away then drinks a large glass of cold water.

And feels better. Breathes out. Calm down, he's just a guy, a dozen virtues, you are a mean, mean, self-pitying woman.

Or just tired, anyway. The carpeted stairs are, under the re-assumed burden of the book bag, stations of the cross. Huffing at the top, she pauses to look at Curt lying splay-limbed in his recliner, the remote commander in hand. She passes behind him, drops her bag at her computer desk, and kicks off her pumps.

"Howdy, podnuh," Curt says. His eyes are on the screen where men are playing baseball in—judging from the calligraphy on the in-field wall—Tokyo.

"I'm hungry. What's for dinner?" she asks.

"I stopped off at the Stoneleigh with Barry and had a burger."

"That takes care of you."

He turns to her, grins.

"I'll bet you think I didn't think of you."

"Prove me wrong."

"Look in the refrigerator."

"You brought me something?"

"I'm no dummy."

He looks expectant, as if for a reward. She wants to say, *So go get it for me*, but instead kisses his forehead.

"I found the brie already. Thanks."

She sits on the couch stretching her neck, and Curt blanks the screen with the remote.

"You have a good turnout?"

"Yeah. Okay. The usual suspects." A boy's face fragments into words that evaporate before her mouth can be shaped to utter them. After a moment, she says, "Thanks."

"For?"

She smiles. "For remembering where I was and what I was doing and being interested in it, for turning off the TV and for asking."

He shrugs. "I was just vegging."

She passes up the opportunity to gig him—*would you have kept on watching something good?*—and says, "How about yourself?"

"Just more Tiny Town. But Barry told me we got a new contract for a train station somewhere East."

"That figures, West doesn't have any."

"It perked me up, though. All those *gares* and *estaciones* we saw this summer gave me ideas."

"How about having little sleazy cabdrivers in Hot Wheels out on the apron or gypsy women grinning with flowers in their grubby little hands?"

"Clients would love that."

"It always killed me how when you walk up to those lay-outs in a bank lobby the little people in them always look like somebody from the '50s. Ward and June."

"You haven't seen the one we did for the business park in Shawnee Mission, have you?"

"No."

"Hey, affirmative action strikes again."

"You're kidding me. No, wait, I get it: the little black people look like the little white people; they just painted the old models to make a new model line."

"You got it."

"Progress."

"Barry says they can't get a sitter, by the way. They wanted to know if we wanted to have dinner there. I sort of said no."

"Sort of?"

"I said I'd check with you, but that maybe we'd just try again some other time."

She sits up a little straighter. "What's wrong with what they want?"

He drums his fingers on the remote control.

"Aw, I don't know. You know."

"Tell me."

"Well, it's that, you know, how they indulge that kid and he's at them every five seconds wanting something like he can't stand for them to pay attention to anyone else, and they always stop talking to you and get up to play with him, for God's sake, and they won't make him go to bed, and it's just impossible to have a decent conversation. You just feel like you're intruding on an Evening with the Family. They act like they expect us to clap and whistle every time he opens his mouth."

"He is cute."

"He's not that cute."

Is too. Is not. Is too. She would call this a sidecar argument; it runs alongside of, but is attached to, another, more primary vehicle. He's afraid to admit this kid is cute for fear she'll use it on him later.

She shrugs. "Up to you."

At this point, they couldn't say whether they're going to be mad at one another. Could go either way.

"Why is it up to just me?"

"Because I don't mind going over there at all, but it won't kill me not to spend Saturday night with your friends."

"My friends?"

"Okay, that was low. I mean we can easily find something else to do if you don't want to go. You decide, I'm neutral, that's all I meant."

"Maybe I'll feel different about it tomorrow."

Zoom. Into the sidecar again. Tomorrow and tomorrow, clock ticking.

"Yeah, maybe."

"I'll sleep on it."

"Okay."

She lays her nape against the couchback, closes her eyes. Blue wall of the classroom, unironed shirt, rumpled khakis, a handsome young face. Something restful and pleasant yet energizing to gaze at it.

"I showed slides of our trip to the class."

"Yeah?"

"The one you took of me and that Englishman was on the carousel."

"Hmm."

She opens her eyes. He's kneeling before the VCR to perform the programming ritual, then he rises, stands before her, a tall brown-haired, brown-eyed fellow in gray gym shorts, a Corona t-shirt, the remote control in one hand. Bare feet, big toe almost touching a corner of a magazine poking out from under the chair.

"Think I'll tinker in the old workshop."

"Curt?"

"That's me."

"Sit down a minute."

He looks worried, like a kid about to be punished. So—she thinks this is so typical—rather than fully comply with her request, he eases down onto the arm of the recliner.

"What do you want?"

"I want to apologize."

"What for?" He knows her too well not to be a little suspicious, she sees.

"For how I've been acting about that night in Nice."

He rolls his eyes—this again? "I told you nothing happened!"

"Yes. But I think I see now why you took off. It was because you were feeling pressure from me—the wedding party. I think you knew I was wishing that was us getting married, and you were rebelling."

He shrugs. "Could be."

Susan swallows, inhales deeply, turns her face away. Her eyes sting.

"Is that all you can say about it?"

"No. You just have to give me a chance to think about it, you know. I mean, you spring something like that on me and you expect me to come up with an answer right this second."

It's maddening that he either doesn't know enough about himself to immediately recognize this to have been his motive or he's simply not willing to admit to it.

Against her will, she tumbles herself out of the couch, drops to her knees and crawls to the recliner—she's only half-clowning—wraps her arms around his bare thighs and lays her head in his lap. The shorts she laundered smell like Bounce.

"Curt, don't you love me just a little?" She hates sounding so whiny but can't help it.

His hand strokes her brow. He chuckles. "Of course, I do, babe. I love you a lot."

"How do I know, Curt? How?"

"I'm here with you, aren't I?"

"Are you?"

"Yes."

She closes her eyes. She burrows her nose into his belly. Around the Bounce there's a rich warm smell of his skin—he's a big healthy fellow—and she can hear her heart beating in the ear that's pressed into his loins.

"What do you love about me?" She knows he hates this, but the impulse to ask is overpowering.

"You're beautiful, for starters."

He's humoring her. It's like he's following a script—what more can she ask for? Fit punishment for squeezing it out of him.

"Maybe I won't always be beautiful. And I'm not always beautiful. So do you love me when I'm not?"

"Sure. I mean, you're always beautiful to me."

"But what about the me that's me?"

"You're smart and funny. I love that, too."

"Am I sexy?"

"A total fox."

"And you didn't fuck her?"

He scoffs. "No. She was a twit. She was just trying to piss her husband off. I didn't mean diddly-squat to her."

This isn't quite what she wants to hear, but she pretends he's really saying that he was faithful because he loves her.

"I think I believe you now." Her nose is clogged; she pulls her head up from his lap, reaches for a tissue on an end table, blows her nose. Her tears have spotted his shorts.

"Good."

"I don't think I ever have before, but I do now." She *wants to,* is actually what she means.

"Good." This "good" has an air of closure. Curt eases up from the recliner's arm and stands on one foot, scratches that calf with the big toe of the other foot. He idly flips the remote from end to end and catches it a few times before tossing it onto the recliner.

"I've gotta go work on my model, Suz. The meet's only two weeks away."

She almost says *What've you been doing all night?* but bites it back. He wants to avoid her.

Can't say as I blame him, she thinks. Crazy woman!

He goes downstairs; she drags herself up and trudges to their bedroom, listlessly unhooks her earrings and plinks them into her jewelry box, begins peeling off her clothes but when the zipper on her skirt hangs on the fabric, she curses and in a sudden burst of rage pops the hook, tears the skirt from her waist and hot-foots free of it, doing a furious dance, flings the garment into her closet.

When she's out of her pantyhose and down her bra and panties, she feels totally exhausted. She falls back onto the bed. Feels vulnerable, small, too nude. She drags a pillow from under the spread and hugs it. Crazy woman! A twenty-eight-year-old crazy woman! Not Married With No Children. With an unfinished master's thesis. Her live-in boyfriend cheats on her and doesn't love her.

Who would want to marry such a crazy woman?

Sobs boil up like vomit and she smothers her face into the pillow, thrashes about on the bed, shoulders heaving, body shuddering, screaming into the dampening goose-down until she runs out of breath.

She sits up. The pillowcase bears damp spots, lipstick marks, smudges of tan makeup base. What a mess!

When she feels the volcano inside rumble up again, she runs into the bathroom, flushes the toilet, and gets under the shower, where she sobs with her hand over her mouth. After a while, the hot water pelting her shoulders melts her sorrow away; she turns the nozzle to a vibrating pulse on her nape and lets her brain go slow-mo, her mind play dead.

Out of the shower, she wraps in a towel and scans her shelf of the medicine cabinet, takes down her pill clock. Forgot it this morning. Again. Play catch-up. Yes, she knows what this means, Dr. Freud.

Nude under her terrycloth robe, she goes to the top of the stairs and leans over the banister. Curt's head is bent close over the dining table, one hand nimbly and skillfully pressing a swatch of balsa firm against a cutting board while the other wields a surgical-looking Xacto.

"Curt?" Meek little-girl voice.

He doesn't look up, but he answers, "Yeah, babe?" From down there he sounds like someone speaking through a child's can-and-string telephone.

"Curt, I'm sorry I'm such a bitch."

"You're not." He lets that hang, then looks up and grins. "A bitch."

"Are you coming up?" She wants to say *Please come hold me. I need you!*

He turns back to the wood. "Be there in a bit."

She tugs a clean case onto the soiled pillow and lies in the bed with her wet hair kelping on a towel laid under it.

She takes up *The Goddess Within* by Jennifer and Roger Woolger from the bedside table. Since Holly pushed the book on her, she was wary at first, but the premise of it has proven mildly engaging—that Jungian archetypes reaching back to Greek mythology have counterparts in the contemporary female unconscious. Susan has reached the part where a questionnaire promises to reveal which goddess rules her dreams, her life. Is she an Athena (very smart, career-driven), Artemis (also independent, but a nature-lover, Sierra Club sort), Aphrodite (wants love), Hera (the power-lover, politician), Persephone (exists more in the world of the spirit than the flesh—definitely Holly!), or Demeter—"She's the one surrounded by kids; the one babies seem to hang on as from a sturdy tree; the one dishing out the peanut butter and jelly sandwiches...."

She scoots up against the headboard, opens to the questionnaire, takes up the pencil that marked her place. Hesitates. Is she getting too old for this stuff? If she had a nickel for every "who am I?" test she'd taken in *Cosmo, Glamour* or *Seventeen* over the years, she could retire a rich woman right now.

Not surprisingly, the first section relates to appearance.

"Since I don't go out a lot, clothes and makeup aren't that important to me." She's supposed to answer with a 3 (strongly applies), 2 (moderately applies), 1 (mildly applies), or - 1 (not true at all.) She'd give this a 1.5.

"My appearance is rather unconventional."

Well, I'd like to think maybe a little, but stylishly so, you know, when they get up close somebody might notice a pin or my socks. But when I think nobody's watching I go around the house in panties, sweatshirt, and flip-flops.

"Being well-dressed and made up gives me confidence to go out into the world."

That's true, but I don't have to be all dolled up. I don't want my clothes to be dirty, or rumpled the way some student, some kid, a boy, might wear an unironed shirt (a blue one).

On to the second section, then: "My Body." Getting down to the nitty-gritty, here.

"I tend not to think about my body."

Uhhhhh. Where's the line between "not thinking" as the result of feeling okay with it and "not thinking" as wanting to avoid the subject? She accepts her body, she truly does, yes. But she does automatically inventory her flaws as she steps out of the shower and confronts the full-size mirror on the door. Right breast slightly larger than the left, resulting in a droop; she'd like more space between her thighs but there's too much between her eyes, and her butt's too square.

But is this question related to thinking about your body as something other people see as opposed to something you inhabit? It's more PC to focus on the latter, right?

Okay, her answer:

I tend to be more aware of it as I get older, more in tune to it. I can hear it better, feel it better, know what's going on in the tissue and muscle and moving parts. Not incidentally, it has been talking a lot lately.

What's it saying? somebody asks. Gurgles, squeak of new green stem against moist earth as the bean pushes toward heat and light. Water trickling. Heartbeats. Blood, the hum of cells happily making themselves more abundant. Getting ready for a party. Something weird happens inside when she spies some tiny face at Tom Thumb, some kid straddling momma's hip, head lolling half asleep, drooling on her blouse while she rolls her grocery cart down produce lane. That face, it's as compelling as that place on your paycheck where it shows the amount.

The book falls flat to her breast, and she crosses her arms over it. When she came to Carver, several other new teachers started, too. Most were single or engged (she was cohabiting, and Crystal was married); they were all like a club of maidens, and during the next few years they watched each other go up the marital ladder as boyfriends become fiancés, then husbands. A round of bridal showers. Then Susan took two years off for grad school, and when she returned to Carver, there occurred a round of baby showers. The club cleaved into those who had and those who didn't have. The ones without griped about the boundless narcissism of the newly pregnant, but no sooner would a complainer get pregnant, then she'd slip to the other side and become the very thing that previously aroused her annoyance and envy. Of the original group, only two are still childless. One is Holly, who seems happy as a *bonne vivante* and bachlorette.

Leaving yours truly, Barren Bertha, the Maiden.

How had they talked their men into marriage and parenthood?

Was she missing something? Having a husband and children had not been a burning aspiration when she was in college; it was something to anticipate with pleasure as part of future that seemed luxuriantly indefinite yet certain. Later, after she and Curt started living together, she set marriage and child-bearing aside for graduate school, then kept it shelved when Curt got laid off at one firm and spent six months searching for another in his field—his present job.

She guesses that scared him. He's got a list of what he calls reasons and she calls excuses. *Aw, why should we spoil what we've got?* Or he says it's money, but together they make enough. If he'd sell his Integra and stop buying gadgets and toys they could pay off his Visa bill, put away one paycheck and afford a nice wedding and a child. He says they need to save for a down payment on a house, first, but he can't save a dime no matter what the purpose. She says poor people get married and have kids all the time; he says that's what keeps them poor.

Truth is, Curt's not grown up enough to be a father. What she fears is that he's the kind of guy who spends his life being just a kid himself. They usually marry women willing to mother not only their children but also their husbands. Like her Dad.

But, "Do you want to be like your mother?"

Answer is a minus 1: "Not at all."

When Curt comes up, Susan has fallen asleep hugging the book. The yellow pencil is wedged between her fingers.

"Suzie?" he whispers. When she doesn't answer, he slips the pencil free, gently parts her arms, lifts the book, closes it with the pencil as a marker, sets it aside. Her mouth is open; she's breathing in quick shallow scoops of air that might be called panting. Her eyelids twitch.

"Hey, you dreaming?" he whispers.

Susan's having a conference with her thesis advisor. Her professor keeps referring to Susan's thesis subject as paintings about the "Denunciation" instead of "Annunciation." The professor's tone is stern and reproachful, as if Susan has made a mistake. Susan frets and squirms on her chair, she's so disturbed by this uncharacteristic error on the professor's part, but she can't bring herself to correct this older woman, a mentor she admires. The professor's mistake is distressing far out of proportion to its importance. She keeps wanting to speak but thinks over and over she has to "keep mum."

Curt leans down, kisses her forehead.

"Suzie, sweetie?"

The professor's office dissolves into Curt's big round friendly face. She reaches out to embrace him, drags him down between her open thighs.

❦ 6 ❦

When Kennedy was assassinated, Jeffrey Robbins, Jr. was a decade away from drawing his first breath; even five years later when Martin Luther King and Robert Kennedy were murdered and the war raged in Viet Nam and Woodstock came and went, this young man was still only so much genetic potential asleep in the cells of his male sperm-donor and female egg-bearer, who were then unknown to one another.

His mother watched the Watergate Hearings from her bed in the maternity wing of Baylor Medical Center. When Nixon resigned, the boy was not yet speaking complete sentences. When he entered the first grade, his mother had to put their '78 VistaCruiser wagon in a long line at a filling station, but at present the boy has never connected his own vague memory of being hot, restless and bored in the back seat with any event of national significance. He's never dated his memory "1979," and he's never encountered in his meager reading any reference to "the 1979 energy crunch."

More things (a sampling) that Jeffrey Robbins, Jr. does not know:

—Given a U.S. map with the states' names blanked out, he can correctly identify only California, Texas, Oklahoma, Florida and Georgia. On a globe test, he can find the North and South American continents, but cannot locate a single African nation except Egypt, believes that Scotland and England are separate islands and that Ireland is a country on the European continent.

—He has never heard of Spiro Agnew, Joe Louis, Lenny Bruce, Florence Nightingale.

—He does not know the boiling point of water or why the ocean tides are influenced by the moon; he could not tell you which travels faster, light or sound.

—He can recall that our government is divided into three branches, but he might answer "Congress" and "the President" and "Cabinet" if asked to name them. Within a few months, he'll be eligible to vote.

But he's not different from his peers. His ignorance is largely the result of youth, of course; even so, there's little chance he will catch up, exactly, though the vessel of his being will naturally fill with the substance of his own time, his life, his sins or crimes, achievements and accidents. Sometimes it seems a serious flaw in the design of nature that we aren't born knowing all that humankind has learned on its trek through history. However, to have it that way would require this slender, freshfaced boy to be born bearing a very heavy burden not only of useless information but also of collective dark deeds; a congenital awareness of the genocide in this century alone might encourage even the most optimistic and energetic two-year-old to commit suicide. Besides, it seems sufficiently burdensome that we are born trapped in the house built from our genetic blueprint. The "I" learns quickly that the house will go up in flames—not by accident but by design—and that the grand plan requires that "I" stand inside while the house of the body is—how do the papers put it?—*burned beyond recognition.*

That's occurred to Jeff only in the abstract. Naturally, he experienced childhood traumas associated with death: his father's mother; his terrier, Timmy; a ninth-grade school chum drowned in a local lake. Though Jeff has not personally known any suicides, local school counselors anxiously survey the psyches of their students for alarming signs due to an national epidemic of such cases. A Northern suburb of Dallas, Plano, was recently dubbed the "teen suicide capitol" of the U.S.

Given the obvious signs of his mortality, you might think that he lives in fear and trembling. However, he wards off harm by using the famous magical incantation: *not me.* His senses may claim that the world perpetually churns into the maw of death, but his youthful soul denies it vociferously.

Suppose, though, that he lost a parent or a sibling and that the trauma has penetrated his defenses. Suppose he sees he might be next, say, and that nature itself has shape-shifted into a god-like maniacal killer running amok, tinkering with auto brakes, coaxing drunks behind the wheel, and whispering sweet nihilisms into the ears of sleeping psychopaths.

Where can he find aid and comfort? His church? Have his parents given him spiritual guidance to help him thread his way through the difficulties ahead?

His father is a Jew who has drifted into a complacent, half-conscious agnosticism; he spends the Sabbath of his fathers working at his office and playing basketball with old fraternity brothers. On the Christian Sabbath he meets Gentile friends at the Church of Brunch and the New York Times.

At present, the father's religious impulses are devoted to picking apart the mother's evangelical Christianity—she had been a Presbyterian but was "born again" into a fundamentalist sect shortly after the divorce. When the boy visits, his father relishes any opportunity to subject the mother's beliefs to the cold light of rationalism: Speaking in tongues? Walking upon the water? Turning fishes into loaves? Conception without intercourse? Adam and Eve and talking snakes? It doesn't occur to the father to discuss the suffering of the innocent. Nor does he talk about the profound gap between explanations about how and why death came into the world and the deep suspicion that such a scheme of things is, despite the cold comfort of the text, an abominable cruelty.

The ridicule merely makes the boy uncomfortable; to him, his mother is being attacked unfairly. She's not there to defend herself, but he can't take up her cause by arguing for the literal truth of walking upon water or turning it into wine. To him, the Bible stories are no more or less outlandish than the stories of talking turtles who are named after Italian Renaissance artists and are skilled in martial arts.

Whether Bible stories are history or myth seems unimportant; his most serious problem is that his mother's Christianity makes her weird. She is unlike his friends' mothers. She reads the Bible constantly; she preaches against rock-and-roll (will not allow tapes of heavy-metal or rap groups in the house), and is distressingly vocal in public about the fate of drinkers, dancers, and gamblers. The church services she forced on him when he was younger were an excruciating embarrassment. About twenty people met in an Oak Cliff apartment; they were blue-collar types who favored polyester clothing and out-of-date hairstyles and eye-glasses and spoke with poor grammar, and even though they were complete strangers they'd clasp him in their sweaty embraces.

Were it not for his father's legal rights, his mother wouldn't have allowed the boy to spend weekends at his father's apartment when he was younger, since the father's girlfriends often lived there. The mother insisted to Jeff that only a court could force her to risk the boy's damnation through exposure to the father's sin. His mother told him to wash his hands thoroughly when he visited and to wipe off the toilet seat before sitting on it.

In the matter of religion both parents campaign for Jeff's vote. The mother's platform—there is one way and all others are damned!—precludes his somehow accommodating both or offering a compromise candidate. The father's campaign is altogether negative; he can try to sway the boy to vote against the mother, but he offers little reason to vote for him.

Neither knows Jeff's true feelings. He observes that his mother derives enormous comfort from both her church and her religion, and Jeff's deeply grateful that she gets it. To him his Dad is his connection to the normal territory of the planet. He's like everybody else's Dad. He lives in the regular world, where divorce is common and your father reads the newspaper every day and keeps up with the stock market and buys neat cars and gets tickets to the Mavericks and goes to all the hit movies and has girlfriends (some nice) stay over at his apartment; he reads *Sports Illustrated* and buys tapes for the stereo Jeff keeps at the apartment or lets the boy play tapes on the big system in the living room with the Klipschorn speakers, lets him watch R-rated films on his twenty-five inch Sony. (The mother knows nothing about this.)

Which brings us to what Jeff's mother calls "carnal knowledge." Though the boy and his peers are ignorant of what adults do in public, they are very knowing about what is done in private.

Shortly after the divorce when Jeff was nine, he discovered a *Penthouse* between a *Newsweek* and a *Forbes* in a stack of magazines beside his father's couch. His father was outside washing his car. The boy opened the magazine to the center-fold. The woman had giant bosoms and hair all over her thing, and since she was lying with her legs open he could see it was like a pocket, sort of, or a mouth, a bearded mouth, with a little tongue sticking out.

He slapped the magazine shut and jammed it back into the stack.

He had heard something. Only a squirrel on the roof. He went into the kitchen, anyway, where he sat at the table playing his video football game, the tiny screen reflecting back the roundness of his cheek, his mouth.

On visitation weekends thereafter he would see the new Miss Month, and he got used to it. On paper they were about the size of Barbie dolls, but he got the impression that the camera had diminished them; to his mind's eye the real women depicted belonged to a race of giantesses. Their hairy things might be big as catcher's mitts, their bosoms the size of basketballs.

When he was twelve his father's girlfriend noticed the magazine and said, *Aren't you worried Jeff might see this?* It hadn't occurred to the father that Jeff might be rooting about in the magazines, but he said, *Yeah, what's to worry about?*

There was nothing to be ashamed of; the kid's mother was a bluenose Bible-thumper, and the kid should know that human sexuality was where life came from, and it was good.

Two years later when he had a buddy sleeping over and his Dad and Sybil were at a business dinner, he found a film called "RimBo" in the stack of tapes. They presumed it was a satire like "Airplane." But it was about a guy with a huge dong. He kept sticking it into women's butts or their pussies, and the camera would zoom in so close the dong looked like a big greasy arm sliding in and out of what looked like something from the bottom of the ocean that pulsed as it tried to swallow whatever ventured into its hideout. The woman screamed and the guy grunted off-camera; it was like the monkey house at the zoo. The guy had another woman suck his dong, and since it was bigger than anything any woman ever put into her mouth, it distorted her whole face, made her look unlike any woman he'd ever seen. When, later, Jeff went into the bathroom, his own pink finger of a dick looked pitifully ineffective even when stiff, and after the goo was gone and it was curled in his lap like a worm, despair swept over him. He yearned to do all he saw; he was terrified that one day he would be *required* to do it all but would lack the equipment, the knowledge, the determination. He envied the guy's way of carrying himself, the way he stuck out his dong and there appeared—without question or without anybody's objecting—a hole right there to put it in. This required a way of being in the world, a posture, that he feared he could never master. Some guys could stand at the plate and take a fast ball without flinching or stepping back when the pitch came inside; some guys could dive, not jump, off the thirty-five-foot tower at camp. These guys grew up to have big dongs.

That his father had the film suggested that his father was among those men for whom sex was like a meal you ate with relish and complete unself-consciousness. Though he'd never caught his father and a girlfriend in the act of love, he'd seen them kissing, and he knew when they went to "nap" behind the locked bedroom door, they were probably doing It.

But like this "Rimbo" stuff? It was inconceivable. He knew he was born from his mother's egg fertilized by his father's sperm, but he couldn't picture them doing what he saw on the screen. His father had girlfriends (and later Sybil became his stepmother), but his mother was celibate. (She's a "bride o' Christ," joked the father, the way you'd say "Land O' Lakes Butter.") The boy couldn't even picture his mother alone without clothes; the attempted projection of that image generated static like TV interference.

The film only visually corroborated the locker room gossip of junior-high boys, only illustrated or clarified a hundred jokes he'd heard but only half-understood; the film merely made explicit the accumulated implicit promises of a thousand television commercials and music videos. Soon the guys he ran with at Lakeview—most living with their single mothers—were borrowing such tapes bootlegged by older brothers and were staying up on weekends, the innocent mother respecting their privacy and offering them popcorn while behind the locked door they're watching "Cum On My Tits." They gave themselves an informal course on the sexual practices of Western industrial societies: sodomy, bondage, sado-masochism, domination, cunnilingus, autoeroticism, fellatio, transvestitism, tribadism, etc. By age fifteen Jeff had seen demonstrations of practices that ninety-nine percent of the Earth's people would consider even in this day and age to be inconceivable, unbelievable, only apocryphal or legendary. (Or unthinkable. And in many cases criminal.) He took it in stride; he laughed with his friends; they yelled encouragement to the players; they made vulgar remarks about the slabs of anatomy bared to the screen.

He grew six inches during that year, leaped four shoe sizes and added fifteen pounds. Now people he didn't know treated him differently. Three times grown women, complete strangers, have told him he should consider modeling, and they offered to help him. A woman in a fur coat who accosted him at Neiman's told him that he could be her "house boy." When he and his buddies stroll the malls, flocks of junior-high girls giggle and cut eyes at him as they pass, and one might yell something unintelligible to his back, and if he turns around they'll be scurrying off, mockingly chastising the one who spoke so boldly. When he worked concessions at the theater, guys in tank-tops and neat-cropped hair and mustaches smiled too much and tried to snag his fingers when he gave back change.

The result of this attention on his personality? Cheryl, who couldn't keep her eyes off him this evening at the art club meeting, thinks he's "conceited." Becki presumes he's gay. His mother presumes from his apparent lack of interest in earnest courtship that he is too serious-minded for the frivolous girls who call at all hours (even though she can tell he doesn't encourage them); she thinks he is shy and is waiting for the right girl. She believes that he will find his true sweetheart at The Church of the Gospel Truth. Some day when he is ready. To her this is "returning," as if he's now an unbeliever or a backslider.

They're all mistaken. The truth is that despite all his bawdy talk with Todd, he's terrified. And, secretly, he is terrified of being terrified: is there something wrong with him that he doesn't feel he could be like the guy in "Rimbo"? Is there something wrong that he's not accepted any proposition? He's so skittish that he's learned to detect them before the other party has even spoken, sometimes before the other party has even understood that he or she will offer a proposition.

He thinks he's supposed to be pleased by these approaches, but all he feels is dread. They call for a response; he lacks the guts or the desire to say yes and saying no obviously wounds the other person; part of him says it's not his worry how a stranger feels when he says no; another part feels guilty. He longs to talk to someone about this but that requires revealing that something's wrong. Is he a weirdo? A pervert? A retard? Something wrong with his hormones? (If that's the case, why's he have wet dreams?) Does he need a psychiatrist?

Listening to him talk about this would evoke your pity. Because his problem seems so clear, a few smart words from someone he respects and trusts—his father?—might set his mind at ease. Someone wise might tell him he's just not ready to lose his virginity; he's not physically or psychologically mature enough to feel ready deep inside. He's sensitive and bright enough to be aware of what others about him are feeling, and everywhere he turns the culture screams at him to join the fun, to surrender his childhood. Someone wise could say, "Hey, you're just green, you know, like trees and fruit, it's natural, for God's sake. Be patient. When you're ready, you'll be ready, and it will happen soon. And then you'll have several decades of this stuff."

But he doesn't seek help from anyone he knows. He goes it alone, waiting with antsy impatience for a defining event to arrive and resolve the tension. You might say that his adolescence has been like a bad dream, that he "woke" to find himself thrashing about in deep dark water and screaming for help, but no one came, and so he had to flail his way to safety before he drowned. That's where he is right now, still in the water but clinging to the bank and looking out to the depths where everyone else is having so much fun.

Now, at his desk, he finds himself absently doodling in the margins of his history notes.

Drawing, he thinks. Told her he's taking private lessons. You're a lying dick.

Do you just pick up a pencil and start in on it?

He's been drawing since he was old enough to grip an instrument; he can't stand to talk on the phone without making pictures on the notepad, and his class notebooks are always festooned with garbage in the margins he's put there while half-listening to a lecture.

He reviews his meager repertoire by skimming his class notebook: Yoda, Tic Tac Toe, a hand pointing to a star, more stars, Darth Vader, a guitar, the profile of a woman with huge lips. A man in a robe with a long beard and a staff. A Star Wars fighter. M-60 tank. *FUCK YOU* altered to read *BOOK YOU*.

Clears his desk, sets clean typing paper directly on the top. The rough surface of the old wood will screw up the drawing, so he slips three more pieces under the first. He rummages about in the clutter of his top drawer until he locates a lead pencil—nobody would draw with a ball-point, would they?—finds one ("Shamburger Building Center"), but it's dull. Leaning over the wastebasket, he shaves the soft pine with a razor blade, feeling like a surgeon.

The point breaks the instant he touches it to the paper, and after two more sharpenings he sees that a slightly blunted point will withstand the pressure.

He can't do his stupid margin scribbling, of course. He needs an official subject. He stares at the paper for a moment. A house?

But when he's finished the roof and the chimney, it looks like a fourth-grader's rendering, so he leaves it without doors and windows and goes on to the second sheet. He tries a horse, then the face of a cat, then a pirate with scar and eye patch. It seems his lack of talent makes him scrawl cartoons instead of drawings. It's very, very hard to make anything look the way it does in real life.

He tries drawing an empty Dr. Pepper can. This requires more concentration than doodling out of his head: he's seeing the can with a clarity he's never experienced. The results are better than when he drew from his imagination, but he's impatient with it: even if it's a really good job, when you finish you've only got a drawing of a Dr. Pepper can.

Tool poised over a fresh sheet, mind drifting. His pencil hand is the habitat of drawing memories, so, while he muses, it idly rehearses what it knows: profile of a woman with big lips, then a bust of a woman meant to look beautiful, long lashes, high cheek bones, feathery bangs. The hand adds eyeglasses on the woman.

The pencil drifts lower, tickling the paper with downy strokes as her breasts, then her nipples, appear; it's as if they've been present but invisible on the page, and the dark shaft of lead has caressed them into visibility. Then she's lying on her back with her legs spread like the M-women on restroom walls, and when he shades in her pussy his erection strains against his jeans. It's weird, he thinks, to be aroused by the sight of something he is drawing, and yet be also aroused by drawing it. There was a blank page and that throbbing pussy in his brain, and the image has leaked out of his hand onto that surface, where it's even more potent.

He wads the paper, tosses it into the wastebasket, then immediately retrieves it and jams it into his book bag.

New sheet. His left hand keeps kneading the stiffened flesh, so he decides to solve two problems at once: he sets the offending hand onto the desk beside the paper and pulls the gooseneck lamp over it like an examining doctor would.

Studying his left hand, he begins to draw it with his right. It's weird; the hand the right hand is creating on the page looks thick-fingered and primitive like a sturdy ape's paw made of wood, and when he moves his gaze back to the "subject," the living hand looks pink and naked, complicated and slender, vulnerable as a sea creature tossed alive onto shore.

He sighs and gets up, turns off the lamp. He lies back on the bed and stares at the ceiling. A water-stain Rorschach. Doctor, I see a wingéd creature. No, wait, it's the outline of a fried egg, no, wait, doctor, it's a rusty coathanger bent out of shape, somebody's weird sculpture. The stain is old, but a damp gray spot the size of a quarter in its center reminds him of the rain. He rolls over, looks through the window, then scoots to the sill and raises the sash. The wind has stopped, the streets and sidewalk gleam, but the drizzle, so light it's more like a saturated mist that gravity is tugging down, makes only the faintest sibilant rustle on the leaves of the silver maple in the front yard. A car goes *ssshhh* as it cruises by.

Miss Hart, her scarf! Panicky, he gets up, feels in the book bag and pulls it out. Christ, he probably ruined it wadding it up like that. What was he thinking of, keeping it? He better fold it up nice and take it back tomorrow in a Ziploc bag.

He throws back the rumpled covers, tightens the bottom sheet, then spreads the scarf flat into a large smooth square where he usually lies. Perry Ellis. It's expensive, then. It's a beautiful black, gray and red abstract design. Naturally, her scarf would match her taste as an artist, art teacher. It's delicate and too thin to keep a fold. He lifts the scarf in his left palm and holds it as if weighing it. It feels very light and soft to his fingertips.

He lies back on the bed with his feet on the floor and sets the scarf on his bare chest. He blows on it, and it unfolds, cascades down his ribs. Tickles.

He drapes it over his face to keep out the light. When he breathes out, it poofs up, then back. He keeps his mouth closed so he won't get spit on it but inhales hard to smell her perfume. It sends chills zipping along his arms. He goes back to being stuck in a flood with her, having to remove their wet clothes and get under a blanket in the dark cave of the car with the radio playing. Then, with his eyes closed, he pulls down his pajama bottoms. They're together in the car. He touches her breasts. He trails the loose folds of the scarf over his erection. It feels cool and silky. He kisses her nipples and touches her under her skirt; he coils the scarf about his erection, pulls it slowly, slowly, so it rubs him as it unwinds free, then hears moaning.

"Oh shit! You fucking pervert!"

Too late he tried to buck free, and now the scarf is soiled with great damp spots that stink like ammonia.

Curt's always fast. Now he's fast asleep. The boyishness that Susan used to find endearing as the source of his playful spontaneity often makes him romp like a puppy when the situation calls for more delicacy. (We might say he dogpaddles his way furiously across the water where a calm Australian crawl would get him there with more grace.)

What of Susan's expertise? She and her high-school sweetheart, Nathan, were eager amateurs but not given to experimentation beyond timid explorations of oral sex as a prelude to missionary intercourse. She was so much in love that whatever they did could be sanctified by the rosy glow of her swelling emotion, and so she had no need to taint her love-making by admitting it to a priest. But when Nathan broke up with her just before she left for college, she was deeply ashamed and did confess. Losing him served her right for breaking the rules.

She arrived shortly thereafter on her new campus in Austin

heart-sick and angry, and that not surprisingly led to depression and the dark urge to commit acts that would correspond with her opinion of herself, confirm her utter lack of worth. She drank too much (vodka with mixers); she smoked too much marijuana ("too much" being her own eventual judgment), and usually boys were her companions; usually they became sexual partners for a single occasion, or maybe for a weekend, once or twice for a fortnight. Most of them she hardly knew, though one or two might have been called "friends" in that way the young identify one another solely on the grounds of, say, both liking the same hit song. The graduate teaching assistant for her huge introductory psychology class was a married man with a small child; he hit on her after the course was over, and she met him secretly at the La Quinta on I-35 on a weekday afternoon.

She was hardly ever sober when she was with these partners. And it didn't matter much if they wanted her or only sex, because the sex had little value to her—it rarely led to orgasm—so she felt no loss if they took it for granted. Many partners sought return engagements. (And why not—she was a smart and beautiful girl who'd go down on you when she was stoned.) Sometimes she went out with them again; it depended mostly on her schedule, since her feelings seemed to be irrelevant.

She was almost falling-down drunk at a fraternity house one Saturday night with a boy she'd dated once before, and he was leading her by the hand through rowdy, tipsy students down an upstairs hall toward his room, when they were separated by an upheaval in the crowd. From an open doorway, the Bee-Gees were crooning the soundtrack from the recent hit "Saturday Night Fever"—*Oo oo oo oo stayin' alive*...A cute, sturdy-looking fellow boldly wearing an Aggie sweatshirt was leaning on the door frame. He said, "You don't wanna go in his room." She said, "Whose room?" He jerked his head toward the end of the hall. "You're with John Robert, right?" She said, "Yeah. So?" He said, "You don't wanna go in that room." He wasn't smiling;

he wasn't flirting. His brows were scrunched into a frown. She grinned, trying to stay playful. "Why not?" He blushed. "Because there's other people in there, other guys, you know?"

She took his advice and, already queasy from drinking, went home. When she discovered this Galahad the very next day in her Art History class, she was floored by the sensation of fate or, at least, fateful coincidence—as if he'd been assigned the role of guardian angel and had been given her schedule and the mission of following her about. He had saved her from what she believed would've been an attempted gang rape. His warning seemed so wholly fortuitous, so random, that she'd come to her senses altogether and was astonished that her luck had run so good for so long that she hadn't met the fate of the woman in *Looking For Mister Goodbar.* She realized that she'd been at great risk from her own recklessness—at risk of pregnancy, herpes (she hadn't heard of AIDs yet), gonorrhea. Her Catholic teaching rose up to condemn her; she had a reawakened awareness of herself as soiled, as a sinner, and her shame burned deep.

He spoke to her, asked if she were feeling okay.

His name was Curt. It turned out that he had been admiring her from across the room in this large class for some time.

With Curt she felt safe. He didn't seem to know she'd been acting like a stoned-out slut for months. They started dating. Her fidelity to him was the gift she offered in exchange for his compassionate inter-est in her welfare. For a long while she thought Curt had sort of, well, "saved" her, but then, once their ardor cooled from months of expo-sure, and rational considerations (nagging doubts) had crept in, she wondered if his gallantry hadn't been self-serving even as it served her. He's standing in the hallway, sees this girl he'd been admiring in class coming along with John Robert, feels a twinge of jealousy, de-cides to intrude. Her question was: if she'd been a homely fat girl he'd never seen before, would he have spoken up? Did it matter? And wasn't she ungrateful to undermine his courage this way? And was this her low self-esteem working to negate a deserved gift?

Now, several years later, what she can recall most clearly from this period is this: when they got ready to graduate and started talking of moving in together, she wondered if she hadn't given up her freedom hastily. Had she merely been faint-hearted? Had she *really* been in any danger? Or was she just timid from religious indoctrination and the cultural influences on females? Was sober, steady, reliable Curt really what she wanted in a mate? Truth be known, she'd felt safe long enough to miss her wildness.

Susan rises from the bed and goes into the bathroom to finish what Curt started. When she emerges wearing her terrycloth robe she pads softly out of the room. She feels too wired to sleep; she might as well work—the dream about her professor nags her.

In the study she threads her way in the dark to her desk, sits, clicks a few keystrokes, and a file blinks onto the screen. The room seems too much like a cave with only the screen's gray glow like underwater light softly bathing the nearby pad, a clock, books, so she hits the button on a goose-neck lamp and cocks the shade to shunt the light away.

Being too restless to sleep and being alert enough to work are entirely different states, of course, and Susan's mind is momentarily paralyzed by her own hieroglyphics made earlier on the lighted square twelve inches from her nose. Curt has said that this thesis is an albatross around her neck, and she replied, *Albatross? I'd call it a pterodactyl!* It's all she needs to finish her M.A. in Humanities, and that M.A. means a raise of $3000 a year. The trip to Italy fired her up, gave her the jump start she'd hoped for. But, she doesn't know what—is it dog days? Too many distractions at the start of the school year? For whatever reason, she can't get cranking on it. She drags a huge tome under the light: Frederick Hartt, *History of Italian Renais-*

sance Art. Turns to p. 335, a 4" x 4" black and white reproduction of Botticelli's Annunciation. She eagerly looked forward to seeing the original in the Uffizi in Florence, carried note cards into the museum; she came away deflated—it seemed dark, dingy, and small compared to her imagined projection of it—but she was willing to blame all that on the very poor lighting. The text says that the painting shows:

> ...*the gathering intensity of Botticelli's religious fervor. The event takes place in a room furnished only by the lectern at which Mary has been reading. Through the open door one looks into Mary's closed garden. From behind the lily held by the angel a tree rises, as if to fulfill the prophecy of Isaiah, "A shoot shall grow from Jesse's rod," and to foretell the Tree of the Cross. The buildings in the background, intended to be read together with the garden and the tree, may likewise be symbolic. The barrenness of the architecture, like a draftsman's rendering rather than a painting of a real room, provides a strangely unresponsive setting for the emotionality of the figures. Mary, whose pose derives from the Annunciations by Donatello (see fig. 245), Fra Filippo (see colorplate 29), and Baldovinetti (see fig. 317), now sways as if caught in a rushing wind....*

She fidgets, rubs her eyes. She wishes she still smoked. Since she's working on a degree in interdisciplinary studies, she plans to treat the depicted material as narrative or story to be interpreted using at least three theoretical templates, each like a different lens: one is the traditional scholarly exegesis from a Roman Catholic perspective; another interpretation is broadly psychological, and a third treats the story from a feminist-political point of view.

She's put off digging into the Catholic reading—for one thing, there are volumes of source material to pore over, since this interpretation reaches back to the early Church fathers. For another reason, as a lapsed Catholic, she tends to take an ironic, even sometimes frivolous, attitude toward this interpretation. She recalls with distaste her Catholic upbringing and gets angry when she considers that the guilt and shame she carries concerning her body and sex are the vestiges of that childhood indoctrination. Thinking of the Annunciation in a flip and sardonic way is a kind of revenge. She protests too much and knows she does; to convince herself that she is *not* overly sensitive and defensive, she struggles to adopt a stance of scholarly serenity, of Olympian detachment, but maintaining it is like trying to stay upright while you're walking on one rail of a train track.

When the Pope came to Denver, she made fun of the outlandish hoopla (like others, she called his Plexiglas-bubbled limousine "The Pope Mobile") and jibed at one Anglo friend who made a pilgrimage to see him. (She said nothing to her Hispanic colleagues, as they might have considered such teasing racist.) When the friend returned, Susan longed to hear all the wickedly ironic details, but the friend merely smiled at her—beatifically, she thought—and told her that the pleasures of a pilgrimage were for pilgrims to discover. Susan felt a twinge of regret that she could no longer be swayed or moved (remade, reformed) by being blessed, even if only in a crowd of 10,000 worshippers, by the Holy Father.

She fingerstrokes on the keyboard to bring up her draft.

...these paintings dramatize the cycle of emotional and physiological response that begins in quiet solitary repose and turns to arousal, then to orgasm, then to guilt and judgment. Because paintings can only suggest but not depict a temporal progression, we must "read" them the way we interpret props that appear in dreams; that is, we see that multiple and contradictory psychological states which we normally consider to be sequential have been compressed and layered onto one static picture; a painting may be considered a kind of palimpsest of symbolic events.

Just prior to the moment depicted, Mary is closeted in a room alone, engaged in an activity (reading) that itself removes her one step farther from everyday reality. Ostensibly, this setting and Mary's activity suggest prayer or a meditative state of receptivity that prepares her for the angel's visit—it has opened the door for the visitation, so to speak.

*But the picture of Mary standing beside her chair or couch after the Angel has appeared also suggests what has happened immediately **before** the arrival, or as of the arrival: often the book she was reading has been knocked to the floor. From this, we presume she was startled by the angel (say she bolted up from her chair), but, more importantly, Mary's posture and that book on the floor testify not only to a violent physical reaction of Mary's just before the "moment" we "see" her in the picture, but to a reaction that suggests that just before the "opening" of the painting, she experienced an uncontrolled **physical** response that grew out of meditation.*

The angel—often gloriously blond, androgynous, other-worldly—is a figure from her fantasy, a figure with an aura supercharged with Eros. The angel who has arrived at the "moment" depicted in the paintings represents, simultaneously, at least three different things:

1) The angel is the object of Mary's lust, the result of her arousal and likewise the cause of its continuance; that is, the angel is the objectification of her arousal.

2) The angel represents Mary herself in the state of transport or orgasm. The androgyny of the creature harks back to polymorphous infancy when self-arousal has no connection to differentiated genders or other persons: the infant Mary was both male (fingers, hands, objects) and female (genitalia) for herself. The angel hovers, glowing, off the floor, in flight, or if not literally in flight, clearly able to achieve flight by wings. The connection between flying and orgasm is a psychoanalytical commonplace.

3) The angel represents the post-orgasmic self-condemnation. Bursting in upon her privacy, the angel is the "world returned," the inevitable landing after the flight. That the angel comes as a spokesperson for God is significant. The angel's specific message is not as important as is the fact of the intrusion: startled by the unexpected interruption, she per-haps jumped to the conclusion that she had been caught. Perhaps "he" (God, her father, the Moral Authority who has sent the angelic deputy) is pretending not to know what she was up to but wants her to be aware that he is always within knowing distance.

But the angel's message—that Mary will give birth to the son of God—is ambiguous and complex, the usual condition of messages that come from dreams or within. The message expresses Mary's maternal longings even while it represents her acknowledgment that her self-grat-ification cannot produce a child, and the idea that Mary will conceive without the aid of mortal man more firmly speaks to her unconscious fear that masturbation will "harm" her by making her barren (require a God for impregnation). The message from God is not the annunciation of a gift: it is a complicated "Denunciation," a "message" that embodies her own guilt and even delivers a sentence for the crime: for thy sin thou shalt be barren.

Her mind goes fuzzy. When she tries to retrack the idea, it dis-sipates. Screened on the back of her skull comes up a glowing slide of another, much later *Annunciation,* by the 19th century painter Maurice Greiffenhagen, this one very secular: Mary with one hand dreamily languid, loose-wristed, in the air, her head back, face uptilted, eyes closed, red-lipped mouth parted. Kiss me. The angel's downturned face over hers, his eyes closed too, his mouth parted. Movie moment. I will in-spire (breathe).

Child-bearing. The angel's beauty. The angel's face, almost al-ways seen in profile, is difficult for the modern eye to call masculine. Like a girl's, or a boy's. Mary's blue robe, pale face. Mary, Mary, quite contrary, shouldn't you say no?.... Little boy blue, come blow your. Little blue boy, little big horn, little-horn boy. Unicorn.

Her eyes close, though she's not sleeping, only slipping into the zone where dreams walk out to meet us and draw us inside, where the imagination and memory consort and confuse one another. Figures move there. She's awake enough that if you spoke, she could answer, after a moment, but not alert enough to be put behind the wheel. What happens now behind her eyes, it's not her fault.

Is an idea a dangerous thing? Can an idea move or restrain us? Should she be warned? If we could thrust our hands through the fictional framework we could perhaps scribble on her notepad. As she so obviously knows, there are ways to interpret an Annunciation scene. But she has overlooked one. She tries to see how the figures stand for us all, Everyman and Everywoman, but it could be said that the scene between Mary and God or God's messenger dramatizes a moment when an ordinary person (Mary before) is called upon by an outside force (God, the State, another person) or an inward voice (she was meditating, soul-searching) to perform something extraordinary; the scene illustrates a moment when a small and anonymous individual whose life is the same size as everyone else's suddenly steps onto the public stage of history because of an act of heroism, a heinous crime, or mortal sin.

Before the Angel singled her out, Mary was a person no one knew; afterward, she belonged to the Romans.

*O*n a Wednesday morning Susan whipstitches herself through the crowd in the hall to catch him.

"Jeff?"

He turns, looks panicky. Susan regrets accosting him so boldly. She touches his arm as if to draw his attention.

"Could you drop by my office right after sixth period? There's something I want to ask."

His cheeks flush with a burnished glow on each smooth hump. He looks around as if they're being watched, but the other students stream blindly by, and they're huddled in a pocket.

"Is it about the scarf you gave me?"

"Scarf?"

"I didn't mean give me. I meant you loaned it to me that night to, you know, dry myself off."

"Oh, oh!" she cries. "No, I'd forgotten all about it."

"You had? I, well, I was going to come talk to you about this as soon as I could, today, but like what happened was I accidentally left it out because I wanted to be sure and bring it right back to you so I put it on my chair by my desk, and that's how my dog got a hold of it. He chewed it up pretty bad. I know it cost a lot, and I'm real sorry. I saw one just like it out at the mall, and I was going to go get it as soon as I could, you know, to replace the one you loaned me. I'm real sorry."

"Oh, it's all right. I'd had it quite a while. It was a gift." She meant to minimize its importance but sees she's implied the opposite. "From no one special," she adds. "Don't worry about it."

"Thanks." He grins, his shoulders drop, his hazel-eyed gaze meets hers. "I'll come see you after school," he vows, smiling. The bell rings and people dash to cross their proper thresholds.

On the way to monitor study-hall, she anticipates their conference. Last night he missed the club meeting, and she worried that the others scared him off. She has always taken pride in going an extra few steps to make the shy kids feel comfortable or to be a good listener when some kid's too upset to attend to business—you never know whether Becki, say, is crying because she's had a spat with Jory or whether her Mom's back in jail and her Dad's insisting that she come live with him in Montana. Point is, each kid is a unique case.

She meant to lure him back to the club by offering him drawing lessons. Now, though, she sees he didn't come because of the scarf. The air's been cleared about that, so he might return without any extraordinary measures.

But by their conference time, she has forgotten the scarf and has returned to believing that she has to reach out to bring him back. He's shy. He needs to be encouraged. It's a terrible thing to be a new kid, alone, in a new school.

After sixth period, she strides into her office meaning to grab her purse and zip off to the lounge to freshen her lipstick and comb her hair, but when she wheels to leave, she almost bumps into Jeff. He does a little bashful two-step over the threshold, his book bag slung over his right shoulder. Can of Coke in his right hand.

"Come in!" Her voice—is she shouting?—shocks her. He's early. She's rattled.

"Thanks."

There ensues a dance of such bumbling choreography that her heart warms to the charm of it: letting the shoulder strap to the bag slip to his elbow, he simultaneously passes the can to his left hand, all the while trying to sit in her visitor's chair, but bag's fall to the crook of his arm jostles the can hand, and soda sloshes onto his wrist.

"Oh, Jesus, I'm sorry!" he murmurs, though the damage is only to himself.

She plucks a Kleenex from a box on her desk, gives him the tissue and takes the Coke, holds it until he's safely seated and takes the damp tissue back, passes him the Coke. Patty-cake. She smiles, and he grins crookedly.

She smoothes the back of her skirt and slips into her chair, aware that her skirt-hem flutters up off her knees. In the hall, students stroll by chattering. Maybe she should shut the door.

He looks about. "This is a neat place."

"I like it a lot. I'm lucky. Most of my colleagues don't get offices, but I was friendly with the custodian who used it as a supplies closet, and I just sort of appropriated it when he retired."

"Sure doesn't look like a janitor's closet."

His gaze flicks from wall to wall. Maybe he admires her decor, maybe it's flattery. She scrubbed the space, repainted the walls gallery-white, hung prints and posters, and brought in ornamental bowls of potpourri to override the vestigial whiffs of mildewed mop and linseed oil. She brought a cheap Dhurri to cover the trowel-swirls in the concrete floor, a nice oak secretary with a drop-front at an antique shop for a desk. Her chair is a spindleback her grandmother used for sewing; it's like a rocking chair without rockers (rocking nauseated her grandmother), so to Susan this chair offers comfort and stability.

"I like that desert scene with the lion and that woman, that's neat."

She waves toward the poster. "I thought about maybe painting what the French call a *trompe l'oeil*: on that wall, an optical illusion, a window frame with a scene, maybe what you'd see if a window were there—you know, the tops of those highrises on Turtle Creek, the Crescent, and the freeway."

"You wouldn't want something wilder?"

"Wilder?" The way the boy pitches in pleases her, and she beams at him.

"Well, you know, like Mount Everest poking up out of the middle of North Dallas."

Susan laughs. "Well, that's a great idea."

He leans forward. "Or a jungle scene maybe."

Susan crosses her legs, and her right foot juts into the space between their chairs; she wore Birkenstocks today but neglected to freshen her toe-nail polish. She sees his eyes trace the line of her bare shin from the sandal to her knee. She raises her hand to touch her cheek with her ring and middle finger, and his eyes follow the hand. He seems alert to the smallest nuance of movement in any part of her body. Maybe he has a little crush. That's cute; when the boys do that, it's always a little flattering to your ego, likewise when the girls admire your jewelry or your clothes. She and her female colleagues have a tacit, publicly unacknowledged competition for the regard of students, and though no one would confess it, this is one way to win—to be admired, even adored. In return they wind up treating some students as pets but never call them that; instead, they find ways of making allowances for transgressions—he has a single mom, she works two jobs, his father's in jail, she's A.D.D.

Jeff is poised perfectly in her mind to assume this role. He's an underdog because he's new and because he seems like a refugee, the human detritus, from a shallow, materialistic culture, a wash-out from a private prep school but not yet an "artistic" kid. She wants to help him; she loves to think of herself helping him; she loves to feel his admiring regard, it's like sunlight. And he's awfully easy to look at himself.

"What I wanted to talk to you about was that, well, you remember our conversation about taking private drawing lessons?"

"Yes, ma'am."

"Jeff, you can call me Susan, remember? You can call me anything but ma'am."

"Okay. Sorry."

She smiles. What a bashful fellow! "It's no problem. What I was going to say was I've been thinking about taking it up again just to keep from getting rusty and I wondered if you'd care to sign on."

"Really?"

He looks excited? No, he looks interested, or at least he's putting on the face of someone who is supposed to be pleased. Whatever—it's less than she hoped for.

"If you're worried about the fees, we can work something out. I've got lots of things that need to be done around here or at my apartment, you know." Her offer sounds indulgent to her ear, and she's annoyed that she has to sell him on it. She adds, "You'll have to buy some supplies initially, of course, and I don't think I can help you with that," though she instantly recalls that everything he might need is here.

"Thanks," he says politely.

Much to her irritation, he seems blasè, even indifferent.

"Do I hear a 'but...'?"

"Oh, no." He frowns at his feet. He's wearing scuffed leather deck shoes, sans socks—Euro-trash style—but his tanned dusty ankles suggest to Susan a montage of Norman-Rockwell boys treading barefoot down the trail to the fishing hole, a beach on a lake, an aroma of coconut, Nathan's water-beaded skin. "It's just that it puts a lot of pressure on me, you know, and I don't know if I have the talent that would make it worth your effort."

"Oh, Jeff! Jeff!" She bends forward, laughing, and touches him gently on his knee with her fingertips; his leg gives slightly to the pressure. "Let me worry about that, okay?"

"Okay."

They stand and face each other as if an orchestra just struck up a tune. "Well, you'll need some Ebony brand pencils with jet-black lead, and a couple erasers, one gum the other just pink, you know, I'm sure you've seen them. You could probably get some Venus drawing pencils with different shades of lead—they come in different degrees of hardness: HB, 2B, 2H, etc. Later on you can get some calligraphy pens and some charcoal, but—"

He looks bewildered. "Well, I tell you what. You just show up for your first lesson and I'll bring pencils and paper. Then I can make you a short list of necessities, how's that? When would be good for you to meet?"

"I can basically meet any time," he says, then frowns. "Except when I have to help my mother."

"Okay, that's fair. And me, too. How about after school this Wednesday?"

He shrugs, beams at her. "That's cool."

They do-si-do and glide toward the door. He is tall, taller than Curt; the tag on his shirt sticks out above his collar, and she almost reaches up to tuck it in but catches herself. The dog hairs curl on his nape, arousing, strangely, her pity.

"Well, I'm glad we had a chance to talk, Jeff, and I'm presuming that you won't drop out of the club?"

"Aw, naw."

At the threshold she hastens to add, "You'll be glad you stuck it out, believe me, we're going to be doing some very interesting things and I'd hate for you to miss them. I just talked to some people about our doing a mural on a fence that's around a construction site a couple blocks away, so we need lots of designers and painters, and I know the others would appreciate your ideas and your help." Her sudden bubbly garrulousness is inexplicable, embarrassing—he's agreed to come back, so why is she cheerleading?

Despite herself, she says, "I'm also going to give a Halloween party at my apartment. I've been doing it for the past couple of years. Everybody comes in really weird costumes and we go watch the parade on Cedar Springs, you know? Even I come in costume. I haven't figured out what I'll be this year." She smiles brightly into his face; he has one foot in the hall, one in the office. Is she being tiresome?

To her surprise, he asks, "What were you last year?"

"A cat. A black cat."

"Were the same people in the club then?"

"Yes, some."

A smirk plays on his lips, a light in his eyes: he thinks it's corny, and he's caught the others at it.

"Look, we're not talking bobbing for apples. I don't know if you've ever seen the Cedar Springs parade, but there's some very resourceful costuming, these female impersonators, you know? The parade is pretty wild, lots of drunks, punked-out people, good bands, floats, and a ha ha beauty contest at midnight. But suit yourself. Come as you are, if you like. Nobody'll mind."

"Okay," he says, into the hall now and backing away. "Thanks a lot, I really appreciate it."

"No problem."

She hangs in the doorway, waving back; one might be on a train that's begun to move and the other's been left behind on the platform, but she couldn't tell you who was which.

At the first lesson, Susan gives Jeff an Ebony pencil and a large swatch of newsprint paper and seats him on a stool at a drawing table in the studio next to her office. She sets an orange on the table. She stands beside him and explains that she wants him to draw not the orange, but, rather, the light values around and on it; she wants him to pay close attention to the "colors" of dark and light.

She takes a sketch pad and sits on another stool, legs crossed, giving herself the same exercise. Later, she critiques his drawing. Talking to him, their faces very close—Curt says her breath is "different" during her periods. She would slip a mint into her mouth, but Holly and two sculpture students are working after school on projects in the studio, and to put something in her mouth to freshen her breath would just seem, well, misleading.

The first lesson doesn't take him very far—he has talent, but with so little training he'll remain far behind his classmates without a passionate commitment to practicing. He seems eager to learn; he listens with alarming intensity to her every word, making her aware of speaking each one. They don't chatter or joke; he seems so grim and determined that she considers turning on the radio to relax him. You have to stay loose, she says. Right-brained. Joking with him, she picks up his right arm and shakes it. "Loosen up!" she commands, and she keeps shaking it until he laughs and lets his hand go limp so that she can make it flop back and forth on the end of his wrist. But she doesn't feel very relaxed, herself, and her own supposedly superior version of the light values about the orange is the worst piece of drawing she's done in years.

During the next week, he brings her, unbidden, drawings of a Dr. Pepper can, an egg, a softball, a book standing on the two legs of its opened cover. They show improvement, and she is especially pleased by his effort at rendering the book, how the spine forms a triangular brace to support the weight of the pages, and so the drawing works not only with light but with space, perspective, gravity—he has an engineering streak, somewhere.

Once when he comes, she makes tea, and he drinks from his mug as if doing this is a curiously pleasurable novelty like dancing with one's mother at a wedding.

She phones him twice to arrange their second lesson. Once she talks to his mother, who, to her surprise, isn't aware of Jeff's interest in drawing. The woman doesn't sound enthusiastic about the enterprise; the coolness in her tone can't be attributed to any particular cause, but it arouses Susan's curiosity, and she presumes that the mother is overly dependent upon her son and is jealous of any activity that takes him away. Susan feels the presence holding the other receiver rear up like a ghostly embodiment of maternal concern; Susan resents being resented without the woman's having any knowledge of her own professional (also maternal, in its own way!) concern for Jeff's best interests. Susan considers giving her number to Jeff, then imagines the phone ringing in her apartment and she balks. But she's not sure why: she could easily explain to Curt that Jeff's a student, and there's no reason to hide anything. But maybe because of Curt's behavior in Nice and how they're walking on eggs around one another these days, she doesn't want to do anything that he might imagine has evened the score.

During the second lesson, they have the studio to themselves after four-thirty. Holly, waving good-bye, says, "Ta-ta, kids, ya'll be sure to lock up," which Susan feels is unnecessary. Has she ever been irresponsible?

She has an old cowboy boot with a flopped-over top that she poses and sets Jeff to work on. This is tough, she knows. He immediately falls prey to the beginner's tendency to draw small and centered and much too carefully.

"Jeff?"

He looks up, a glaze in his gaze that speaks of too much concentration.

"Draw big, take the whole sheet, and loosen up. Don't look at your pad so much, just look at the boot more."

"Okay."

He attacks relaxing with that same tense grit, so she turns on the radio. It's usually tuned to WRR, and a flock of notes from a piano soar brightly about from one sunstruck corner to another like trapped birds in search of an opening. Mendelsohn, maybe.

"What kind of music do you like, Jeff?"

"Aw, I'm just your basic grunge fan. Seattle bands."

"Curt Cobain?"

He chuckles, as if her asking amuses him. "Aw, a little of everything. How about you?"

"Mostly classical. Or Windham Hill, that kind of stuff." She checks the impulse to say Curt likes rock and roll.

"New Age?"

"Well, okay, yeah. I guess so." She eyes the boot, glances at her pad. "But I'm not into pyramid power and I didn't go to the Harmonic Convergence. I think I was washing my hair that weekend."

He doesn't know she's made a joke. He says, "Most of my tapes are at my Dad's. My Mom is kind of weird about religion, and she doesn't like most stuff to be in the house." His head bobs as he looks from boot to pad, boot to pad. He snickers. "She thinks it's all full of Satanic images and commands from the Devil."

"Huh!" says Susan. She's feels she's been handed a key to the kid but doesn't yet know the location of the lock. Light from the north window falls on one cheek, leaving the other in shadow. She quietly turns to a blank page of her sketch book and watches his cheekbone collect the waning golden light—October light, she thinks—and his lashes dip into it and come out dewy and dripping. Probably all his girlfriends envy his lashes, his cheekbones.

"Thing is," she hears him say (she can't look at him for a moment), "You can't talk to her about it. She's kind of weird this way. In a lot of ways she's just like a regular person, you know?" He looks up at her suddenly, breaking the bifurcation of his face by shadow and light. The question might have been a plea. Susan doesn't know what to say, so she says "Uh-huh," and after a minute he goes back to his drawing. Susan traces his jaw line now that it lies again in the full light. His skin is smooth, so smooth. No zits. Is this fair?

"She gets into these spells, these weird moods, you know, where she can't seem to get anything done, and she just sleeps all day and night. She's a clerk at the car license bureau, and when she gets behind in her work, she needs me to help her so she won't get into trouble."

"What do you do for her?"

"Typing, mostly."

"These spells—is this something that she's being treated for?" Susan can't tell if he's referring to procrastination, depression, or psychotic episodes. His hair is roughly the shade of balsa wood. Wavy. Is this fair, too? Portrait of a perfect specimen. So perfect he's almost a cliche. Where was the interest in this face? His nose—slightly crooked. Maybe it was broken once?

"You mean like a psychiatrist or something?" He has stopped drawing and is frowning at her.

"Yes, I suppose. Or whatever." Under his lighted eye are freckle-flecks like the mica in mountain streams. Fool's gold.

"No. She'd never consider that—that's just more Devil worship."

"You think she needs it?"

She's pushed too far? He draws for a moment, then, looking up, he grimaces, shrugs. His helplessness arouses her pity.

"I don't know," he says.

She hears *Do you know?*

"Are you worried?"

"I guess." He sighs. "Yeah, sometimes."

"What's your Dad think?" She inwardly holds her breath; she's poked her nose about one millimeter across a line, here.

"He thinks she likes to make a victim of herself."

"Would you like for me to talk to her?"

His gaze darts up instantly; he looks horrified. "No. I mean, you know, not about that."

"Well, about the club, then? About coming to the meetings regularly or about your lessons." Maybe with that excuse to talk to the mother, she could also encourage the mother to seek help for what sounds like a debilitating depression. She adds, with little chuckle, "By the way, half the people I know are on Prozac or some other anti-depressant."

"My Dad already suggested that. My mom's against all drugs. It's hard enough for me to get her to take aspirin. She fainted at work and found out she was anemic, but I have to put her vitamins right beside her plate or she won't bother to take them."

"She's lucky to have you worrying about her. That says good things about you and about how she raised you."

"I guess."

She's about to ask again about talking to the mother when he says, "Hey, this is hard!" and bows to the task with an intensity that clearly means he wants this subject closed.

Susan hopes she helped by listening, at least. And while she can't intercede, she can keep these facts in mind when looking for a way to cut him some slack. She goes back to work on her portrait. Light pours in upon his face, basting the right half yellow, yellow-gold, and the music swells. Portrait of a boy. Sweet, innocent, helpless. But troubled. Lighted half is youth, the shadowed half what lies ahead. The person the youth has conjured with his story of worry, that's the one she wants on the page, that's the feature of interest she's looking for. Her hand moves swiftly, easily, connected to the subject, that boy, passing into her eye and onto her pad without her stopping to consider it, her brain a conduit for the imagery, like a court artist working to capture the emotion of a witness who's testifying.

"This sucks!" He sneers at his pad. He straightens up, pushes his shoulders back and stretches his arms.

"Don't judge it." She looks at her own pad, at the boy. What she's done is good, but he's broken the spell.

He sits frowning at his pad in a theatrical way that makes her know he's beckoning her to appraise it; his faint smile tells her he has pleased himself. Should she show him her portrait?

"How are you doing?"

"I dunno. This is a lot harder than eggs."

"Lemme see." She hops off her stool and goes to his table, pressing her pad to her breasts.

"Gosh, Jeff, this is so much better than last week! You're really making progress. You've really got a good eye, I can tell from this that you see what needs to be done—" She leans forward into the space between his head and the pad and watches her arm move down to his drawing, her index finger tap the rounded heel of the boot, aware of his gaze on her arm like a lamp. "See, here, where the heel is round, you did just the right thing by treating it as if it were a sphere or globe, you know, where the light falls with greater intensity because the surface is closer to the source. You're really learning fast!"

He gives her a cocky, sidewinder smirk. "You think I'm ready for life studies?"

She blushes, looks away, caught unaware by this appearance of the man in the boy. It's a joke, sure, but she feels he's dropped the mask of helpless innocent to show the face of a leering adult male. And she resents it. It makes her uncomfortable. Matt does it sometimes—is Jeff copying him?—but never in private.

"No. You're not ready for life studies," she says flatly. She then goes on with the critique, pointing out mistakes of perspective that cause confusion in the spectator's vision. The drawing is amateurish, of course, but he has indeed made considerable progress, and she tells him so again.

Then she pauses and stands back slightly with her pad held to her chest. If you were to ask her at that moment if she's encouraging him to ask for an exhibition of her portrait, she'd deny it, of course. But just as his body language told her he longed for her to examine his work, so the prominent display of the pad clutched to her breast suggests she's hiding something, and since it's also the most prominent object in his vision when he looks at her, the thing hidden is clearly being advertised as such.

He grins. "Okay, let's see yours now."

She's not certain his double entendre was deliberate. "Well, I didn't do the boot," she says earnestly. "I was working on something else." No doubt he knows what she's been drawing—the intensity of her gaze as she worked surely would have felt like a source of heat to him. "I like to do people because after you've been at this a while you'd rather accept the challenge of capturing a living subject than an inert one." She waits a beat for effect, then says, "I did one of you."

"Oh!"

She cants the pad toward him, her hands holding it like clamps and framing it on an invisible wall in the air.

"Wow!" He blushes. "That's great! Could I buy it from you?"

She laughs. "Buy it? Of course not, I'll give it to you, if you like it that much."

"Yeah, it's great!" He keeps grinning. "Would you sign it?"

She laughs again. "What do you think I am, an artist?"

"Well, it looks like real art work to me."

Without asking, she squeezes the end of his pencil between her thumb and index finger and slips it out of his grasp, signs her name on the bottom of her sheet with a flourish, a parody signature.

"Great, that's just great. Thanks a lot!" His head bends over the sketch, his possession. The instant he begins to study it she ceases to exist; he gazes at it with the absorption of someone inspecting his face in a mirror.

Minutes later, after they've put away their tools, she says, "I hope someone's coming to pick you up?" Before he can reply, she adds, "I've got to get right home, and I'm almost out of gas."

"It's okay. I'll call my Dad."

She waits until he leaves so that she can determine which exit he uses, and when he heads to the front, she goes out the back door. She refuses to look toward the curb where he might be standing; instead, she keeps her eye on the fuel gauge. It registers Full; she gassed up this morning in case she had to take somebody home.

$\mathcal{S}$aturday morning Susan wakes expecting that she and Curt will drive to the Canton monthly flea-market to find chairs that match their dining table. But he doesn't recall talking about that; well, he does remember talking but not deciding. Meantime he's agreed to play softball; his firm doesn't have enough guys as it is. She says, well, you could've discussed that with me before you said yes.

"Aw, I'm sorry. What's the big deal? We can go to Canton tomorrow."

"Maybe I have plans tomorrow."

"Like?"

"Maybe I've agreed to play in a softball tournament without consulting you."

"Well, maybe you could get somebody to go with you today."

He leaves before lunch, and she calls Jennifer then Holly to ask if they'll make the hour's drive with her. Their rejections only make her more irritated at Curt. After all, these chairs were to be theirs.

Also, it isn't just that they need to consult about the chairs; the point is—and this makes her furious enough to scream—that it's not just a goddamn shopping trip! It was a date, and he stood her up.

Little things like this sometimes make her glad they're not married. She imagines being married one day to someone who is not like her father. This husband would be stronger, more responsible than she, more dependable, a man who does not have to be arm-twisted into taking responsibility for aspects of their mutual life. This husband would be the Susan in the partnership, and she could let go and be the Curt for a while. She'd have a bunch of babies and go barefoot around her house and never take off her apron except when he's about to come home. She could revert to an infantile state and baby-talk her man and if any women friends clucked their tongues she'd beam beatifically and plug her baby's hungry mouth with a ripe and ready nipple. That idea seems appealing but it'd be hard with a partner who won't go whole hog and change a dirty diaper. Sure, women do it, anyway, always have.

But she's not sure she could. Does she really want children? Or is Curt's resistance the primary appeal to her, the way his resistance to marriage itself makes her want it?

Maybe what she wants is not playing house with Ward Cleaver but instead how about waltzing off to Mexico with some amblin' gamblin' guitar-plunkin' rascal you'd never in your life count on for anything more than whatever fun you could have. (Come to think of it, Nathan played guitar but he waltzed off alone.) Or maybe she and this phantom could be Professor Mister and Professor Missus toiling elbow-to-elbow on a dig in Kenya's Muldavi Gorge, 50-50, one-half plus one-half, Yin and Yang, the two amulets. Played by Hume and Jessica. You have your Golden Anniversary in a tent surrounded by dusty shards of unparalleled significance.

Anything else is preferable to what is, sometimes. Her mother has taught grammar school nonstop for thirty-five years because nobody could count on Susan's father to be employed. Her mother saved money, made long-range plans, had long-range goals, (sending her children to college), used her common sense (favorite saying: "Use your noggin, for gosh sakes!"), is immensely practical: a gift received from one distant relative is rewrapped for another; she clips coupons, takes hints from Heloise. When Susan was a teen, she hated how unromantic her mother was, but when she reached college, then her mother seemed mushy-headed, and Susan had running arguments with her about feminism. Her mother was the core of the family's emotional and economic support (her father was just another kid, one who didn't have to mind), but her mother would be the last on her block to call herself a "feminist." (She actually said, "Lord, I wouldn't be one of those bra-burners!" which infuriated Susan.) At the time Susan was too young to realize that her mother was a feminist whether she believed it or not: her mother had behaved for all those years as if she were. Susan believed then that she herself was too smart to step into the traps that lay ahead. The ideal Susan's children will have a Dad they can count on. So far, though, the real Susan has avoided her mother's error solely by default—she picked a man who balks at marrying her and fathering children.

Deserted by Curt, Susan will indulge herself. Maybe she'll get her sketchpad and a blanket, make up a picnic basket and go to White Rock Lake for a few hours. Hello, come here often? I have some chilled white wine, would you like some? Yes, I come here often by myself, too.

No, do something useful, at least. (She is her mother's daughter.)

Maybe she should call Jeff to see if he is interested in taking a lesson this afternoon. Would that seem strange to him, to hear from her on a Saturday morning? (And is it too early to call a teenager on a Saturday morning?) Well, of course there are plenty of kids at *rehearsals* on the weekends, and shows as well; they're used to that. It's not so peculiar for them to interact outside of official school hours.

And it would give her a chance to see how he's doing. No harm in it, surely.

When she calls, to her surprise, he answers.

"Oh, Jeff! It's you!"

"Huh?"

"I mean, I wasn't sure you'd be up."

He laughs. "Oh, yeah. Some days there's no sleeping in around here."

She presumes that veiled comment refers to his mother. She proposes that they have a lesson today, maybe later this morning. Unlike Curt, the boy has no prior commitments and is pleased to be asked, pleased to have her attention.

He says, "Where should I meet you, at school?"

To her surprise, she blurts out, "Well, why don't I pick you up? We can do something a little different. We can sketch outside." And she pictures the lake, the picnic basket. The lesson doesn't have to be formal.

Dressing for the lesson, she's inexplicably paralyzed with indecision. Lipstick? Why lipstick? Well, her lips get chapped outside, for one thing. Earrings are a habit; if you're going out into the world with another person (no matter who) then you wear earrings. If she and Holly were going to Canton this afternoon, she'd wear earrings. Actually, now that she thinks of it, you never know who you might run into, anywhere. Cologne? Yes? No? If yes, which? No, then.

She decides to wear the maillot she bought in Nice (wear it under shorts and a cotton blouse) because it's sunny today, and she can touch up her tan on her shoulders and legs before the weather turns cold.

On the way, she comes to believe that she suggested picking Jeff up just to meet his mother. See what's going on here. Far better for them be allied against all that can harm a kid than to be mutually suspicious. A teacher's biggest surprise often comes when you meet the parents—you never know what they'll be. And your most effective tool as a teacher is a parent who's on your side.

Jeff's mother answers her knock wearing cut-off blue-jean shorts with a ragged hem, a Dallas Cowboys sweat shirt, and child's pink bunny slippers. A safety pin is holding one corner of her black-framed glasses together. She looks at Susan through the still-latched storm door expectantly but without speaking. Has no idea?

"I'm Susan Hart, Jeff's art teacher?" Susan smiles widely, like a hostess.

"Oh." Mother turns away into the darkened interior and yells, "Jeffie! Jeffie! Your teacher is here!"

A muffled shout from inside. The woman's face appears again at the glass. Knowing she might only have seconds, Susan says, "I want you to know how pleased I am to have Jeff come to our club meetings. He's making a lot of progress with his art, and he really seems to be enjoying it."

The woman unlatches then stiff-arms the storm door open, but remains in the threshold, leaning forward. She's several inches shorter than Susan's 5'6" and mustard dots one corner of her mouth. Her short brown hair might have been cut with pinking shears. Her eyes busily flick about—to the street, the yard, Susan's Reeboks. She's like somebody who gave up chain-smoking an hour ago, Susan thinks. Would this be what Jeff calls her "supercharged" state?

"Jeffie said you're painting a fence?"

"Painting a fence?"

"Yes!" pounces Mother, targeting Susan's gaze with an intensity that unnerves her—it's as if the mother believes she's trapped a liar. "Painting a fence."

"Oh. You mean the mural at the construction site." Susan looks away, to the street; inexplicably, the mother's scrutiny makes her feel like a liar. "Yes, we are." Planning to.

"He should worry about his math and English grades."

Is this an oblique criticism of her? Or Jeff?

"Is he having trouble in his academic subjects?"

Mother leans out to point at a black box fixed to the wall. "He got two failing notices this week. I'm supposed to go talk to his teachers but I just don't know when I can make time for it. It's hard working day in and day out and then people expect you to show up during *their* hours."

Susan smiles, politely. "Maybe you could catch them on the phone?"

"I've tried calling down there at that school. I let the phone ring twenty-six times the other day, but nobody answered. And I can't just stand there at my desk with a dead phone to my ear all day long. There's people watching and waiting."

"Well, that's certainly understandable. And I know that sometimes they leave the phone off the hook in the office because they get too busy to answer it, anyway." She doesn't suggest bringing in Jeff's father—Mother seems one millimeter away from spontaneous combustion. "Maybe I could talk to Jeff about this. I'll remind him that students at Carver are privileged to be there, and if they don't keep up their grades, we send them right back to their home school!"

Susan's tone of stern authority—not wholly fabricated—seems to appease the woman, and she steps through the door and onto the porch. Her heh-heh smile—Susan's seen that twist of lips on Jeff, just before he cracks sarcastic. "Well, I can guarantee he wouldn't like that," Mother says, and she shunts the smile Susan's way so that seen at this angle it's from one conspirator to another.

As they're driving away, Susan plays back the conversation and her suspicion clicks on with a hum.

"Jeff, did you tell your mother that we were working on the mural today?"

"Uh, yeah. I thought we might be doing that."

She looks at him; he stares through the windshield. His shorts show long skinny legs matted with hair a shade darker than that on his head. The muscles in his thighs are firm, likewise in his calves, as if he ran track or played a lot of soccer. Though maybe not: it's amazing how lean and fit they can look sometimes just because they're young. Natural washboard abs, at sixteen; after five years of keeping company with a keg, the flab sets in.

"I told you we could have a lesson."

He darts a glance her way, then shrugs.

"Jeff, does your mother know I'm giving you lessons?"

"Well, I said it was my Dad's and my deal, you know?"

"Why don't you let her know? She seems concerned about how you're doing at your new school. That's natural."

"Okay, I guess I will."

Too easy—caving in to get her off his back. She can slide off to the side or push forward, here. Duty says get real.

"She says you're failing English and math."

"What??"

Bluster, outrage: ergo, he's guilty. "You got failing notices. Who are your teachers?"

"DeKoont for English and Mr. Keebler for algebra. The thing is," he says hotly, sitting forward, "Miz DeKoont won't give me credit for a paper I gave her that she lost, and Keebler? Man, every time I show up for a makeup quiz, he's never there!"

He crosses his arms, all puffed up.

"Would you like for me to talk to them?" She means will they corroborate your story?

"Aw, no. It's my problem."

Yes, and the sentiment is laudable, but Susan knows it's designed to divert her.

"Sometimes when teachers seem unreasonable, you just have to grit your teeth and go that extra distance to make up for it."

"I know. And it… it's part my fault, too. Thing is, I am missing some homework assignments and I flunked four of Keebler's daily quizzes."

"What's wrong? Do you need a tutor?"

"I don't know." His tone is plaintive, though not whining, as if he too is worried, perplexed. "I can't seem to keep my mind on the right stuff."

"How's your mother doing?"

"She's okay."

"No recent bouts of depression?"

He sighs. "She's in a prayer group for it now."

"You think it helps?"

He shrugs. "I dunno. Maybe. Sometimes. It's hard to tell, because you can't know what she might be like if she weren't going to it, you know? But she's been okay lately." He cracks a grin. "If she can push your alarm buttons about my grades, then I'd say she's coping just fine."

Susan laughs. "Well, that's good."

"Yeah. Thanks for asking about her. I can't talk to just anybody about it. My friends...."

She waits, but he doesn't finish and she has to supply speculative predicates: *think she is strange? don't know about her? don't like to hear about her? wouldn't understand?*

"You're welcome. If your Mother's okay, are you worried about something else?"

He laughs, groans (histrionic irony), wags his head and bumps it twice against the glass. "You might say that."

"Would you like to talk about it?"

He chuckles. "Oh, I don't think I could do that."

She smiles teasingly. "Are you having trouble in your love life?"

"Yeah, I guess. The trouble is I don't have one."

"Oh, now, it's hard to believe that a kid as presentable and nice as you couldn't get hooked up with whoever you wanted to."

He squirms under the heat of the compliment. "Maybe. I guess so. Trying's what's hard, you know?"

"Yes, sure. I remember—"

He looks expectantly at her, but she can't bring herself to verbally sketch the girl sitting by the avocado wall phone in her mother's kitchen with clenched fists while her brother stood by gleefully taunting her, *Jesus, Susan, call him—how hard is it to dial a phone?*

"—I remember that."

"Did you have lots of dates in high school? Were you like a cheerleader or something?"

"No, I wasn't a cheerleader." Susan laughs. "I didn't go out much with jocks."

"What were your boyfriends like?"

"Well, I didn't have many, really. We all kind of went out in groups, you know. Then I had one boyfriend my junior and senior year. You kind of remind me of him."

"Really? How?"

She's blurted this out thoughtlessly, and, now forced to find a comparison, realizes any likeness shared by Nathan and Jeff is probably incidental, or so general as to be meaningless: their vibrant youth.

"He was a musician."

"I'm not."

"No?" She plays dumb. "I thought you were."

"No. But what'd he play?"

"Guitar, of course."

"Huh! What kind of music?"

Susan laughs again. It sounds so silly now. Though she's not yet thirty, she can see herself as an old crone in a rocker jawing about the good old days. "He liked Hall and Oates."

"Who?"

"Never mind. Sort of mainstream, top forty, FM stuff."

"What happened?"

"What happened?"

"You know, to him. And you? Where is he?"

"I… Say, you're pretty sneaky, Jeff. I believe we were talking about your grades."

"I wasn't trying to change the subject." He grins. "It was just a lot more interesting than my grades."

"Well, I promised your mother I would nag you. I'll tell you straight out—the school won't keep you if you don't do well. There are too many kids wanting in. Even the prodigies get kicked out. I'm a cluster teacher, and I can go to bat for you, but there's a limit to how much we can sway the administration. And to tell the truth, it's hard for us to fight unless we feel somebody's really working to do their best, you know?"

"Yeah. That makes sense. I can't argue against that. I just have to try to focus better."

"That's right. First thing you should do is go to Miss DeKoont and Mr. Keebler and ask them what you need to do to pass this six weeks, and then do it!"

"Okay. I will."

Whew! Susan hates this stuff. Too parental. She'd rather be a pal. And she knows just by having this little chat she's become his champion. No doubt he'll come to her if there's further difficulty with Sally DeKoont and Bob Keebler. Of course, every kid needs a mentor, especially those who are floundering. She'd be glad to fight for him. She's gone toe-to-toe with the dean and the principal for a lot of them over the past years—they get under your skin, wedge their way into your heart and head, and they pop up in your dreams and you wake up at 3 A.M. worrying about them and can't go back to sleep, and, next thing you know, you find yourself too deeply invested in their future and their welfare. You have to watch out for keeping this side of the line and not be an enabler or a patsy the kid manipulates when he's in hot water.

At White Rock Lake, they lay a blanket by the shore, eat her tuna salad sandwiches, chips and Cokes, then she tells him to draw the scene before them. A regatta is afloat, white boats with white sails bob on the light breeze in the distance like strung-out ducklings. Nearby, three grackles sheening in the light high-step through the grass and hammer the turf with their strong black bills.

She wears sunglasses, he doesn't. She meant to sketch too if only to keep him company but can't get going. They sit in full sunlight, so at last she feels too warm. She sets her sketchpad in the hollow of her crossed legs and tugs her blouse free from her waistband. This attracts his attention, but the instant he realizes she's pulling her shirttail out, his gaze skitters back to the front. As if he accidentally burst in upon her taking a bath, she thinks. She unbuttons the blouse.

"It's really hot today. I wore my bathing suit under my clothes so I could get some sun."

"Oh."

She folds and lays the blouse on the quilt. Under the strong, harsh light, the skin of her upper arms looks mottled, pitted, an expanse of lunar bumps and tiny lesions. Her tan has faded to the hue of a squash whose name she's never sure of—butter something.

"I had pretty good tan when we were in Italy this summer. We stayed in this place in Assisi that had a balcony you could sit on."

"Yeah?" His gaze sweeps to and fro like a lighthouse beam from the lake to the pad, over and over.

"Don't look at your paper so much."

"Okay."

But he doesn't look at her. She's certain he's trying to keep from it. Hard to say exactly what she feels about this. Her exposed flesh embarrasses him, arouses discomfort, and she is touched and a little amused by his apparent innocence, the virginal modesty implied, because this stands in vivid contrast to the response she'd get from hard-hats eating lunch along a downtown sidewalk. Jeff's not-looking is another instance of his extreme attentiveness to her every motion, and that, too, pleases her. The boy seems to have a space in his mind reserved exclusively for her, a space much larger than all the sensory information he presently has collected about her, and the space is like a vacuum that sucks and draws his senses toward her: when she's within range, his nostrils and pupils dilate, his internal antennae quiver. He hears and records every word she utters, and he observes everything closely. (He recently brought her a Milky Way, and she remembered that she'd been eating one during a conference they'd had.) His posture toward her is precisely the opposite of Curt's: Curt can't record any more data about her on his hard drive. A single stroke on his keyboard from her results in a "destination disk is full" message.

But the boy's refusal to look at her is faintly irritating. Maybe it says, You're too old, you're like my mother or something. Maybe he misinterprets and she'll become the antagonist in an ugly anecdote, the old broad with wrinkles and bags and sags. No, surely not. She's too young. Still, to them…

She plants her palms behind her, elbows locked and fingers outstretched going the opposite way she's facing, like somebody crawling away from herself. From Jeff's POV—pup tent shape. Old Hollywood cheesecake pose. Don't toss your hair.

She lays out her long legs knee to knee. Her khaki shorts cover her thighs—slip them off? No.

Cants her face to the sun and shuts her eyes. An airhorn blast from the regatta like a truck barreling through a busy intersection. Scrawww…clack! says a grackle. Birds. *Little Birds.* One of Nin's stories is about a painter who wants his wife to pose nude but she's shy. Finally does. He falls in love with his painting, and she catches him literally making love to it. Another story, Susan's favorite, is told by a novice artist's model. Her employer is painting a horse running away with a Godiva and asks the nude model to mount a dummy horse that rocks; the pommel rubs to and fro against her clitoris, and, knowing the painter is watching, she struggles to hide her growing arousal but soon surrenders to her orgasm.

Just Nin's fantasies. Of course. Susan knows better. In real life, an artist observing the nude form for an aesthetic purpose is engaged in an activity that transcends vulgar lust.

Sweat trickles down her neck and tickles between her breasts. Wind caressing the hair of her arm makes her shiver. Nin's stories arouse Susan, but that response repudiates her claim to the supposed innocence of life studies, and the stories (by a woman) embody an attitude toward women that is officially repugnant. And, anyway, isn't she supposed to *analyze?* So: the stories in *Little Birds* playfully flirt with the idea of how male artists translate human models onto a canvas, so that, like Pygmalion and Galatea, the artist constructs a version of the living human that constitutes his ideal, his Jungian anima. The magic in the painting comes from that mysterious electric connection between the real and his ideal, and the art is charged with libidinous energy. So is male art, a boy's art, the portrait of the male libido controlled via objectification?

That air horn—two blasts, a truck careening through the intersection *watch out!* Eyes click open, she turns, catches Jeff off-guard, and he hastily corrects his errant, probing gaze.

"How are you doing?"

"Okay. But this is kinda boring."

"Art is 99% perspiration and one percent inspiration," she jokes.

"Like you said, though, human subjects are more interesting."

"You have to work up to that."

"You don't think I'm advanced enough?"

"Who do you want to draw?" Even as she asks, she knows.

"Whoever's available." He's got that one-side grin on.

When she doesn't answer, he pleads: "Couldn't we try just a little? Look—" he grins, tilts his sketchpad toward her—"I've already started." A form, a woman's form, that pup tent shape, upended V, the triangle of torso and arms and the ground. She looks off. It's too coincidental that this request interrupts her reverie about *Little Birds*. Must be the situation set them both off. What reason could she have now to refuse?

She pushes up, wraps her arms about her shins, chin atop her bony caps.

"What could it hurt?"

"Well, nothing, really, Jeff. It just might, well, if you take on too big a challenge prematurely then sometimes the failure is too damaging, and you can lose what little confidence you've gained. Makes it harder to move forward."

He laughs. "Aw, gee, Susan—it's not like we're doing high wire tricks without a net!"

He turns back to the vista assigned, flips over to his original drawing and returns to work, not sullenly, but with good humor. And now her resistance seems inexplicably rigid, unreasonable. Maybe even suspicious to him.

"It's hard, you know."

"Sure," he says.

She smiles at him when he turns to look at her. "Maybe we could try a little gestural drawing. But you have to promise not to expect too much of yourself and don't be upset if it doesn't turn out right."

"Believe me, I won't slash my wrists over it."

She talks for a few minutes on the aims of "gestural" drawing: capturing the basic lines of the figure, the distribution of weight. He nods as she speaks, a nod for each period at the end of her sentences, punctuating for her.

Then she stands and smiles down at him. When he averts his eyes, she suddenly feels modest, so she turns her back to him while she unbuttons the waistband of her shorts. After they've fallen about her ankles, she steps free of them, bends to pluck them from the quilt, and lays them atop the folded blouse. Her motions are ceremonial—deliberate, self-conscious—as if "gestural drawing" were a ritual that included this prescribed way of disrobing.

"I'll only hold a pose for about a minute at a time, Jeff. The point is just to sketch free and fast, without thinking too much about it, okay?"

She's watched a hundred models, but she's not used to modeling and has trouble striking poses that feel natural. She's aware of the maillot's cut (feels the air on the naked wedge of hip), and she's afraid that no matter what attitude she assumes, it will smack of a centerfold pose. She does not want to arrange her parts in the most advantageous way, no, that's not the point. The point is to serve impersonally as a figure model, to help the boy develop technique.

He is looking at her, tracing the lines of her hips, her legs, her torso, neck and head. The maillot feels too tight, too constricting. She holds a pose that gives him a side view, then turns her back to him, weight on one leg, hip cocked, then after a moment turns to face him, swinging her shadow away from his face. He squints, sunlight burning his eyes like the flare from arc-welding. She leans back to shade his eyes, and he looks at her, draws.

This goes on, minute by minute, and she tries not to consider that he might be grading her (she's an "8"), the whole point being to get them beyond this kind of thinking. When his gaze alights on her form, there's something wincing yet eager in his expression, and she thinks they'll just keep doing this until he's able to shake off his inhibitions and view her body only as a form in space, with curves, shadows.

Above them, on the road, a pickup passes, and over its wake soars a hoot and cat-call.

"Maybe that's enough."

Again she turns her back to slip her shorts and blouse on over the suit.

He clears his throat. "I'm going to get something to drink. Want something?"

"Yes, please, diet Coke." A warble of nerves alights in her voice.

She's anxious to look at his sketches. She watches his back as he walks toward the boathouse concession stand, strong-skinny youth's legs, a t-shirt, khaki shorts, bare-headed, tanned limbs. The two girls behind the counter stand close, murmuring to one another about him, no doubt. She wonders what they will say to him, what he'll say back. She pictures herself working there, a girl their age, though knowing what she now knows. What would it be like to do it all over?

Sitting on the quilt, she furtively tugs his pad toward her. What has he made of her? The side view—her form is thick in the middle, the lower limbs too long, the arms short (this because he was sitting almost literally at her feet, she guesses), the forward hip centered large on the page (thus it would be to his eye), the undercurve along the back drawn in an unbroken line from her spine to her thigh; on the next page, the back view, the canted, rounded hips centered again, a line down their center splitting into a crooked smile at the bottom.

She looks up to the concession stand. Jeff is holding two cylinders, but has not lifted them from the counter. One girl leans toward him, the other has disappeared. Go on, say something to him! Be bold, maiden! He's shy, you'll need to lead him. Give him that drink for free, ask him what he's doing here.

What would he say? *I'm with my teacher.* No, that might make him a nerd. He might say *I'm with a friend.* Or *she's my sister.*

The third sketch, the frontal view, shows breasts that are larger than her own, she thinks, hips that are likewise. Between her thighs is a checkmark V where his pencil speedily recorded what he allowed himself only the quickest glance at. She smiles. The very awkwardness of the visual expression charms her; his inarticulate pencil is so much bashful stammering to her eye. A trembling hand made nervous by inexperience and excitement. She is pleased that he's no expert, and tracing the lines that approximate her form she drifts off to when Nathan first fumbled with the buttons of her blouse.

⤳ 10 ⤳

*P*laying Gulliver in Lilliput is a weird way to make a living. But it takes Curt back to Lincoln Logs and Erector sets and the fleets of model planes he built. Sometimes he can't believe that he actually gets paid for doing something he has loved since he was a kid with a Lionel train: *perspective,* you see, that's the point. You get your train set up, and you lie down beside it with one eye on a level with the track, or with your chin on the carpet, and watch the train come right at your face, and you're just a tiny helpless little dude, *help! here it comes!* but then you can reach out and stop it like Superman.

Sunlight pours into the loft space and onto the sheen of the polyeurethaned oak floor. Curt's hovering over an intersection in Indianapolis, a god stroking his chin, considering, while below on acreage off the southeast corner, a human carrying a briefcase is passing under an earthtoned archway of what will now be called "Galleria Norte."

Curt's thinking of how he wants to people it. Deal is, this shopping center started life as a boring arrangement of two tall blond-brick boxes joined by a low rectangle—though he's not convinced this version is an improvement. The center had been slipping from competition out on the burb-ite fringe, so the clients want to upgrade, get more class. Boutiquify, give it a Mediterranean aspect, and never mind that the place will be under a foot of snow all winter. Result: big square box covered in faux-adobe, red tile roofs, big hole in the center for a huge glass-covered atrium courtyard. Loggia running all the way around the outside (that'll be a boon come the snow!).

Unless they're by a crafty postmodernist like Portoghesi, malls are vanilla-looking. Curt likes to model skyscrapers designed by people who want to make a statement; he likes for the buildings to have a manly thrust up from the modeling table, with balconies or mezzanines high up where you can put people looking out over things just as the viewer looking at the model does, get instant identification with the mannequins and womanneqins on location.

He's holding a shoe box of little people supposedly "from all walks of life" but they're not, really. It's all he's allowed to work with. Dioramas he'd really like to do—a couple of guys in hard hats seated on a bench under the loggia here with open lunch boxes; out back, an overflowing dumpster and an old Cambodian woman poking around in it; a plumber in a battered white van trying to put a Band-Aid on his finger; in a restroom, a woman with morning sickness bowing to the old porcelain god. A car with a vent window smashed and a gap in the dash where the radio used to be; another car with a couple steaming up the windows with a quickie.

A new style: Indianapolis-Mediterranean. Curt roots around in the shoebox until he finds a woman, stands her against the wall of the back parking lot between two cars. Puts a dude beside her. She's willing to have at it then and there, right upon this faux Mediterraneo. The models are old, so she's got a hat and a shirtwaist dress and looks like Mamie Eisenhower and Dude's in a suit and a fedora so he's a

Marcus Welby type. Tourists, no doubt. So she wants to party hearty. Out of joint with her time and place. Dude says, really whiny, *What about your husband?* Because her husband's right inside the mall buying a pound of Earl Grey or something. And she says, with a smirk, *Are you daft? Believe me, he knows! I tell him everything! I've even gone out without him and called him on the phone right in the middle of something.* Dude says, *Really?* Makes his skin crawl to hear this. *Hmm, yes,* says she. *Every little thing. It's what we agreed on. We're honest. I may do whatever I wish so long as I tell him all about it.* She's got her hand lodged in his butt crack by this time and is humping his leg like a spaniel, but Dude is like really freaked out to hear this latest news. This bird—that's what the English call them, eh?—and her chubby hubby are way too sophisticated. He's a veritable virgin in the arts of adultery, never even planned this, and here he is, going limper by the minute while she squeezes it like she's milking a goddamn cow, and then sneers, *What? I thought you American boys were the very epitome of masculine vigor,* only it's "viggah." Maybe it was the Diana Rigg accent that put him off. Or knowing that his old lady would read the crime on his face the second he saw her again. What do the English say? "Sorry!" and it sounds like "soddy."

"Viggah!" he says to the Dude in the display.

Enter Barry. Curt thinks that he and Barry could be Elliott and Michael on *thirtysomething* if their wives were better friends, or any kind of friends at all. And if he felt more free to talk to Barry about things that were really bugging him. Like he could really say he was terrified he might lose her. Might as well say by the way my dick just shrunk two inches shorter than yours.

Barry strolls across the floor, surrounded by the shining blonde context of space and air, shoes creaking.

"These dudes are so boring." Curt plucks another Businessman from the box.

"Stand him on his head."

"I think I'll have another dude walk beside him reading out loud from Heidegger."

"It might permanently disable him."

"He's in a lot of trouble already and doesn't know it. Check out the fedora and the briefcase. He's a hundred years out of style. He's going into the mall to make a Business Call. Little does he know that when he stops off at that Chicka-Fil kiosk I'm going to give him salmonella."

"And he's thinking the worst thing that happened today is somebody laughed at his hat."

"If he survives the salmonella, though, he might get away with the hat. You see 'Dick Tracy'?"

"Yeah. Eminently forgettable."

"Yeah, but gangster fashion, '30s and '40s stuff, it's coming back." Curt thinks about wearing a fedora. Nah. After "Indiana Jones" made that safari-styled hat hip to wear, he got one, wore it a half dozen times. He was always having to double back to retrieve it from a restaurant booth, a movie seat.

"Let me see that." Barry takes the shoe box, riffles about as if in a Whitman's Sampler. Barry seems in a pretty good mood; Curt thinks he must have things under control at home, even considering the kid. Kid's in daycare, anyway. Nikki probably makes even better money than Barry as a CPA. That a problem? Does Barry ever feel undermined by Nikki? Bewildered? Maybe it's that marriage thing again, and kids. Maybe he should think harder about it. She's been acting so squirrely. She's so sure something went on that night in Nice with the English bird that you'd think she has some *need* to believe it. Seven years and not a single instance where he strayed! Give him some credit!

He has to admit, though, something about her being jealous is gratifying. At least it makes her sit up and pay attention! Her jealousy is the best proof he's still got a hook in her.

"Need some chicks," says Barry. "Ah!" Barry holds up by one leg a woman wearing a skirt and blazer and carrying a briefcase; she's about as tall as Barry's middle finger. "She's smiling."

"Of course. She just unloaded some really lame stock on a widower."

"Where shall we put her?"

They stroll about the display. The layout is mounted on a low platform and will be sectioned for shipment.

"She articulated?"

Barry holds up the figurine, waggles her stiff leg. "Nope."

"Poor thing's been on her feet her whole life, then."

"Here, how about this?" Barry lays her supine in the parking lot. Curt laughs. "Bring your guy. Let's get it on," says Barry.

"No, dipshit, she's still got her briefcase. Turn her over on her stomach."

Barry complies. Curt says, "Now she looks like she passed out and fell on her face. More realistic."

"I think she's too big for this set." Barry picks up the woman, plunks her back into the shoe box. After rummaging about for a minute, he comes up with a Woman-and-Child, two figures molded on a single base, holding hands. Without comment, he leans over the roof and gingerly places them into the atrium beside the fountain. It doesn't escape Curt that this seems protective, even tender.

"How's Nikki?"

"Fine."

Curt holds out his hand and Barry passes him the box. Curt wonders if Nikki really is fine. Maybe he should ask about the child. How's the wife and kids? Shh. Jeez. Sounds like the guy in the fedora making that Business call.

"She still like her job with, uh—"

"Mobil. Yeah. She got a promotion."

"Oh, hey! Great." Curt's enthusiasm stands in contrast to Barry's low-keyed announcement, and he's at a loss to follow up. Is Barry gnawing on this deal or what? Other people's lives are such a mystery. His own life is such a mystery.

"How's Nicholas?" He recalls the name because Barry and Nikki argued about it before the child was born.

"Fine."

Curt strolls to the window overlooking the West End parking garage and the phalanx of silvery shafts of the Allied Bank Tower and its water fountains. Nice space. Always people sitting down there. Peaceful to look down on people sitting serenely on benches in a sunlit space surrounded by greenery and water. You can imagine yourself there. Principle of his trade.

"How old is he now? Three?"

"Three-and-a-half."

Yuppie parents, thinks Curt. Once Nikki called Barry and made him drive all the way out to North Dallas because he'd forgotten to move the child's car seat from his own Acura into his wife's Volvo wagon and she couldn't take the kid to the doctor five blocks away without it even though her mother was staying with them and could've sat with the kid in the back seat. They say "three-and-a-half" like they're counting the minutes.

"How long were you guys married before you had Nicholas? I forget." Curt tries to sound casual, off-hand, as if only musing.

"This Mediterranean idea is really stupid for this location," says Barry. "I forget, too. I think it must be, uh, I dunno—Nick is three-and-a-half, we just celebrated our eighth anniversary. Why? You guys thinking of taking the big step?"

"Yeah, I guess. Who knows. Maybe." Barry's not aware that he and Susan aren't legally married.

Barry laughs, and the sound bounces into the high empty ceiling of the room. "You wouldn't regret it, Curt. It's great being a Dad."

"Yeah, maybe so." Curt thinks of Elliott and Michael on *thirty-*

something again. Barry's had stocks and bonds since college, and he's already in a retirement program. He was born being fifty. It's different with Curt. It's great being a Dad? No, it's great being a *kid.* His Dad was strong and stupid/stubborn: it took three heart attacks to kill him, but, by golly! He won, didn't he? He has his Dad to thank for the civil engineering gene and the hefty life insurance policy that paid for college. Curt's mother's theme song about his father has always been: *He never knew how to say no to people and they worked him to death.*

Barry leaves to make a meeting, and, alone in the quiet, sunlit space, Curt moves as if in a hot-air balloon over Galleria Norte. How about a rooftop sniper? Then a few peoplettes scattered about the parking lot, glued to the board by splashes of crimson nail polish?

Oh, my children! he breathes into the face of the box. Their little lives, wholly in his hands. When he was a kid he used to take his plastic soldiers and dig them into a fortification, then he'd assume a prone position several yards away to pick them off with a BB gun. *Ka-Blam!* It was more fun to zap sparrows, grasshoppers, lizards. He can recall the sensations of innocent blood-lust—man, talk about *Lord of the Flies!* Never thought of it then, how guiltless all that killing was, just leering cheery fun, a little Freddy Krueger on the loose.

Stomping roaches still brings him that old thrill, but these days it bothers him to kill a wasps' nest or feed their mice the D-Con; he'll do it, but he's always aware of the mystery of their existence, the complex cosmic arrangements that brought their molecules and cells together in this time and place for reasons no one has yet to determine. Killing them without knowing why they were alive in the first place seems a very foolhardy thing to do, like blowing up a building that could turn out to be a bank that has your money in it.

"Curt? Call!" yells Barry from the door.

"Who is it?"

"The old ball and chain." Barry's head turtles away.

In Curt's cubicle, the receiver lies out of its cradle and, loose and askew on his desk, it looks like the aftermath of an accident. What's her mood?

"Hello," he says mildly, pretending he hasn't been told the caller is Susan.

"Hi, Curt," she says, "it's me," she adds, unnecessarily, putting a little distance between them. "I just wanted to remind you to stop by Marty's on your way home and get some cheeses and crackers for my party."

"Oh sure. I didn't forget it."

"I didn't say you did."

"Well, you are reminding me, you know."

"See you later," she says. "Gotta go."

"Bye, babe," he speaks to a dial tone.

This is like yesterday's argument about the meat on the counter. You see, Dr. Counselor, while we're eating breakfast standing in the kitchen, I say, like I always do, "What do you think we should do for dinner?" Now, Doc, I swear I didn't mean that she was supposed to be responsible for it, I only meant that we should think about it now in case we need to defrost something, and she says, in a very undefrosted voice, "Whatever you want to do." And I think, uh-oh! So I say, "Well, hamburger helper's all right with me." And I go to the freezer to take out a pound of round ground, and she says, "I've got other plans for that," so I cool it, back off. I make a couple of other suggestions, and each time she shoots them down. The game is this: she's going to punish me for presuming she has the responsibility for deciding (I didn't) by forcing me to decide, but she'll protest the decisions to let me know that the responsibility is really in her hands, get it? You see, Doc, she has to be in charge of what we eat for dinner, but I'm not allowed to see that or mention it. She can't officially be in charge because that'd be a sexist presumption on my part, but I can't be in charge because having the kitchen as her stronghold gives her the control she needs. So right before she leaves she says, very annoyed, "Well, just take the ground beef out of the freezer. I'll probably be home before you are, and I will take it upon myself to do something with it, but it won't be Hamburger Helper!" I say, "If you want something else, just say so, I'm not particular." And, get this, Doc, she says, "What I want is for you to quit trying to control every goddamn thing we do!" You see my problem? When I say I don't care, I'm accused of letting her shoulder the responsibility; when I say I'll be glad to do it, I'm accused of trying to control. Get it, Doc? Help!

Their European trip jarred something loose in their relationship. They argued a lot during the weeks they were there. Where to go, when to go there, what mode of transportation, how long to stay, where to visit, what to do when there, where and what to eat, where to stay and sleep, what to take: Doc, our vacation in France and Italy was a movable fist, ha ha ha.

You know the Jack Spratt philosophy that opposites attract and that they're good partners because each fills in the other's gap and makes up for what the other lacks? Hey, Doc, it's bullshit! Example: I'm a laid-back kind of guy. I wanted to make some plans, sure, but I also wanted to let the situation from day to day govern us, keep flexible, loose, spontaneous, as much as possible. Doc, I wanted to schedule some unscheduled time, you see? And Susan thinks that this unscheduled time is really a vacuum that needs filling by plans, her plans, so I'm forced to struggle for a hole in the schedule while she's trying to plug it with an activity. Unless things are planned, she worries.

Curt thinks he understands this need for control in Susan; he blames it on her father, how he was so undependable and her mother had to take care of things. She lacks confidence in men; at an early age she learned that men couldn't be relied upon, so it makes her nervous when Curt tries to lay claim to an area of responsibility (she doesn't believe he'll do what he says he'll do or that he'll do a decent job of it). But she also can't stand it when areas lie fallow and unclaimed. Their most common disagreement lies in whether something needs to be worried about, and, if so, how soon should they start? And she equates his desire for spontaneity with incompetence; she mistakes going with the flow for being irresponsible. It's not just the little stuff like whether to defrost the goddamn meat they quarrel about: more and more it's the big stuff—getting married, buying a house, having a child. Everything's so sour between them lately it makes him regret having been so goddamned virtuous.

"Here kitty, kitty, kitty!"

Curt, coming down the stairs. She shoves the icy bottle far into the back of the freezer, shoulders the door shut, swallows.

"Meow, meeeoowww!"

A man materializes in the doorway, a black patch over one eye, one of her bandannas—a red one—looped dashingly about his head.

"Ahoy, mate!" she says.

"Avast ye timbers. Hizzen up the mizzenmast!" The pirate brandishes a slim cardboard crescent wrapped in tin foil. "I need a scar, kitty, right here." Points to his cheek. Hands her one of her own eye-liners.

She steadies his chin with one hand and pencils in a scar from jaw to temple.

Curt says, "You smell boozy."

"And you're most devil-may-care." Curt looks cute. He's wearing a white shirt and black bicycling tights sashed with one of her old scarves. Wearing a dumb costume renders a man harmless, therefore endearing. She purrs like a cat and, finished with her artwork on his cheek, mounts his thigh.

"Aye! You like my manly costume!"

"Meow!"

His hand goes under her hips, and he pulls her close. "I'm glad you wore this again."

"It was just, you know, lack of time and imagination," she says hastily. She doesn't want to be accused or even suspected of exhibiting herself, even if that may well explain her choice of costume.

"Whatever."

"Curt, I'm sorry. You know, calling about the cheese. You've been great about helping."

"I like your little rascals."

Because Curt doesn't extract any quid pro quo promise from her, she feels generous. "So let me know when I have to play the Little Woman for Ralph the Moneybags and his lovely wife Ursula Upchuck."

"It won't be until I feel we can't get out of it, believe me. Nice thing about him as a silent partner is that he's pretty invisible, too."

He kisses her, passionately, and they both feel a little woozy; they're pleasantly tippled and feel the piquant conjugal arousal that comes when desire far outstrips the opportunity immediately available to gratify it. Her hand moves.

"Wow! Long John Silver."

"Now I'm glad you talked me out of coming as George Bernard Shaw."

She laughs. She hugs him, presses her cheek against his chest.

He bends; they smooch, again. If he's surprised to detect vodka along with their dinner wine he doesn't say it. She had a little tiff with herself over buying it, and she doesn't want to argue about whether it's proper for her to take a swig when the kids are in the house. It'd been a good while since they'd had any. A grown person ought to keep a bar stocked. And when she's nervous, she just needs a little something to calm her down. Social situations always unhinge her a little. But sometimes when she's had too much of anything in public Curt looks at her funny, as if he's recalling how she was the night they met.

"Mmmm!"

"Mmmm!"

The doorbell chimes.

"Damn!"

"Later, Irrigator!" Susan flits light-footed in her black ballet slippers down the carpeted stairs, her tail—one of Curt's old ties and stitched to the seat of her body stocking—flicking at the wrought-iron rails as she passes.

Matt is at the door dressed as a Burger King counterperson. With him are two fellows who both look like Ozzy Osbourne. He introduces them as Carver students who play in a local band called Kiddie Porn.

"Believe it or not," he says to his companions, grinning, gesturing toward Susan from head to toe, "This is my art teacher."

When Susan congratulates them on their costumes, Matt says, "Aw, they always look this way!" and they all three laugh.

Leading them back to the walled courtyard off her dining room, she chatters over her shoulder, dances, skips, making herself a moving target. Inward squirming, ill-at-ease. Their masculine gazes are puffs of breeze that set her spinning like a dry leaf.

In the courtyard, the pirate is stirring a kettle of Hawaiian punch and 7-Up. She wishes she could've bought a keg to get the party rolling, but no kid here will be within three years of legal drinking age. Besides, they'll probably have been drinking, anyway. When she was in high school she swilled gallons of rum or vodka diluted by Sprite or Coke, mostly in Nathan's company. Tonight host and guests alike will find excuses throughout the evening to sneak off for a furtive snort. The absurd hypocrisy troubles her, but not much.

Curt waves his sword, says, "Yo!"

The bell chimes again. This time it's Becki and Cheryl, the former wearing what looks like a '50s prom dress and holding with vaguely papal dignity a wand topped by a large sequined star; the latter has on baggy men's overalls, a baseball cap worn backwards, one tooth blacked out, a pipe wrench protruding from one pocket. With them is a short person in a Batman outfit, complete with cape.

"This is my little brother," apologizes Cheryl. "I had to bring him. I hope it's okay."

"Sure. Batman is welcome at my house any time." She smiles like a den mother welcoming a new scout, though she's thinking that a warning would be nice. She's planned a short hike down to the Halloween parade on Cedar Springs for later, and she's not sure Cheryl's mother would appreciate Susan's exposing this child to the raucous, bawdy ramble of a thousand cross-dressers through the heart of the gay ghetto. Would Curt mind staying behind and baby-sitting? (Yes? No? Maybe?)

She flags the trio to the courtyard and steps into the living room, where she has moved her compact stereo for the party. She hits the switch, gets a blast of Bartok (as usual it's set on WRR) and immediately scans the dial, second-guessing student tastes, thinking she'll alight on whatever sound pleases her the least. Here—way too much drums and guitars amplified into howling distortion, somebody screaming words.

Five minutes later, when she's in the kitchen sliding a tray of egg rolls into the oven, the bell chimes again. Jeff? No, it's one of her Madonna wanna-bes, Jennifer, tonight appearing as The Nerd, Vitalised hair, black-rimmed plastic specs, a dozen pens in her shirt pocket.

"Hey!" says Jennifer. "You look neat, Miz Hart. I heard about your costume from last year, it's great! You look really, uh, like you know."

"Thanks. I was going to wear something else, but I ran out of time."

"No, I think it really makes you look sleek and sneaky, cool, you know?"

"Come on in, the party's out back," Susan says to squelch the talk about the costume. Is it such a surprise that adults can have sex appeal? *Sex appeal?* Sounds like something from *The Donna Reed Show*.

In the courtyard the groups still adhere to the forms of their arrival, separate, with poor Curt dutifully wandering from one to the other trying to unravel them but only succeeding, it would appear, in hypnotizing them. He's trying to talk to them, but they can only nod and murmur, "Yes sir" or "No sir." Led to the patio by Susan, Jennifer stands looking from group to group and weighing their relative social importance before attaching herself to one.

Responding again to the doorbell, Susan finds Lillian from her Drawing class in a ballerina costume standing on her stoop between someone in a mask and an unfamiliar boy in street clothes.

"Hey, Miz Hart!" chirps the masked man: Jeff! He's wearing a cape, a hood with sharp ears. She smells liquor. The three are beaming at her happily, Lillian rosy-cheeked. She'd never have put this girl and Jeff together.

"Batman!" she says. "You've arrived just in time. There's an impostor inside wearing your costume," she utters before thinking. She hopes seeing an eight-year-old dressed in a similar outfit won't wound Jeff.

Jeff waves at the other young man. "This is Todd."

"I'm here as Bruce Wayne," says the other. He's a handsome blackheaded kid with a slanted smirk, and when that's all either has to say about his being an uninvited guest, Susan steps aside and murmurs, "Come on in" to the trio without singling him out.

Susan moves her stereo to the patio, and soon the kids are dancing. For a while she's too busy to observe anyone closely to see who hangs close to whom. She slow-cooked a brisket earlier today and now she shreds it, while Becki helps by grating cheese, then they cut tomatoes and warm flour tortillas to make burritos. Once when Becki goes off to the bathroom, Susan opens the freezer again for the icy bottle.

Meanwhile, Curt keeps the chips and dip, the cheese and crackers, in proper order on the picnic table and piles ice on the drinks in the cooler. Susan's aware as she moves through the apartment and the courtyard checking on her guests that some vanish for minutes at a time—in her study making out? In their cars drinking, smoking pot? As she works in the kitchen, she resists pouring herself another glass of wine.

Then around eleven-thirty, she catches Curt in the living room.

"How're you doing, ace?"

"Pretty fair, Toots. How's about yourself?"

"Good so far. Thing is, though, we're going to be walking down to Cedar Springs to the parade in a few minutes, and I'm kind of worried about that kid."

"The one in the Batman suit?"

"Uh-huh. Curt, would you mind staying here with him?"

He looks out of the window and onto the stoop as if hearing something. "Aw, gee, Susan—"

"Never mind. It's not a trap designed to get you cozied up to the idea of having kids, Curt. It was just a simple goddamn request, a favor I needed done."

"It's not like I'm not doing anything for you otherwise," he tosses at her back as she goes out of the room.

They all agree to make the three-block trek to Cedar Springs for the Halloween Parade. When Susan volunteers to stay behind and baby-sit, Cheryl says her brother will be fine with her: "He likes to protect me," she adds.

The neighborhood is noisy tonight. It's unseasonably warm—in the high seventies and humid—and she'd hoped that Fall would have begun by now and had looked forward to the usually chilly breath of Halloweenish air. Apartments nearby are flaming with light and music, people weaving in and out of doors, shouting, singing, drinking on the stoops, the landings, the balconies. The police have blocked off surrounding streets to vehicular traffic, and no sooner has the group left Susan's apartment than they meld into a swarm of pedestrians and revelers in costume: a man dressed as Dolly Parton, a woman with a mustache and tuxedo and top hat, a devil in red satin, a man carrying a wine bottle and wearing nothing but a huge blond wig, shower shoes, and a jock strap. Becki and Lillian and Jeff's friend Todd walk behind the fellow, giggling and snickering. Curt seems unduly attentive to Jennifer, has seemed so all evening, she thinks. It was just such a festive night in Nice he and that woman slipped away in the crowd and came back hours and hours later and he claimed he "got lost." Matt and his buddies have swept up two girls(?) in cheerleader outfits and have surged on ahead, while Susan and Jeff and his pal, Lillian and Cheryl and the little Batman lag behind. For a moment she considers offering again to escort the little brother so Lillian and Cheryl and Jeff will be free, but the offer never makes it out of committee.

For a while they elbow through the throngs on both sides of the street, waiting for the parade, gawking at the other costumed revelers, worming past the al fresco terraces of cafes and bars, inching by the fire station where blue-shirted men sit as always in chairs before the open bay bemusedly witnessing an annual outbreak of "alternate life-styles." Susan sees a brace of dominatrixes leading handcuffed, all-but-naked men on leashes, and she counts at least two dozen males clad in black leather outfits sporting studs and motorcycle caps and knee-high boots. Balloon breasts with painted nipples, balloon breasts with attached nipples; phalli fashioned from foam rubber, fabric, rubber hoses, foot-long hot dogs; Mickey Mouse and Goofy sporting long and floppy dongs; several Marilyn Monroes, two Judy Garlands, a Whitney Houston. The floats inch by, moving party platforms, and the crowd squeezes between them, pass bottles and joints from the street to the floats and back. On top of the two-story buildings lining Cedar Springs people stand or sit with legs dangling to watch the parade. Music pours into the streets from the floats, the bars, windows of stores.

At one point Susan loses touch with anyone from her party; she was trying to stick close, but a wedge of drunks parted them. She's not tall enough to see over their shoulders. She thinks she should be heading home in case someone wants to go back there, and when she turns she's inadvertently shoved into the chest of a pleasant-faced fellow dressed in a cowboy outfit.

He in turn is pushed toward her, and he smiles apologetically as they're mashed like passengers in a rush-hour subway.

"Long as we're here," he says, grinning, "Why don't we dance?" He takes her hand in both of his in a courtly fashion. "I thank you're a real purty kitty."

She laughs, charmed. "You're not just dressed up like a cowboy, are you?"

"No ma'am," the fellow says. "I just come into town from Vernon to see the sights. Would you know where a man could git uh honest drank and like maybe a blue-plate special? If yew did, I'd be proud to take yew to it."

The cowboy has hoisted her right hand as if to lead her in a waltz. His belt-buckle, the size of a saucer, presses against her ribs. The crowd weight thrusts them up against each other like the halves of a continental fault. She's always liked that look—boots, clean ironed jeans, and a starched white Western shirt with pearl buttons. She surrenders just an instant to the crowd pressure and lets herself be ground against the fellow. *What's guh guh guh good for the goose…*

But the crowd sweeps her out of the cowpoke's arms; she ducks her head into the Crossroads Market and spies a clock. It's 11:55. Back on the sidewalk, she's moving toward home as best she can through the throng when she happens upon Matt, his two buddies, Cheryl, her little brother, and Jeff.

"Hey, hey, wild scene!" says Matt.

"Yes. But I should go back home now. Have you seen Curt?"

"Way up there—" Matt waves south, toward the Melrose Hotel.

"Oh. Well—" she looks around, helplessly. "Guess I'll just go back now."

"You're not afraid?" asks Cheryl.

Susan smiles too brightly. "There's lots of people out. I'll be okay."

She squirms free of the crowd and turns down Throckmorton toward her apartment. Immediately, it seems, the crowd dissolves into the solution of the night; lights from the parade are swallowed by the gloom, and Throckmorton street is the setting for a charcoal chiaroscuro. The street lamps leak their dappled light through a scrim of leaves onto parked cars and other singles or couples drifting to or from the parade. She doesn't like to walk alone in her neighborhood at night, but her costume is camouflage, and though the atmosphere is vaguely noir-ish, tonight she's of it, not just in it, slipping along in her sleek black cat's skin. Sleek and sneaky, quick and agile. Got sharp teeth and claws, too, and a nimble way of leaping (well, there is the problem of warped perspective and a certain numbness due to alcohol.)

"Miz Hart! Susan!"

She whirls on little lithe feet, almost trips. Jeff is trotting to catch up to her.

"I thought maybe I'd walk back with you."

"How gallant! *Trés gallant, monsieur!*" As they say in Nice.

"Well." They walk side by side a moment. "I've got a headache, and I thought maybe you had an aspirin."

Susan laughs. "Oh, then you're not protecting my virtue?"

"Aw, uh," he murmurs. It amuses her how she can strike him awkwardly speechless by being so mildly flirtatious.

"I mean, yeah, I didn't want you to have to come back by yourself if it made you uncomfortable."

"Did I say that?" She touches his shoulder with her fingertips: I'm teasing.

"No, but when you left, Becki said she'd be afraid in this part of town and that made me think maybe you just didn't want to be a bother to us."

"You're sweet. But I don't want you to miss anything you want to see."

"It's okay. You've seen one drag queen you've seen them all."

They stroll in a companionable silence. She wonders where Lillian is and why she and Jeff aren't together. A couple cross-dressed as Rhett and Scarlett pass by arm in arm, and Susan resists a playful urge to hook her arm through Jeff's and skip down a yellow brick road. Where before the dimly lighted street offered ominous shadows, now that darkness softens angles, and the solitary figures hurrying past are looking not for victims but friends and lovers.

"I didn't know you were married."

It's not a question, so no answer is required, thank God, but even in replay she can't tell if he's disappointed or only surprised.

"Did you think I wasn't?"

"I guess. I mean you don't wear a ring."

She hears You fooled me and it wasn't fair. "I don't wear one because my skin reacts to gold."

"Oh."

"Curt and I have been, well—" she stumbles, decides to lie, "married for eight years." The lie bothers her because she doesn't know what motivated it. "I mean, we've been together that long. Well, seven years, actually."

"He seems like a neat guy."

"Thanks. Yes, he is."

"What's he do?"

"He works for an architectural firm. They make models of houses or buildings or whole shopping centers or malls."

"Huh! I always wondered who did those. Is there good money in that?"

"Well, it's like anything else. The man who owns the business seems to do very well."

"Are you guys going to have kids?"

"Oh! Well! Uh, sure! Sometime." Inwardly, she reels from the unexpected question. No overture such as *Hope you don't mind my asking* to suggest he's even aware of a breach in etiquette. Should she respond in kind: *You plan to stay a virgin forever? Are you and Lillian sexually active?*

"Why did you wonder?"

"I don't know. I just think you'd be a good mother, you know. You guys'd make good parents."

"Really? What makes you say that?"

"Well, you know, because you're nice. You're a good listener, and you care about people. And you know stuff."

"Know stuff?"

He sighs, exhausted, it seems, with the effort of making himself understood. She can tell he doesn't want to be grilled; he'd rather simply utter what's on his mind or convey it telepathically without having to explain himself; in this, he's very much like his peers.

"You know how to get along with people."

"Well, I sure appreciate it that you think so, Jeff! Speaking of that, are *you* getting along okay, now? Are you feeling a little more settled at school?"

"Yeah. I guess."

She hears a plea for follow-up questions, but they've stepped up onto her porch and the light beside the door blinds them both. She squints while reaching up to retrieve the key they leave on a narrow ledge over the door frame; she's aware while stretching up on tiptoe of how her form is extended in space to his gaze as he waits behind her. Though her body stocking goes from her neck to her ankles she feels as nude as when he sketched her at the lake.

The muffled *ta-ta-ta-ta-ta* of a police helicopter washes across the porch then a breeze lifts it away.

She goes first to the kitchen cabinet and gets two aspirin, then pours Jeff a glass of water.

"Here."

"Thanks."

He pinches the aspirin with his fingertips, sets them on his tongue, sluices down the tablets. A cool washcloth? Rub his head or neck? Her mom always massaged a headache away for her, and she did it for Nathan. Curt just squirms to be free.

"Would you like to lie down?"

"What?"

"Would you like to—"

"Oh! Oh, no, thanks, I'll be okay. Aspirin usually works."

"Do you have a lot of headaches?"

His lovely brows are furrowed. "I don't know. What's a lot?"

"Every day or so."

"Yeah, I guess."

"Have you been to a doctor?"

"No."

"Why not?"

He shrugs, looks away. "Aw, I guess because it costs money."

Okay, she gets it now. He wants her to feel sorry for him, wants her to baby him. She does feel sympathy, sympathy for how the poor kid is having to work so hard in trying to manage Susan's sympathies, and she's at least three steps ahead of him. She'll tease him.

"I guess if aspirin usually works then a doctor's not necessary. My philosophy is to never go to a doctor unless someone else carries you there because they're afraid you're going to die on them."

"No kidding?"

She grins. "Yes kidding." They stand looking at one another, though his gaze has that wincing squint: that light's too bright! Just as it did that day at the lake, that look pricks her mischievousness. It's so rare that someone male is intimidated by her. No, abashed is a better word. Merely being a teacher gives her sufficient authority for intimidation; this is something else. And he has absolutely no idea how handsome he is. She sees that her wine glass sits empty on the drain board and feels a sudden need to fill it, does so, takes a slug of it. It was a cheap California cabernet, and when they had it for dinner it had an acidic twang. Now it seems very smooth.

"Are you hungry, Jeff?"

"Not really."

"You want something to drink?" Instantly, she pictures the bottle of vodka in the freezer, but she's got her wine glass in her hand. This kid rattles her; she wants to feel relaxed.

"Yeah, that'd be good."

"Why don't you go on out back and get something out of the cooler? I'll be right there."

"Oh, okay."

He walks back through the dining room, and when he reaches the sliding patio door, she calls out, "You'll have to unlatch that door."

"Okay."

When she hears the door hiss on its runners, she takes a tumbler from a shelf, opens the freezer, pulls out the frosted bottle and pours herself two fingers of ice-cold vodka. She tosses it back in one gulp, grimacing with the cold shock against her teeth and palate, then she goes outside to the patio carrying the empty glass. He's standing beside the picnic table with a diet Coke. She dips her hand into the freezing water of the cooler, extracts a Sprite, opens it and pours some into the tumbler, thinking this is kind of like high school except that she's just drunk her vodka straight and is belatedly using the soda as a chaser. She lifts her hip and eases onto the top of the picnic table, and Jeff sits very near her on the bench, his head level with her breasts. He has taken off his cape, the mask. His hair is tousled cutely. The shifting breeze brings them the sound of a band on Cedar Springs. Curt and Jennifer dancing?

"Sounds like everybody's still having a big time."

"Yeah, I guess."

His *Yeah, I guess* sounds whiny, dog-sorrowful. She thinks he's trying to hint that he's feeling down, but he can't bring himself to say that and explain what makes him blue, so the mournful sound is calculated to inspire her to dig the story out of him.

"I wonder how the others are getting along. I hope they're not getting into trouble." She coughs up a nervous chuckle. The vodka makes her head a little whirly.

"Aw, don't worry. They'll be okay."

"Did you lose your friend?" Maybe he and Lillian had a spat, she thinks. Maybe that's what's troubling him.

Jeff snorts. "Todd? Oh, I'm sure *he's* okay!"

Rather than amend her question, she says, "I've always thought Lillian was a really nice girl."

"Lillian?"

"Yes, the girl—"

"Oh!" Jeff laughs. "Hey, we weren't together! We just came at the same time."

"Oh." To her surprise, Susan feels her cheeks burning. "My mistake. Sorry."

"I'm flattered, though. She's popular. Todd's really scamming her."

"How's that?"

Jeff smiles, amused. "My friend is being quite friendly with her in hopes of having serious physical contact with her on a regular basis."

They both laugh.

"How come you're not 'scamming' her?"

"I don't know. I guess because to her I'm slime."

"Jeff! What makes you say that?"

"I can tell. Girls like her and Cheryl and Becki at Carver think no-talent guys are loser slime."

"Oh, Jeff, it's just not true, believe me."

"You're a teacher, you don't know."

His burning look of injury stabs her. She says, coolly, "Jeff, I think I know them as well as you do, and I guarantee you they don't think you're slime. Besides, I meant that it's not true that you're a no-talent loser."

"I'm not?"

"No, of course not." The wonderful thing about really young men, thinks Susan, is that they have no idea they're not supposed to let their needs be so naked. By the time they reach Curt's age, they will be claiming that they're geniuses and winners but will secretly suspect otherwise and expect you to know that and reassure them even though they don't officially need it and would be the last to admit they did, and if you give them reassurance they don't have to thank you because, after all, they didn't ask you for it. When you compliment them they act like you're trying to overfeed them, make them fat; Jeff, on the other hand, is a puppy eager to gulp down whatever tidbit she'll toss him.

"I think you're very talented, Jeff. I'm sure that given a little more time you're going to feel very much at home at school. You'll make friends soon, I just know it. You're charming and very attractive."

"I hope so, I mean I hope I can make friends at Carver. Todd is one of the few people from my old school who'll still have anything to do with me."

"Why is that?"

"Because I got kicked out and people there are embarrassed to be seen with me."

She looks down at his face. Seated on the bench with his shoulders against the table, he stretches his head back so that his face lies horizontal, eyes closed, as if he's floating in a pool of moonlight. She's sitting on the table top, her feet on the bench near his hips, and his left cheek is only inches from her right thigh. She knows she's supposed to ask what he did to get kicked out of Lakeview; he's offering her intimacy of a peculiar kind—I'll tell you all about my troubles but only if you promise to feel sorry for me.

But that in itself stirs her compassion, that he feels such an extortion is required: it was like using a crutch to gain sympathy when you also couldn't walk without it.

"What happened?" she asks softly.

He's silent for a while, and she holds back the urge to coax him out.

"I'd hate for people at Carver to learn about it, you know?"

"Jeff, please don't feel you have to tell me this right now. I want to be here for you, I really do. And of course I believe you can trust me. But—" she pats him on the shoulder—"if you don't feel like saying anything, don't."

"Okay. Thanks."

They're silent for another long beat and she considers suggesting that they go back inside and busy themselves preparing snacks, making more burritos. She doesn't want to make him uncomfortable, but, then again, she also doesn't want to abruptly end an opportunity for him to talk if he needs to.

"Thing is," he says, "I stole a credit card from this girl's purse.

Then I went shopping at Neiman's and bought a whole lot of just *shit*, you know? Just crap I didn't need or nobody else did, and I started giving it all away as presents, and it only took about a day to get caught. I mean, I wasn't even smart about it."

When he doesn't go on, she says, "Do you know why you did it?"

"Yeah, I think. I just wanted either to fit in or get kicked out. I couldn't stand being in between."

He bows his head, puts his face in his hands. He's very still, so she doesn't think he's crying, but his body language speaks deeply of his shame to her. She slides her hand across his nape and squeezes gently.

"Jeff, you *will* make it with us, I promise!"

"Please don't tell anybody," he murmurs between his fingers.

"No, of course I won't."

She wants to comfort him. Her hand lifts from his neck and moves across his back, patting him gently on his shoulder blade, as if saying *there there*. Her hand moves back to his neck, to his head; she gently strokes his tousled hair. She pities him now the way you pity that one kid in a kindergarten class who clings to the teacher's side.

He bends his head back, drops his hands. His eyes are watery, and he smiles weakly.

"Thanks."

"You're welcome."

"You're a really good friend."

His face is uptilted below hers, with the white moonlight playing in his long lashes, his mouth full-lipped. *Endymion*, she thinks. She bends toward him. An image pops to her mind of a plate with a cupcake on it. Kiss the hurt. What harm would it do? His own mother doesn't give him much, what he needs, an intelligent, sympathetic ear, an understanding of what it means to be young and in a state of yearning.

"How's your headache?"

Since she's perched on the table top and he's sitting on the bench below facing out, his shoulders almost touch her knee. It's easy to move her hand to his forehead, and when her palm settles on his cool skin, he lurches with surprise but quickly settles back to let her stroke his hair.

"Better."

"You feel a little warm," she says. She strokes his forehead for a moment. "You'll be okay, Jeff, I promise," she whispers. She can make the hurt better. A mother's kiss.

She hovers over his floating face and dips down to brush his lips with hers, gently, bestowing grace upon him like a blessing: *you will be fine, believe me, trust me.* Before she pulls away he strains up to secure the match, and someone moans. Her head swims; they are both paralyzed in place except for their faces, their lips, and his mouth is a tender well from which she thirstily draws something she didn't know she needed until this instant.

$\widehat{~}12\widehat{~}$

The bar of the Melrose is normally a sedate, clubby place with wing chairs and shelves of leather-bound books no one has read. To-night it's bedlam, but Curt and the old frat brother he accidentally stumbles into manage to elbow their way to the counter for a drink. They're both surprised to find the other here, and only Curt is in costume. He hasn't seen this brother for five years, and the guy has a paunchy look. A neatly trimmed mustache, though, and he's wearing a starched oxford-cloth button-down fastidiously tucked into the beltless waistband of Calvin Klein jeans, and pointy-toed lizard Justins.

After they have drinks in hand, Curt says, "Susan and I live near here." He wants to allay suspicion regarding his presence in the gay ghetto on Halloween night.

The brother—his first name is Jacques but everybody called him "Jack," which he wrote as "Jac"—smiles with pity.

"You're still straight, then."

"Well, yes." Curt's scotch and water is one part the former and twenty the latter, and he peers over Jac's shoulder into the milling throng for Susan's students.

"I'm not."

What do you say? Jac sounds vaguely defiant, and his grin is twisted.

"Huh!" Curt coughs up finally. "When did this happen?" He tries to treat it as, say, a promotion, but he sounds as if he's asking about a car wreck.

"When I was little bitty."

Curt wants to be sympathetic, but Jac's irony mocks him. Even knowing the sarcasm rises from defensiveness, he doesn't like the smug implication that he's a moron for being heterosexual.

"Oh, for Christ's sake, Curt, get that look off your face!" Jac laughs. "You and I were never in the shower at the same time."

Curt almost says *I wasn't checking* but, indeed, that's what he was hurriedly doing. Instead, he asks, "Should I offer my congratulations or what?"

Jac lowers his horns. "Well, I am happier now, Curt."

Very deliberately, Curt lays his palm on Jac's shoulder (he didn't want Jac to think he's afraid of getting AIDs), claps him once (*I dub thee...*), then removes his hand (he doesn't want to appear eager to touch him, either.)

"Hey, bud, I'm happy for you, then."

"Well." Jac smiles. "Now that that's out of the way, let's have a drink."

They're already holding drinks. The way Curt sees it, now that that's out of the way, there's no reason to keep talking. They lamely rehash old times, but the anecdotes fail to rekindle fraternal feelings. Not that the memories aren't without interest; in fact, past events now have a new, startling coloration in Curt's mind's eye, and, despite himself, he does wonder again if he and Jac have ever been naked in the same room or stood elbow-to-elbow at a urinal. Or how about the night they were pledges and blindfolded and he had to hold someone's hand to be led upstairs? Was that Jac?

Jac works now as an engineer for the city of Dallas, he said. Curt's about to explain his work when he spies Becki homing in on him, so he waves her over.

"I've lost everybody. Maybe I should go back now. You think they've all gone back?" The star's gone from the end of her wand, but the bodice of her old prom dress still does a delicious push-up number on her breasts. When she catches Curt glancing at them, she blushes; he feels guilt but is also oddly heartened by this wordless exchange.

"I better go with you in case Susan's not there."

Turning to Jac, he sticks out his hand. "We're giving a party for Susan's art students. It was good to see you, Jac."

Jac shakes his hand firmly. "You too, Curt."

"We'll have lunch sometime, okay?"

Jac laughs. "No, we won't, and you know it."

Curt laughs back. Two could make honesty a weapon. "Yeah, you're right. Let's not have lunch sometime then, okay?"

"Fine with me!" Jac chortles. He waves Curt off with a sweep of his hand that goes from Curt's head to his knees, as if to say, *That pirate get-up is just too, too preposterous!*

When they get outside, Curt wonders what Becki thinks of what she'd witnessed, but he doubts he could explain it. The unexpectedly candid conclusion to their conversation was bracing—the instant he and Jac acknowledged utter indifference to one another's futures, it seemed possible they might be friends again, but that instant depended upon a mutual pledge of abstention based on mutual disdain. Susan will appreciate the irony of it.

At the apartment, they find the others dancing or chattering on the patio about the sights witnessed on Cedar Springs. Susan's at the kitchen sink washing a platter. Her body stocking holds her ass high and tight, so he presses against her and tongues the nape of her neck.

She yelps.

"Ooop! Sorry!" he says. "Just me."

She whirls and grabs him about his chest and squeezes him hard. "Hold me, Curt."

He holds her tightly. Her damp, soapy hands bleed through his shirt and burn cold to his back. Her hug has the urgency that means she's had frightening thoughts or is upset. It's how she hugs when he's leaving on a business trip.

"Everything okay here?"

Her head, nodding, bumps his chin. Then she strains up and shoves her face into his neck and kisses him.

"I love you, Curt."

"Love you too, babe."

Every time he relaxes his arms around her shoulders as if to signal he's ready to let go, she just clings more tightly. He waits, patiently, for her finally to release him.

"I've gotta pee."

She gives him one last squeeze, then twists back around to the sink. He shoots a quick glance about to make sure no one's looking and strokes her ass. Poor Jac.

"Mmm, mama!"

"You want to help me make some more burritos?" she says quickly.

"Yeah, be right back."

In the downstairs bathroom, it looks like a kid has gotten sick and hasn't cleaned up very well. The toilet bowl and rim sport a Jackson Pollock array of colored bits. His fingers feel cold to his cock, and his cock feels hot to his fingers. Tonight's the night…. Poor Jac. Any sign, back then? Who'd he go out with? He had a stormy deal with a violinist, weird girl, not like anybody any of them ever dated, though she was in a sorority but he couldn't recall which one. Oh, well. Different strokes. Boy, wasn't that phrase loaded?

He has almost exited when he realizes he has a decision: to clean or not to clean? One part of him says you were almost out of there without even thinking about it—just keep cruisin'. These are her students, after all. She normally does the downstairs bathroom, anyway. His duty's the one upstairs.

But she'll freak out if she comes in and sees somebody's puke. Okay, so do her a favor. She'll owe you one, okay?

Whistling, he scrubs the bowl clean with brush and Comet, even sponges the belly and the base for splat-over. He feels happy, like a good guy doing a good deed. He'll get his reward later. He has his reasons for wanting to finish the clean-up as soon as possible after the last kid leaves.

Later, at 2:10 A.M. by the beside clock, Curt lies grinning in the dark. Poor Jac. All in all, Curt's pleased with his role in their impromptu little drama, though he would prefer to have been in street clothes. He hasn't gotten around to telling Susan about it, but soon as she gets out of the bathroom, he will. He'll hold her close while they smoke imaginary cigarettes and chuckle over the fate of poor Jac, who'll never know the manly joy of inflating your babe pump by pump like a balloon until she explodes and comes with groans and moans then starts blubbering from that weird combination of relief/joy, that come/cry/laugh stuff—man, aren't women truly fascinating? Endlessly mysterious!

One day during his senior year he was shopping in Foley's in Austin for a shirt, and after he bought it, he deliberately walked through the lingerie, perfume and cosmetics departments on his way out. This was a habit; seeing the mannequins in panties or teddies and seeing the nightgowns and lacy brassieres hanging from the racks, seeing the pretty sales clerks and the beautiful women lined up at the counter to buy, and smelling the perfume wafting on the air—well, all this gave him a lift, like a whiff of pure oxygen, put a little extra bounce in his step. It was a very cheap and harmless high, like sunshine.

So he had a La Coste knit pullover in the bag—they were still big, the ones with the alligator logo—and he was cruising this pleasant avenue humming, serene, when, at the frontier between panties and belts, he spied a rack of beautiful scarves standing on the display counter. Beside it, with elbows on the counter and her hands propping up her chin, was a short, freckled redhead with green eyes and mulberry-colored lips, who—right as his gaze slid off the rack and onto her face—beamed winningly.

"Hi!" said she. "Can I help you?"

"Hey, these are really pretty!" He stopped to finger a scarf.

"Yes. How about one or two?"

They grinned at each other. Full-scale flirtation. Now, Curt's heart was already chock full of Susan on this day. But flirting with this girl didn't detract from the adoration he felt for Susan—it was a spillover, so to speak. The night before, it was great. Their dozenth date, fifth time to make love. She spent the night for the first time, they'd had breakfast two hours ago at IHOP before she went to the library.

"They're nice!"

"Yes, they're really really pretty! Feel!"

The clerk was very cute, Curt thought; she warmed his heart. He had no interest in asking her out, but exchanging smiles was enjoyable in its own right, and he wanted to please her.

"I think I'll get one for my girlfriend." He wanted the clerk to know he'd buy a gift on impulse just to make Girlfriend feel good, but he knew that this might warm the clerk's heart, too, make her feel enriched: the scarf he bought right here and now was for all of Womankind.

"Oh, that's nice. I'm sure she'll love it. Gift wrapped?"

"Oh, yeah! You bet!" Curt crowed. At the register counter, he discovered that the scarf was seventy dollars. He hid his shock behind the facade of a cheerful big spender and wedged the purchase onto his smoking Mastercard.

When he gave the wrapped box to Susan that night, she said, "What's this for?"

"I don't know. Just because."

She unpeeled the wrapping carefully, folded it and set it aside.

"Oh, God, Curt! This is really beautiful! It's a Perry Ellis—hey, you can't afford this!"

"Aw, don't worry about it. I just wanted to buy you something nice."

She started laughing. "I get it now!"

"Get it?"

"You know—how come the gift."

She was grinning. He was baffled but pleased to have pleased her. (Lying in the dark now, years later, smiling, he realizes that these feelings are familiar fixtures in his relationship with her: puzzlement mixed with pleasure.)

"Yeah?" he asks.

"Yeah! It's because of—well, you know."

"Huh?"

"You know—last night."

"What about last night?"

"Currrt!" They were sitting on her sleeper sofa, and she moved close to nuzzle his shoulder with her cheek and stroke his bicep, parodic but nonetheless effective gestures. Kittenish.

"We made love?" he asked.

"Well, yes!"

"And?"

"You sure have a short memory! You don't recall it was different in any way?"

He blushed deeply. "Oh, you mean because you, uh, had, uh -"

"Yes." She held up the scarf and laughed again. "That's just how sweet you are. You brought *me* a reward for coming."

☞ 13 ☞

"So, Dad, I've got this problem, see?"

"Yeah, son, what is it?"

"There's this teacher, and she's hot for me."

"Sounds like quite a problem, son."

"It is. What should I do, Dad?"

"Well, how do you know she's hot for you?"

"She Frenched me."

"That's a pretty good sign. What did you do?"

"Same thing."

"Who started it?"

"She did."

"How'd it end?"

"We were at a party, in her back yard, and we heard some people coming."

"What'd you say after that?"

"Nothing."

"What'd she say to you?"

"She said, 'You're such a sweet boy.'"

"So what's next?"

"I don't know, Dad. It was like over three weeks ago."

"Has she said anything since?"

"Nope." To tell the truth (is this possible?) he hasn't talked to her since.

"Maybe she's waiting for you to make the next move."

"What should I do? What would you do?"

"How old is she?"

"Twenty-five, maybe."

"Good looking?"

"Yeah, very."

"Well?"

"Huh?"

"Hey. You have to ask?"

"Well, I was wondering because, well, she seemed kind of upset later that night and I think maybe she's been avoiding me."

"Probably just hormones, son."

"So I should just fuck her brains out and not worry about it?"

"Yeah, that's it. You got the picture. Good boy. Here, take this rubber for luck."

He sits in the downtown Wendy's alone during Thursday afternoon rush hour eating a small Frosty and doodling on a napkin with a felt point pen while waiting for his Dad's black Saab to pull to the curb outside and honk. He'd like to ask his Dad about this problem but suspects he can't bring himself to do it. What would his Dad say? Imagining the part about "hormones" was no exaggeration—to hear his Dad tell it, hormones rule the kingdom of women: if his mother calls his Dad to complain about the support check being late, then it's hormones, because, see, he's explained it to her a hundred times that she should call the Dallas County courts and climb their ass, not his, because that's where he sends the checks, and if the check is late getting to her, it's not his fault. (His mother would have already called that office and discovered that his father was late getting the check to them.) His Dad says the word hormones this way: HOR-mones. He'll look disgusted and snicker. To be fair, Jeff has to admit that his father uses the word to account for his stepmother's fits of temper, too. If, say, Jeff's supposed to go to dinner with them and Sybil doesn't show up, then, when Jeff asks where she is, his Dad'll make that face and say, "HOR-mones," and Jeff knows they've had a fight. Hormones are like insects whose bite causes rashes, fevers, irrationality, volcanic upheavals of temper, crying jags, though the way his Dad says it you get the idea that females voluntarily cultivate these bugs as pets so the bites are, in a way, self-inflicted.

The girl behind the counter—Tamara—waves to get his attention. She must have been in the back when he came in.

"Hey, Jeffie!"

"Hi. How's it going?"

"Great! You done your algebra yet?"

"Yeah."

"What'd you make on that mid-term?"

"I think it was eighty-three, something like that."

"Wow! I'm like barely passing in there. I wish I could study with you before the next test."

He can't recall what cluster she's in—he thinks it's Dance, though she looks too stocky for it.

"You work every night?" he asks, thinking it must be hard to work and go to rehearsals, too. Then he realizes it sounds like he's trying to arrange a date.

"No. I'm off on Monday, Wednesday and Sunday."

"Must be hard to make rehearsals, then."

"Rehearsals?"

"Oh. I thought you—"

"No, Visual arts."

"Oh. Okay." He's embarrassed to have forgotten this, but he's also relieved that the conversation slid away from "helping her with algebra," hint hint. He likes how she's full of pep, kind of a bubbly kid, with a moon-shaped face and springy reddish-blonde curls that bounce when she bobs or shakes her head. And yes he's been coming in here since the semester began because she's friendly and slips him free fries and because sooner or later he might've asked her for a date.

But things are different. Now. He's got beaucoup new stuff on his mind. Everything he ever thought about dating and sex has been up-ended, cut into bits and shuffled in a hat, and poured back out onto the table as scrambled nonsense. When a desirable grown woman you know, like and respect unexpectedly slips her tongue into your mouth and rubs her tits against your cheek, it profoundly colors your picture of her.

Dreams do come true. He can't stop thinking about that kiss, her tongue, her lips, her soft black hair falling over his face, her warm breath with its faint aroma of wine, the uuhhh sound she made in her throat and chest, her small tight ass in the body stocking. Every night her ghost alights in his darkened room, and he lays her on his bed and slides between her legs, and she says *oh you sweeet boy!* in his ear, and the way she says *sweet*, it doesn't mean he's merely *nice* any more: it means his dick feels good (big) to her, like a craving satisfied by a rich dessert. He can still smell her perfume in parts of the scarf he hasn't fouled, and when he eases it over his taut flesh and remembers their kiss, his dick and balls turn so stone hard his stomach aches.

Without her knowing it, he has followed her down the halls at school watching her hair move, her trim calves flex when she walks in her low-heeled pumps. He drafts in her fragrant wake only half-aware of his surroundings. He sits all the way across the cafeteria from the teacher's table but his gaze never leaves her face. When she cocks her head to listen to somebody, her bangs hang over her brow and bother her, and she rolls her eyes and blows a huff of breath up to move them, lips parted, cheeks frogging for a second. It's really cute. It kills him.

It's not true she's avoiding him. It's the other way around. What happened has made it impossible for him to stop by her office and speak to her. He has avoided going out the building by that route since the party. His hands shake merely to imagine being near her again; he is dead certain that his desire, his guilt about having her over and over in his bed, will flag itself on his face, and even if he might say *well, you started it!* still, it's shameful that he's a wuss who lacks the courage to face her and follow through.

And the longer he stays away, the harder it is to imagine being with her. What she might be thinking is beyond his comprehension but not his speculation: it meant nothing? She's forgotten it?

Next to Susan Hart, Tamara is a silly child. Weird as it seems, what he wants now in a female is a woman, not a girl. In his mind's eye, his fingers delve to that V and encounter a thick black bush of luxuriantly curly hair, fleshy wet labia. How does a woman differ from a mere girl? Hard to say, exactly. There's an impression of bigness, somehow: hips, breasts. Yeah, but Susan Hart was not actually larger than, say, Tamara. You think they know something, that's part of it. They know all the mysteries; they've had a lot of sex, so they're, like, practiced at it. And the thing that they're so knowing about is so mysterious and powerful that it makes them like priestesses, that they possess those secrets. With a girl you're always thinking that maybe they wouldn't want to do it or would be disgusted or afraid, but with a married woman, you know that they know about it already and they've been—what's the weird word his mother uses? Soiled. Another thing is, like Tamara or the girls at school, everybody talks about whether or not they're virgins or whether they've been boffed, and it's all guesswork. Rumors go around—has she or hasn't she? Will she or won't she? If you're really liberal, you say what's it matter? If you're a nut-churcher like his mother, you say (as he's often heard), *Once a girl unlocks the door, anybody can come through it.* Whole armies. The National Football League. So what it comes down to is that when he looks at Susan Hart, he knows she has. She lets a man do it to her, maybe whenever the man wants. She wants a man to do it to her. The idea of that certainty sets him afire.

When you go backpacking in the wilderness for the first time, do you want to accompany a child or would you prefer being taken by a guide who knows the way? Like you could either play the big stud and pretend you know what you're doing and enjoy the admiration of the kid and you both might get lost and die, or you could admit from in front that you're ignorant and need help. Even if it means swallowing your pride and suffering humiliation.

His aimless, errant pen has been drawing pairs of breasts all over the napkin; they look like owl's eyes, so he jots in brows, frowning brows, and a beak just below the cleavage to disguise his original intent. Owlishly, the breasts peer at him, looking angry, so he wads the napkin and tosses it under the table.

His watch reads 5:15. His Dad is late. He pats his shirt pocket, then lifts the flap to glance inside again, where a folded piece of paper rests, on it a message in a florid, blue-ink cursive:

Wed. Nov. 28th

Jeff, we've missed you in the last two meetings! We have only two left in the semester—next two Tuesdays (Dec. 4 and 11)—so I do hope you can make them both. Also, if you're not too busy and you're still interested, we could have another lesson or two before the term is over. Hope to see you Tuesday!

Next to Susan's scripted initials is a drawing of a head, very stylized, could either be a cat or a man in a cat mask. When he got the note through Miss Cartling yesterday in last period, he thought the little face was her self-portrait, a reference to her Halloween costume, then later when he looked closer it seemed like a rendering of the masked face of Bruce Wayne. In either case, it set his mind spinning: she was not trying to forget Halloween, anyway, though she still could be trying to ignore the importance (if it was important).

His hands suddenly feel cold, sweaty. Another possibility (oh, dream on!) is that the face is meant to remind him, to let him know she's thinking of that kiss, too.

Does she want to kiss him again? The suggestion about "lessons," does it mean more? What do I have to do? she whispers. A scene from a dumb porno flick: a would-be "lady" professor "interviewing" a male "student," and the professor is playing coy and teasing at the same time: It's not nice to make a lady beg, gentlemen don't do that. The idea is that at some point you're both supposed to pretend that the guy's the aggressor and the girl's only a passive victim, too surprised and helpless to ward off an advance she has no idea is coming. Sometimes when he recalls the kiss, he sees her sort of pained and bemused smile when she broke it off, then when she said *such a sweet boy!* it meant *harmless child*, and the insult to his masculinity is like a blow to his gut.

So. It could be different: her office? The other students have gone home, her skirt lifted to her waist, she lies back on her desk. *Give it to me, big man!*

His mouth is dry, his groin aching. He pushes the images away and moves to another setting, another set of characters, another time between now and then. Him and his Dad. A father-and-son talk. The Beaver has to initiate it. Dad, I'd like to learn to use my dick. Will you teach me? Son, a dick can be a dangerous thing. You want to make sure the safety is on, and never point it at anybody because it might go off by accident.

No, he doesn't need to learn how to use it, really. Thing is, what he wants to do is be able to lay an accomplishment on the table so his Dad can praise him, so his Dad won't keep on thinking he's just some weirdo wimp always hanging to his mother's apron-strings (over-heard: ...*she protects him too much against everything...*). But he also wants desperately to get advice on what to do—not the mechanics, that's simple, known to all: a hard dick in a wet pussy, you go up and down until everybody's howling and panting like they've run an 880—but how to proceed, how to feel, what to think.

He can't very well brag about making a conquest then ask if he's supposed to go ahead and try to make a conquest. He can't have it both ways, can he? If he lies about already doing It, then he can't ask if he should. What he wants to know the most is not should he do It, but, rather—

—Is it likely that this beautiful married woman will let me do It with her?

—Will I be completely humiliated if she says yes and I can't?

—Will I be completely humiliated by her saying no?

—Will any harm come of this?

—Will it be discovered?

—Will it get me into trouble? Say I go ahead and follow up and act like I know that she really wants me to be a big manly stud, and it turns out that not only does she *not* want this, she's so angry about it she has me kicked out of school? She calls the cops?

What to do....

You have to ask?

Yeah, Dad, I have to ask.

Todd would say, Chris would say, Dad would say, the whole world would say—*Go for it, dude!*

⌒ *14* ⌒

A parable: Deep inside a sultry, moonless night, an ocean liner churns through tropical waters. The passengers slumber in air-conditioned bliss. Up on the bridge, a crewman has one eye on a radar screen whose blips are regular as the heartbeat of a healthy patient, and one eye on a chess board whose configuration he changed an hour ago after a radio message from Lisbon. The officer on watch is perusing a magazine; while his eyes slide across glossy text, his ears and shoe soles note a muted thump. Someone stepped down to the bridge from a ladder? Glances up. No one. The crewman remains unaware: N-B5 looks A-OK. One passenger three decks below heard it, too, felt it against the back of her head. Could be disaster but probably the crew? Seven stories below the bridge and under the waterline now is a ten-foot rent in the skin of the ship, an arterial wound as it were, gushing, gushing. A trapped-rat grease-monkey gurgles Help!! just as his last air-space is elevatored out by tons of surging water. Meanwhile, the boat glides onward, otherwise undisturbed.

Some facts:

1. Susan had her hair trimmed on Monday, Nov. 12, the day before the next scheduled meeting of the Art club after her Halloween party. (They didn't meet Tuesday, Nov. 6, because of the elections.)

"What do you want to do?" Kelly asked her.

Kelly's done her hair for as long as Susan's lived in Dallas. First time she went her hair was permed in big curls, the style those days. The last couple of years she's worn it just below her ears with a natural wave, a part, and bangs, the right combination of convenience and style, she thinks.

Normally she'd just tell Kelly to trim it. But on this day, she said, "You think I'd look as good as Sinead O'Connor with my head shaved?"

"Uh, well, I think being famous helps a lot. Are you feeling rebellious or just bored?"

Susan looked into Kelly's mirror as if the answer might appear on her face. Susan was swathed in the pink protective drape; her wet hair was plastered to her forehead and cheeks, the condition of utmost neutrality before decisions are made. An unfinished portrait. Shave her head? Why? In France they shaved the heads of the village women who fraternized with the Nazis. You could really unsex yourself this way, couldn't you?

"I don't know," she said.

She settled for the usual. Because she left the salon vaguely dissatisfied, she stopped in at Espirit on McKinney where she tried on blouse after blouse with steadily plummeting spirits. She eventually paid for the dubious entertainment of shopping by coughing up too much money (thirty-two dollars) for a kooky lapel pin—an enameled international prohibition sign—circle and a slash—without an image behind it.

2. Later that Monday night, the twelfth, she called Jeff's house.

She planned to say she was reminding him of the meeting tomorrow night. She planned to ask if he'd been feeling well. She planned to ask if he'd been busy studying or working on a play. The phone call had purpose. She was the faculty sponsor of the club, after all. It was her responsibility to motivate students to stay involved. When and if they dropped out, it was usually or almost always from lack of faculty encouragement or because they were very busy doing other things. A boy such as Jeff who is officially in the theater cluster, for example, would doubtless become too busy working on a play to attend meetings. It was seldom anything personal. Susan was well-liked; there was no reason why Jeff would take a dislike to her, as friendly and helpful as she has been to him, with him, as far out of her way she has gone to keep him interested. She couldn't think of any reason why Jeff would avoid anyone in the club—he seemed to have a good time at the Halloween party, seemed to fit right in. Nothing happened between him and the others that she knows about, anyway.

When his mother answered, Susan hung up.

The mother wouldn't have known the answers to her questions, anyway. And the reason for his absence was probably the obvious one: he was busy.

3. Saturday, Nov. 17th: She bought a brighter shade of red lipstick at the cosmetics counter in Dillard's. While waiting to have her hair done on the 12th, she had browsed through *Glamour* and got caught up in a feature about lips, big juicy bee-stung lips, how, because mega-star Kim Basinger had large lips, some aspiring actresses were considering collagen treatments, lip-jobs. That seemed ridiculous. She liked the name of her new lipstick: Luscious Lips.

4. Saturday, Nov. 10, she told Curt: "Goddamnit, Curt, I'm tired of you building models on the dining room table—it's my table too, you know! I can't even sit here and eat a sandwich because you've got all your crap here all the time!" Since this was the first inkling Curt

had ever had that Susan wanted or needed part of the dining room table or that his using it annoyed her, he was (first) shocked at her vehemence then (second) abashed, then (third) annoyed that she acted as if she'd warned him before.

5. Even though she had just tossed out all the leftover Halloween candy, on an inexplicable impulse she bought a five-pound bag of Hershey's chocolate kisses and put it in the freezer thinking she'd have a tiny little treat every now and then. But she had eaten every one by the time she and Curt went to Longview for Thanksgiving.

6. She expected to see Jeff at the meeting on Tuesday, Nov. 13. It did seem a little odd that he hadn't come by her office since Halloween, that she hadn't even bumped into him in the hall. It would be easy to duck into the attendance office or check his enrollment record to see what other classes he is taking then say something off-hand to another teacher—*By the way, Jeff Robbins is one of your students, too, isn't he?....*

Well, if something were wrong, she would know about it, wouldn't she?

Was there any possibility however remote that he might have misconstrued that kiss? God forbid that he might imagine that she would want to prey on him—he was a student, for God's sake! And she a teacher! Most likely, the kiss meant nothing to him: he was a savvy teenager; they were all sexually experienced, and he probably had a concubine here at Carver already, and that explained why he suddenly lost interest in art. Any kid who could kiss like that wouldn't be long without a steady girlfriend. (Lucky girl!)

Still, if he were to have misunderstood, what should she do? Would it be better to explain it as just a maternal impulse, friendly kidding, like under the office mistletoe, or would that just put undue emphasis on it? Wouldn't it be better to ignore it, and as time went on whatever misunderstanding he might have would simply evaporate from inattention? If she forgot it, no doubt he would, too. Since he'd probably forgotten it, she might as well.

He wasn't at the meeting on the thirteenth. She said at the end of it, "We won't meet next week, because that's the Tuesday before Thanksgiving, but then we'll meet the Tuesday after—that's the twenty-seventh—and twice more in December before the term is over. If any of you know Jeff or see him, you might tell him." She watched their faces. She expected someone to explain his absence. No one did.

"Oh, well," she said. "Mid-terms are coming up next week. I guess you've all been studying."

"I can't do it until the last minute," said Matt. "It's a religious conviction."

Cracking a grin, she said, "Some of us don't procrastinate," as if referring to Jeff, though she had no reason to think his study habits were better than Matt's.

A parable, cont'd:

The officer on watch has put down his magazine. A strange vibration has seeped up from his shoe soles, his calves, his thighs, up his spine and into his cortex. Now he cocks his head, listening. Faint sound of *Mac the Knife* from the all-night lounge aboard the ship. Funny, the ship feels, well, heavier, in the water.

More facts:

7. Curt was shaking her. "Suzie! Wake Up!" When she stumbled to consciousness, she said, crossly, "Whut?" Curt told her she was having a dream—she was moaning and whimpering. "Yeah?" He asked, "What were you dreaming?" She stared into the darkness inside her skull. Figures were fleeting about in shadows, like people in the bushes at a park, at night, scurrying away as the police cars screech up, sirens howling. She couldn't recall anything specific, but her

body harbored the glowing sensations of great arousal coupled with fear—a combination she hadn't experienced since her teen years. She was amazed that her body could recall these sensations so vividly when her mind had forgotten them; they had once been so familiar, when she and Nathan groped in various furtive pockets of darkness. Having that old familiarity suddenly return without any images to pin it to was mysterious, stirring, upsetting. It was a little as if her body were another person reminding her of an intense and rich experience they once had together. This "familiar" tingling in her nerve-ends was like a scent that instantly penetrates to that portion of the brain that stores a memory, but the conscious mind cannot either put a name to the scent or locate the setting or object in which it resided.

"I don't know," she said finally.

"It sounded like a bad dream," Curt said, defending his decision to wake her.

"Maybe." After a moment, Susan thought of asking Curt to make love to her, but he had already fallen asleep. Then for the second time that week her body refused to submit to her will to sleep, and the struggle the two waged for control went on until 5 a.m., when her body at last surrendered.

Perversely, though, when the alarm went off at six-thirty and her will said *Get up!*, her body then did not want to be awake. Her will and her body were in need of family counseling; they were like spouses with deep-seated grievances who need to be dragged to the arbitration table. The will said, at hers and Curt's dinnertime, *Time to eat!* but the body said, *Not hungry!* The will said, *Not another chocolate kiss!* and the body said, *Watch me!*

8. She said to Curt, "Why do I always have to go down first thing in the morning and start the coffee?" He had never heard this complaint in all the time they had lived together.

9. On Sunday, Nov. 18, the day after Susan bought her Luscious Lips lipstick, Curt asked her, "What time do you want to leave Wednesday?"

"Where are we going?"

"You know, Longview. For Thanksgiving."

"How come we always have to go to your mother's house for Thanksgiving?"

Curt frowned (not angry—perplexed). "Well, we always have." Time was 9:45 P.M. Susan was at the bathroom sink, Curt lying on the bed.

"So?"

"Well, I guess I just presumed that's what we'd do this year."

"What if I don't want to?"

Curt said, very slowly and carefully, "I suppose we should discuss an alternative."

"How about Acapulco?"

He leaned across the bed and eased the bathroom door open a little more so he could see her face. What is this?

"Turkey fajitas and cranberry guacamole?"

She didn't laugh. "It was just a metaphor, Curt."

"I'd have thought you got traveling out of your system for a while this summer."

"Traveling's not the point. We could just stay here, you know."

"And have them come here?"

"No. Have them stay there. Just the way it is with my relatives."

"But yours live in St. Louis. My mom lives about an hour away. I guess I didn't know you didn't like to go there for holidays."

A sigh glissandoed from the bathroom. "It's not really your mom, Curt. It doesn't matter, really. We can go if you like."

He mulled over the past few moments. "Are you thinking about Kenneth and Vivian?"

"Not unless I can help it."

Her belligerent body defied her wishes and the daily ingestion of anti-contraceptive hormones; it flaunted its ability to confound her scheduling and dumped her period unexpectedly into her life an hour before they left for Longview on Thursday morning in Curt's Integra.

On the way, Susan said, "I bet you a dollar I can tell you exactly what we're going to have for dinner, and maybe even the dishes that things will be served in." Curt side-stepped the bait her sneer offered. He laughed, instead, and said, "It's nice to know that in a world of uncertainty some things never change."

Mavis was pleased to see them. After Kenneth and Vivian and their two children arrived and all were seated at the table, Susan smiled vacantly while Curt's older brother described in minute detail how he successfully defeated the problems of remodeling a bathroom in their new/old Victorian home in Longview, during which his wife persisted in sharply slapping her children's hands (girl, five; boy, three) to encourage better table manners. As Susan had claimed, the menu was as predictable as a planetary orbit: roast turkey, cornbread stuffing with too much celery, giblet gravy, canned green bean casserole (add sautéed onions, one can Campbell's cream of mushroom soup, bread crumbs, bake, sprinkle with sliced almonds), sweet potatoes, mashed white potatoes, lime congeal, Parkerhouse rolls, green salad, pumpkin and mincemeat pies. Where ordinarily Susan might have been cheered (as was Curt) by this show of culinary tradition and its attendant hallmarks of order and stability, she was vaguely disheartened by it.

It was not a great task, though, to elevate herself above the melancholy sadness of banal repetition and the mild dislike she harbored for Curt's brother and his wife. She had a peculiar sensation of being on auto-pilot. While her visible person behaved as if everything were normal, her self detached and hovered. She felt quizzical and perplexed, the way you're disturbed when you walk into a room knowing you're there because you intended to do something but now can't recall what that was; you can't summon up anything more than an unattached sense of urgency. It was the way you also feel when an intriguing piece of mail arrives while you're having company and protocol prevents your opening it.

After dinner the men collapsed onto the couch for the Cowboys game. Susan knew to offer to help Mavis with the dishes, but as soon as she set foot in the kitchen, Vivian turned on her to say, "I'll dry and put them away because I know where Mavis keeps things," so Susan excused herself. She went to the bathroom to change her tampon and remembered just in time that she'd once caused a ruckus here by flushing one into the antiquated, rural septic system, so she had to wrap the bloody thing in tissue and bury it in the bottom of the bathroom wastebasket.

Curt's father had bought this little "spread" of five wooded acres and a pasture only shortly before he died, and his mother hardly ever wandered beyond the vicinity of the house. The afternoon was truly golden, lovely, unusually warm, and since Susan hadn't overeaten for once, she felt like walking in the woods. She passed through a grove of ruddy-leafed Spanish oak, thickets of dewberries, under huge sycamores with lemon-yellow leaves. She came to a clearing of shin-high grass surrounded by woods.

She stood in the middle and revolved slowly. Center stage, theater in the round. If she could find a ring of mushrooms, she could pretend this was where fairies met in the moonlight.

"Hello!" she called out. She giggled.

She couldn't remember the last time she had been alone with herself in the outdoors. It wasn't like being alone in a room. The air had a whiff of woody musk but was cool to her skin. Her heart beat hard and shivers rippled along the nape of her neck. She was alone but not lonely. But the sense of blissful solitude had an undertone of melancholy.

She sat on a stump in the clearing and turned her face to the sun, closing her eyes. She unbuttoned her blouse and drew it off her shoulders. Then she unhooked her bra. The breeze goosebumped her arms; she shivered. Her skin felt deliciously sensitive. Once she and Nathan made love in the woods. What if she were a girl again and she was with a boy here in this warm and sunny clearing, with a blanket, some illicit wine, a free, fanfared afternoon ahead like a childhood destination: the fair! the carnival! the parade! Christmas! To be a girl and enjoy the kissing without too much thought of what lies beyond, all hazy romantic pictures. Then, anyway. Who knows what girls like her students think? Or are doing on a day like today, in the woods. The Beckis, Jennifers, Cheryls, the Matts. The Jeffs. If she were Cheryl but knew what she knows now, and Jeff were here with her. A bottle of wine, a blanket. An afternoon to kiss away. Such soft lips!

Head tilted back, feeling the heat against her lids, thinking of this, her heartbeat slowed, her blood thickened and she felt a soft caressing throb inside her temples. She was calm for the first time today, the "calm" one feels when lost connections are made: that errand at last remembered while standing in the room, that intriguing letter opened at last.

Soft lips. Tip of his tongue on hers. Shaft of his warm breath down her throat.

She shouldn't be thinking about this. She'd gotten off the track. It was Nathan and she in the woods. And when they made love, the blanket they lay on wasn't thick enough to keep sticks and rocks from gouging into her back, though she didn't notice them until they were calm again.

A cloud-shadow ghosted across the clearing, chilling her bare skin into a prickle. Shivering, she put her bra and blouse back on. The shadow might have been cast by a giant hand, and the way it loomed so large and swept so swiftly across the space alarmed her.

She should not have kissed that boy!

10. Usually when they spend Thanksgiving at Curt's mother's house, they leave on Saturday to avoid a hassle about going to church on Sunday. This year, though, on Friday night when Curt told his mother they'd be leaving in the morning, Susan said, "Any reason we couldn't stay until Sunday, Curt? I mean, so long as Mavis wouldn't mind."

At that moment Mavis looked like the winner of Publisher's Clearing House Sweepstakes, but before she could burst into assurances that their presence would be welcome, Curt shot Susan a narrowed glance and said, "Well, I'm right in the middle of a project and I need to go in Sunday to work on it."

Later, when they were alone, Curt said, "What the fuck, Suzie? What's going on? You blindsided me in there. How come all of a sudden you want to stay until Sunday? You never did before. We never did before. And that wasn't kosher at all to weigh in without discussing it first. You made me the heavy."

"Well, there really isn't any reason we couldn't stay."

"Jesus! You were the one who didn't even want to come in the first place."

"So now that we're here…"

"What about church? What are you going to tell her about that?"

"I thought we could go."

Curt, wide-eyed, sank to the edge of the too-narrow mattress in his old bedroom. "You're kidding me! You're not even Protestant, let alone Baptist. I can double-guarantee you it won't be worth staying for even as a hoot or an amusing dabble in Southern sociology. Did you forget we've been living in sin all these years? We show up in that church and somebody'll haul us up to the altar by the scruff of our necks, believe me."

Susan was looking out the window. Moonlight bathed the pasture in a coldly silver light, but she couldn't make out specific objects because her reflection and the lighted room at her back were etched on the pane. Curt was being insistent. She'd spoken up in front of Mavis without thinking; he was right, it wasn't fair. She didn't know why she'd had a notion to go to church; it was hard to fight for something when you didn't know why you wanted it. She had a vague picture of being a family and getting dressed (Mavis wears white gloves), singing "Rock of Ages" in good Southern Baptist style and letting the wind of a good hellfire jeremiad curl her hair, being introduced to dozens of red-faced burghers, or to cohorts, colleagues or peers of Kenneth, gal-pals of Vivian, then they'd all troop off to Luby's cafeteria where they'd stand in line with others in their suits and Sunday dresses, get the vegetable soup (oversalted but underspiced), sliced roast beef and gravy, mashed potatoes and peas, the cherry Jell-O with peach chunks, the coconut cream pie, while humans on either end of the life-span inched along in aluminum contraptions of one sort or another: strollers or walkers. Inching off to Bethlehem. One minute it sounded like a prescription for good mental or spiritual health, the next for madness and despair. Either extremity seemed desirable, but why?

"Didn't you grow up here? Maybe I want to know more about how you grew up, did you ever think of that?"

"I left here the minute I got out of high school. When did you develop this interest in my origins?"

She thought *Since I realized I don't know you* but instead said, "Okay, you win. Forget it."

"What's with you?"

She shrugged. She didn't know. Hormones, maybe.

11. When Jeff didn't show up for the post-Thanksgiving meeting on the twenty-seventh, Susan was alarmed. It could mean that he was avoiding her; maybe he had indeed misinterpreted that kiss. It might be necessary to discuss it, to clear the air. She needed to apologize for it—whatever the motivation, however innocent or lightly impulsive, it now seemed terribly inappropriate.

She went to the attendance office on Wednesday the twenty-eighth to check on his absences from school and found that he was apparently in good health. Naturally she couldn't demand that he come talk to her about this, but she certainly didn't want him to be walking around school thinking that kiss meant something it didn't. Or—God forbid! - talking about it. His misunderstanding about it, if multiplied ten times over through gossip, might have the student grapevine shaking with gossip that could be twisted into God only knew what shape.

In any case, she could no longer ignore his abrupt disappearance from her field of vision and from the club, no longer pretend that it wasn't peculiar, at the least.

12. On Wednesday night, she wrote a note in hopes of encouraging him to attend a club meeting, where she could at least judge by his demeanor and behavior whether further action on her part was desirable or necessary.

Her draft of the note was as follows:

Wed. Nov. 28

Jeff, I've we've missed you in the last two meetings! ~~*I'm a little worried that I or someone in the club has done something to offend you, or somehow I've we've not done the right thing to encourage you in the best way.*~~ *We have only two left in the semester—next two Tuesdays (Dec. 4 and 11)—so I do hope you can make them both.*

She intended to stop there, but it seemed odd to omit mention of the lessons, as if they hadn't made vague plans to continue them. She was afraid that he might think she'd lost interest, that he lacked the talent or didn't deserve her attention. So she added:

Also, if you're not too busy and you're still willing or interested, we could have another lesson or two before the term is over. Hope to see you Tuesday!

Finding the correct way to sign it was as troubling as writing the text. The formal "Ms. Hart" would reimpose a distance that she herself had removed by asking him to call her Susan. "Susan" would be fine if this message were not being delivered through school channels; prying eyes would not find anything scandalous in the message, but the breezy "Susan" might possibly raise someone's eyebrow a millimeter or two. She settled on "SH" despite how it seemed like a clandestine code signature. Then, on impulse, she scribbled that figure of a cat or a bat-mask that later captured Jeff's imagination. She meant for it to be a cartoonish self-portrait, an offhand embellishment to ameliorate that too-stiff double initialing. Feeling overly constrained by circumstances to keep her note business-like, she had unconsciously sought to signal something beyond the text that couldn't be deciphered by all.

To her, that cat-face meant *Still your friend despite the impersonality of this note!* To Jeff, it said, *Do you remember Halloween night? I do!*

13. A brief essay on desire:

Unless they are ill or starving and are thus preoccupied with pain and death, the most engrossing sensation humans experience is desire. While it lives, desire is frequently the most interesting thing in our present. Also the most demanding: it asks for our undivided attention. It rewards that attention by suffusing the physical self with a glow that affirms all creation; it reawakens our interest in life. It affirms life because fulfillment requires that life be continued.

Paradoxically, desire saturates the brain with enzymes and agents that induce a waking sleep or a conscious trance, and in this condition we leisurely relish weaving the desire into a narrative (fantasy) that both expresses or dramatizes the desire but also further fuels it.

Desire has a self-perpetuating momentum; it seeks its own end. It therefore creates its own future; it could be said that it uses our bodies to write its own script to bring its "story" to a satisfying climax and denouement. It is single-minded in its determination to survive and overwhelm our other interests, plans, intentions. It feeds on itself by encouraging behavior that further inflames it; it drives furiously toward only that which can satisfy it; our desire locates sources for potential fulfillment with an instinct so swift and unerring and wholly indifferent to our conscious wishes that we are sometimes as surprised to recognize its choices for us as we are to learn those of our friends.

14. One more fact: On Friday, Nov. 30, Susan received a note in her mailbox in the main office:

Thursday November 29 (I think!)

Dear Susan,

Thank you for the invitation! Yes, I have been busy. But I've been drawing, too, though, so I haven't given up or anything. I think too much of your help and your time to do that, even if I should give up for lack of talent. I've missed all you guys, too. You guys have all been great to me, made me feel really at home. Especially you. I really appreciate all your help and stuff. I hope to pay you back some day soon. I'll be there Tuesday night. Maybe we could have a lesson after?

p.s. I want you to know I really appreciate all your special attention.

Sincerely,

JR

He, too, had included a drawing at the bottom of his note. It was a caricature of his own face, with big round eyes and exaggerated lips.

A parable, cont'd.:

SOS SOS SOS SOS SOS...

⸙15⸙

*H*is hands. *He's got the whole world in his hands…* As Jeff drives, she watches him supposedly to supervise but can't keep her gaze from locking onto his hands. They are aristocratic, with long slim fingers and rectangular nails that curve nicely on their ends like a trenching spade. She can't see his left very well; in good weather he likes to steer with his elbow on the window sill, but she won't allow one-handed driving, so he complies with her rule by putting his left thumb along the wheel rim. She'll say, *Two hands, Jeffie!* and he'll say (teenage exasperation), *Count them, Mother!*

They're cruising I-30 East toward downtown boxed in on both sides by eighteen-wheelers so that it feels like they're in a noisy canyon.

"Don't go by way of Central. I don't want to get onto that freeway."

"Mom, it takes too long any other way."

His right hand curls more tightly, a knuckle swelling. Veins on the back of his hand are manly in their prominence. She can remember when he could hardly make a fist around her index finger.

"I don't care. We're not in a hurry. Go up Stemmons to Oak Lawn and take Preston."

His jaw tightens. As always, always in a hurry. To be somewhere else, with someone else. She'll drop him at North Park, and he'll probably meet his friends and they'll do who knows what for most of the afternoon. *What do you do? We just hang out. What does that mean? Aw, Mom, you know. Talk to people, sit around. How's school? Fine. How was your club meeting? Fine, Mom.*

He doesn't have any idea how difficult it is to be a single mother with a teenage son. People say it's normal for teenagers to clam up, turn moody, skittish; people say it's normal for kids to get low down on themselves, but that's also when they're vulnerable to peer pressures, demon forces out there over which she has no control but to pray for safety.

He lies to her, she knows that. She tries not to let it upset her. People say kids his age lie not necessarily to cover things up but sometimes merely to control some aspect of their lives, if only the information you can get about them. She understands this, wants to be understanding. She doesn't want to be an alarmist.

What is he thinking? He drives the way his father does, shutting you out, squinting through the windshield in a way that fools you into thinking that he's concentrating on the road, but you can surprise him by saying, *Aren't you supposed to turn there?*

"Jeffie—"

"I see it, Mom. He's got his signal on, for God's sake."

She lets the swearing pass. She lets his lying pass some of the time. She is sick at heart that he will not let Jesus Christ enter his life, but a faith embraced unwillingly is a weak force. She lets many things pass by, holding her breath. He doesn't know that she asks her Fellowship to pray for him. She prays every day for him. Life is full of dangers to body and soul, so each day that goes by without Jeffie's falling prey to sin or death is a day of rejoicing. If he catches whatever she has—if it's in his genes—that drags her spirit down into depressions, dear God please let him have discovered the power of love to soothe!

But she can't let her worry show. He's very, very touchy and the slightest criticism sends him into a fury; he's at an age where he doesn't want to be supervised, scrutinized, interviewed, interrogated, or even thought about. It's as if his need for privacy is so ferocious he has thrown up a transparent force field about his person, and if she so much as even glances his way, it sets off his alarm. *How come you're looking at me?*

People say it's normal for boys his age. But if you read the papers or the brochures the schools send out, you know those things are also warning signs of involvement with drugs. Changes in mood, routines or habits; secrecy; irritability; falling grades; disturbed sleeping and eating patterns. Every parent has memorized these things. Since he won't tolerate hearing her read Scripture to him, she has studied the fortune-cookie sayings in the suicide pamphlet the school district sent out in case she needs to give him advice: *Suicide is a permanent solution to a temporary problem; suicide is like a cold—it's contagious; suicide is the easy way out; suicide is not fair to the ones who love you.*

Not that he would likely turn to her in his hour of greatest need! But that's why it's so important for her to keep quietly trying to show him the way. And to stay vigilant. When he comes down to breakfast, she gauges his intake. Cereal as usual? *Sleep well, honey?* Does he suspect? *How're your grades? Won't the first six weeks be up soon?* It's hard to watch someone closely when they don't want to be watched and are themselves watching out very closely to see if you are watching them. Even the most innocent question becomes loaded. For that reason even the most simple ones are evaded: *how was school today? Fine.*

He never talks to her. He always seems angry at her. She doesn't know why; she tries her best to please him and to provide a good home. True, sometimes she gets sick and can't function, and he's such a good boy, then, the way he takes care of her and the house. Yes, and she knows he gets impatient with her. It's not a normal situation, a young man like Jeffie living only with a mother and sometimes having to take care of her. Sometimes she worries that it will have an ill effect on him, that she is cheating him out of a carefree time of life. But then sometimes she thinks it is good for young people to learn to take care of others. He does a good job of it, bless his heart!

They are stopped at the light where Armstrong and Preston merge with Oak Lawn. Ahead are the mansions of Highland Park, even an ex-Governor lives on this street. Mostly, she thinks, they're just crooks. They belong to a church—probably the First Baptist Church downtown—but they're godless. Money is their god. Mammon. Their revered pastor Reverend Criswell owns a Mercedes-Benz and wears thousand-dollar suits. She used to drive through this part of town and envy these people. But that was part of her other life, the life with Jeff, Sr. She pities them now. When she thinks of how much time and energy she and Jeff wasted worrying about cars and sofas and clothing, she is glad to be free of it, glad that getting free opened up a space inside. She sometimes envies Catholic women—they may choose to be nuns.

Jeffie taps his fingers on the wheel in time to a song in his head. He smiles a little twisted smile.

"What're you thinking about?" she asks.

"I'm wondering if you're happy now."

She is startled; thinking of nuns had made her think about marriage. Her ex lives not too far from here, in a condo with his whore. She's driven by it dozens of times. Was Jeffie thinking of that, too? No, the tone was different.

"What do you mean?"

"This is the world's longest light. I'm going to be late meeting my friends."

"Getting there late is better than not getting there at all."

"Have you ever been killed on Central?"

"No."

"Well, me either. And I've been on it a million times."

"Let me remind you that when we're in my car, we go the way I want to go. I let you drive it. When you have your own car, you can drive anywhere or anyhow you want."

"That'll be a cold day in Hades."

"It's none of my concern," she says cheerfully. "Take it up with your father."

At last the light turns and he guns the engine unnecessarily, lurching impatiently along in his slot within the sluggish caravan. The speed limit here of thirty m.p.h. is strictly enforced, so they are locked into a dutiful train. Ahead is a battered pickup towing a flat-bed trailer bristling with lawn care machinery. Seated in the pickup's bed are three young men, Hispanic, all in sweat-stained cowboy hats, dirty shirts. Jeffie and his friends don't know how easy they have it. These young men, yard workers, have come no doubt from Mexico and send back much of their pay to their families. If they get sick or hurt there's nobody to take care of them, no money for doctors, hospitals. She sees them riding old garage-sale Schwinns to and from the Kroger store not far from home. Jeff Sr. has a $400 mountain bike he rides at White Rock Lake for exercise and about $200 worth of special cycling togs. He mounts the bike on his expensive car and drives two miles to the lake, takes the bike off and rides ten miles around the lake with several other rich men. Decadence, utter decadence. It's hard to believe she was so caught up in that. It was a profound pleasure to give away her gold necklaces and the diamond earrings and let the Salvation Army come take away half the furniture they had in that house on Briar Meadow in north Dallas. It's hard for Jeffie to understand why someone would *not* want money, why someone would *deliberately* be poor.

Jeffie has an expensive bike Jeff Sr. bought him years ago; it has hardly been ridden. Naturally, now he wouldn't be caught dead on a bike. All his friends have cars. *Come now, Jeffie. All of them? Yeah, Mom, it's true, I'm not lying.* Then he'll catalogue the motor vehicles, some with names not familiar to her. Then she can zing him: *Well, since they all have those cars, why would you need one too?*

In her lap is the day's mail, handed through the window by the postman while they were backing out of the drive. There's a letter from the Christian Children's Fund. No sense in turning down an opportunity to remind Jeffie of what he has to be thankful for and of his responsibility toward the wretched of the world. He acted so sulky on Thanksgiving Day; she didn't ask any more of him than to sit beside her at the table of a very kind and decent Christian family. It saddened her how he squirmed just to hear people praying.

She's in luck: the packet from CCF contains not only the monthly sponsorship bill, but also a letter from their "child" in India, Althea. Years ago she and Jeffie's father signed up because she had believed that it would teach Jeffie about children in the world who were less fortunate and make him feel he had a sibling, also. For the first year or so, he did seem interested in his first Indian "sister," whose name eludes her now but whose face—homely, round, unsmiling, spectacled, her hair in two braids—comes vividly to mind. That girl soon graduated and the sponsorship passed to the present Althea, whom Jeffie has no interest in. However, he retains enough respect for the enterprise to nod and adopt a neutral expression when she subjects him to news from the girl's missionary school.

The letter was written on thin, crinkly paper and the feel of it evokes dusky faces in starched white shirts and dresses, red dust, white frame buildings, snake charmers, Nehru jackets and servants waving fans over Englishmen dressed in khaki. The girl writes in

Urdu or Hindee, whatever that language is, and someone unnamed translates the letter into a peculiar English that she finds charming: *At present we are keeping well. Hope you too are fine. I am writing to you after a long gap.*

"Oh, Jeffie, look. It's a letter from Althea!" She holds it up until he is forced to glance at it. "She says, 'On the 23rd September we celebrated Our Sponsor's Day. Two days ahead we were given time to draw the picture of their sponsor—' Oh, she means our sponsor, of course—'and to write a short essay about them. I have drawn your house and flower garden.'"

In the letter is a space where the girl drew a picture from a snapshot. Checking an impulse to make Jeffie look at it, she goes on. "'On the 23rd morning there was Eucharistic celebration. After this was a short programme.' She spells it British, you know, em-em-ee. 'Those who drew well or wrote nicely got prizes. It is winter season here now. It is also the season of harvest. All are busy at harvest. Our annual examination will start from 4th December to 14th December. I am working hard to pass nicely. Now I end this letter. My family and I wish you A Very Happy Christmas and Happy New Year.'"

"Well, that's sweet, isn't it?"

"Yeah."

As usual, the child didn't reveal anything essential. She probably wouldn't be allowed to say, for instance, *Dear Sponsor, my father has drunk too much and my mother is cursing him.* She can picture the child, Althea—this one is less homely and doesn't wear glasses, has her hair in a page-boy—bent over a desk, drawing hers and Jeffie's house and "flower garden"—here the child must mean the beds along the porch: she sent the child a snapshot of herself and Jeffie standing on the front steps it must be, oh, three years ago, taken in the summer, when she'd planted beds of petunias and coleus and periwinkle in front by the steps. In the eye of the child, there stands a big wooden house and a flower garden and a smiling mother and a smiling youth, her American sponsors, having a happy life.

Seeing herself as that child must see her—this lifts her spirits when she reads these letters.

"Jeffie, do you think you'd ever like to go to India?"

He scoffs. "I'd be happy if I could go to Vail over Christmas break."

This is a dig at her. His friends will be leaving town during the holidays for ski resorts all over the planet, but he won't be joining them.

His friends. Is it good or bad that he still runs around with Todd and those others? It speaks well of him in a certain way, though those kids have poor spiritual values and permissive parents, and no matter how much she believes each person is responsible for his or her own actions, she still believes that the trouble Jeffie got into at Lakeview Prep was not his fault, really, it was the fault of Jeff Sr. for putting him where godless children with more money than is good for them were his only choice of companions. It was inevitable that he became like them, if only for a time.

She worries that he's not making friends at his new school. She's glad he's interested in his art club and pleased that he works at drawing. His step seems light these days, and he seems anxious to get to school and likes staying there. She does not want to spy on him. She does wish he would keep the door to his room open, though, simply as a sign that she's welcome to visit. Sometimes she hears the music playing from his radio behind the door, and he comes out and goes to the bathroom, and she will whiz by and glance into his lair. A drawing under the light at the desk, an opened can of Dr. Pepper. So far as she can see, all he was doing was drawing, listening to music, drinking a soda: so why does it have to be done behind a locked door when there's only one other person in the house and that's she?

She unwads the papers in his trash can but isn't proud of it. His silence, his closed door, his elusive "fine" to any question, provoke her to pry. She has found little or nothing. No drugs. A filthy magazine under the mattress, probably brought over from his father's house. She thinks she handled that right. After she touched it, she left it there. Then she decided that she should turn the mattress over before putting on clean sheets, so when she flip-flopped the mattress, she "found" the magazine (where she'd already discovered it when she deliberately stuck her arm under the mattress). She threw it in the trash. She said nothing to him. She knew he wouldn't ask about it.

So it didn't exist, never had.

In the back of his bureau drawer was a woman's scarf smelling of semen. She couldn't bring herself to touch it. On the margins of his notebooks were names he has not uttered aloud: Tamara, and Susan here, Susan there. Someone named Susan is on his mind. She hopes Susan is a nice girl.

"Who are you meeting?" They've reached Boedecker and Northwest Highway, and he's in the left lane waiting to turn into the acres of parking lot outside the mall.

"Oh, you know. The usual suspects."

He's in a better humor now the mall's in sight; it's a little as if he didn't actually believe he'd get here, and that urgency makes her wonder if he's not meeting a girl (Susan?) here.

"And that would be?"

"Todd, Chris."

Is he lying again? His profile, the cheekbones, the long lashes. Who can tell? People say a mother always knows when her child is lying, and, while that's true when the child is small, when they reach adolescence they get more skillful, learn to push your buttons, study up on the art of being credible. Like his Dad. Until the very end, he had her believing that his nightly absence from home was occupational only, and even when he moved into his condo, she was still so gullible she believed he was trying "to find himself" and was only having "a career crisis." How stupid can you be? Pretty stupid.

Well, like father not like son in respect to how far she'll go in buying a story.

Otherwise....That's why she keeps looking at Jeffie's hands, she can't help it. They belong to a boy she fell in love with a thousand years ago. She was just a freshman and her folks thought a non-coed college like Texas Women's University would be the safest place for her, but her first semester wasn't six weeks gone before she met Jeff, who was a senior across town at North Texas. She didn't know then she could have those kinds of thoughts and feelings, have them so strong they'd overwhelm and overpower you. And she had no tools, no weapons, to fight them off the way she does now.

Looking at Jeffie is frightening sometimes. Jeffie's hand on that steering wheel is like a little hole in the warp and woof of time and his father's hand is sticking through it there, his father as a young man a little older than Jeffie now, putting his hand on the wheel of a '68 Chevy, her putting the ring on his finger at the wedding, then his hands on places of her body only doctors have touched since, she's glad to say, his hand on the wheel of the Chevy—the wheel was an odd opaque gray, like the color of a bowling ball—then when they parked at the drive-in movie those long fingers would slip past the top button of her blouse and snake under the bra and—

She clenches her jaw. "Watch out!"

"I've got a hundred yards' leeway, Mom."

Hands that she loved, kiss the knuckles. And when Jeffie was tiny she'd slip his whole hand in her mouth when she kissed it. Now she sees his hand on the wheel and thinks of the boy those many years ago who put those hands in places that would be shameful to her now, but never mind. She sees Jeffie's hands and falls in love all over again with Jeff then her mind rushes the tape fast-forward and he's left her and she falls into hate with him. Loves him, hates him. And the boy, he's part her, too, not separate like his father. He'll never desert her. He'll always be her son. But then he acts just like his father these days—hard-willed, resistant, argumentative, secretive, elusive, closed off, dying to cut the cord. He is a man-sized person, a male, larger than she, resisting her, struggling with her, using his will and his size, his new-found man's ability to control her with silence and her own need to please him and to appease him, to rely on him, so that she loves him desperately and hates him, too.

The truth is that the boy will follow his father's footsteps. First by lying to her. Then by leaving.

"Mom?"

She opens her eyes. "Move the seat up for me before you get out."

This irritates him because it makes it hard for him to get out from under the wheel, but he complies; he's too eager to get away to waste a second on arguing. He yanks the lever under the driver's seat, and they both lurch forward. He gets out of the car. She scoots under the wheel. He's walking away from the car toward the entrance, but she drills her gaze into the back of his head and zaps him with a telepathic message: *You'd better not just walk away!* He stops, turns, strides back to the car.

"Thanks for the ride, Mom."

She smiles. "You're welcome, dear. Have a nice time."

"Okay. I will."

"And be home by four to rake the lawn or you can't go out tonight," she adds as he's walking away, and he waves behind his back to acknowledge that he heard her.

She eases her old Chevy into a line waiting to exit the lot. Very crowded—first Saturday in December. Christmas shopping. Lots of Jaguars, Cadillacs, Mercedes, a hundred Jeep station wagons. Car phones. Dallas Museum of Art and KERA - Channel 13 decals to show support for culture. The women strolling into the mall look as if they've spent all morning primping: makeup, expensive slacks, cashmere sweaters under tailored blazers. Over the roofs of the cars in front of her rise the twin gold spires of an office complex whose reflective glass panels shimmer in the sunlight like the vibrations of a rocket just lifting off. In the summer the sun reflecting off the building bakes dead the grass berms along the freeway beside it. It's as if the building emits rays that poison vegetation, organic life. Inside the gold spires are platoons of conniving S & L executives, like that Dixon who spent his investors' funds on buying whores for the board on their outings. Out here in North Dallas, Mammon rules. She has just delivered her only son unto Babylon.

⪥16⪤

Susan agonizes in Victoria's Secret choosing a gift for her professor's bridal shower. A saleswoman listens with mounting interest as she explains her problem: the invitation declared lingerie to be the theme, but the honoree and first-time bride is fifty and, frankly, stands a little on the stout side. The saleswoman, chipper and undeterred, says, "No woman's too big to be sexy on her wedding night!" The clerk shows Susan a lacy red silk teddy that unsnaps in the crotch but Susan blushes and blurts, "She's my professor!" Susan can't picture the highly educated, dignified professor welcoming her man's thrusts through a manufactured gap in her underwear.

The clerk suggests satin pillow slips with embroidered flowers, to which Susan gratefully pays twice what she meant to spend.

"What'd you get her?" Susan asks on Saturday morning while Holly drives them to the shower. They both took the professor's Renaissance Art History seminar, though only Susan got an A. Holly's dislike for the professor made Susan surprised that Holly has accepted the invitation.

"I considered something racy but I just got some handkerchiefs instead. Do you know who the guy is?"

She means *Who in the world would do it?* but Susan ignores the subtext. "No, not really." Once Susan went to her professor's apartment to borrow a book and while she was leaving, a man coming up the walk passed her. Salted beard and spectacles, nice wide shoulders. Younger by ten years or so. Maybe he? "I heard he teaches history at Colgate."

"Will they have one of those long-distance deals, or what?"

"I don't know." Susan hasn't considered the possible effects of her professor's marriage on her own thesis. Now she's drenched in fear: what if she has to find a new advisor?

By the time they reach Richardson Susan is struggling with the ethics of querying her professor about her plans, but she decides this is not the proper occasion. The shower is hosted by a colleague in English in a home that hasn't been dusted in a decade, and the guests are female faculty at various area universities, the professor's younger sister, and selected graduate students. Susan sits in a metal folding chair in the living room with her plate on her knees. She picks at the quiche and fruit salad but has more than her share of Mimosas and a rather distressingly large portion of the ubiquitous Die For chocolate cake.

She's wearing black pumps and a blue silk dress that she bought to wear to an architectural awards banquet two years ago and hasn't had on since. She isn't sure what possessed her to unearth it from her closet, but now she feels overdressed. The honoree has on the same black polyester stretch pants and nylon jersey blouse with faux scarf and gray blazer she usually wears while lecturing. It has always struck Susan as ironic that a woman with an international reputation as a scholar in art history should have such little concern for personal adornment, and this has never been more apparent than today. Where that self-imposed uniform has always seemed a reassuring constant in Susan's experience with her professor, it seems in this context wildly aberrational, as if the professor is not aware of being the honoree, or refuses to submit to her condition or situation, or merely dropped by.

However, inwardly the professor seems to have undergone a tectonic shift. She eats nothing, but, like Susan, soon dispenses with the tiny paper umbrella as an obstruction to serious drinking. Her lank gray hair is plastered along her flushing cheeks, and her perpetual grin is loopy, crooked, her large blue eyes as strangely burning as those of the awe-struck Annunciation Marys. She laughs too loud too often, and when she twists on her chair, her pants squawk against the vinyl cushion like a fart. She's giggly, spills her drink on the cuff of her blazer. She doesn't seem happy so much as goosey, giddy, half-hysterical. Although she's used to being before a classroom, she's obviously very unaccustomed to having her mating self be the subject for consideration.

Of course, she has to suffer a public exhibition and approval of her future undergarments. Gifts include a satin bathrobe, a camisole, pajamas, a flannel nightgown with a high, lace-trimmed neck—all properly oohed and ahhed and dutifully recorded by the appointed secretary—then, an extra from her best friends: a black merry-widow corset and silk stockings that inspire howls of laughter and the usual bawdy allusions to a wedding night. The professor blushes like a maiden and titters with her hand to her mouth. Susan feels then as if she is older than her professor, that she's the professor (The Professor of Love) and her professor the student. She pictures herself behind her professor's desk with the professor seated in the student's chair. The older woman asks questions that make Susan extremely uncomfortable, even though she knows the answers: *How do you tell your husband what you like? What do you do if he ejaculates prema-*

turely? That fantasy takes a sudden detour and cuts to another location: Susan's office at school. Jeff's face pops up suddenly, though he's been on her mind since she got his note yesterday. What's she going to say to him?

She jerks herself back to the present. Her idea of her professor's innocence is presumptuous, of course: just because she's only now marrying doesn't mean she's virginal—after all, Susan has yet to walk that aisle.

Will her professor be content as a wife? After all, someone her age, settled, has habits and rituals and routines; she has her own income, pursuits and interests. To many women, the professor's single life is a condition to aspire to.

After the gift-opening, Susan and Holly hover about the professor and the hostess with other guests to wish her well and to take their leave. When Susan approaches her professor, the woman says, brightly, "Why, hello!" as if noticing Susan for the first time (though she greeted Susan at the door), then, after Susan wishes her professor all the best and they've hugged (a first, for Susan), her professor says, "Did you get that book on Max Ernst?" When Susan looks blank, the professor says, in confusion, "No, of course you didn't! I'm sorry!" then turns abruptly to greet another friend who stepped forward.

On the way home, Susan replays the exchange. "You know," she says to Holly, "I don't think she recognized me. I think she confused me with somebody else." She doesn't want to admit this to Holly (after all, she took pride in being favored), but she's so crushed by the possibility that she can't restrain herself. "She thought I was somebody working on Max Ernst."

"Oh, what the hell, she was half-plastered and rattled by all the attention. Forget it."

Susan licks her lips and catches a faint taste of chocolate. After a moment, she says, "I don't know what I'm going to do if she goes off with her husband and I have to get a new advisor."

"Well, don't worry, Suzie. They won't let her just bolt from her position, you know, and besides it's not like she's a receptionist who's marrying a lawyer—I heard that her groom's not even tenured yet. She's a full professor here. More than likely, he'll come be the housefrau, you know."

They lapse into silence for a moment, and Susan imagines Salted Beard in the professor's kitchen, stirring a pot. *I'm home, dear. What's for supper?* How nice it would be to have a man so willing to take on those responsibilities. This afternoon was cleaning time. Curt would cooperate, sure, but it was always her responsibility to initiate it, even though they agreed that every other Saturday afternoon was cleaning day. Tomorrow she can work on her thesis: if there's any chance that her professor is leaving, then it'll be very important to get something solid underway—if worse came to worst, they could confer by phone or mail?

Then Monday, then Tuesday, the Club meeting.

And Jeff. What to tell him?

Susan says, "What would you do if you had a student who had a crush on you and you wanted to discourage it?"

Holly laughs. "Why would I want to discourage it? Oh, never mind! Hey, it would depend on the student—male or female?"

"Male."

"Is he cute and is he shaving yet? Are we talking fifteen or eighteen? Is he taller than me? Can I imagine actually dancing with him at a club?"

"Let's say he's very handsome but still somewhat boyish. He does shave, yes. And he is taller than you. And I guess that if the lights in the club were dim enough that people couldn't tell how old you were, then yeah."

"Have I had any contact with him that's out of the ordinary?"

Susan crosses her legs. "What do you mean?"

"I mean did I inspire this crush by doing anything unusual?"

Susan licks her lips. "Well, yes and no. Maybe. Let's say you were at an extracurricular function and you gave him an innocent peck the way you might, you know, be playful at an office party under the mistletoe, or like the way you greet a friend or something."

Holly gives Susan a sidelong glance. "On the lips?"

"Uh, well, yeah."

"Huh! How long?"

"What?"

"How long did this kiss last? A nanosecond or a while?"

These questions are unexpected and Susan regrets having brought up the subject. "Well, just a little bit, you know."

"Is my mouth open and are we using our tongues?"

Susan looks out the window at the high, enclosing concrete walls along the Tollway. Graffiti tag of the *East Side Locos* elongates in her vision as they speed past.

"Uh…yeah."

"Wow! I *am* being a bad girl! And what happens then?"

"Nothing. The boy sort of disappears for a while, then you get a note that lets you know he's smitten."

"Huh! And what am I feeling? What do I want to do about this?"

"Well, Jesus! You want to set things straight, of course! You don't want this to go any further, for God's sake! I mean, you can't afford to get involved if you're a grown-up and attached and you care about your career as a teacher! What else could you want to do? Of course the thing you want to do is figure out a way to make it all go away quietly at the least cost and pain possible to you both!" Susan hears her voice grow strident and she wills herself to shut up.

"Oh," says Holly. "I just wondered."

Susan's unprovoked vehemence calls for an ameliorating follow-up. "I know you've probably had a lot of practice in letting guys down easy. And I don't know what I should say to him."

Holly laughs. "Well, even for a professional, though, this is a tough one. A tender youngster's going to be wearing his heart on his sleeve. The good part is how quick he can bounce back. Since you did sort of inspire it, then it's pretty hard to tell him he only imagined that he was being kissed. I mean, you can't just say, 'Sorry, this is all in your head.' I think I'd go for flattery—you know, tell him you had a weak moment and you felt vulnerable and he was very attractive and desirable and so things happened that you wish hadn't and you vow never to allow anything to happen again, although of course if the world were different, if people's lives weren't so complicated, blah blah blah. Let him go off believing that he's such a powerfully magnetic dude that he could sway you from your intended course of fidelity and upright professional behavior, and that this was all unexpected. You didn't know you were so susceptible, but knowing his power as you do now, of course, then you'll be on your guard and steel yourself against it, and so on. Treat him like an almost irresistible adversary—he'll love it."

Even delivered in a flip and cynical way, it seems like sound advice, partly because it's close to the actual case. Susan considers paying for the wisdom by revealing Jeff's identity, but she resists the temptation. "Thanks, that's very good."

"Does it sound true to you, though?"

"True? Well, maybe."

"Why did you kiss him? I always thought you and Curt had a solid thing."

"No, well, I mean yes, we do, or we did have something. I think maybe I'm mad deep down at him."

"Because of that thing with that English woman?"

"I'm not even sure he did anything, and I'm not sure that's why I'm mad at him."

"Do you still want to get married?"

"I thought so."

"Wow! You're not so sure now? Does this kid mean something serious to you?"

"Oh, no, it's not…him at all! He's like a, a *mascot,* Holly. I feel tender regard for him, that's all. Like a big sister. He's not at all the kind of guy I'd choose to have a serious relationship with, for God's sake. And I was very wrong to have stirred up anything in him. It was very inappropriate and unprofessional!"

"I'm glad to hear you say that. Spares me from giving you the lecture."

They fall silent for the time it takes them to creep through the tollway exchange and for Holly to toss quarters into the basket.

When Holly doesn't introduce a new subject, Susan says, "I don't want it to mean anything, this kissing business. It was just a mad impulse, I was a little looped, and I wasn't thinking, and he seemed kind of blue and very cute and I felt sorry for him, that's all, and it really doesn't mean anything! The last thing I'd want is to go any further with this, believe me! For God's sake, I have enough complications in my life already, you know? I mean, who needs something like this?"

⊱17⊰

ℋurrying through the throngs, Jeff glances at the display windows—it's worrisome that the season started already and he has yet to choose something for his Mom, Sybil and his Dad—but as he passes Victoria's Secret his gaze snags on a lacy underthing, and he has a fleeting picture of having a gift box in his hands then passing it to Susan: how surprised she'd be! How pleased! What would it be?

Yeah—what would it be? This gift would be a hundred times harder to choose than something for just a girlfriend. Maybe Tuesday night he could be sly and fish for an idea.

Chris and Todd are already waiting for him at a table in El Fenix next to a window that looks out onto the fountain in the atrium. Chris, the lineman, has already gone through a basket of chips and a cup of picante sauce.

"Hey, dude, what's happening?"

"Hey, dude, nothing much."

He slides into a chair by the window. Chris and Todd are watching girls coming out of Dillard's. Todd frames them between his hands like a movie director. He thinks he's the Steven Spielberg of the camcorder, and sometimes when they sit here he burns tape just to flatter them. Or if the girls they're watching go across to Thirsty's for frozen yogurt, then this'll be an exciting development—walking away, they face the guys' table, where, unseen and unheard, the guys can remark on the technique they employ to lick their cones. Todd has a collection of clips, cream-coated tongues lapping at the phallic mounds.

"What do you think?" Todd asks him.

"About what?"

"Which one of the Heathers would you want to fuck?"

Jeff's memory produces the faces of two girls with that name at Lakeview, but both are unlikely candidates as a subject of this discussion. Todd must mean the movie.

"Winona Ryder, I guess."

They fall silent. Jeff looks out at the tiled arena surrounding the fountain, where a clown is accosting children and their mothers and forcing them to take balloons with a store logo. The fountain has a timed cycle that begins with a tiny bubbling column in the center that rises like a hard-on until it's about twelve feet high and the side jets are shooting into the pool, then it dies away again. Sometimes when they watch it, they make accompanying sounds ("Aaaahhhh!" and groans), especially if a captive audience is at a nearby table.

At the moment the fountain is detumescent. Two old farts in jump suits and running shoes stride by the window, getting their aerobic mile and a half in for the day, guesses Jeff. The mall is favored by heart patients as a place to hike for rehab, and they blow by at a pace that'll knock you down if you get in their way.

"Check it out." Chris nods. Two girls in matching sweat-shirts with Greek letters on their breasts go by. SMU. A mousy blonde, a cute brunette, but neither speaks to anything in him. The whole ritual seems juvenile, like video arcades, skating rinks.

"Woof," says Todd.

"Oh, man, you're so particular," Jeff says with more spirit than he intended. Todd raises an eyebrow that quivers like an antenna. Jeff grins at him. "Like you'd turn it down, right?"

Todd says, "Yeah, unless your mother called for a date."

Jeff snorts. "Chris, how's Paige?"

Chris waves so-so. "She's pissed right now. She wanted me to go shopping with her this morning. I told her I was going to sleep until noon."

"Five bucks says she shows up right here—" Todd presses his thumb against the table top. "And twists your ear."

Chris yawns. "Could be."

Todd turns to Jeff. "He's forgotten what it's like to be a hungry bachelor." Todd squints at Jeff, bends forward slightly. "Like us, right?"

"Yeah." Because Todd seems to be studying him, Jeff adds, "I have to use the family Hoover."

"A pound of liver," says Chris.

"I like a good hot watermelon myself," Todd says.

"What happened to your blow-up love dolly?" Jeff asks.

"He got carried away and bit her one night," jokes Chris.

It's like a Three Stooges routine; these lines have been delivered in this order before, by the same speakers.

"Did you hear about the guy down in Duncanville?" Chris goes on, seriously. "He was doing that deal where you sort of hang yourself and reduce the oxygen to your brain while you beat off—"

"Yeah, yeah," says Todd. "We know. Sure. And this guy was going along the road one night and picks up a hitchhiker who disappears mysteriously at the next truck stop, and when he starts shooting the shit with the waitress she asks him what the guy looks like, and, sure enough, the hitchhiker is like some dead dude from ten years back, right?"

Chris seems offended. "No shit, Todd. There was this court case down in Houston. This guy read how to do it in *Hustler* and now his parents sued for wrongful death or something."

A waitress arrives carrying a huge metal disk that she sets on a nearby table, and, using towels as oven-mitts, she lifts two steaming plates and puts them in front of Todd and Chris. She places a basket of fresh chips and sauce on their table.

Todd pokes at his enchiladas with a fork.

"These are beef. I wanted chicken," he tells the waitress, "Rosa" by her name tag. She looks at her pad.

"I must have got it wrong," she says, not looking at him. "I'll take it back."

"No, I'm too hungry."

"Sorry." She looks at Jeff. "You want something?"

"Ice tea, please."

When she whisks up the metal disk and strides away, Chris says, "You ordered beef and you know it. You were just setting her up for a no-tip situation."

Todd grins. "Sure. I didn't say I *ordered* chicken; I said I *wanted* chicken."

They laugh. Seeing and smelling their food, Jeff feels his stomach growl. He had a sandwich before leaving home. It sometimes kills him how the kids at Lakeview have money to eat meals out any-where and anytime they want. If they don't have cash, they use plas-tic.

Jeff dips a chip in the picante sauce and nibbles delicately at its edge. He watches the other two eat; now they're as single-mindedly intent upon their food as they were on sex a moment before. It's like a cartoon—open a door in their skulls and there'd either be a throb-bing pussy inside or a steaming twelve-ounce steak. They're like dogs or cats, their concentration is so primitive and intense. Chris cut himself shaving; they both reek of cologne. Why does he feel like fifteen years older than his friends now?

Rosa brings his iced tea, and he makes a point of looking her in the eye, smiling pleasantly, and saying, "Thanks." She's around Susan's age, Hispanic, has a wedding ring, probably a couple *niños*. She looks a little haggard around the eyes and a little overripe in the bust and hips, but she has a womanly quality he's begun to appreciate in females. To his own surprise, this quality is very appealing, but mysteriously so: he couldn't defend his finding Rosa the waitress sexy to these guys without suffering their extreme derision. White bimbos and sleek rich schoolgirls only. Others need not apply. His new-found ability to locate a source of sexual interest in the likes of Rosa the waitress makes him feel like a man of the world. No question as to whom he owes this enriching expansion of his awareness.

"What's on your mind?" Todd has wiped his plate with a tortilla and lit a cigarette. Chris's still chowing down, head over his plate. Jeff realizes Todd was watching him while he was musing about the waitress.

"What?"

"What?" Todd mocks. "Jesus, you had this look on your face like you just became the Ultimate Cool Dude. You know, smug."

"I was probably just thinking about how your sister gives me such good head."

This time, Todd won't bite. "So what's going on?"

"What's going on?"

"How come you've been so hard to get a hold of? I call your house and your mother says you're at school."

"Been studying, you know, I know you don't believe that people actually go to class and do their work at Carver, but—"

Chris looks up. "Todd thinks you've got something going."

"Something going?"

Todd and Chris both hee-haw at his attempt to act innocent, and, even though he tries very hard, he can't altogether squelch the smirk that tugs at his mouth. He wipes it away with his fingers.

"Yeah, like you've got some punch who's either so hot you're afraid to show her to us or she's such a dog you're ashamed of her."

"No, I've been busy, that's all. I'm not like you guys. I've got to make my grades. My dad's not going to run down to the school with a big check if I start to flunk out."

"Whoa, dude!" Todd's eyes widen.

Jeff sees he blurted out something better left unsaid. "I'm sorry, that was a cheap shot."

Todd doesn't seem to have taken offense but he does look at Jeff with great curiosity. "What are you so touchy about?"

"I'm not."

Chris and Todd roll their eyes.

"Okay, you're not touchy. I just asked you why you've been hard to get a hold of lately, and you answered that I'm a dickhead whose Dad has to buy his grades."

"Sorry." He looks at the chip basket. "Maybe I'm just tired of not getting any."

That sets the other two back for a good ninety seconds. Although he spoke without much thought, it seems like a brilliant stroke, since their speculations about his "mystery woman" were hitting much too close to home. His "confession" has a lot of reverse English. It's rare to hear that sort of thing among them, anyway, so uniqueness alone gives it credibility. It flatters them—Chris, anyway.

"So who is it?" Todd asks.

"Who is it?"

"This girl you're not getting any off of."

He panics but takes the easiest path from this point. "One of those Carver chicks, you know."

"That one at that party?"

He gives Todd a "blank" look, furrowing his brow. Party? That one?

Todd snickers. "I think her name was Cheryl."

"Oh!" Jeff shakes his head. "No." Too late, he sees that he should've said yes.

"Was it another one who was there that night?"

"Uh, no, you don't know her."

"Well, shit, of course I don't know her! I don't know any of those Carver chicks, no thanks to my buddy Jeff."

"I meant you hadn't seen her."

Todd's antennae-like brows quiver again.

"What's she like?" Chris asks.

"She's just this stupid girl in algebra who works down at Wendy's and she gives me free fries and I thought I could score, you know? I've been out with her three-four times now and I can't seem to. Well, some stuff, you know, it's not like she's some weirdo about it or anything. I think it's just a matter of time and opportunity."

"What's your problem?" Todd asks.

"What's my problem?" Jeff shoots back. "Jesus, you ask me what my problem is that I can't get laid?"

"Gentlemen," says Chris.

"My problem number one is I don't have a car. You want to lend me yours?" It's only a rhetorical question; Todd claims his father won't allow anyone but Todd to drive Todd's car. Considering the driving record of the Lakeview crowd, it's a reasonable restriction. "My second problem is money—neither one of us has any. There's nowhere to go to take her. I can't just check into a motel. She lives in an apartment with her Mom and a couple of brothers and sisters, so what do I do, you tell me?" He's worked himself into a pose of indignation with credibility; he successfully backs Todd off.

"My parents are out of town a lot, and you know it. You know you could ask me to bring her over to my house."

"Yeah?"

"Yeah." Todd looks hurt. "How come you didn't even ask me—are we friends or not?"

"I thought about it," Jeff lies. "I just didn't think she'd go for it, you know? And this is all a very recent development."

"Dump her ass," Chris says cheerfully.

"Easy for you to say."

"So you've got a thing for her?" Todd asks.

"Well…," Jeff sighs, toys with the chips in the basket. "Yeah, I guess I do."

"What's she look like?" asks Chris.

"Short, blond curly hair, very nice eyes and a great smile," says Jeff.

Todd smirks. "A girl other girls insist is cute when they try to fix you up?"

Jeff's arm is being twisted so he delivers up the obligatory assessment of her parts with ill-disguised distaste for doing so.

"Good tits and ass." It sounds like a lie to his own ear, and even he believes that the girl at Wendy's is attractive. Susan's much sexier, which Todd must have noticed on Halloween, but Jeff fears even hinting that she's the desired object.

"Your enthusiasm is underwhelming," Todd cracks.

"Hey, you guys, I don't like doing this!"

They stare at him. "Doing what?" Todd asks.

"Hey, I like this girl, okay? I respect her. I enjoy talking to her, and she understands me. She's not like Lakeview bow-heads, she's very intelligent, very grown-up. Okay?"

Chris and Todd laugh.

"Gee, excuse me," says Todd.

"Okay, okay," Chris says. "So you're in love."

They sit quietly, Todd and Chris lighting new Marlboros, while Rosa comes to remove their plates. Now that Jeff has established this "girl," he itches to tell them the truth: *not some girl, you guys, we're not talking about wrestling in the back seat or getting it on with some stupid cheerleader, no, man, I'm talking real woman. She French-kissed me, see, that night at this party? Then she started begging me for it, couldn't get enough.* (Get real!)

Claiming to be ga-ga over that kid at Wendy's makes him feel disloyal, and it also undercuts Susan's value as a prize. Besides, he's so in love and he's so proud of her, he longs to lay claim, make it public. But not to these twits.

Barring that, the least he can do now is get them to think that he and the girl are like Chris and Paige but he's too chivalrous to officially tell it.

"What's her name?" Chris asks suddenly.

"Name?" He can't remember the girl's name; his whole head suddenly glows hot as a light bulb, and Chris and Todd both guffaw. "It's Susan," he announces, glad to have located a name but immediately horrified to hear it spoken.

"Susan?" Todd's brows, squiggling again.

"Yeah, Susan… Katz."

"A JAP?" asks Chris.

"Uh, yeah. No, I don't know. No, not a JAP."

"Hmmm," muses Todd, grinning. "Very grown-up, very intelligent, named Susan."

"It's not what you think!" Jeff says hotly.

"What do I think?"

"I don't know. What do you think?"

Todd turns to Chris, smiling. "What do you think?"

Chris says, "I think Jeffie is acting very nervous here on the witness stand."

"I don't like to be cross-examined," Jeff says to Todd.

"Okay," says Todd. "I think the case is closed, anyway."

"What's that supposed to mean?"

Todd winks at Chris. "I think I know his secret."

Jeff almost rises to the bait; instead, he gives the other two a feral grin but utters not a word. His hands slicken with sweat, and inside he's crawling. He curses himself for being so stupid. He meant for them to believe that he's doing it with the girl at Wendy's, and now it appears that Todd's on another track: he believes Jeff and Susan??? It's very scary (yet also gratifying) to think that Todd pairs them in his mind as lovers. Jeff's strategy has been inside-out; he should've bragged about boffing his art teacher, and the other two would never believe it. Trying to hide the object of his desire, he may have revealed her.

But so far it's only something they (or Todd, anyway) suspects. So if they "know," it's only, like, unofficial. He hasn't *told* them anything. If they "know," it's not his fault, really.

"Uh-oh," says Chris. He nods toward the fountain. Paige and a girl Jeff doesn't know are approaching El Fenix; they're carrying big Neiman's shopping bags with handles, and Paige shades her brow with her hand to peer into the dimness of the restaurant.

"Hen-peck alert," says Todd. "Told you."

"Pussy-whip alarm!" Jeff declares with grateful relief.

The girls come into the foyer and stand squinting like moles until Chris, knowing that he's about to be spotted, hails them with a papal wave.

"Who's that with her?" asks Todd.

"Her cousin from Wichita Falls."

"Arf."

"Tell me," says Chris.

The two girls thread their way among the crowded tables with their bulging bags held aloft as if fording a stream. When they arrive, everybody exchanges a chorus of "Hi's" and Paige introduces her cousin, Alex, a chubby brunette who wears far too much makeup.

Jeff lowers his visibility by adopting a spectator mode while Chris and Paige and Todd and the cousin banter.

"Alex likes to come to Dallas because the shopping's better," says Paige.

"They don't have malls in Amarillo?" asks Todd.

"Well, sure. Actually, we've got Dillards and everything just like here. Actually, except for the Neiman's this mall's just like the one down the street from my house. But we don't have the Galleria, and everybody comes to Dallas to shop there."

"So how come you're not shopping at the Galleria?" Todd asks her. Jeff knows the answer and presumes Todd does too. Todd's just making trouble. "Paige wanted to come here," Alex declares before she catches Paige's warning glance.

"My mom needed something from Woolworth's, sewing stuff," Paige says testily to Todd. She turns to Chris. "I bought you something," she says coyly.

"Yeah?" Chris seems embarrassed by the implied intimacy.

"Don't you want to know what it is?"

"Uh. Sure. You going to show me?"

Paige blushes. "Well, not here."

Todd and Jeff laugh. "Victoria's Secret!" Todd says. "She bought you a nightie to wear, Chris."

"Aw, up yours!"

"Todd, you're such a dick!" sighs Paige. "I pity the poor girl."

"He's just jealous, Paige," says Jeff, but then immediately regrets entering the banter on the wrong side.

"You'll have to excuse Jeffie; he's in love."

Paige blooms like a flower unfolding in fast-action photography. "Really, Jeff? Who with?"

"He's just bullshitting you."

The spotlight of communal attention sweeps restlessly on; the girls are hungry. Paige promised to take Alex to the Galleria where they're going to eat at Uncle Tai's. She wants Chris to go with them. The cousin is then observed sending pathetically obvious signals that Paige is a little slow in receiving due to her pique with Todd. But, at last she catches on, looks at Todd and Jeff and says, "Why don't you guys come with us? Chris is going to get bored with only us."

"I'd rather come alone." Todd yawns.

"He needs a nap," Jeff says to undercut Todd's rudeness.

"How about you, Jeff?"

Jeff shrugs. "I'm sorry. I've got to go home and rake leaves."

Todd hums a few bars of *Leave It To Beaver*, but Jeff doesn't let it push his button.

Chris leaves with Paige and Alex, giving the other two boys a sheepish grin; Todd and Jeff spend a few minutes perfunctorily rating the females who parade past the window. On the way to the cashier, Jeff digs two quarters out of his pocket and tries to pass them like a relay baton to Todd while they're walking.

"What's that for?"

"My tea."

"Shit! Get serious."

"I want to pay for my own tea."

"Yeah?" Todd whirls on him. "Well, how about the chips, too, dickhead. You owe us for some chips."

Todd's not smiling.

"How much?" Jeff reaches for his wallet.

"Will you get serious?" Todd ignores Jeff's outstretched hand and steps to the waiting cashier. Jeff swallows, closes the two warm, damp quarters in his fist, and walks through the foyer of the restaurant and into the atrium. At the apron of the fountain, he blinks back the strong light. He feels inexplicably sorry for himself. Someday he'll be as rich as the Hunts and he'll buy all his friends whatever they want whenever they want it.

They walk without speaking to the parking lot. They take their seats in Todd's 300SX and strap themselves in wordlessly. Todd starts the Nissan's engine, but then, before putting the car into gear, he shuts it off. He looks through the windshield. Jeff wonders if Todd is about to order him out of the car.

"Hey, man," Todd says after a minute. "Look, I'm a turd most of the time. I know it. I just can't seem to control it. I don't have many friends and I seem to abuse the ones I do have." He turns to Jeff. "I am just jealous of Chris. What it is that you and Chris have, I'd like to get it. If I thought there was a school for it, I'd go register, you know? I just step all over myself with chicks, man. They hate me."

"You're a good-looking dude."

Todd's look says *knock it off.* "I'm not asking to be pumped up, here, buddy. I need to know what's real."

Jeff smiles. "You're going to ask me how to become a great lover?"

"No," says Todd. "And pardon me for making you nervous with my confession. I'll think twice next time."

He starts the car. They drive several blocks down Northwest Highway toward Preston Center without speaking. Jeff was pleased to see Todd drop his guard, especially since implicit in it is the presumption that Jeff is Todd's superior, that Todd admires Jeff's ability to relate to girls. Women. Todd obviously believes that Jeff is older and wiser in the ways of love. So now Jeff feels guilty about dancing away and refusing to acknowledge this request for a show of true friendship. It's hard to trust people, especially people you're always parrying.

"Okay, I'm sorry, bud," Jeff says when they reach the light at Preston. "There's nothing really wrong with you and women, man, that wouldn't be completely solved if you'd just behave a little nicer around them, treat them with respect. Watch what you say. Say things that make them feel better, not worse."

Todd clears his throat. "Flatter them?"

"Well, you don't have to flatter them all the time. You can make people feel better without sucking up to them, you know."

Todd nods. Jeff sees he's acknowledging the point but doesn't know exactly what it means.

"Sometimes you can tell somebody is feeling shitty and if you just tell them you can see it and encourage them to tell you about it, then it makes them feel better."

"Chicks like that?"

Jeff's frustrated that Todd consistently misses the point, yet Todd's ignorance makes him feel supremely superior, like an older brother who's been through experiences that have led to a wisdom he can share. Share as part payment for past debts, even.

"I'm not talking about a make-out technique, see, dude? That's the thing I mean. Not everything can be, like, focused on that, or they know, or they sense it, and it puts them on guard."

"But it's always on my mind."

"Yeah, yeah." Jeff chuckles. "Now we're at the heart of the problem. Sometimes you've got to think of women as your friends, or just people with pussies, if you know what I mean."

"Yeah, but this is like telling somebody 'Don't think about a polar bear!'"

Jeff laughs. "Yeah."

Todd seems content with the sagacity of the advice for the moment; he wheels the car South onto the Tollway, and when they've leveled off at a brisk seventy-five, he says, "So do you feel like this girl Susan you were talking about is a friend, or what?"

Jeff's momentarily electrified; he looks out of the window, shifting his weight. "Uh, yeah, I do feel she's a friend. I mean sometimes we just talk." Talked, that is, before he turned into a complete wimp who couldn't face her.

"What about?"

"Other people. Ourselves. Art. School. Family. Trips we've taken."

"But you're also…" Todd sighs. "Well, getting it on?"

He sounds so wistful that Jeff can't resist laughing.

"Did I say we were?"

"No, you said you weren't getting any, but I didn't believe it."

"Okay. Some." He's so buoyant he strains like a hot-air balloon against his seat-belt. He never imagined it'd be so gratifying to win recognition from Todd for losing his virginity. (Too bad it's not true!) He adds, merely to add still another support under his credibility, "But, it's like I told you, it's hard for us to get together."

"Hey, if I can help, let me know, man."

"Okay."

"I'm sorry about the car—" Todd dips his head toward the dashboard. They're approaching the turnstiles at the end of the Tollway. The downtown skyline looms in the windshield green as Oz.

"It's okay."

"But if I'm doomed to be a dork, at least if I can help a buddy, I will. I mean it, dude. Matter of fact, my parents are going to be out of town all week. *Mi cama es su cama.*"

"Gracías, hombre."

"You know what I was thinking? This is going to sound really weird, man."

Todd's grinning at him as he slings quarters into the turnstile basket without looking.

"What?"

"I was thinking you were getting it on with that art teacher. She seemed very friendly to you."

"Really?" Jeff barks out a laugh, shakes his head. "That's wild!"

"I wouldn't mind."

"Oh, hey! Me, either!"

They're on Stemmons now, merging with the Saturday afternoon traffic. He longs to reveal what actually happened and to lie about the rest, but all he can do is to emit an aura of suggestive pretense.

When he turns his head, he discovers his ghost smirking at him in the side window: Oh, you're the Ultimate Cool Dude with a secret? Well, the secret right now is this—there's actually less to reveal than there is to hide.

⤳*18*⤲

On Sunday afternoon, Curt says he has dibs on the upstairs study to watch the Cowboys - Vikings game, so Susan relinquishes her half of the space to work from a clipboard downstairs in the living room. There, she toys with the following notion:

Mary, the dutiful student, is alone in her room, meditating or reading. Significantly, she is "inside," because of the ancient associations of the female with domiciles, protection, safety. Her Mother is no doubt downstairs in the kitchen. Mary is engaged in a quiet, passive activity in keeping with the cultural expectations of her gender.

Her brother "Gabriel" appears in her room; he has come in through the window, or perhaps, more conventionally, through the doors. He's been doing something with the Father outside. He brings her a message: Her Father is inviting her to come outside to play with him, to come outside the rules of the family, to violate the rules, even, and lie with him, conceive a child. She would please Him by doing this. The Father has chosen the daughter over the Mother for this; thus the daughter moves up one notch in the hierarchy, and the Daughter knows from this invitation that in the eternal struggle between Mother and Daughter for Father's attention, Daughter has won. This is her reward for pleasing the Father, along with membership in the "club" to which the Brother already belongs.

But this child he wants her to have with Him: it will be a male. The gender is the Father's choice. He will not leave the matter to biological chance, which might result in a "mistake"—a female. God the Father intends to use Mary as a brood cow to be serviced when a new male deity is needed. When the "family" portrait is painted, one would see God the Father, Gabriel the Brother (the "Little Father"), Mary the new Mother, and the Son. (Mary's own displaced Mother is still down in the kitchen.) The ratio of men to women in the portrait would approximate that of the anchor teams on the usual nightly newscast.

All her life, males have managed to get Susan to please them. She learned this from her mother, who treated Susan's father like a special child in the family. Although day-to-day authority clearly resided in her mother, that authority only extended to Susan and her brother, a year older than she, and that authority could be overruled by Susan's father, though it seldom was because Susan's father lacked sufficient interest to assert his opinion.

Her mother made rules for the family, but her father didn't have to follow them. Dad didn't have to keep his room clean, Mother did it for him; Dad didn't have to put things away that he had gotten out of cabinets; Dad didn't have to work unless he wanted to, which was maybe half the time. When he was between graphics jobs at publishing and printing firms, he called himself a free-lance illustrator. Any employment he took soon grew boring, and he'd quit. Susan's mother would complain. He'd say, *Life's too short to do what you don't want to do, and as long as I was working there, I didn't have time to find some-*

thing better. If Susan or her brother said that they didn't want to do something because it was boring or they didn't have a sufficient desire to do it, her mother would always say, *You've got to do it whether you want to or not. We all have to do things we don't want to, that's part of life.*

Dad also didn't have to finish what he started: the house where Susan grew up was a veritable demonstration home of half-completed do-it-yourself projects—unpainted moldings, a wall sheet-rocked but not taped and bedded or painted, an uncovered switch box hanging loose from its niche in a wall. Dad was also allowed to be foolish about money, and Susan's mother frequently argued with him about buying gadgets or tools that might be used only on an uncompleted project. He spent $1500 on an old pickup, but it sat in the driveway for two years, hardly driven (both parents had serviceable sedans), though once he used the truck to bring home plywood that he stored on the back porch for another two years before using half of it to half-finish an attic study.

To Susan the child, her father lived in an enviable bubble of exemption. It stood to reason that by pleasing him she might be selected to stand beside him under that umbrella. She tried to please her brother, too. If her brother was reading and she wanted him to play with her, he would snarl, "I'm reading, dummy," but if she were reading and he wanted her to play, she'd put down her comic or book and comply. If he wanted to play "Scrabble" and she "Life," then he'd say, "Well, we can play both." But they'd play "Scrabble" first and then never get around to playing "Life," unless, of course, days later he might decide he wanted to play it, then he'd make it seem he was just fulfilling his earlier contractual obligation. Their parents worried about him more, but they seemed grateful that she gave them little cause for it. He got into trouble at school, she didn't. He sassed his teachers, she didn't. He failed some classes, she never. He and her Dad got white meat chicken. He controlled what they watched on TV on Saturday morning.

When they reached adolescence, her father invited her thirteen-year-old brother to go on a four-day sail in the Gulf with another father and his son on a boat owned by the second father. It was the beginning of the summer after her sixth grade. The reason given for not including Susan was that the other father had only a son. (This implied a need to preserve a numerical balance.) When six weeks later, they went again, she protested that it was her turn. Her mother said, "Susan, honey, this is something the men are doing. It's good for boys to be alone with their fathers."

Susan didn't know enough then to argue that it was good for daughters, too. Her reward for sacrificing her father to her brother's good development was that she got to help Mother clean the house.

As her brother advanced into his teenage years, less was expected of him, while more seem to be expected of Susan, such as learning to cook while the brother lay on the living room floor watching TV. More and more her brother told her mother that he didn't want to do what she asked him to do, or that he was busy doing something else or that he would do it later (but didn't), and her mother wouldn't make an issue of it. Susan, however, was expected to complete chores and tasks assigned.

While her brother worked on the car that her Dad helped him buy, her mother made her help scrub the bathrooms, and she had to polish the silverware, too. The lines of power shifted. Brother became Little Father, and the family hierarchy looked like this in Susan's mind: 1) Father; 2) Little or Assistant Father; 3) Mother; 4) Susan. Under this system, her Brother also became someone for both females to please.

Susan blamed her mother for this arrangement. Her father's preference for her brother meant to Susan that she and her mother were deficient, short a part or two. She didn't want to be deficient; she wanted to please her father. Being like her mother prevented it. She despised her mother and her mother in herself. She resented her mother for expending so much energy in trying to please the father and getting so little reward for it. She despised her mother for falling behind the brother in her father's regard.

When she reached dating age, pleasing males came to mean that if she gave them what they wanted, then they would "love" her, give her their attention, make her important to them, perhaps marry her or ask her to live with them. (All true of her relationship with Nathan, she knows: he had a list of needs or desires long as that of a scavenger hunt and her need to please sent her scurrying out eagerly to find each item.)

In college, she realized that despising her mother for complying with the system was tantamount to blaming the slave for slavery. She learned to blame her father for his unthinking presumption that as a man the others in the household should have to please him, and she decided she wouldn't repeat her mother's mistake.

Has she succeeded? Her situation is not nearly so clear-cut to her as was her mother's, partly because the person perceiving (Susan the angry daughter) is the same person engaged in the relationship (Susan the domestic partner). Curt is not her father. For one thing, notwithstanding a lay-off, he has kept a job since graduating from UT several years ago; for another, Susan tries to maintain vigilance over certain, well, slippages in regard to housekeeping rules and tries not to allow Curt to presume anything in regard to sweeping, dusting, mopping, washing windows, vacuuming, grocery shopping, laundry, meal fixing, etc. She has him fairly well-trained; she doesn't have to please him as a means of coaxing him to "help" her with the housework—no, she stands up for herself, here, though their relationship in Household Maintenance is still manager-to-trainee. This arrangement gives her the power of decision and organization, but it likewise keeps her responsible for seeing that things get done, so in that way, hers is like her mother's relationship. She has to say, "Curt, it's time for you to go to the store," or "We need some fruit and cereal and milk if we're going to have breakfast tomorrow," and even though he'll get his car keys and leave immediately for the store, still, it'd be nice to have him look in the cupboards and the refrigerator and notice what was needed without being told.

Her mother pleased her father by taking care of things. She anticipated his needs and knew more about them than he did and produced things he needed even when he didn't know he needed them. She also pleased him by bringing home a steady paycheck and by having, thanks to her job, a group health insurance plan for the family, and a retirement program, though Susan never once heard her father thank her mother for supplying them. He said, "Good thing we've got that insurance!" Her father considered himself a new-fashioned man: "I don't care if my wife works outside of the home, it's fine with me." He was too cagey to add the unspoken corollary though it was apparent: *so long as she also does those things that my mother did for her family.* What Susan's mother might have done to please her father in the bedroom Susan doesn't care to explore, though she suspects that, given her mother's pragmatic and unflappable nature, she performed whatever acts were required with dependable grace, maybe without enthusiasm but likewise without complaint. Once Susan was at the dining room table doing her homework and saw her father step up behind her mother at the kitchen sink and put his hand on her butt. Susan's mother half-turned and gave her husband a quick but preoccupied smile. Susan thought the smile said: *I'm supposed to be grateful for the attention, so I'm acting like I am.*

That's not Susan and Curt, either. And since they don't have children, issues about parenting roles haven't arisen. So far she and Curt have managed to be what she thinks of as "40/60" equals, with her the forty. He still gets to decide too many things, often by not deciding or by balking about having a decision made—getting married, having a baby, buying a house.

More of her tally:

—They go to see films only Curt wants to see more than ones only she wants to see. The same holds true for eating out vs. eating at home. But the bigger the choice—say, in how to spend a vacation—the harder it is to concede wordlessly, of course, and she will surrender only after a struggle. Her desire to please him, or her habit of pleasing him, sometimes leads her to keep her own desires to herself, so that often he's not aware that she had a preference (for a film, restaurant, etc.) that isn't his.

—They spend more time socializing with people at his job than at hers, people who are his old friends than hers.

—They have sex whenever only he wants it but not when only she wants it; that is, she cannot say no but he can.

—He can go to the kitchen and fix himself something to eat without asking if she wants something, but she can't bring herself to do this.

—When her parents visit, she has to treat Curt as if he's a guest who has arrived with them: for instance, he's exempt from having to prepare for their visit. But when Mavis or Kenneth and Vivian come, she's expected to play the hostess, if not explicitly by Curt, at least implicitly. Curt expects Susan to set aside temporarily who she is in order to become the kind of wife who will play hostess to her in-laws, the kind of wife who will make herself responsible for the experience her in-laws have as guests, though their blood relative lives here, too.

—If he has a bad day, she will try to baby him to make him feel better; if she has a bad day, he will invite her to describe the day's events, then he will try to argue her out of feeling bad about them; rather than trying to please her (that might require an effort), he will act as if she is practicing faulty mental health by feeling bad.

—When on occasion they settle on a preference that is declared to be hers and not his, then he'll make it known that he's setting aside his choice and expects a quid pro quo in the future. Their trip to Italy this past summer is an example. So far as she can determine, their trip has cost her the right to choose their vacation spot for the next two decades.

She tries to stay alert and stand up for herself, but at the same time it secretly pleases (or appeases) her to be the one who gives in. Curt rewards her by liking her; he gives her his attention. That, at least, is an old and familiar pattern. If she were to become too big a "bitch"—a woman who thinks of herself first—he might reject her, leave her, find a woman who wants to please him. It's easy to find women who want to please men; they're everywhere. It's not "right" for a woman to want to please herself; it's "selfish," and the "best" women are those who think of others: Mother Teresa. The "best" man—as in "may the best man win"—is the one most able to secure what he wants for himself from other men, including their women. She feels comfortable as The Pleaser, even when she recognizes how she's fallen into the role out of habit (bad habit); it's a little like the comfort of nail-biting or the way you might call a friend whom you're tired of and who bores you, call just because you need a predictable conversation with another human being and because you're afraid that friend might think you're bored with her if you don't call. (Q: Is Jeff only another "man" in her life? Does her conditioned response to male needs explain why she foolishly bent over him that night in her back yard and kissed him "to make him well" when he didn't ask for it?)

She knows all the ins and outs of being one who pleases the men in her life. It's like a neighborhood she grew up in and all her memories good and bad are associated with it. Her identity itself is connected to the role and the memories of playing it.

Going outside of that neighborhood, moving away, as it were, brings risks, dangerous adventure, the terror of unfamiliar sensations, unforeseen consequences. It isn't easy giving up the comfort of who you are, particularly if the world constantly reassures you that this "nice" way you are pleases them.

What Susan wrote:

Dear Mary Mary quite contrary,

Couldn't you say no? I know you got the word from the highest Authority, no less, but wasn't it a cheap trick for him to send that gorgeous fellow with the message? Didn't that arouse your suspicions? I mean, he could have made the dove coo it in your ear or your car radio sing a special tune, or—now, here's an option! Let's say you've missed your Visit two months running and you upchuck seven mornings in a row and get a sudden yen for hardtack and kosher dills but don't know why; all your friends start winking and nudging you with their elbows, but you feel altogether baffled because you've never so much as kissed a fellow. (No, not sensible; after all, she's married, she's not necessarily a virgin, it's a virgin birth, there's a difference.)

Anyway, there you were minding your own business, meditating, introspecting—okay, call it praying—alone in the room, uh, receptive may be the word, not expecting (ha ha) visitors, least of all this gorgeous hunk, when all of a sudden blam! a laser beam from the blue blue sky shoots down through your window like something from a Speilberg movie, you blink, and presto! there's an angel in your bedroom!

This creature has red hair and white robe (Memling), or maybe fuchsia wings and gold hair (Fra Angelico), carrying a Madonna Lily (Bartolommeo della Gatta, et al), and before you can scream, it goes down on one knee (Gherardo Starnina) or hovers about a yard off the floor (Pablo Callari e Bottega), and this Heavenly Hunky Helicopter is lusty, busty (got to check into the tradition of angelic androgyny here), a zaftig angel with pink fleshy limbs and blonde curls, a very healthy human glow, with big cardinal-red wings, very feathered (gobs of small brush strokes), peach-fuzzed face, bare arms and throat, a calf coyly revealed below the robe; somebody's heartthrob for sure, this Gabriel, maybe only the pederast painter's own squeeze....

And says to you,....what? That you're preggers, or will be. Or, as of right now: Hello, you've just been knocked up by the Word.

Maybe you didn't scream because we all know it's common for a woman to hear some man tell her she's going to do something she hadn't had the vaguest prior inkling of. Nothing new in that, for sure. Maybe you couldn't tell if this was a prophecy or a command: with Omniscience and Omnipotence balled up into one, when does "I know what's going to happen" become "because I make it so?"

But if he was so cock-sure about it, why send that fine-looking fellow?

Here's where it gets interesting to me. You sit there in your tangerine robe (Tintoretto), and on hearing this news, you bow your head and submit, presumably with gratitude (Fra Angelico), or maybe you sneak a look outside into your garden (pardon, that's Garden) where the famous First Couple are wading like gate-crashers through the shrubbery, or maybe you're flung back on your chair when that angel and those putti come bursting through the wall (Tintoretto), or you demurely cast down your eyes, or—well, some hope here!—you strike an attitude that's a trifle sullen and put upon (Simone Martini, in the Uffizi). Anyway, point is I don't recall your ever being like a contestant on The Wheel of Fortune who just landed on that $5,000 pie wedge—with one notable exception: in the aforementioned example of Sr. Callari e Bottega, you're sort of scrunched behind a pillar, hiding while you peek at this awesome angel who has just man-i-fested out of nowhere to hover right beside your chest of drawers, and the look on your face says this—"Wow! There's an angel in my room! How scary! How beautiful he is!" (What do you expect, he's Italian, and, worse yet, he's better looking than you.)

But this exception proves the rule—your expression shows you haven't heard him speak yet. That brings me back to my original question, about your suspicions or your possible after-grousings when the band's gone home and the concessionaires have folded up their stalls and you're left to face your condition all alone. If the outcome was a foregone conclusion, why'd the boss bother with the flattery, the razzle-dazzle of a PR campaign, the insidious seduction?

There's this to consider—If the Authority had sent a crone or a hunchback, wouldn't you have rung 911 or at least asked for time to think it over?

Would you have nixed a talking frog?

～*19*～

Saturday after Susan returns from the shower, Curt wants to see "Good Morning, Viet Nam!" but Susan insists upon "Dangerous Liaisons." Curt wants to eat at Mia's but Susan prefers Al Dente. They argue for several minutes, but Susan stays uncharacteristically stubborn until Curt offers to concede the movie if he can pick the restaurant. She accepts this settlement, since she's much more passionate about seeing "Dangerous Liaisons" than eating at Al Dente.

Even though Mia's is Curt's choice, Susan eats all of her sour cream chicken enchiladas with green sauce, beans, rice and guacamole salad, as well as a basket of chips with picante sauce. She washes it down with two Tecates. She eats and drinks so much she's in pain.

But during the movie she forgets about being too full. In one scene, the cynical and jaded seducer, Vicomte de Valmont (played by John Malkovich), successfully deflowers the innocent maiden played by Uma Thurman, and Susan writhes inside with sorrow.

Alarmed, she wants to scream to the girl, "No! Don't believe him!" Then Valmont takes on the greater challenge of seducing the faithful, convent-raised Madame de Tourvel (Michelle Pfeiffer) merely to prove that even a loving wife is corruptible, and at that point, Susan astonishes Curt by bursting into tears. Likewise, when Valmont, redeemed at last by allowing himself to love, is killed in a duel by the young music teacher (Keanu Reeves), Susan weeps copiously to the point of embarrassing herself. She has to keep Curt sitting through the credits until she can regain her composure.

"God, that was maybe the best movie I've ever seen in my life!" Susan calls out while washing her face at the bathroom sink prior to retiring. (Curt is already in bed.) She can't get over it. So powerful! She hasn't cried that much in a movie since she saw "Bambi" as a kid. "It was really moving. What a great story about being too smart for yourself! I wonder how much they changed stuff from the book, did you hear? All that maneuvering and lying and there Glenn Close and John Malkovich believed that they could be honest with one another because they didn't really care about each other or anything but, you know, the conquest, but in reality they were hooked up in ways they didn't realize! And so many good performances, didn't you think? What'd you think, Curt? Didn't you like it?" She waits, listening, hears nothing. "Curt?"

He's asleep.

The next afternoon is the aforementioned Sunday when Susan relinquishes the upstairs "study" so Curt can watch the Viking - Cowboys game on their sole TV. She goes downstairs to work from a clipboard on the sofa. For a time she doodles and wonders why she gave in so easily—what's more important to their mutual future: her thesis or the goddamn football game? Why didn't she insist he take the TV into another room? After all, it's called a portable TV! Why didn't he volunteer to do that? Most of her text and her notes are stored on files in her computer, and she can't easily move the machinery. His insistence on being in there this afternoon to watch this game is really unreasonable. He said, "I'll turn it down low, and you can stay here and work if you want to."

Oh, sure! Goddamn it! Well, he did offer to use the earplug. But having another person in the room, even a silent one, can be distracting.

If he hollers down the stairs at her to bring him something from the kitchen, she'll take a butcher knife and stab him right in the heart with it.

For a while her anger is like static on her mental radio and she can't get a clear station for her thesis. It isn't just this business about the room. It's an accumulation of minor grievances:

1) He thought the movie was "okay."

2) He insisted on spending Thanksgiving the way they always had, at Mavis's, with Kenneth and Vivian and their children.

3) He balked at trimming his toenails and they raked her legs while they slept.

4) He did a half-ass job of cleaning the upper bathroom yesterday while she was at the bridal shower, and she felt compelled to redo it.

5) Once again he'd fudged on his half of the household expenses and she wound up paying the electricity bill.

She could go on with this niggling little piddly crap, but doing an inventory neither makes her feel better nor truly justifies what she feels. If she were ga-ga over him and they were spending their first weekend together, none of these things would be noticeable, or, if they were, they'd be endearing.

Winter has at last arrived; she closes the mini-blinds to shut out the cold and the awful gray light of a rainy afternoon. Because the heat rises up the stairwell, and she can't raise the thermostat without Curt's complaining that it's "steaming" up there. She has to wrap in a blanket, in addition to wearing a sweat suit and Curt's thick wool hunting socks. She wishes they had a fireplace. Someday the house she owns will have one. And a big kitchen. And a workshop so that the husband can pursue his hobby somewhere other than on the dining room table. Curt won't want to talk about owning a house, of course. Or about getting married and having children. (And if he did, *she* might up and run!)

It's as if he lives in a perpetual present, the way he's content to go to work every day and watch ESPN on weekends, and his idea of recreation—or progress—is to buy new toys. Living without any apparent regard for a future. By avoiding discussion and action, Curt effectively controls their future, even though he only has one of the two votes. By doing nothing he determines that nothing will be done. This is like a sculptor's laying claim to the best block of marble in the quarry but then letting it sit idle because he has neither the inspiration nor the ambition to work with it.

This makes her feel they have no future; if you have no future, then the present does not lead to it and is therefore dead. The past is dead, too, of course. If your past is dead, and your present is dead and your future is aborted, then what's that make you?

Dead.

Grim thoughts for a gray and rainy winter afternoon.

Something more cheerful, then. When was the time in her life that she felt the most alive? That's easy—from the time she and Nathan met to the moment she realized he no longer loved her, most particularly during their honeymoon period. They spent almost every moment petting and fondling and kissing in his car, did it during stolen afternoons and nights at various houses, once or twice a motel (all night! how delicious that seemed!), on a blanket in the woods, on a dark dock on a summer night, once in a hammock. Learning to please him, learning how to be pleased. It hadn't taken him long to break her down: she too ached for consummation, though less urgently—it was more as if being in his arms and kissing him in the dark cozy womb of his heated car filled a void she hadn't known was empty, and she eagerly welcomed his hands and fingers, tongue and cock as a means of feeling more of whatever it was that he alone could make her feel. She was not driven toward a particular destination so much as she was looking for an intensification of an already intense experience, greedy for a bigger bite of what already tasted heavenly.

Mary, Mary, quite contrary, why couldn't you say no?

The past was dead. But it can be relived. In memory. What would she do different?

Give in sooner.

She sound of her own laughter in the empty room startles her.

If she were a kid now, she'd be just like they are, her Cheryls and Jeffs—eager to burn up her youth, torch it, bust it open to see what's inside, toss it off a cliff to see if it would fly.

Too bad the choice is not available for adults. Of course, if she weren't attached....

Holly's advice, the speech to Jeff, nicely expressed the agony and the ecstasy, didn't it? *I would if I could, but I can't; I almost did but didn't; I'd love to but I won't; you're the one who could make me break my vow; you can't make me break my vow.* (Was this the same as daring someone to try?) The teasing tension inherent in the polarities—it reminds her of those panting sessions with Nathan before she finally gave in.

She's got to clear the air with Jeff, and do it soon. Tuesday night. She needs to dispel any fear he might have that she plans to take advantage of him, and she wants to be sure he isn't crushed that she can't reciprocate his infatuation.

If he even has one. Isn't it possible she's just being vain and dreaming up his adoration because it's so nice to be adored? And so he has a crush, so what? Kids have them all the time; they're as temporary as mood swings. Same as all their other likes and dislikes, they're easy-come, easy-go.

But she can't take any chances about a misunderstanding. She *will* talk to him about what happened Halloween night, and she *will* make it perfectly clear that it was a mistake that she *will not* repeat.

But, in rehearsing this vow, she instantly regrets the lost possibility of his eager attention, their flirtation. Well, that kiss again. Since now there's no possibility, she feels free to compensate herself for the loss by indulging in the idea of it. What could it harm, after all, since she *will* set him straight on Tuesday night.

What if she and Jeff were students together, like she and Nathan were—classmates, contemporaries. Maybe it's a painting class. They're alone, after school, working on projects. They're using finger paints to make mock children's art. The room is warm. He removes his shirt; she is wearing shorts and a halter top. He kisses her. Just lightly, playful. And she... kisses him back. Then they kiss a long time. Her knees grow weak, her calves tremble. Her hands shake. The kiss has a power of a strong drug. When they finally break off, Susan dips her fingers in red paint and smears his chest. While she's kissing him again, he unclips her halter top. His hands move over her breasts, and he fondles her nipples. He dips his fingers in the blue paint and dabs her nipples with it.

If someone saw Susan on the couch minutes later, she'd appear hypnotized; her gaze is glassy, her mouth parted slightly. The rims and lobes of her ears are the color of beets.

She flings off the blanket and goes up the stairs and into the bathroom, where she strips herself naked except for the thick wool socks then puts on her bathrobe.

At the threshold to the TV room she stands leaning on the door frame.

"What's the score?"

"17-3, Minnesota."

"What quarter?"

"A minute to half-time."

"Good!"

He looks up at her. "I can turn it off, if you still want to work in here. It's too disgusting to watch. I can take my radio down and listen while I work on my model."

"Thanks. But I've got a better idea."

"What's that?"

"Come here!" She takes his hand and tugs him up from the recliner. Now he knows. He looks a little panicky. Not on his schedule. He's caught between balking because he wants to keep up with the game and agreeing to this because as a guy he's supposed to be ready any time any place. For her, it feels peculiarly heady to be in charge here, acting gruff and bluffing her way along, and she thinks *better go quickly or you'll lose the element of surprise!*

"Don't worry, it won't take long!"

She tows him into the bedroom, pushes him back on the bed, straddles his hips and unbuckles his belt, wrestles down his pants. It doesn't take much manipulation to get him ready, then she slips him inside her, rides him, raised up, back arched; she opens the robe to flash him whatever he wants to see.

But as usual his eyes are closed. She stares at his fleshy moons of eyelid as she rocks back and forth. If she is to be his alone, she wants him to see her, damnit! and she wants to be seen! Wake up, Curt! She rides him roughly, bouncing and landing hard, as if desperate to get his full attention.

When her climax breaks, she collapses on his chest, kissing his neck, weeping and murmuring, "Curt, don't you love me even a little bit?"

⁓20⁓

*T*uesday, Susan eats in the cafeteria, and while she tells Holly about "Dangerous Liaisons," Jeff stops by their table. "I'll be able to come to the club meeting tonight!" He beams at her, then looks sheepish. "But I was wondering, you know, whether you could give me a ride home again?" His voice, cracking, sails up on the end of his question.

"Sure! Fine!" she says, shaking inside. This meshes perfectly with her plans to let him down easy.

Holly's eyes bore into her, and as soon as Jeff walks away, she grins. "Have you got your speech ready?"

So Holly has deduced the identity of the Mystery Man! "Near as I can tell," Susan mutters. She bends to her plate where a stalk of emerald broccoli lies in a puddle of melted orange Crayola.

Although she told Curt that she would stay at school until after the club meeting, when the 3:40 bell sounds, she hotfoots out to her car and is at her front door in fifteen minutes. Curt won't arrive until

six at the earliest. She can freshen up at her leisure without interference. Not that she wants to be, well, *alluring* or anything; it just seems
as if the occasion calls for putting on something that makes her feel
strong, in possession of herself.

She showers slowly, then goes through several costume changes
before eventually slipping into her best old Levis with one knee
cutely ripped, a narrow belt with silver cowboy buckle. Finding the
right top was harder but she winds up in a forest-green t-shirt that
reads *The French Connection* across the chest. She changes bras twice
to get one that doesn't let her nipples show.

She stops at Taco Bueno on Lemmon for a bean burrito without
onions to go, holding it like a banana in one hand and bolting it down
while driving with the other. At school, she drinks two diet Cokes
and a cup of coffee, so by the starting time for the meeting, she's jit-
tery, wired. Jeff didn't stop by her office before the meeting, but he's
there at seven-thirty when she goes into the classroom.

Fresco night. She describes how they're made, then shows slides
of various artifacts at Pompeii, including copies of the statues of
Apollo and Diana originally found on the site, and a huge fresco
from the Villa of the Mysteries depicting the initiation of a young
bride into the cult of Dionysius. Not to her surprise, the class seems
most interested in the would-be bawdy frescoes on the walls of the
bordello. She tells them that the Italian guides keep the door to the
bordello locked and allow only members of their tours to view these
frescoes—"they're such hot stuff." Naturally, the images are so tame
to the kids they snicker at the idea of locking them away from children's eyes.

On the same carousel Susan mounted slides that Jennifer shot
Halloween night. Susan lets them comment freely among themselves as the snapshots click up onscreen: Becki as a plumber; Jeff in
the Batman outfit, his friend Todd looking superior; Curt holding up
his sword and snarling, squinty-eyed; close-up of Susan and her

cat-face; another of her posing with a fist on her hip, her tail in her other hand, legs crossed, imitating the famous photo of Chaplin; one of Susan sitting atop the picnic table, Jeff standing beside it—this was hardly two minutes after they had kissed and the others had come barging unexpectedly through the patio door in high spirits and eager to relate their adventures; other slides follow but Susan has little awareness of them.

When the meeting ends a decade later, she lifts her voice loud enough to be overheard and asks Jeff if he minds carrying something out to the car. In her office, she gives him a stack of oversized art books—"for my thesis," she says—and she carries a large portfolio of student drawings. She leads Jeff to her Hyundai in the faculty lot. Normally, she strides from pool to pool of security light as if connecting giant flagstones, but tonight she threads the shadowy spaces between cars and hugs the flanks of vans.

Inside the car, they both buckle up without speaking, the sibilant hiss of the belts and clack of latches a welcome metallic cacophony, and she quickly starts the engine for auditory continuity.

Jeff says, "I hate to ask you this, but I'm spending the night with my friend? Would you mind taking me there instead of to my house? It's about the same distance only a different direction. I hope you don't mind."

"No, it doesn't make any difference to me. Where to?"

"They live out near the Galleria. You take the Tollway to Belt Line."

"Oh." The location is several miles out of her way and much farther than his home in Oak Cliff. Inwardly, she balks, but after all, she has something hard to say to him, and the extra time might help.

"I really enjoyed the slide show on Pompeii tonight."

"I'm glad. It was an interesting place to visit."

"I'd like to go to Europe after graduation, college, I mean. My Dad and Sybil—that's my stepmom—they go all the time, usually for my

Dad's law firm, you know? He told me I'd like it a lot, especially being a young guy and just bumming around with a backpack."

"Yes, that would be something you wouldn't want to miss."

"What is your favorite country?"

Her answer to this (Italy) is no sooner given than Jeff shoots in a
follow-up. He's obviously going to interview her, maybe because
he's too nervous to let a silence stand, she thinks. As they head north
on the Tollway, she answers questions about her trip by telling him
tourist anecdotes, deliberately dropping in Curt by name once or
twice then wishing she hadn't because it seems a little cruel. Traffic
on the Tollway is heavy; headlights from behind strike the back of
the boy's head, her hand on the wheel, illuminating them, and she
pushes on the accelerator to outdistance the lights.

She keeps thinking that any minute they'll quit talking about her
trip and she can bring up what happened Halloween. But he says
he's always had a lot of questions that nobody could answer—what
do you do about money? How can you eat if you don't know the
language of the country? How do you take trains? His friend
Todd—"it's his house I'm going to, by the way"—goes to Switzer-
land in the spring to ski, and his family goes to London like every
Christmas, but Todd never seems to have to cope with anything foreign when he goes with them. Susan says that it's quite possible, if
you have the money and the desire, to go all over the world and
never quite leave the U.S.

"Why go, then?" laughs Jeff.

"Good question!"

The topic at last spins off into the void of silence, and Susan takes
several slow long breaths very quietly in preparation for introducing
"the" subject, but by now they're near the end of the Tollway. She
has outdriven her instructions; leaping ahead, she pictures the car
parked at a curb, engine idling, Jeff about to step out at Todd's house,
and she detains him. Saving her speech until that moment would

mean no distractions from driving (and no uncomfortable afterburn, either).

At the north end of the Tollway, she exits east onto Belt Line, and Jeff says, "Keep going straight for a while then left; I'll show you where."

After they've gone a mile or so, he says, "There!" and she takes the left turn. It puts them on a wide suburban street lit by tall aluminum stanchions bearing on their stalky ends fluorescent orange bulbs that turn the intersections a Martian hue. No tree taller than the many wooden fences stands in sight. She guesses that they're beyond the Dallas city limits and now they've entered the affluent suburb of Plano. Out of principle she isn't familiar with the northern burbs, those Republican bastions built on the lunar foundation of bulldozed prairie, with streets designed by a French curve and named after a developer's daughter or mistress—Tiffany Drive, Heather Lane. The houses are sprawling brick ranch-style with an acre of front lawn whose close-cropped expanse is broken only by fake gas lamps and, at streetside, wide sidewalks that it's hard to imagine being occupied. She feels like an alien out here.

He looks ahead, squinting. "Uh, next block, turn right up the alley."

"The alley?"

"Yeah, I'll go in the back."

She turns up the alley and hits her high beams. Her lamps shine up the empty concrete ribbon; she steers the car up a pristine narrow canyon whose walls are cliffs of redwood fencing upthrust from the turf the precise six feet allowed by law; the garbage cans stand uniformly on platforms, secure, their lids on chain leashes. She almost says something to Jeff about how squeaky clean it all is but lets it pass.

"Next house."

A break in the fence lets onto an apron of concrete, and she wheels

over it to face a four-car garage. The doors are large white squares
wholly unblemished by hardware. They fling light from her headlamps back into her eyes; she shoves the gear shift into P and clicks
off her headlamps, leaving on the parking lights.

"Well, here we are," says Susan.

"I'd really like for you to come in," Jeff says as he slowly releases
his seat belt. "Todd's mom paints, you know, and when I told her that
you might bring me home, she said she'd really like to have your
opinion. Besides, I'd like to offer you something for coming all this
way. It was really nice of you to do that. You've been very nice to me,
like I said in my note, and I want you to know I really appreciate it."

"Well, that's flattering, of course."

"So please? His mom would fall all over herself to think that
somebody official had looked at her stuff, really!"

She understands that he wants to show her off, that being shown
off was to be her reward. His pride in her makes what she has to say
even more difficult.

"Maybe some other time. Jeff?" She averts her gaze and looks at
the blank garage doors that glow yellow like an underlighted wall. It
has been years since it was this hard to tell someone something.
Maybe since her last confession to a priest.

She sighs, swallows. "I'd like to talk about what happened Halloween night, if you don't mind. I just feel like things might have gotten
confused or maybe misunderstood."

She waits, but when he doesn't respond, she glances at him. He
looks stricken.

"What do you mean?"

"Well, I mean that I just feel bad about what happened. I want you
to know that I've been feeling horrible about how I acted that night.
What I did was extremely inappropriate, and I regret it deeply." Unexpectedly, her eyes sting, and she blinks back tears. "It was a very
regrettable impulse. I've never, never done anything like that before!

I realize that it put you in a very uncomfortable position. There are words for what I did that I can't bring myself to use."

"Oh. But I don't feel bad about it! I don't! To tell the truth, I liked it."

His face is turned to the passenger side window; he sounds anguished. Just as she feared he would be. How can she ease out of this and leave his pride intact?

"Well, Jeff," she smiles and tries to strike an ironic or playful note. "I didn't say I didn't like it, you know. I said I felt bad about having done it because it was so inappropriate. And because I took advantage of our relationship and abused it."

He turns toward her. "You did like it, then?"

She looks away. "Yes, I said so."

"Is there any chance you'd ever want to do it again?"

"I'm sorry, Jeff, but this just wasn't right. Look, you're a very attractive young man and you seemed to be needing something then, and I guess I was in a weak moment and wasn't thinking very clearly or I wouldn't have done something so impulsive."

When she turns to look at him, his face is a gaunt oval giving back jaundiced light from the garage doors; his eyes glimmer damply, and he's staring at her.

"You think I'm just a kid."

"Jeff, you're a student. I'm a teacher. It's against the rules. If I were a student, too, maybe things would be different. I think you're a very sweet young man and lots of girls—"

"I'm not sweet!" His jaw trembles. "I said I liked what we did. I can't think about girls my age any more now. And I thought…. Oh, I don't know what I was thinking. Stupid, it was all stupid. I just don't want to be sweet any more. I liked what we did, I liked it a lot. I've thought about it a lot since then."

"I'm sorry."

"I just thought, well…" His shoulders jerk upward convulsively, approximating a shrug. His jaw wags once but no sound comes out his mouth; he might be drowning but is unable to yell for help. "Just, you know—"

"Oh, Jeff! Don't worry! Really! It's okay. Some girl, some really nice girl is going to be a little less shy than you are, soon, believe me. It just takes time. You're such a good-looking kid, so many girls out there, all they do is take one look and you make them melt, I know. You've just got to see how desirable you are."

"If I'm so desirable, why don't you want me?"

"Jeff, this isn't the point. I—"

"But did you want me?"

"Jeff, I think you should go in now."

"Before I make you puke?"

She refuses to be moved by the sight of his wet cheeks. "Now you do sound like a kid, Jeff," she says gently.

"I just wish you'd tell me one thing, Susan."

Against her will, she asks, "What?" when he doesn't continue.

"Why did you kiss me?"

Hasn't she already answered this? "Maybe because I felt like a big sister, or a mother."

"My mother never kissed me *that* way!"

"No, of course not. Maybe I was a little drunk, too, and the story you told me about what happened at your old school touched me, made my heart go out to you."

"You French-kissed me! Was that for my own good? Was that just to make me feel better?"

His unexpected boldness strikes her dumb.

"At least be honest with me, okay?"

"Jeff, I don't know what to say that I haven't already said. I'm sorry for what I did. There was something about the moment, about you, that moved me, you see?" She gives him the smile—coy, apologetic, playful—that women give men when they ask to be excused without being comprehended: *I'm too stupid to understand, let alone explain, myself.* "It was, well, thoughtless."

They fall silent and stare through the windshield at the blank yellow wall. She restrains an impulse to shut off the engine. Why *did* she kiss him? Certainly not to wind up engaged in a sex act, as the newspapers would say. His youth conveyed the possibility of a tender nongenital sensual contact, that was all. And she had moved—gravitated might be a better way to put it—toward that like a cat chooses to lie in the chair you've just vacated because the cushion is warm. She had basked in his gaze, enjoyed his regard, his attention—yes, maybe she had realized that she could arouse him, and maybe that too was appealing. And it was nice to be aroused, to feel desirable—the innocence of it had had a rich but distant familiarity. The instant she had kissed him she had felt more alive, more awake somehow, than she had in months—was it the danger?

"Did you think of what it would do to me?"

"No. I said it was thoughtless."

She presses the brake, moves the shift lever into Reverse; the car humps convulsively in place like a cat coughing up a hair ball, and a halo of soft light bathes the back of his head.

"Oh, man I can't believe this," he whispers. His jaw is clenched and his lips quiver. She thinks he might burst into tears. She can say *I'm sorry!* again but it'll only be to extort forgiveness, and accepting the brunt of his injury without further comment seems the least she can pay for her folly.

He yanks his book bag from the floorboard then clutches it in his lap.

"Shit!" he bursts out. "Man, I had champagne and flowers and everything…"

A wild flurry of motion startles her as he grabs his door handle, jerks it, bumps the door open, and clambers out of the car, leaving the door yawning open on its hinges; he stumbles headlong as if half-blind toward the gate, fumbles with the latch, opens it then flings the door to behind him. It bounces once against the sluggish lock and creaks slowly away from the frame. Through the crack she sees a slice of a glimmering blue pool, ghostly ominous shadows of shrubs. A darkened wing of the house.

Probably best to let him work it out alone. Let his pal console him. She sits frozen for a moment, then stretches across the passenger seat to close his door. Upright again, she lifts her foot from the brake, checks the rearview mirror. Her backup lights conjure up a growing redwood wall behind her, then she swings forward and drives toward the mouth of the alley. Relieved, but uneasy: she has done her part!

But champagne and flowers? For God's sake! He planned a seduction!?

If so, then…If so, then this trip to his friend's house has been part of the plan. Going inside to look at the mother's paintings! Good God!

It also means that Jeff's alone here.

Fear washes over her, and for the first time since kissing him she's shaken by the possibility that what she initiated so thoughtlessly could easily rocket to an uncontrollable and unfortunate conclusion. These kids are so stormy, so unpredictable, so impulsive.

And Plano is the teen suicide capital of the nation!

She can't leave without reassuring herself that Jeff can accept this rejection. She's got to do more, because she failed to let him down easy and leave him with his pride intact, as Holly advised her.

She u-turns in the wide boulevard, heads back up the alley and parks the car before the four garage doors. Leaving her purse in the driver's seat, she locks the car then steps to the gate and pushes it full open to disclose the pool and the rear of the house. As she presumed, the house appears to be empty, the windows darkened. Her breath condenses in the chilly air. A large patio attached to the house is enclosed in glass and abuts the far end of the pool; inside it, a light cocked toward the wall illuminates a wrought-iron table and chairs, large potted plants that give off shadows.

She spies a cottage apart from the house on the opposite side of the pool. Lights burn in the windows, and shadows move across the blinds. She treads softly around the pool and across the narrow strip of lawn to the cottage, where she stands at the door and peers through the glass.

Jeff sits on the bed with his head in his hands. Candles burn behind hoods of glass on a dresser. She knocks, his head swings up, mouth open, in surprise, then he hurries to the door.

His eyes are red, but he's smiling. Instantly she sees that he misunderstands her motive in following him.

"Jeff, I want to talk to you. I can't leave you like this. I was worried."

He nods, steps back, and she slips over the threshold. When he closes the door behind her, he says, "I'm glad you came. I was really acting like a dork. I'm not a baby, Susan. I owe you an apology for my behavior." He sighs. "I really had things sort of built up, you know?"

He smiles bravely and, doing his best to imitate an adult host, gestures toward a low-slung leather chair. Susan sits on the edge of it, her knees cocked high. A door to somewhere, another room? Two black windows like square jack-o-lantern eyes along the back wall. On another wall an amateur's watercolor seascape, no doubt the mother's. Posters, a stereo-set, speakers mounted in the corners, a headless camera tripod, an oak "entertainment center" with a TV, shelves of video cassettes and Nintendo cartridges, a desk—this is obviously his friend's lair, borrowed for the evening.

He follows her gaze to the desk and blushes. On it—a silver ice bucket with a green bottle's neck erect above the rim, a slender upright vase rising to a bursting ruby spray of roses, a dozen most likely.

"See?" He rotates, gesturing. Then he grins. "I even cleaned the bathroom."

She smiles. Is she wrong or does he seem a little, well, relieved? He steps over to the shelving holding the sound equipment and, grinning over his shoulder, picks up a CD, waves it. "Chopin, too. And Schubert. Your stuff." He nods toward the desk. "There's a fridge under there. I got this special cheese," he says sadly. Then he brightens. "Would you like some? It's that kind you like that you had at your party."

"No thanks."

"There's diet Coke. Todd won't drink anything but Pepsi, but I knew you didn't like it."

"Oh, God, Jeff! Some day, some girl!"

He slips the silver disc into the player. "I wish you'd quit saying that," he murmurs.

"But it's true! And I'm touched that you went to all this trouble. Everything's right, Jeff!"

Now he gives her a searing look. "Except for one minor detail."

He eases down onto the bed near her chair, forearms on his thighs, staring into the gap between his knees. Bruised again. But otherwise he seems less upset here than in the car. She'd gently chide him for his self-pity if she weren't so afraid of it. The faint piano music softens her agitation into melancholy.

"Do you want me to take you home?"

Her wording is unfortunate—sounds like something a mother would say to a misbehaving child. His head swings up, and his look says *you don't need to coddle me.*

"No, I'll stay here."

"Will you be okay?"

"Sure." He holds his palms up as if to read his lifelines, then lays his face into them; he seems to press hard; his right heel jitters restlessly against the carpet.

She stands, wanting to leave, then sits beside him on the bed, taking care not to touch him.

"I'd be glad to take you home, Jeff. You might feel better there."

He raises his head. His eyes are red and damp, but when he speaks his voice is clear. "No, really. I'll be okay, Susan. I know you've got to go. The thing is, though, see, I have to tell you the rest."

"The rest?"

"Stuff I was going to say." He expels a huge, ragged sigh. "Like I know I'm just a kid and you're married and I'm a student and you're a teacher. And maybe when you were my age or in college you had lots of guys who were probably crazy about you. You're probably used to having guys fall all over themselves, I realize that."

"No. Your feelings for me are very special, Jeff."

"Okay, maybe so, maybe not. I know you don't want me to feel bad. I just want you to know that nobody, *nobody* has ever thought about you as much as I have! It's all I do. I have this picture of you in last year's annual? I stare and stare at it. And you thought that I wasn't coming around to see you since you kissed me at your party? I wasn't exactly hiding. I was sort of watching you come and go but I didn't want to embarrass you or myself by hanging around like some dork." He sighed. "God! You're so damned beautiful!"

She sits uncomfortably stiff, not knowing how to respond. Somewhere deep within is a muted hum, a slight vibration, an oddly electric thrill, as if she were fourteen and has never been in this situation before—though has dreamed of it—and is skittish, alert, half-alarmed but also pleased and excited. She wishes he'd stop jiggling his foot; it makes the bed tremble. Curt has these fidgets, too. It's in their genes.

"Thank you," she says finally. From somewhere far away a siren curls over the suburb like a finger of smoke. She hears the metal ticking of a furnace, then a blower rumbles on and smothers sounds from the street. She observes with detachment as he bends toward her hand that is flat on her thigh and, with his fingertips, gently strokes the skin on the back of it.

"God, you're so so beautiful!" he whispers. "Can I see your hand up close?" She shivers, then swallows. Very gently, he takes it. A priceless bracelet, perhaps, the salesclerk standing by observant while the customer drapes the final gold strands over his own palm, stroking the fabric-soft metallic strand.

"Your fingers are really beautiful!" His warm breath brushes her palm. The sensation of his fingertips stroking her lifeline shoots right to the center of her lap. He bends closer as if to inhale a fragrance and softly kisses the heel of her thumb. Her mouth comes open but a word catches in her throat.

"I know you probably think that I haven't been doing my art work, but I have. I've been drawing a portrait of you." He looks up into her face and smiles. He's obviously so ecstatic to have her here this way that he seems about to swoon. "But I've had to use that photo in the annual or try from memory. Do you remember when you modeled for me that day at the lake?"

Susan feels her cheeks burn. "Yes."

"God, you were so beautiful! You are so beautiful! I think maybe that was the happiest day of my life!"

Gently she pulls her hand out of his lap. "Oh, Jeff! I'm sorry you think that's true."

"But why?"

She looks to the back wall of the room, the squared black blank windows. She shrugs; it's impossible to explain this without hurting him.

He takes her hand again. Her arm is limp, paralyzed. Her hand is like a detached object that she has passed to him, a borrowed thing. Every time she turns to look at him his face is beaming in admiration, adoration, his eyes round with awe; she feels oddly hypnotized by this adoring gaze, as if it is a tangible connection that requires her to pose as a model of whatever perfection the gaze is both perceiving and requiring. His sweetness, his gentleness, this *awe* of her!

She turns forward and feels his eyes on her profile. Then his heated face presses into her neck.

"So beautiful," he murmurs against her throat. "Help me to draw you, please? I know this will be the last time you'll let me get close to you. I know it's wrong, and I know you're a good person. But we're here now, together. Let me see what I'm trying to draw. Help me. Please?"

His hand slides softly and slowly to the lapel of her blazer and bends it back from her throat. She whispers, "Jeffrey," and leans away, but he presses forward. "Please! I'll never bother you again, I promise!"

He tugs gently on the blazer so that it's off her shoulders, pinning her arms, and he then traces the muscle from her neck across her bare flesh. "So beautiful! I can't believe how beautiful you are!" Then she feels the heat of his open mouth as he kisses her there. A voice says: *Stop this, right now!* But she's paralyzed, mesmerized. Her will is engrossed in the slow churn of her blood, watching it stir and bubble and steep…Yet meanwhile, his will has risen: where does he get this ability to insist, the sheer courage? The maleness of it is a wonder.

With his mouth and fingers he learns to draw her shoulder; he learns to draw the hollow of her throat under her jaw when she tilts back her head to give him access. She opens her eyes and feels dizzy. She props herself on her arms and her elbows quiver. Then she is slowly melting back on the bed. On the ceiling, a puzzle of acoustical tile. She can't bring herself to be a partner to this, can't lead or guide him. But she can let it happen if it will. For now she is only the sentient thing under close observation, trembling, allowing the exploration as he studies her bared midriff with those same soft tools of measurement, the fleshy tender calipers, the wet probe making its way millimeter at a time over her form. A firm tug on a waistband, a muted puht! of a button freed.

When she closes her eyes, there appears a stream flowing through a valley that is lush, green and pristine; the untouched meadows lie open and unprotected, the grass waving in the wind; a buck comes down to feed, nibbling on tender shoots, and the mouth of the animal leads the sleek brown body slowly to the water's edge, where it laps, gratefully, to its fill.

⤜21⤝

$\mathcal{A}$t midnight, Susan checks her gas gauge while pulling out of the alley behind Todd's house. She'll risk driving home nonstop even though she's afraid of having to call Curt if she runs out. Getting home—she needs it, desperately; she dreads it, terribly.

Is Curt worried? Should she stop and call? She pictures him in the TV room, watching David Letterman, drinking a diet Coke and eating microwave popcorn.

Curt, in the meantime, working on his seventh beer, is nowhere near home himself; he's standing in the doorway of Phillip's refrigerator, blinded by the light from within, trying to recall why he opened it. Came to get something for himself and somebody else at the table. He looks up, to think, and his eye makes a wobbly landing on a kitchen clock. Midnight. Susan's probably home now, has been for awhile. Should he call? Is she worried? He pictures her lying in their bed, reading, or lounging in the TV room watching David Letterman and drinking a caffeine-free diet Coke. He wishes he were already there, at home. The image of her lounging on the sofa in her sweats is appealing. He stretches out with his head in her lap.

If he calls, though, she'll probably figure out that he's been smoking cigars, drinking too much beer, and (the biggie) consequently dropping a hundred bucks in just two hours, lousy lousy cards. Yeah, she's gonna know sooner or later, he won't hide it, but no point in giving it away before he has to.

Susan and Curt—each envisions the other already at home. So, now, in their TV room, two ghosts of the couple, their imagined creations, watch David Letterman, sunk into a soporific domestic bliss. You might call them the "caretaker" couple because they serve to preserve the union itself. They are the faithful ones. Curt's imagined Susan does not lie to him, and Susan's imagined Curt does not lie to her. The caretaker couple has scruples and upholds the integrity of the relationship, while the actual Susan and Curt are liars. It's important to Curt that Susan will be home waiting and will punish him for his transgression; it assures him that the reins of their relationship are still held in someone's hands, if not his own. Likewise, it's important to Susan that Curt will be sitting on the sofa munching popcorn and will interrogate her when she arrives home late, after being unfaithful. It reassures her that Curt, at least, still has his funds in the bank of their union. (If they both withdraw their deposits, the bank will fold, of course.)

The ghostly caretakers are like parents quietly maintaining hearth and home while the errant adolescents rebel against the constraints of parental rule. The actual Curt and Susan will feel betrayed if both arrive home late simultaneously; each will discover that the other was not fulfilling the tacit agreement to relationship-sit while the other was out for the evening.

Curt arrives home first. Not finding Susan's car in the driveway, he experiences, almost simultaneously: 1) relief that he won't have to reveal where he was unless he wants to; 2) irritation that she won't be curled on that sofa waiting for him; and 3) concern for her welfare and safety. Within the next several minutes, each emotion will return like a musical theme to be developed with variations, but first he's very busy: he tosses his smoke-drenched clothes into the washer, jumps into the shower, leaps out, brushes his teeth, puts on a clean t-shirt and shorts, socks and moccasins, ducks into his terrycloth robe, and clicks on the TV, then he goes downstairs thinking he's gotten away clean and is rooting around in the refrigerator and also wondering whether he should call the police, when he hears her car door slam. Relief in a new key, then anger (what right to make him worry?), then a below-C pedal tone of fear: what if she came home earlier? What if she's been calling to let him know she's late? Is there time to check the machine?

Susan sees Curt's car as she expected. Her feelings are less complicated, though stronger: guilt over her infidelity, guilt over the lies she's about to tell, shame for knowing in advance that she'll lie.

When she comes up the stairs and into the TV room, there he is just as she imagined he would be, though without the popcorn. His hair is wet. Just showered—then he just got home?

"Hi, Babe," he says. "I was worried about you."

"Sorry I didn't call. I had to take a bunch of kids home after the meeting and they all live way to hell and gone." She considers adding the names of far-flung suburbs but fears it will sound like overkill.

They smile at each other uncertainly. Perhaps their inventions are not skillful enough to hide minute nuances of body language that can be detected by receivers fine-tuned by the years of cohabitation. So each has his or her suspicions about how the other spent the evening; each is reluctant to make an issue of this, though, for the obvious reason that any attack can boomerang.

Testing the waters, Curt says, "I wound up over at Phillip's with Barry and Michael and Rick."

The volunteered information makes her nervous, as it tacitly calls for reciprocation, so she goes on the offensive.

"What'd you boys do?"

"Watch football."

"It's Tuesday night."

Curt looks panicky, and she regrets having pinned him down.

"ESPN," he adds after a moment. "Phillip's got cable. Canadian football."

"Nice," she says, smiling. "Well, I'm beat. I'm going to shower."

Susan shuts the bathroom door, locks it on second thought, and begins the tedious nightly ritual with a Cetaphil wash of her face before getting into the shower to scrub away the evidence of her liaison with Jeff. Because she really doesn't like to go to bed with wet hair, she showers at night only when she wants space from Curt. Before she steps under the water, she wonders if he will read her showering as a sign of anything. She stands outside while the water cascades against the shimmering curtain, shivering in her nudity, struck sad by the realization that now even something as natural and simple as taking a shower has been consumed by the voracious cancer of her deviousness. And so long as she keeps this secret from Curt, it will be a chasm between them filled with such questions as, *Will my taking a shower reveal more than I mean to?* And yet will things actually be "better" if she tells him?

Jeff kept saying she was "so beautiful." It makes her cringe now. Sometimes when he said it he wasn't looking at her or even in her direction; the true horror was not that he was mistaken about her looks but that the word was connected only to how he felt, to the sensations he was experiencing; and, beyond that, not how he felt about her, the real Susan, but the adored one he has invented and has such a crush on. When she replays his gushing, "Oh, God, you're so beautiful!" she hears only an expression of his infatuation entirely unrelated to any aspect of her actual person. It is iconography, fetishism.

There is such disparity between her feeling for him (or for herself!) and this rhapsodic outpouring of praise that it gives her an uncomfortable insight into the lives of movie stars and their difficult relationships with obsessive fans, some of whom—and it's frightening to remember this—murder the adored object when their attentions are spurned.

She has aroused in him just the sort of grand passion and consuming, burning "love" that, by legend at least, women imagine it would be gratifying to inspire. Seeing the first signs of it in an admirer, a woman might be inclined to stoke the fires, give the coals a little huff of her breath, and so aggrandize herself still further in his estimation, see herself grow larger and more potent in his eyes.

But all she sees in her mirror is a trashy whore. If she were a man maybe she'd think *sly dog!* But she's not, so she just feels crummy and defensive and dirty. And very very sad.

Oh, Curt! Why did I do this to you? To me? To us? To Jeff!

⟨22⟩

*J*eff lay awake most of the night, brain stewing in hot juices, but when Todd comes in at seven, he's lapsed into a coma with his clothes on and has to be shaken back to life.

"Well?" Todd grins.

Jeff tries to play it cool but his lips curl into a smirk.

"Mission accomplished."

Todd pokes around the room, sniffing for clues. He heaves up the wet green bottle from the silver bucket like an angler showing off a catch; the soggy label has slipped off-center and is torn, but the cork is still wired down, holding in the pressure.

"What kind of hot babe is she? Is this too cheap for her taste?"

Jeff yawns. "To tell the truth, we didn't have time for it. We never got around to it."

He drags through the school day numb with fatigue and his mind knocked askew as if from a pleasant concussion. English, Algebra II, World History—what did they have to do with anything now?

Mixing among the children in the halls makes him feel he's been flunked back to grammar school. The only subject that interests him even remotely is Jeff's Experience 101. He itches to see Susan again, but when he checks his appearance in the bathroom mirror—the same rumpled clothes from yesterday, his cowlick a truculently erect finger of hair, his eyes raw red, the lids swollen—he's afraid she'll take one look and regret even knowing his name. Since he has no idea how or why he's been so lucky, there's no way to assess his strengths: flukish chance, being in the right time at the right place, what? So he can only spoil whatever appeal he has by walking up to her office and seeing her. The context alone might scare her now.

She is absent on Thursday. That night, after an hour of agonizing hesitation, he calls her apartment. A man—her husband?—answers. He almost hangs up, but instead forces himself to say that he's one of her students and he wanted to ask her today whether there'd be a club meeting next Tuesday night, but she was absent.

"A touch of the flu," says the male voice. "She should be back to-morrow."

The guy wouldn't sound quite so knowing if he, like, *knew.* "Oh, I'm sorry to hear she's sick. Please tell her I hope she gets to feeling better. It's Jeff, my name is Jeff."

On Friday he combs his hair five times in the restroom, takes ten deep, slow breaths before walking past her office after the last bell rings. Her door is open, but Ms. Calco is with her. Susan has her back to the hall. Her black slacks are tight on her hips and hint at hollows and curves underneath. He's been there—it seems a marvel to him now; it seems remote and impossible, as if she were now another person entirely and this so-called memory is only a wet-dream he confuses with life.

He leans with one foot up flat against the wall and apes the ennui of a student waiting for a conference, willing her to turn around. He's prepared to outwait the other teacher but his confidence is housed in a container that begins to leak as the minutes crawl by. Should he leave then come back later? No: he'll miss her.

Ms. Calco spots him first. She flashes him an inexplicably peculiar smile, murmurs to Susan. Susan twists about with her feet still in place, smiles like a hostess.

"Oh, hello, Jeff! How can I help you?"

The impersonality rattles him, but circumstances justify if not excuse it. He leans forward until his head is across the threshold. "I was wondering if we're still having our meeting Tuesday night?" When something dark crosses her face, he rushes on. "The party, the last club meeting party?"

"Yes."

"Well, should I bring something?"

"If you like."

Then they wait motionless, watching him, as if they've been speaking to one another on the telephone before he interrupted. He can read their body language (have they been talking about him?), but can't resist holding the tether of their attention long enough to let her know that he's been thinking of her.

"I hope you're feeling okay now."

Ms. Calco and she exchange a darting glance. Susan says, "Much better. Thank you," but she isn't looking at him.

"I'm glad. Well, see you then."

Saturday he goes shopping for Christmas presents. From money he got from his grandparents, he buys his Dad a mileage gadget at Brookstone and he gets Sybil perfume at Dillard's. His mom is harder to shop for; he usually saves her for last because it requires his undivided attention, and he usually gets her several small items. But this year he wedges her into the same trip and finds furry house slippers and a book of illustrated Bible stories she can use for her Sunday school class. Are these enough? Short-changing her on his attention nags at him. He wanted to leave himself sufficient time to dig into the richly engrossing but anxiety-provoking task of finding the right present for Susan, and having sacrificed some of his mother's time for that bites at his conscience. He promises that when school's out for the holidays, he'll come again solely for his mom.

The present for Susan seems more urgent, as if she's a fleeting phenomenon or plans to be elsewhere for Christmas. He has to come up with something to knock her back, really open her eyes. He has mentally catalogued her taste in perfume, jewelry, accessories, music, books, and (of course) art and has scanned the inventory many times in search of something suitable and affordable yet still impressive, but everything seems so woefully ordinary that it leaves this huge gap between what he wants the gift to make her feel and his fear it wouldn't work. He yearns to give her lingerie but can't bring himself to buy it.

Sunday he wins back his conscience by asking his mother to help him bake cookies for the club's Christmas party Tuesday night. She says she'll be happy to do it for him, but he insists they do it together. They make a special trip to the store then spend the afternoon as companionable coworkers. The aroma of browning cookies billows in the oven-warmed kitchen, and he sits at the table eating the raw dough off the sides of the bowl with a rubber spatula while his mother drinks coffee. He feels charitable toward her, appreciative. He sees that she is a woman, not merely a mother. Furthermore, she's a woman with a limited life and reduced possibilities, and he sorrows for her. He can tell she loves having his attention; her appreciation of that inspires his generosity. He knows if he gives her enough of it she'll reward him by a compliment, and true to her nature, while they're boxing the cookies (leaving the broken or misshapen ones for themselves), she says, "Jeffie, I'm proud of you, you know that? You are so many things your father isn't."

Tuesday night, at the party, there are so many cakes and chips and dip to eat that he frets Susan won't try his home-made cookies, so he ties one in a bow and presents it to her. "I made it myself!" Looking elsewhere, she bites into it. "Very good!" she claims, though it might be praise given to a fourth-grader. He yearns to have her to himself and talk; he longs to know the answer to the question branded into the gray matter of his cerebrum that night exactly one week ago: will it happen again? Is what we did the start or end of something?

She doesn't exactly avoid him, but neither does she engineer an opportunity to be alone. Well, he understands how discretion is required—he can be as cool as the next person. In fact, acting cool when in truth there is a web of pleasures and impossibly rich emotions invisible as gamma rays crisscrossing in the air between you—this is a pleasure in and of itself, this special knowing. He keeps watchful and hopeful, aiming his gaze near her face in case she looks his way and he can send out a fine tentacle of recognition unseen by others. But she's so good at this that her awareness of him shows only in her not looking; her glance goes everywhere except to the vacuum in which he stands. He forms the hub; she's the ever-circling rim.

So he ducks out a little early and hangs around the parking lot in the darkness. When she eventually emerges from the building, he steps out from behind a car. She jumps, yelps.

"I'm sorry!"

"I wasn't expecting you, Jeff."

"Can I talk to you? Could we go home together?"

She looks back into the building. "I'm taking some other kids home tonight. They'll be along in a second. I was just coming out to the car to get a box to put things in. You can join us if you like."

His heart falls. "Oh, that's okay. I'll call my Mom or my Dad."

Her face is in the shadows. It makes him uneasy that he can't see her eyes. "Is there any way we could, like, talk sometime soon?"

He hears her sigh. "Jeff..." she whispers. "Jeff, this won't do. I'm sorry. I've done a lot of thinking these past few days. I don't know why I let it happen, I really don't. But what I do know now is that it was some sign, you see? I mean it was a signal like an alarm that something is *terribly wrong* with my life. I just can't let myself blunder on without first trying to understand why I would do such a thing to you or to me or to Curt. What I did doesn't make sense to me, and until it does, I just can't let this happen again. I have too much to lose. You understand? It's not you. It's the situation. I'm very sorry, but you and I can never be alone together again. Do you understand?"

"Yeah. I guess."

Something in his tone offends her, he sees too late. "Don't feel sorry for yourself or sulk, Jeff! It's not becoming at all!"

"I'm sorry. It's just that you're so beautiful and I—"

"Shhh!" She puts her finger to her lips and leans toward him, and her lovely face materializes in the soft light. "Now, none of that!" One corner of her mouth turns up—she's wryly wise to him but heart-warmed, too—and he feels reprieved.

"Jeff, some day—"

The double doors to the building crash back against the wall as a flock of students bursts out, and the prediction, or prophecy—or is it a promise?—is never uttered; instead, she murmurs, "I have to go," and steps away to her car.

All night he worries her words, twisting and pulling them like taffy into all the conceivable shapes they might take. They can be endlessly debated and interpreted, but the polarities are:

1) There is no hope.

2) There is hope.

As the sleepless hours speed on, he nurtures the possibilities for a future with all the desperation of building an elaborate argument on top of a shaky premise.

She has to stop—*but only temporarily.*

She cannot do this again—*for now.*

She needs time to think—*and then she can return to him.*

Some day—*she'll be ready to resume.*

After school, he naps and wakes when Todd calls to insist that he go to Klub Video about nine: Wednesday night is weekly "amateur" night, and they're in the habit of going every month or so just for campy laughs. His mom is working late on this Wednesday as usual and will go directly to church from her office, so he fixes himself a sandwich.

Groggy, he perks coffee, and, while he's drinking his first cup, he has an inspiration. He understands that it's very important not to make a nuisance of himself while Susan is in her necessary cooling-off mode, but he can do something to keep her thinking of him in a special way. He turns over in his mind the possibilities for a definitive gift for Christmas, then, at last, he realizes that nothing *purchased* will work.

From there it's only a hop to this: the portrait that he claimed he's begun a few weeks ago will be the perfect gift, the one he claimed he needed her to model for. Okay, so he's not the world's greatest artist, but he's good enough (he's a lot better than he was when he started!), and he'll put in hours and hours of work until he gets it right, make up for what he lacks in experience by using elbow grease, as his mother puts it, and the inspiration born of love. The way he feels about her: that's got to count for something, too, doesn't it? If he pours his passion, his soul, into the drawing, isn't that what art is all about? Won't the love he feels for her guide his clumsy hand, compensate for his inexperience?

He copped last year's annual out of the library earlier in the semester so that Todd could peruse the photos and pick out somebody for Jeff to introduce him to. At his desk, he pulls it out and turns to the faculty pages. He's looked at this photo of Susan a thousand times; it's the size of a postage stamp. Her hair is shorter now. It isn't a good likeness; it doesn't do justice to her dimples, the complicated, sinuous curvature of her lips, and, of course, altogether fails to capture the stunning clarity of her gray-blue eyes. Even still, as he peers at it now, he goosebumps along his nape. *This* woman he lost his cherry to! *This* woman he kissed all over! He would die for this woman!

He sighs. He gets out his tools. He drifts off, mooning, then returns abruptly to himself, his desk, room, house. He feels all swoony from love and grief, and a painful erection strains against his jeans. The clock says fifteen minutes have gone by. Where was he? In a trance.

His right hand holds a drawing pencil. Under his elbows on the desk is a piece of sketch paper, heavy and expensive, about eighteen by twenty-four inches. It glows under the white light from the desk lamp. Big gum eraser in his left hand; the pencil and eraser are poised for use, like a knife and fork.

The big white space produces the blankness you get in your mind if somebody points at you out of nowhere to say: "Quick, what's the square root of 144?" That panic surrounding a void, a vacuum where nothing will sprout.

What if you fuck it up?

That's what the eraser's for, stupid.

Maybe he should wait until he finds more snapshots?

No—he can't spare the time. Today's the twelfth—thirteen shopping days until Christmas, but only a week until school lets out and he won't see her. So he has to finish this right away. Finish it quick as he can and get it to her before something happens, before she…

Okay, just draw, goddamnit! Try one out. There's a dozen sheets of paper and a lot more where they came from, okay?

He looks at the photo. He recalls now that there's a system for this, beginning with the head shape rendered onto the page, like a large oval or circle, depending. Susan's face is a basic oval with the sides squeezed in a bit. You draw the big oval on the page, then the cross-hairs sort of deal to position the eyes, nose.

He works on the large oval, drawing, erasing, drawing, erasing, until he believes he's gotten the basic shape of her face. The photo shows her bangs short and evenly combed across her forehead; now, though, they're so long they fall into her eyes unless she pins them back. The shape of the top of her head in the photo, then, is what you might call out of date. The woman he loves, the woman he made love to, came to life after the one in the photo. The Susan who sat for the yearbook snapshot is the pre-Jeff Susan and thus seems, with those short bangs and the squint, a stranger.

What he wants to capture is his own Susan, the post-Jeff Susan. Labor of love. He sets his pencil to the pad along the upper curve, stroking the page in a effort to draw how her hair falls down from the pole of the oval and hangs over her forehead, thinking, as he does, of touching her cool soft hair with his fingers, then he moves on to her cheeks, his pencil struggling, clumsily, to go the right way, to make the right lines, marks—it's a little like being blind: invisible on the page is the ideally executed portrait of this beautiful woman he adores and it's his task to discover where those ideal lines lie by copying over them, though, being blind, he won't know when he has found them. Other people will, however, and that doesn't seem fair. He won't show the portrait to anyone but her, but of course if she has it in her possession he can't control who sees it. Will it seem "true" to her? Or does the fact that she's the subject mean that she, too, will be blind the way he is? Like how you look in a mirror and don't see the same person everyone else sees. This weird "blindness" is frustrating. Does every artist feel this?

Blindness. Braille, he thinks. The pencil stroking the page in an effort to discover the invisible line underneath, and his finger tracing over her cheek, through her hair, her earlobe, her jaw line, her lips. When he's trying to draw Susan his pencil is like a finger of love impressing on the page his feelings for her, just as when he touched her he wanted to imprint upon her actual flesh a code of his love, let her skin and flesh absorb the message so that it is, well, inescapable for her, undeniable. And must then be accepted.

Yet the awkwardness of his pencil hand makes him grieve with frustration: the distance between his conception of the portrait and his execution is like the distance between his love for her and his fear that it won't be enough to hold her.

He peers at the little snapshot; it draws him closer, inviting him to scrutinize the details on a larger scale, and as he leans into the tiny square on the page, the snapshot's borders widen, making a window that expands as he leans still farther, then the window is like a door into a Susan-world and he crosses over the threshold as if into a dream, where he relives the very first time he saw her in the hallway. He thought she was so stunning and beautiful, and she looked so young, like an older student to him, or a student teacher, and he followed her down the halls for ten minutes, ducking behind the Coke machine near the auditorium, strolling fifteen paces behind with students between them right into the main office, where she went to the mail boxes and stuck her hand in a pigeonhole and that's how and when he knew she is faculty.

And that's why he went to the first club meeting. Oh and then such incredible luck that neither his Mom or his Dad picked him up, and it was raining, and she asked if he needed a ride...Then, in the rain in her car when she brought him home, then, later, kissing her mouth, her neck, her breasts, the fragrant nest between her thighs.

It's not you, Jeff, it's the situation. But what is the situation if not him and her? She must be afraid he's going to tell somebody or that they'll be caught. She said, *I've got too much to lose.*

As if he doesn't!

That stings. He has a world that can be lost: he has her to lose.

⁓23⁓

On her way to school the morning after her sin with Jeff, Susan stops by the Catholic church on Oak Lawn near the house. She's lived here in the neighborhood for a few years but has never set foot inside this church, though her mother walked to Mass one summer morning when she and Susan's father came to visit. Her mother had found the church altogether on her own without asking Susan for a recommendation; ever since Susan decided to live with Curt without benefit of wedlock her mother has not spoken to her about church-going.

When her mother returned from Mass that sunny summer morning, Susan felt obliged as a hostess to inquire about her mother's experience at Holy Trinity, as if she were responsible for it. Her mother said, matter-of-factly, "A lot of Spanish people."

Sanctuary, Susan is thinking now. Like where people go during revolutions to keep from being caught and killed. She remembers from her childhood the persistent rumor that priests have to take in the perpetrator of even the most heinous crime if he asks for it.

Forgive me, Father.

This isn't going to be easy. The last time she went to confession? She was in high school. She and Nathan—

"May I help you?" asks an older woman, who might be a nun to judge by her shiny, makeup-free skin, plastic-framed spectacles and gray smock. Susan has entered the door nearest the parking lot and finds herself suddenly awash in screaming knee-high humans: she has blundered into the school wing, and her disconcerted expression must be a distress signal.

"Uh, well, I was looking for, uh, the sanctuary—"

"Up the hall and to the right."

Actually she's only looking for a bulletin board where a notice might be posted about hours for hearing confession, she wants to say, but the teacher/nun is quite busy herding kids into classrooms. Checking her watch, Susan sees she'll be late if she spends more than a couple more minutes here—of course, she can call later to inquire.

The children's uniforms, the omnipresent crucifixes, rocket her back to being a kid in St. Louis. Her first confession. She read about the saints and received instruction from elderly nuns whose lives were a tantalizing mystery to her. A collage of memories relating to her mother and the other women in the church. They stood behind tables to sell cakes and cookies; they went in a gaggle to visit nursing homes and hospitals; they consoled widows in their homes. Susan pictures them hugging one another, talking, all the while she and the hordes of children surge about their legs like whirling surf; the women's hands fly and flutter, touching and stroking one another, their children, the sick and lame they visit. They sat in a sewing circle repairing clothing to be given to the Salvation Army or Catholic Relief; they arranged flowers, they made coffee. She sees her mother and the other women of the church in almost any room of the building except for the sanctuary, where the priests held forth assisted mostly by boys, though nuns and lay women were allowed to dress the altar. She remembers her mother's "church" as a gathering of women talking to one another in the auditorium where people played Bingo and put on the Christmas and Easter pageants, in the kitchen where food was prepared, in the classrooms and dressing rooms.

Her father often said, "Wild horses couldn't get me into a church!" He called himself a "Transcendental Pantheist" sometimes and at other times a "Universalist Agnostic." He disdained meeting in a preordained place and time to worship. He said, "I can worship my God any time I want to in a better place." Where was it? "Everywhere," he said.

In college she believed that her father's notion of religion was far more sophisticated than her mother's, and preferable to it. She could picture her father walking alone in the woods and communing with Nature or staring up at the stars on a cold clear winter night and having a private but meaningful conversation with, say, the Emersonian Oversoul (not an old white man with bulging veins in his forehead and a big white beard!). He gave her the impression that "true" religion consisted of a man's using his mind to confront the enigma of the cosmos and to appreciate the structure of the mystery, the scope and cleverness of it all: God was a creator whose creation was to be "read" or "heard" or "seen" the way critics admire and judge masterpieces of literature, music, or art. Above all, it was a profoundly private experience best had in solitude, akin to a one-man crossing of the Atlantic. You might invite a gaggle of cake-baking women aboard to see you off or greet you when you landed, but you would not want them along for the journey.

But by her junior year it dawned on Susan that her father never went walking in the woods alone or pondered the stars on a clear, cold winter's night. Such a night would generally find him in his study—since it was the half-redone attic room, the house heat rose to it—now and then hollering downstairs for her mother to bring him tea or hot chocolate. And then she concluded that his "religion" all too conveniently matched his character and temperament—it cost him nothing.

She's about to abandon her search for information when she finds what she's looking for: the bulletin board near the Oak Lawn entrance. While she stands scanning it, she catches a glimpse of someone in black passing behind her and she freezes in fear the priest will speak to her—though of course if he were to, she could establish a footing. Against her will, her gaze clicks right just as the priest—a young Hispanic fellow—turns to enter a door within arm's reach of the bulletin board.

"Good morning!"

"Morning, Father," she says, eyes averted, as he disappears.

There. That wasn't so hard!

Confessions can be heard weekdays on Wednesday evenings, by Father Montejano, says here. Was that he?

On her way back to her car, she imagines seeing him through the scrim, the grill. *And when was your last confession?*

Uh. Over ten years. *Over ten years!*

When she and Nathan first started dating, they'd do what her mother might call "heavy petting," but the prohibition against going all the way was too strong in her to surrender early on to his begging and pleading. He was a great kisser and made her hot, yes, but Sister Catherine's voice went *tsk-tsk* in her head and when she closed her eyes she saw the big nun's wagging finger and the frown. But then she sank deeply and madly in love with him, and her love seemed more holy in her heart than anything she'd ever felt inside a church. Once he said, "I love you, Suzie," then her resistance to giving in was only brief, mostly *institutional*, you could say (pregnancy notwithstanding), and in the end she recognized that the only arguments she had to counter Nathan's own came out of her mother's mouth. Naturally, that was enough to discredit them.

But she didn't go to confession the first Sunday following that first time, or the next. Or even a month later, she remembers now. No, there was a period like a honeymoon, when, once she'd given in, she and Nathan went at it fast and furiously for weeks like gleeful little gold-miners who'd stumbled onto a secret claim. She glowed for weeks, juices dripping, tissues swelling, panting and groping, and they used their fingers and tongues on each other in the most absurdly public settings. When they were enveloped in their cloud of love, anything and everything they did seemed *holy, holy, holy.* Sometimes, though, after they'd said goodnight and she lay awake alone in her bed going over what they'd done, she'd imagine someone, a nun or a friend of her mother's, saying that she was a tramp, a slut, that she *ought to be ashamed!* Her pulse would race and she'd clench her fists and make up angry speeches to defend herself. Doubt would seep into her anger. She'd curl up to make herself small and pull the sheet over her head.

Still, she didn't go to confession until the Sunday after the Saturday that Nathan said he needed more space. She can recall hurrying into the booth, ashamed but also half-hopeful that after doing penance and getting absolved, Nathan would be delivered back to her and they'd be together, but not as before, no, they'd be chaste, she would promise that, and, yes, oh God, she felt so horribly guilty and she realized now, Father, how the punishment for her sin was that Nathan no longer loved her, that if she hadn't *soiled the vessel of her precious womanhood* then he would still respect, love, value, treasure and cherish her.

Her penance was a few dozen Hail Marys. How many exactly she can't recall now, but it seemed a light sentence at the time, and she remembers how ardently she had wished for a tougher chore (such as climbing a mountain on her knees) to cleanse herself—because her confession, penance, and Act of Contrition didn't bring him back. He moved with his family to Chicago, and he never wrote.

She started college soon after and hoped that the disruption in her cycle—she had dried up and missed two periods—was purely the result of emotional distress. In the dorm a girl she barely knew said quinine and a super-hot bath would bring on her period again, if you're like late *for some reason.* The quinine made her ears rings horribly, but her flow came back, copious in volume and lasting three days longer than usual. She told herself that being upset and going off to school was why her periods had stopped. For a few days she walked with a light step; it was as if she'd had the flu and now she had been restored to health. She slept hard for three nights running as if it were an Olympic sport and woke almost yearning for a lumberjack's breakfast.

Then she realized that if she had been actually pregnant, she had induced a miscarriage. Inducing a miscarriage was another way of saying she'd given herself an abortion. So for a time she felt like a criminal and the voices of reproach came back and dogged her sleep. Now to them she was (or would be if she had really been pregnant) worse than a slut; she was (or would be if she had really been pregnant) a baby-killer. But she *wasn't.* She knew she *wasn't.* And for them to judge her, well she wouldn't set foot inside one of their effing churches now, not for any reason!

The person she most needed to talk about this with was unreachable. Her desperate epistles to Nathan about her feelings and her problem were lifted by the wings of the post and carried off to a netherworld. She lay in bed nights on end clenching her jaw and fists. His silence pumped her full of rage, and she didn't know how to slough it off, divert it. She stuffed it back, choked on it. She took enormous relish in picturing how his beat-up Impala would skid down an icy highway into the grill of an eighteen-wheeler. (But, naturally, no sooner would he be lying broken and bleeding in a ditch then along she would come by chance, rush him off to a hospital, sit by his bed through the night, and her anguished face would be the first thing his grateful survivor's gaze took in when he emerged from his coma.)

She comes to herself glaring at the bulletin board listing times for confession. Off to that mind-movie again. Sister McArthur always used to say you need to go to confession every week, to stay in practice, like on the piano—you don't wait until the night before a recital to rehearse, do you? Meaning—Susan sees now—that the ritual aspect in and of itself helps. (She understands it now because the prospect of coming back here this evening to a church she's never attended to speak to a priest she doesn't know about the sins *of a decade* is terribly daunting: and isn't staying away that long a kind of sin itself?) Longer you stay away from the keyboard, the harder it is to play the piece! Sister Mac said. And the sins pile up and up until you imagine you can't possibly get them off your chest!

How can she describe her sin with Jeff? Can she just say she had sex with a young man to whom she's not married and not have to say he's only seventeen and she's twenty-eight and he's one of her students? Oh, dear God, this is not a court of law! What good will it be to fudge?

Forgive me, Father, for I have sinned. I have committed adultery.

Except that she's not married.

I have lusted. I have lied. I have committed—how absurdly old-fashioned it sounds!—*fornication.*

24

Todd says Klub Video's a cool place on a school night because there aren't a lot of high school phonies claiming to be college students and using fake IDs. Weekends the place is always jammed with wanna-bes and nerds from the burbs, geeks and twits from little hick towns an hour's easy drive from Dallas on the Interstates.

On a Wednesday like this you're more likely to score with a college girl, somebody cool enough to have her own place, who won't go berserk if you ask her to buy you liquor and might have a stash of X.

No one mentions this; it's a tacit credo among them, and Todd arranged this visit presumably because he's on the prowl. For his own part, Jeff feels not the slightest need for persons or substances in those categories—on the contrary, he holds himself lightly, as if inwardly humming, as he and Todd and Chris and Paige stroll up Elm after parking; he's feeling a spiritual version of being well-fed. But his contentment has a slippery floor when he recalls her exact words last night. Sounded like good-bye, but the thing is—didn't she say all that before, more or less, after they only kissed? And didn't she wind up making love to him?

At the door they pay their two-dollar cover and breeze through the cursory check of doctored IDs. Todd seems antsy, gleefully mysterious to Jeff, and he leads them directly to a table near the huge video screen at the rear of the bar, where across the silvered expanse Janet Jackson and a group of dancers are miming a tune booming from the overhead speakers. The place is about half full, but the crowd is light compared to a weekend night. In a front corner is a DJ booth, though tonight the music's unassisted. A dozen couples on the dance floor work at what might be an aerobic routine if the setting were different. This isn't the best club for dancing—the house specialty is videos, professional and home-grown—so the hard-working semi-professional hopefuls sometimes use Klub Video's dance floor to rehearse routines they'll display at Club Barren in the West End on Saturday, when they engage in unofficial shoot-outs with other hopeful couples on the dance floor.

To Jeff it looks as if Todd has slim pickings tonight; every female in the place seems to be escorted save two girls with multi-colored spike do's and leather jackets who are sharing a cigarette at the bar. Pierced nipples, probably. He's seen these girls at Carver.

One cinder block wall plays canvas to a giant mural done by local artists that depicts in bold colors and a cartoonish style the fronts of clubs and cafes along Elm street and a cast of street characters. He's seen it dozens of times, but now he has new eyes, and the mistakes in perspective and design are apparent—two characters are lumpy forms obviously executed by someone other than the artist who did the storefronts. He should bring Susan here. Wouldn't it be a kick to have her sit with them? Total freak-out.

"What's so amusing?" Todd asks him.

"Huh?"

Todd's giving him back the same smirk he realizes he's been wearing. Paige has gone to the bar to get their drinks because the waitress on duty knows Todd.

"Uh, that mural. The perspective's fucked."

"Oh, wow," says Chris. "Jeff's become a Carver kid."

"An artiste," says Todd.

Jeff smiles serenely. They're children. "Fellows, one could do worse."

Paige comes back with Todd's Absolut on the rocks, Chris's Budweiser, Jeff's screwdriver, her own Miller Lite. She sets the tray on the table.

"That's the last trip I'm making, you guys. This is pure retrograde chauvinism. I'm not your handmaiden."

Todd says, "That mean you won't give any more hand jobs?"

No one laughs. Paige looks at Chris, who shifts his considerable weight, and says, "Todd."

"Okay, okay, I'm sorry, Paige," says Todd.

Apparently what Jeff said to Todd that Saturday afternoon about how to talk to girls didn't stick. It hardly matters, though. Jeff feels distant from these friends from his former life, as if he's only marking time before stepping ahead into a future that doesn't include them. His sense of himself as a future stranger increases when the other three spend the next twenty minutes talking about a science teacher new to Lakeview whom everyone hates with a passion that's positively inspirational to judge by their anecdotes about her bitchy behavior. To be courteous and because he hasn't heard the stories, Paige keeps including him through little verbal overtures - *God, you wouldn't believe this Jeff, but she...* or *Oh, Jesus, Chris, tell Jeff about how she....* To return the courtesy, Jeff tries to stay tuned in, but he soon drifts off to Susan. Aside from being his lover, she's a great teacher, he believes. And popular. He is *so* very glad he got kicked out of

Lakeview! It's the best thing that ever happened to him. Next-best thing.

Paige makes Chris get a second round, but Jeff's still sipping on his first. It makes him uneasy to be drinking on a school night because it's more likely his mother might detect it on his breath, though, really, she seems to have no sense of smell. He drinks screwdrivers because supposedly vodka can't be detected on your breath and because the orange juice makes the drink go down more easily.

When Chris returns with the drinks, Paige says, "Dance with me, Chris."

He and Todd turn to watch. Paige looks good; without those extra fifty pounds, her legs look longer and her pelvis has a sexy rock and she obviously studied the steps the dancers used on *In Living Color*.

"I like coming here on Wednesday nights," says Todd.

"Yeah?"

Todd smiles, half-turning. "You know whose videos are on tonight?"

"No."

"I'm surprised you didn't know, being a Carver artiste and all."

"Fuck you," Jeff says pleasantly.

Todd laughs. "As a matter of fact, I think there's going to be one that a Carver kid's starring in."

"That wouldn't be unusual, you know. They've got a whole film-making department and about fifty students walking down the halls all the time carrying video cameras. It's what we do, you know?"

"Hail to thee, Carver High School."

"Hey, give me a break, Todd! You guys don't know anything about the place! I sit here and listen to you guys bitch about this weirdo woman science teacher, and all I got to say is that I've been to both schools and you guys haven't, and I can tell you firsthand that my teachers are very excellent."

Todd smiles. "Well, that's not in dispute."

Paige and Chris return, huffing and sweating, and, once they've caught their breath, they argue about whether Chris can copy Paige's study questions in history. Jeff sneaks a look at his watch: ten-thirty. He's bored, wants to go home, where he can think about Susan and work on the portrait.

At the microphone, the manager is bending toward the metal head, his earring glinting in the light. He wears a t-shirt and a black leather vest with a cluster of slogan buttons posted on it.

"Tonight, as always, we're featuring the video talents of four local artists," he says without fanfare. "There's a big fat grand prize of twenty-five dollars"—here, everyone whistles and claps—"so use a wet cocktail napkin to record your vote on and drop it by the bar on your way out. The videos are by"—here, he raises an index card to the light—"Jim Baca with something called it looks like *Home On the Rain?* And the second is by Laurie Peterson: *Night In The City;* the third by Tom Swap is called *Boning Up For the Final;* and last is Becky Monday's *The Wheel Is Gonna Get Ya!*" Cheers shoot up in response to the last entry's announcement, and one of the Carver girls at the bar jokingly thumbs her nose at the nearby table of friends.

The first video is three minutes shot ostensibly during a rain, though the shower might have been made by a garden hose: the camera follows a leaf as it falls from a tree onto a rooftop, washes into the rain gutter and down the spout, then gushes across a driveway and into the curbing, where it speeds away in a tan rivulet and into a storm-sewer opening at the intersection. Mild applause, snickering at the table. Todd says, *"Formidable!"* and they all laugh. The second video is by two girls who took turns holding the camera on each other while they primp to go out. They begin in their bras and panties. They're both thirty to fifty pounds overweight. They mug lasciviously for the camera—lolling tongues along their newly painted lips, winking, pushing up their tits to plump up their already considerable cleavage—and at first it looks like they're poking fun at themselves, but then it looks like they only want people to think they're poking fun, that they really hope that underneath the mockery everybody'll think they're really sexy, the way guys, in trying to get a laugh by flexing like Arnold Schwarzenegger, really hope girls notice their muscles. But the piece has quick edits like a commercial and it seems intended to be funny, anyway, and not artsy-fartsy.

Chris says, "My favorite so far!"

Paige sneers. "Geez, I wonder why!"

When the third video comes up on the screen, the grainy black and white footage shows a blinking neon "Motel" sign, then cuts to an interior, two grainy figures seated side by side on a bed. A man and a woman. The man has his face buried in the woman's throat like a vampire.

"Hey!" exclaims Paige. Jeff shoots her a glance. Her face registers shock, and his gaze leaps after her own back to the screen. He recognizes the male now. The setting is Todd's bedroom.

If he had a gun he'd shoot Todd then and there.

"You asshole motherfucker!"

"What??" Todd protests, all innocence.

"Get your ass up there right now and tell that guy to take that tape off." He's trembling all over. Paige and Chris stare intently at him; none of the four is watching the screen.

"Okay, okay," Todd says, rising, his face white. He's no longer smirking. "It was just a joke, you know? I didn't really get much of the good stuff!"

When Todd scurries off to the DJ's booth, Jeff shoots up from his chair and storms out of the club, knocking over empty chairs and flinging them aside as he goes. Outside, he blinks back tears, his fists still clenched, and hurries around to the side of the building, where, in the darkness, he vomits vodka and juice propelled by his half-digested supper. Knees shaking, he leans back against the wall, closes his eyes and grinds his head against the brick. Todd was outside in the yard the whole time, then, looking in the back window. No wonder he was so eager to be helpful.

"Shit! SHIT SHIT!"

People passing the entrance to the alley look into the darkness quickly but then hurry on.

"You stupid SHIT! You fucking MORON!"

His head spins, and a thousand images of that night in Todd's room return, but now he sees them not through the eyes of his own experience but through a camera, what they must look like in black and white to a mocking stranger, Susan's bare breasts and belly, him on his knees with his head between her legs, what they said, how it would make Susan look.

He bursts into sobs of fury, whirls and slams his fist against the brick wall. Pain cracks through his knuckles and he raises his fist to the light to see ragged threads of bloody flesh and dark gashes. He grabs the injured hand with the other, cups both between his thighs, bends over, coos and whistles through his teeth.

"Jeff?"

Paige ventures into the dark alley and calls timidly as if afraid to awaken him.

"What!" he shouts.

She comes forward. "Are you all right?"

"Of course not, stupid!" His hand aches.

"Jeff, I'm sorry it happened, really. Chris is really pissed, too."

"I'm going to kill that fucker! Jesus, I mean I thought we were friends. Why would he do that?"

She lights a cigarette; the flare from the lighter makes her face an orange cameo hanging in the darkness for an instant.

"He's just a thoughtless guy without any feelings for other people. He was probably just jealous. He said he'd trash the tape."

"It doesn't matter, anyway. He's already done all the damage. Everybody's going to know, now."

"Well, maybe not."

"Oh, be serious, Paige!"

She smokes, stays mute, apparently at a loss as to how she might console him. He should appreciate her effort, but the fury raging inside radiates outward onto everything and everyone, including her, and he hates having her offer easily punctured illusions about the serious consequences.

"I don't care so much about people knowing about me. That's not the point. But she has a husband and a career. She's got a lot to lose." It seems strangely mysterious to refer to Susan as "she" to Paige. "And if she gets into trouble, it will be my fault, all because of my friends." When he thinks of Susan's losing her job, he imagines lunging at Todd and kicking him savagely as he lies on the ground, in the face, in the nuts, in the gut, busting out his teeth, screaming at him: *it's all your fault, you fuck!*

Being her champion, leading a line of pickets marching in front of the school.

"Well, maybe nothing will happen."

"Aw go fuck yourself. You're just a Lakeview bowhead, what the fuck do you know about anything!"

Paige flips her cigarette, and the head bursts into a tiny shower of sparks against the pavement. After a moment, she asks, "Do you need a ride?"

"No."

Paige shrugs. "I'm going home. See you."

"Good-bye."

From Klub Video to his home in Oak Cliff is a hike of about four miles. He takes the first mile fast as an Olympic walker, muttering, yelling "Shit!" every so often, using his anger as a protective shield when he moves under Central Expressway and sees forms huddled around a fire near a concrete pillar; he passes through the tall cold canyon walls of the downtown buildings, where the sidewalks are empty stretches of narrow runway on which crazed wings of newspapers do touch-and-goes in the fitful, chilly gusts. Cars pass, exhausts vaporizing. He follows the Kennedy motorcade route down Elm through Dealy Plaza and across from The Grassy Knoll, still striding purposefully, still so angry it feels like the top of his head'll pop. His eyes, aggravated by the dust and wind, bleed cold tears along his cheeks.

For a while he's consumed with getting even. When that burns out somewhere under the notorious Triple Underpass, he settles on never speaking to Todd again, or Chris, for that matter. Paige maybe, depending. Marching toward the county jail that looms over the Trinity's levee—a red monolith of brick with vertical slits where a different building would have windows—he pictures Susan in trouble with school authorities, and he sees himself in trouble with her. Todd now seems irrelevant: the question is damage control, how to keep people from knowing. Should he tell Susan? How? And if he does, how can he ever win her back?

Past the jail he strides up the incline to the narrow walk on the rumbling, busy bridge over the river, his pant legs whipped by the furious rush of wind from passing traffic. Below, in the dark weed-choked bottoms of the flood flats, there might be corpses. Those tiny taillights way off toward where Sylvan crosses over down in the river bed—is that a car with a bloody body in the trunk? Some woman bound and gagged and her wrists taped, about to be shot? Some black dude about his age maybe who's crossed the Jamaican drug-dealers? It's odd you never hear of people jumping off this bridge to their death, but you hear about the bodies found down between the levees, bodies of people who were shot there maybe or somewhere else and were dumped.

Maybe the fall from the rail here wouldn't kill you, like it's not high enough? Or the ground's too spongy down there? There'd be nothing to it, that's for sure. The concrete rail's only as high as your chest, just slap your palm down on it, lift and a heave-ho, there you go over the side. Now and then somebody offs himself by diving from an overpass on Central Expressway into traffic. You'd probably never know what hit you, though the papers say the body "was struck by several vehicles," and so you wouldn't leave a pretty corpse. It'd be a kind of immortality, though, because everybody who hit you with their car would have you show up in their nightmares for the rest of their lives.

The stories never say if people jumped facing oncoming traffic or off the downstream side of the bridge. Which would be better? It's like whether you wear the blindfold or not when you face the firing squad. Whether you're looking at what's about to hit you or not, jumping off a freeway overpass is an incredibly public act, like theater. If you overdose or slit your wrists or blow your brains out, you might make the back part of the Metro section in a little paragraph, but people who go over the railing on expressway overpasses always make the evening news—because they tie up traffic.

When he descends the incline off the bridge and heads up Fort Worth Avenue, he realizes he's been on a morbid little journey while crossing the river; meanwhile, his steady hiking has worn away his angry energy, and he's very tired. His mind is numb, and he can't conjure any useful ideas about handling the problem. Paige wanted to reassure him by saying nothing will come of this, and he tries to think realistically about that: did anybody recognize the "actor" and "actress" in Todd's video? Will they tell? Or tell anyone who matters? How fast will the word spread? The Carver students in the audience—were they watching? Say, in the worst-case scenario, they believe that Susan's the woman. They tell other students, sure, but not teachers or administrators and not parents—they're not the type. No, the danger is that somebody they tell will tell somebody who will tell somebody who matters. Is it possible to track down these people and plead with them not to breathe a word of this? Threaten them? Buy them off? Ignore them and hope nothing happens—like they go around school saying that a Carver art teacher was seen doing it with a student in a home video, who's going to believe them? They're well-known acid heads, coke freaks, speed demons, right? And where's the evidence? (In Todd's hands, unfortunately. He should have kept his cool and grabbed the tape right there tonight and burned the fucker!)

Along the south side of Fort Worth Avenue lie a string of run-down motels. His grandfather on his mother's side once told him that years ago this street was the main route through Dallas for people going West to California, and these "tourist courts," he called them, were always full of cars from all across America. Now, though, the street's only used for local traffic. In the parking lot of The Last Roundup motel are beat-up Firebirds and Camaros and Chevy pickups; people stay here by the week and work construction or as day-laborers. In the seventh grade he had a crush on a girl who lived here with her father, who was a sheet-rocker; her mother lived in Garland and stayed drunk.

Everything seems sad. A blinking sign. *Motel.* Todd might have shot that opening image right here or out on Harry Hines. He was looking in the window the whole time. Why didn't Jeff know? After all, it's Todd's hobby. After he and Todd talked in the car about girls, he'd felt a little more like they were really solid as friends. They'd shared something real. So it was hard to believe that Todd could betray his trust this way.

How much did Todd get? What all did he and Susan do? What all did they say? It's torture to recall postures, acts and words, when each memory is then reexamined for how it appears in Todd's viewfinder. But, then, it's torture to resist recalling each and every movement because he's compelled to inventory what was catalogued by that camera; he has to know how widespread the damage is. Each kiss, each touch, each exchanged word was his private store of secret, bejeweled pleasures to open at will and fondle one by one in awe-struck admiration—and each sweet memory in turn is now soiled as he plucks it up to inspect it. It's like being Midas only everything he touches turns to shit.

≈25≈

When Jeff comes in, his mother is dozing on the couch but awakens when he tries to slip past her.

"How did you get home? I didn't hear a car."

"I'm here," he says.

"It's past midnight, Jeff. It's a school night. I worried about you."

"A lot of school nights I stay up late taking care of you."

He's holding his hands before his chest in an attitude like prayer except that his left clutches the right and rubs it.

"What's the matter with your hand, Jeffie?"

"Nothing."

"Let me see."

"I said it's nothing."

If it were "nothing" he wouldn't display the injury so obviously; he wants her to see it and feel sorry for him, wants to punish her by not allowing her to nurse him. She isn't sure *why*, when it was *he* who stayed out late and made *her* worry. What has she done? His dig about helping her, yet refusing her help....And yet showing her the injury! Draw her in, push her away, draw her in, push...

"Be sure to wash it out good!" she calls out as he goes up the stairs.

She hoped having him home would let her sleep at last, but she lies awake for a few hours listening to the floor creak overhead. What happened to him tonight? If it was just an accident, wouldn't he say how it occurred? Or if it's something to hide, wouldn't he make up a story? No, there's a drama connected to it, a drama he wants her to know without having to tell her. His behavior is a plea for help. But at least he's home safe now. She'll have a heart-to-heart at breakfast.

She oversleeps and when she's up Thursday morning, he's gone. She studies the kitchen for signs of disturbance. His cereal bowl, rinsed, sits in the sink—nothing unusual. Sometimes he sets it upside down in the drainer after he uses it. The spoon's inside it, his usual, favorite spoon with the red plastic handle from their old camp set. He put the Cheerios box back into the cupboard without firmly closing the top, and that's unlike him. He gripes when she lets the flaps fall without tucking the tabs in. How much can she read in something this small?

Since she's running late and has been out sick twice this month, she leaves for work without further investigation, and when she gets home at six on Thursday evening, he's in his room with the music going. She knocks on the door.

"Yes, mother?"—that wry, half-disgusted voice.

"Are you going to eat?"

"I've already eaten."

With no signs of meal-making in the kitchen, she continues to stand at his door in her Burberry and scarf, sweating from the sudden heat, her glasses fogging.

"Maybe I'll go to Wyatt's cafeteria. Would you go to keep me company, honey?"

A rustle over the softly playing music. Her suspicions and her ire are aroused by how he won't open up and invite her in, or at least stand in the threshold to talk: it's incredibly rude.

"Aw, Mom," he whines at last. "I've got to finish my homework, okay?"

Stung, she turns away without answering. She considers going on to Wyatt's because she's too hungry to fix a real meal but also too hungry to eat less than one. She relishes how he might picture her alone bent over her tray amongst the families. But having to eat out alone would punish her far more, so she hangs up her coat and scarf, scrubs her face and changes into her pajamas.

In the kitchen, she drinks a glass of milk, cuts a hunk of Velveeta and puts it on a plate with saltines and a raw hot dog she dries with a paper towel. She sets the kettle on the stove to heat.

At the table, she opens the paper to read, drifts off, ears tuned to the sounds upstairs. She could've called a friend from church to meet her at Wyatt's, of course, though she wanted to have supper with her son to take his temperature, so to speak. But she's irked royally by how he hides from her, and if she accomplishes nothing else by staying home it'll be to hamper his privacy. She wants him to be ill-at-ease and insecure; it does not do to have one's mother totally in the dark about one's life.

And if he's even unconsciously giving signals that he needs help, then she'll stand guard, and every time he opens his door to go to the bathroom or to get something from the refrigerator, she'll be here, loyal to his true best interests and not his short-range whims.

Whether he likes it or not.

She carries a mug of tea into the living room, her footfalls pushing her pulse like a knife into her skull. She's going to have one of those headaches, she bets. She's felt pretty good the past few days, considering how blue the Christmas season usually makes her, but the darkness is always right over the horizon like the edge of a cover being slipped over the world. What's that somebody said? Every silver lining has a cloud.

She turns on the TV. Cosby, already started. She settles into the sofa, sets her tea on the end table that holds her Bible and reading glasses. She considers inviting Jeffie down to watch but doesn't want to face another rejection.

The phone rings once. He's always quick on the draw, but there's no need, really; she rarely picks it up because it's usually for him, though sometimes when she's curious as to who his current friends are she'll answer just to record the voice on her inner ear.

After Cosby her TV Guide shows that *It's a Wonderful Life* is pre-empting normal programming on two channels; likewise, a Charlie Brown special and *The Little Drummer Boy*. Jeffie used to love that show, that story! The last two or three years, though, it's been hard to get him revved up about Christmas short of his giving her a list of things that exceed her budget. That makes her feel helpless to please him, and she has to surrender to Jeff Sr.'s checkbook—he'll buy Jeffie whatever Jeffie claims she isn't going to get for him. She detests how Christmas gift-givings have become a tug of war in which the boy plays them off against each other, and the whole wonderful spirit of the season is swamped by greed and manipulation.

His door screeks open and footsteps go down the hall to the bathroom, that door closes.

Maybe he'll help her put up a tree this weekend. Or help decorate it. The saddest thing in the world is decorating your house for Christmas alone, knowing nobody cares but you.

She has to watch out for seasonal depression: from now until January 1, she'll be prey to the blue demons. Be upbeat! *Lord, give me the strength to appreciate the true joy of thy birth and not lose sight of the meaning of Christmas in my own small problems. And help Jeffie.*

She turns off the TV and picks up her Bible, but the phone rings before she can open it. When it rings again, she cocks her ears and hears the rush of shower water. She walks into the kitchen and lifts the receiver on the wall phone.

"Hello!" she says brightly, struggling to sound as if all in her household are meeting the season head-on with good cheer.

"Hi, could I speak to Jeff?"

"Just a minute. Is this Paige?"

"Uh, yeah, Hi, Miz Robbins."

"Hello, dear. I'll go get him, hold on."

She glides swiftly up the stairs, past the bathroom where the shower's still running, and to his room. He shut his door obviously to discourage her from entering, but since it can't be locked from outside, the shut door is only a insult, not an effective measure against entry.

She leaves the door cocked open. Clothes drape the furniture, his bed's unmade. His desk lamp casts a pool of light onto a large pad of paper, on it a woman's face sketched. Behind the pad a book is propped open against the wall, showing two pages of small photographs. Teachers, Carver faculty. She runs down the photos with her finger until she finds the one he is obviously copying: Susan Hart. Drawing, Design, Art Club Sponsor. BA/BFA University of Texas.

She sniffs the air. The woman is young and beautiful, looks almost like a student. Why is Jeffie drawing her portrait? She lifts the pad, looking for notes, doodles, scratchings. She slides open a drawer, glances inside: jumble of pencils, erasers, a Crackerjack toy, a red crayon.

Paige. She picks up Jeffie's phone.

"Hello, dear? I'm afraid he's in the shower—I'll have him call you."

"Okay. Thanks."

She absorbs the sensory impressions given off by the room for several minutes. The bathroom faucets squeal as he spins them off. She lurches, then calms herself. She came up here to give him a message. Paige called. No, she is not snooping!

To avoid being confronted, she hastily scribbles "Paige called" on notebook paper with the red crayon. As she moves down the stairs without detection, she feels furtive and even a bit vengeful—he'll read "Paige called" as *you can run but you can't hide. I even opened a drawer to get the crayon I wrote this message with!*

She plans to remain vigilant so long as he's upstairs prowling about, but she falls asleep on the couch during the news and wakes at 2 A.M. On her way to her bed, she climbs halfway up the stairs to check on him.

Light under his door, the music still playing.

She sets her alarm earlier than usual to make sure he doesn't beat her up and out of the house without her seeing him, but when she goes into the kitchen to start the coffee, he apparently hasn't gotten up. She raps softly on his door.

"Jeffie?"

No answer. She opens the door and peeks inside. His curled form is hidden under the comforter, only a shock of hair and the tip of his nose showing. His desk is bare. It's cold in the room. He likes to sleep without heat on, so he always shut his vents.

"Jeffie!" she says brightly as she tip-toes up to open the flap in the heating register. "Get up, hon. You're oversleeping."

He groans. "I don't feel good."

"What's wrong, hon?"

She lays her hand on his forehead. His temperature seems normal. He was up late Wednesday night and last night as well—two nights running—so he's worn out and just wants, and needs, to stay home and sleep. If this were once upon a time when they were a normal family, she'd delicately maneuver him away from malingering, bluff him out, ask if he wants to go to the doctor. Once upon a time, she might even sternly order him up and about. But then she also would insist that he get to sleep at a decent hour and would punish him for arriving home after midnight on Wednesday without an excuse or an explanation. In the present, wholly demoralized state in which their lives are mired, it's all she can do to drag herself through one day to the next. The funny thing is he doesn't realize it's not necessary to give a convincing performance to get out of school. Residual patches of her authority still exist in portions of his brain from childhood, though they're will-o-the-wispish and have no predictable pattern.

"Do you want something?"

"Aspirin."

"How about some juice?"

"Okay."

She hesitates at the door. She'll make it easy. "Hon, why don't you stay home from school today and rest?"

"Aw, I've got too much to do."

But he doesn't get up, and she knows he'll eventually say he's going to stay home. It's a typically complicated exchange: his secret agenda is to stay home because he hasn't slept in two nights; to achieve it he thinks he has to play sick. But the moment she shortcuts the outcome by suggesting it, he has to offer token resistance so she won't think the idea was in his mind. So when he voices it, it will seem then to be his. Whew! These kids are hard to work. His father is a master at showing the mask that hides the mask that hides the mask.

It pleases her that he's staying home. During her morning coffee break, she resists the temptation to call him. If he's managed to sleep, she'd only disturb him, and even if he's awake, he'll probably claim she woke him. Or say he's too sick too sleep. Anyway, this would be a no-win call.

But at her lunch hour, she feels justified in checking. After all, if she doesn't, won't she seem negligent?

The phone rings twice.

"Hello?"

The buzz in the line tells her he's on the kitchen phone. "Hi, hon, how're you feeling?"

"Aw, okay, I guess."

"What're you doing?"

"Fixing something to eat," he says, sheepishly. She wants to say *you needn't be ashamed, dear, even sick people eat,* but holds her tongue. There's a beat while he waits for her to speak, though, and menus flicker across her mind: I'm-sick food or feel-good food?

"What're you having?"

"Grilled cheese and tomato soup."

"That sounds good."

"I didn't have any breakfast," he says defensively.

"I know that. Did you sleep well?"

"Yeah, okay. Hold it a sec—"

She hears a pan being set on a burner. He must be taking it off a hot one and putting it on a cold one.

He sounds sullen. Well, she isn't expecting him to admit cheerfully that he feels better: there's the danger she might order him to school. Once upon a time…

She might ask him what he intends to do this afternoon, or she can sound like a true mother and assign chores, but, really, when she is beset by the blue demons he does most of the housework, anyway. She merely wants him to know that she cares about him and worries about him and would do anything to help him if he's in trouble; she wants him to know that here on the planet Earth there is no other human being who has his interests so at heart, who knows what they are, who would make any sacrifice to achieve them for him. In this she is like all mothers, she believes; she can hear this sort of tortured plea for acceptance in her co-workers' voices when they call their latch-key children during those dangerous after-school hours. She can empathize with their terrible tension between wanting to protect your child and knowing that if the child knows this it'll drive him or her away. It's similar to the feeling you have when you're in love with a boy and you're afraid that the instant he recognizes it, he'll bolt from fear of being trapped.

"Okay." He's back. Waiting, again. She can sense his impatience to be off the line. Why does he always seem always angry at her?

"Well, hon, I just worried about you and wondered how you were feeling."

He relents, sensing she might not keep him on the phone. "Yeah, I am feeling better, Mom. I'll probably read some assignments and work on a paper that's due next week."

She thinks he says that to forestall any suggestion that he return to school.

"Okay, that's fine, hon. Don't overdo it. I'll be home around the usual time." Should she risk scaring him off? Well, nothing ventured..."Would you like to eat Mexican food tonight?" she asks, then regrets it immediately.

"Uh...maybe."

"Well, take care, dear."

"Bye, Mom."

Even though his answer has been hedging, she's pleased he didn't automatically say no. Probably he feared she might balk if he claimed he has plans for the evening—even in their current laissez-faire state he can't get away with going out at night after staying home "sick."

Maybe he said maybe just to appease her, buy time. Though it has the sound of a maybe that is only thirty percent in favor and seventy percent against, it's a concession. It's hard not to get her hopes up; it's hard not to look forward to spending time with him over dinner, just talking. You don't want to get your hopes up too much. Even if he can't go out, he can still barricade himself in his room, feed himself before she gets home. When she manages now and then to twist his arm and get him to a cafeteria or restaurant, he'll keep going to the bathroom or play the video machines to avoid sitting with her, and the instant he bolts down his food he's agitating to leave.

Going out with him is like going out with a boy whose mother made him ask you for a date, only in their case she is both the mother who made him ask and the girl he has to ask. He can't remove himself from the venue of the mother's authority altogether, but the power she has to force him to ask this girl for a date will not extend to making him like it.

So, it's pitiful, no? Getting your hopes up about going out on a date that you know has been arranged by the boy's mother?

When she pulls into the driveway in the winter dusk, a light is on in his room, though the rest of the house is dark.

Carrying the tote bag of dirty Tupperware, she gets out of the car and locks it, increasingly irritated and recognizing that it probably comes from knowing she'll have to eat alone, after getting her hopes up. Wouldn't it be nice for him to be waiting downstairs, eager to leave, hungry not just for supper but hungry to talk? You'd think after staying at home all day he'd want company, even if only his mother's.

On the dark porch she holds her key ring to the faint illumination from passing cars until she locates the right key, thinking she could knock and force him to open the door, but he'd know it's a trick to lure him out of hibernation.

The mail box fixed to the wall is stuffed with papers, and she's annoyed that Jeff hasn't taken in the mail but pleased to be first to rifle through it. Inside, she carries the mail and tote bag toward the kitchen but pauses at the stairs to bend her head; as always, light under his door, music on the radio. She wants to yell, "I'm home!" but thinks better of it: *yes, mother, I know you're home.*

She sets the mail on the kitchen table and the Tupperware in the dishwasher. The rolling racks hold his breakfast cereal bowl, a plate and bowl and saucepan from lunch, one mug from her breakfast coffee and another for—she tilts it to the light—hot chocolate. The kitchen's clean. If he's eaten anything since lunch, it's apparently only been cocoa. So maybe he's planning to go with her, after all!

This makes her want to rush upstairs to get a verbal commitment, but she restrains herself. Play it cool—don't tip your hand. *You still want to go out?* No, not that way. *You're still going out with me, aren't you.* Not a question. Not the girl asking for a date but the mother telling the son to take her.

Handling the mail, she separates the wheat from the chaff. Everything's trimmed in green and red and every flyer contains pictures of useless gadgets: Target, Penny's, Montgomery Wards, Sears, K-Mart, everybody selling, selling, selling worthless knick-knacks and gee-gaws. Jeffie hasn't given her his Christmas list and she hasn't asked for one because the commercialism of this sacred holiday profoundly depresses her.

After winnowing, she's left with a Mastercard bill and a square envelope addressed to her and Jeffie, with her mother's name and return address. It is, as expected, a Christmas card—carefully secular, a bird on the end of a snowy bough—but there's a $25 check for Jeffie. Jeff Sr.'s parents sent him $50, but, then, there are two grandparents on that side.

This could serve as an overture. Still in her coat and scarf, she goes up the stairs, then, standing at his door, practices a smile before tapping her knuckle against the frame. He doesn't respond. Sleeping?

She raps more soundly.

"Jeffie?"

Again he fails to answer. Maybe he's gone out and left his light and radio on. She turns the doorknob and pushes, but the door has been locked from inside.

"Jeffie!"

She rattles the doorknob.

"Jeffie, it's me!"

She waits, hoping to hear him groan awake, sullen, complaining about being awakened.

"Answer me, Jeffie!"

The back of her neck prickles. The piercing little knives push harder into her skull. *If he doesn't speak up right NOW, I will...* she thinks, then flounders—what? ground him? lecture him? She wants to stay angry because if he's not being rude, then, then what? Maybe his recent sleeplessness is a symptom of a very serious problem and he's fallen into a fever!

This motherly leap to the worst conclusion is so worn by overuse that she dismisses it. She bangs hard on the door.

"Jeffie! You open this door right now! Enough of this nonsense, you hear me!"

When she gets no response, she yells, "You open it right now or I'm going to get the hammer and break it down!"

She hasn't spoken to him this so angrily in a long while, and she expects to hear him stir and unlock the door, say, *Gah, mom, what's with you, huh?*

When he doesn't answer this time, she turns and darts down the stairs and into the kitchen, where she rips open the utility drawer, grabs a hammer and a screwdriver. Call a neighbor? An ambulance? Someone to help? No, he'll never forgive her if none is needed.

She rushes upstairs, slipping once on the carpeting and banging her knee on a step but scrambling up immediately and running down the hall to his door. She hesitates for a second then swings the hammer and whacks at the wood around the lock, again and again, then, seeing nothing budging, she jams the screwdriver in the slot between door and frame and hammers at the end of it, and when she wedges a gap she can see through, she drops the tools and shoves her shoulder against the door.

It gives, and she lurches into the room. Her gaze darts to the desk, the lighted lamp illuminating that pad, that sketch, then she spies him standing at the closet. She yells furiously, "Jeffie!"

But he isn't standing; he's only upright against the spine of the open closet door. She screams and screams the way you'd scream at somebody to stop doing something; she's holding her hands over her ears, but nothing has changed, and she comes back to herself and rushes to him. A scarf is tied in a loop under his chin and over the corner of the door, holding him up, and she embraces him, half aware that his bare thighs are cold against her arms, then she viciously yanks the scarf from under his jaw and they tumble onto the floor.

"Jeffie! Jeffie!"

She slaps his cheek. His body is shockingly cool, and she pulls his head into her lap, clutches it to her breast, and blows into his mouth, over and over, talking to him; then at last she thinks *ambulance!* and scrambles out from under his body to grab the phone on his desk.

She tells the dispatcher her name and address. "Please hurry, please!"

She crawls back to him. He lies on his back, knees and shins white in the dim room; she sits against the bed, draws him into her lap again, and kisses his mouth, blowing her breath into his chest, pushing it out with her palm, the motion of his breastbone going up and down and giving her hope.

The ambulance howls toward the house and sets the dog to yapping. She'll have to let them in.

She struggles out from under him and rises to her knees. The tails of his long-sleeved shirt drape over his naked loins and thighs. But his sweatsuit pants are tangled about his ankles. She'll raise them up where they belong.

⤳26⤨

*F*riday night, Dec. 14, 10:18 P.M. CST. Susan sits before her clone but is drifting off from the here and now like a rowboat with an un-hitched painter. Minutes ago she was thinking of her thesis and her trip to Italy, then about how they didn't take a cruise to Greece, and now she imagines being asleep on an ocean liner deep in the night, in tropical waters, where she is shocked awake by a jolt and a thump and a *basso profundo* squawk. She lies frog-eyed in her bunk, her body vibrating with alarm, and awaits an official signal that disaster has struck.

Silly thoughts. Wasted time. If the little scenario means anything, it means she better get underway before her professor vanishes un-der a married name and becomes a barefoot Madonna herself.

Susan raises her hands like a pianist and taps out on her keyboard, *Renaissance Catholics belonged to what might be called 'The Cult of the Virgin Mary.'* She's transcribing handwritten notes from the trip into com-puter files. She recalls Ruskin's comment that "The Annunciation is the most widely painted scene in the history of Art," and, quibbling with it, thinks back to the iconography in the cathedrals and museums in Europe. If the Annunciation was number one, then Mary and the Blessed Babe in the Nativity sure ran a close second. Followed by St. Jerome (in Southern Europe) and various chapters from the life of Christ.

What she recalls from her childhood Catholicism is how much she and the other girls were encouraged to follow the example of the BVM, to model their virtues after Mary's—first would be obedience: to God, the Pope, the priest, one's own father. Then came purity. The insistence upon purity had no real meaning to her until the first time she'd found blood in her underwear, and from then on it seemed the nuns and priests could harp only on sin, sin, sin (sex, sex, sex). To be a good Catholic girl meant bowing your head when men talked and keeping your legs closed.

Oh how those early lessons galled her when she got to college and began to realize how much more a woman could be!

Her mother's people were German; her mother took her to parochial school and to Mass on Sundays at a small church in a neighborhood of St. Louis populated by blue-collar Poles and Czechs. Hail Mary, full of Grace, she remembers. Yes, Mary was important. But Jesus on the Cross was front and center in the sanctuary where, if you were a kid squirming in a pew, you could study those violent insults to His flesh for maybe longer than you cared to, longer than was good for you.

Forgive me, Father, for I have sinned, she recited for the priest at the Oak Lawn church on Wednesday. Turned out that her confessor was neither Father Montejano nor the priest who hailed her at the bulletin board—it was an older Anglo, gray-haired, who took his seat behind the screen making that old-man sigh. *Father I have sinned. I have fornicated* and she would've gone on (maybe) to elaborate, but he grunted *How many times?* and she said *Once,* not counting all the years with Curt, of course, and the old priest said, as if moving his hand across a menu to the price list: *two dozen Hail Marys and concentrate upon the holiness of the body of Our Blessed Virgin.*

She sighs, bends toward the notebook, squints. One thing about the Italian trip—she hadn't done so much writing by hand in years, and her cursive improved, but only slightly. The notes concern cathedrals and museums in Pisa, Florence, Venice, Rome, Assisi, Siena and Padua. Looking back on the whirlwind twenty-one-day excursion, all the cathedrals converge into one huge, dark, high-roofed cavern, with echoes of footfalls, chanting, docents prattling in many languages to herds of tourists whose nationalities could be guessed by their shoes and clothing color. The thick damp stone held in a coolness that was always pleasant after the summer sun, but it made her wonder how they were ever heated, which, in turn, made her realize they probably hadn't been. She recalls how stiff it made her neck to scan those ceilings for the frescoes while Curt, beside her or (as usual) far ahead of her, traced the styles of the arches and spines of the domes. And almost everything covered with a half-millennium's dust, the gold-worked ornamentation so dingy the pieces might as well have been painted. The huge columns in the cathedrals showed smooth oiled patches where a hundred generations of human hands had stroked them.

And everywhere you turn—Mary, Mary, Mary. One breast, two breasts, the Babe lying, seated, or standing in her lap, chucking her chin, with or without his genitalia—depending on the date of the painting, sculpture or fresco (pre- or post-Plague). Visigoths buried the images of the Virgin in Spain to protect them from invaders, then, centuries later when the Moors had been beaten back to Africa, shepherds and goatherds stumbled upon the buried images: voila, a miracle! For hundreds of years since, they've been carried about as magical objects and are costumed and dressed and blessed and sanctified and brought out during feast days for processions.

It's very strange, isn't it, that one wooden representation of the Virgin not much bigger than your shoe can still inspire a million Gypsies every year to come from all over Europe to converge upon a place in the southern Spanish desert, to make a pilgrimage on foot to pay homage to a doll?

The inexplicable irrationality of faith, and the occasional absurd manifestations of it, chipped away at her beliefs in high school. She felt embarrassed to be Catholic when she'd hear how thousands of believers would flock to a dusty yard in South Texas to see the alleged outline of the Virgin Mary's hand print on a tortilla. She got saucy with the nuns who tried to teach her that sex outside marriage was sinful: she knew better, she knew that sex in love was holy, holy, holy. Love, not marriage, sanctified sex.

Then, once Nathan left, there came first the shame that she'd fooled herself. She'd believed she was too smart to fall for hokum only to discover that she was too dumb or proud to listen to wisdom. The Sisters would say this was how the Devil operated—by making you think that the rules don't apply to you, that you don't have to be obedient: that's the story of Eve and the apple!

But the shame festered into anger against the system that would judge her. No, there *was nothing to be ashamed of!* She had loved her best and given all she had to give, and the shame was not hers but Nathan's. And if the nuns said otherwise they were wrong.

And so eventually, in the war between her father's pallid but complicated agnosticism and her mother's unshaken and unquestioned acceptance of the Catholic Church, she became her father's ally.

But traipsing about in European cathedrals this summer had been a haunting experience for her, and she felt the Holy Mother Church calling out to the errant child. They met another young American couple in Florence who were also carrying *Let's Go/Europe* and looking for a listed restaurant, and they fell in together. They found it and spent the meal comparing travelers' notes. The other couple,

from Maine, she remembers, had been all through Italy without setting foot inside a single church. Because they were clearly educated,
Susan was astonished and asked why. The man said, "It just pisses me
off to see all that money and energy being spent that way when there
are so many poor people who could have been fed and clothed with
it."

To her surprise, Susan was offended. (She was surprised because
she would've called herself an agnostic and a liberal when it comes to
feeding and clothing the poor.) Later, she wondered if the old Jesuit
saw about making a child a Catholic for life wasn't true. Even splash-
ing about in the puddles inside Venice's flooded San Marco Basilica,
she felt smitten with the romance of past grandeur, the former glory.
Walking about with her gaze on church floors she was made aware
by the elaborate designs of the paving that those enormous stores of
energy and talent and, yes, money of course, perhaps had been foolishly misspent, but only in a way that endeared her to their humanity, their love of mystery, their yearning to worship. Far better to
spend the money on these now all-but-useless hulking repositories
of human aspiration and art than on Stealth bombers. Renaissance
builders made the heavens a place that drew your adoring gaze and
your yearning soul; Star Wars technology will make them a place
from which to hide in quaking fear.

Being in the cathedrals made her want to attend a Mass, take com-
munion (and maybe confession), but it had been too long and that
muscle had atrophied.

She sees that she made a note about Michelangelo's "David" in the
Galleria dell'Accademia in Florence: *what a sweet, sweet tush!* the tourist Susan gushed. Well! She hopes no one else ever reads these notes.
But, after all, the masculine sensuality of the figure is why the sculpture's controversial to begin with, right? That sculpture inspired
both the lofty and the low inside her.

Jeff. Her heart hurts. What is it in the male of the species that makes them elevate some women (Mary) into figures that are bigger than life? Cult of Mary. Cult of Susan, a one-boy cult, anyway. It's very unnerving to be worshipped. If Mary were alive, would she be a spiritual Greta Garbo having to hide from obsessive fans? Or would the debased New Jersey surrogate-Madonna suffice to draw off all that confused energy?

Being adored makes Susan uncomfortable. She feels most comfortable with people who seem to have the same perspective on her as she has on herself, she thinks. That's what it means to have somebody know you—it means their picture of you matches your own (whether either of you has an accurate comprehension is another question), and so you neither feel inadequate to the task of living up to an exalted image nor do you resent being belittled by someone's contemptful cameo. The way Jeff says, *Oh, God, you're wonderful, Susan!* it means everything, so it means nothing. *No, I'm not!* she insists. But he presumes she's only being modest (making her even more virtuous), and replies: *Oh, yes you are, you are!* So, feeling defeated, she mutters, *Okay, have it your way. I am wonderful.* (I am everything and therefore nothing.)

The ancient Mother Church. The Confessor. The Inquisition. The Grand Inquisitor: Do you renounce your sins?

Yes, I renounce my sins.

She knows she must renounce even the temptation to draw him aside where they're alone "to make certain you're okay."

She's haunted by how he winced, squinting, his face responding to her words as if she'd pelted him with ice. Now it's easy to wonder if he'll just rebound like a resilient kid or if he has something of his mom's affliction and this might send him into a nose-dive. Her concern is real, but she's also suspicious of it, the way it could be used by her desire to see him again and soak up more of his adoration.

Making herself keep away now is twelve times harder than any diet she's ever done, harder even than to quit smoking.

You have done the right thing. All that's left is penance, absolution, intones the Inquisitor.

Having renounced not only the past sin but also the possibility for a future lapse, her memory of the night is no longer anything to fear; thus, it glows more rosily with every recollection, as if each time her imagination reconstructs it the costumes grow more sumptuous, the speech more elevated, the tone more dignified. Now everything they said was said for the last time and carries the undertone of bittersweet, anguished renunciation, the already-perceived nostalgia that lies within it. As if they knew then there'd never be another chance. *I must go. Never to Return. We must never meet. I think I shall never see you again.*

An electroencephalograph hooked to Susan's skull would reflect highly increased brainwave activity for the next several minutes as she indulgently skims a book of fragmentary scenes; they are neither fantasies, precisely, nor memories, but a confused melding of both; they are as inexact and inaccurate as dreams (and as telling), and in one such fragment the body of one young man is transported to another's time and place, where he is allowed liberties only another took.

She fails to hear the doorbell.

"Suzie?" Curt's voice startles her back into attention; she forgot he was downstairs, and in her trance had set him outside the house, as if on a business trip.

She revolves in her swivel chair, but the man she sees in the doorway to the TV room is not Curt. Portly Hispanic in a polyester navy blazer, light blue tie. He's dressed as poorly as her own colleagues, and for an instant she wonders if he's someone from the district administrative offices. Curt is coming around from behind him.

"Miz Hart?

She rises to take his hand, though he hasn't offered one, hears him say a name that sounds like "Detective Gabe Ruehl."

"Yes?"

"I need to ask you a few questions."

"What's this about?" asks Curt, edging between them.

"It's all right, Curt," says Susan, moving closer. She feels dizzy but recalls there's a procedure, here; or, at least, the movies and TV say so. "Can I see some ID?" she asks apologetically, hoping not to offend.

Without a word, the man dips swiftly into his inner blazer pocket, flips open the extracted wallet and brings it close to her face. A badge, something that looks like a driver's license.

"I wouldn't know a real one from a fake one," she says aloud, having just realized it. "I mean I've never had to ask."

The wallet vanishes or seems to be transformed by a clever sleight of hand into a notebook. Feeling dizzy, Susan reaches for the back of her secretarial chair for support, but the bearings make it swivel and she has to grab the edge of her desk with the other.

"Would you like to sit down?" she asks the officer, even while she is struggling to secure the elusive chair for herself.

"I'm okay," he says. "Do you know a Jeffrey Robbins?"

"Why, yes!" She jerks as if unexpectedly shocked. "He's a student of mine, at Carver High School. Why? What's happened?"

"When was the last time you saw him?"

"Uh…" Her mind whirls; today is Friday. "Tuesday night," she says, then adds, "At the art club meeting. That's when we meet, Tuesday nights." The parking lot, Jeff coming out of the shadows, scaring her. Then the look on his face. She can't meet the detective's eyes. "But it was the last meeting of the year. What's the problem? Is Jeff in trouble?"

The detective's hesitation makes her succumb to the need to engage his gaze. His brown eyes look invitingly sympathetic, regretful.

"I'm afraid he's dead, Miz Hart."

She sinks into the revolving chair. "Oh, my God!"

Curt bounds to her side and clutches her shoulders, presses her cheek to his belly.

"Was he one of the kids at our party?" Curt asks.

She nods, dumbly. What, is this crazy? But doesn't this name also belong to Jeff's father?

"Are you sure it's my student?"

The officer nods.

"But how?"

Once again, the detective's eyes search out her own, though he has to move into her line of sight.

"Looks like maybe suicide, but the coroner hasn't made a ruling yet."

"Oh, my God! No! How horrible!"

The bottom falls out, and a dark cold wind sweeps over her. She sobs with her hands in her face, dimly aware of Curt's hand petting her and his cooing *it's okay, it's okay,* and something flickers through her memory—her puppy Woofer dead in the street and her sobbing and her father trying to comfort her, and when she looked into his face she remembers his peculiar smile and his air of utter helplessness and embarrassment, the fear of her condition. But the boy, sweet Jeff, dead?

No!

She turns inside out and bawls freely for she doesn't even know how long, the men standing there, Curt stroking her head, her shoulder, mashing her ear against his belt buckle; when she tries to control herself, reaching to her desk for a tissue, she sees that the detective appears to have been waiting patiently for her to finish like a man who has merely raised an umbrella in a thunderstorm while standing at a bus stop.

She tries to assume a business-like air. She blows her nose, nods: thank you. "There's got to be a mistake, officer. I just don't think this boy would kill himself. It must be an accident."

"Did you know him pretty well?"

"Well, uh, he was a student of mine."

"Did you know him outside of class?"

She looks up. She nods. "As I said, the art club…"

She sees now that this man isn't here just to make the rounds of those who knew Jeff and to console them, nor is he merely gathering information by using a wide net. He knows something about her and Jeff? Now—and it makes her feel wretched—she has to set aside her grief and betray him.

"Well, I was his art teacher. He was taking lessons in drawing."

"Private lessons?"

Reluctantly, Susan nods.

"I didn't know that," says Curt.

"Was there anything else?"

"Anything else?" She looks "puzzled."

"Anything of a, well, romantic or sexual nature between you?"

"My God! No, of course not!"

It's as if the detective doesn't hear her denial. "I ask because the kid's mother, she found a letter he was writing—"

"A letter? I didn't get any letter!"

"Yes," the detective says calmly. "It wasn't sent."

"It was to me?" She looks incredulous.

The detective shrugs. "Somebody named Susan."

"Officer, it isn't me. I know that boy liked me and I liked him, he was one of my favorite students, but believe me when I tell you that there was nothing of what you'd call a romantic nature between us."

The detective seems apologetic. "Well, these kids, sometimes you know, they get things in their heads, or they want things to happen or come true, and when they don't, they take it hard. They don't know that most things can be overcome with time. You know what the counselors say—suicide is a permanent solution to a temporary problem. The kids are too young to know what temporary means."

This oddly philosophical tangent strikes Susan as irrelevant and largely rhetorical; not knowing how to respond, she says nothing.

"Maybe he had a crush on you is what I mean."

"Yes, I guess he might have. It happens sometimes. But this is a terrible, terrible tragedy. Why in the world would he want to—" She looks for a way to phrase it that she can bear to utter—"end his life? He had everything to live for."

"Maybe he felt you didn't return his love."

"Oh, my God! Of *course* I couldn't have, even had I known about it!" She watches the detective's face; it is soft, rounded; he might be Native-American, not Hispanic, or even Eskimo, with his almond eyes and his soft, almost beardless cheeks. Sticking out of his blazer pocket is the ruby head of a lollipop new fathers give out in lieu of cigars. With his wire-rimmed spectacles, he looks like a down-at-heels seminary student, not a police detective, and, even in shock, she is struck by his peculiar interest in the psychology of the tragedy (*Maybe he felt you didn't return his love*), as if to his mind she and Jeff were soap-opera characters.

"He was drawing a portrait of you," says the detective. "It was on his desk."

"I said he was my drawing student."

"It was an assignment?"

"Well, no, not specifically, but it was a natural thing for him to try. Officer, wasn't there a note or something? I just can't see why he would do this to himself. Did you talk to his mother or father or his friends?"

He nods. "Mother."

When he doesn't continue, Susan says, "What does she say?"

Again, the regretful, sympathetic look that oddly persists in keeping her gaze engaged with his own. "She thinks you led the boy on."

"No! I didn't!"

"She didn't," says Curt. "I mean I *know* her. I'd know if there was something like that between them."

"The mother wants to press charges."

"Charges?" She rises to her feet, and Curt's arm falls away from her shoulders.

"Yes. Sexual assault."

"What?"

"Sexual assault."

"You must be wrong."

Curt says, "Maybe we shouldn't talk to you any more until we've talked to a lawyer. Maybe you should just leave now."

"I'm not here to make an arrest. I'm just asking questions."

"Well, hey! I don't like these questions, and I guess you know that since you didn't tell us about these charges, whatever we said will just be tossed out!" Curt shouts.

The detective shrugs but looks vaguely embarrassed. "Nobody's pressed charges. Coroner's not through yet. If the mother goes ahead and files a complaint, I'll come back and read you her rights, that okay with you?" Now, at last, he sounds sarcastic and therefore authentic.

When he leaves, Curt stomps about the living room downstairs for several minutes, enraged: *Sneaky sonsabitches! Stupid turds! Talking all around something and trying to get people to entrap themselves without letting them know they're under suspicion!* He's going to call his old frat brother James Nately, get the best lawyer in the city! What horseshit!

She sits patiently on the sofa, waiting for him to run out of angry energy. She wishes she had committed suicide instead of Jeff. If she'd known he was going to do it, she'd have argued him into letting her take his place. It has apparently never crossed Curt's mind that she might be guilty. What a wonderful champion he is! And how dubious the cause.

"God, can you believe that shit!" he groans as at last he falls back onto the sofa. "What do you think? Shouldn't we call James?"

"I guess."

"Hey—" He moves close to her, encloses the nape of her neck with his warm palm, holds her hand, kisses her cheek. "I know what happened is terrible for you. That poor kid! But we've got to think fast about how to keep the situation from being any worse than it is, before somebody makes bad mistakes."

"They've already been made."

"Well, the mother hasn't pressed charges yet. Maybe she's just in grief, you know? And looking around for someone to blame. I mean, Jesus, wouldn't you, if your kid killed himself? The last person you'd want to think responsible was yourself. She's grasping at straws. I think I'll call James right now. What time is it?" He raises his watch. "It's only eleven-thirty. If they're home, they're probably still up."

He bends forward to rise, and she thinks *stop him!* but doesn't. He crosses the room and goes down the hallway to the kitchen phone. After a moment, she gets up and follows him, catches up to him as he is listening for an answer.

Then, in the instant he straightens, face brightening, and his mouth comes open to speak to the party on the other end, her hand shoots up and presses the lever to disconnect him.

He gives her a baffled look.

"Curt," she says. "I'm guilty."

He looks confused, then sickened. "What do you mean you're guilty?"

She leans against the hallway wall in the darkness; she can't recall ever having a conversation with Curt while they stood here.

"Do you mean it's like what he said about the kid having a crush on you and your not returning his love, or what?"

She can't look at him. She looks down the long dim hall toward the rounded archway into the lighted living room, where their furniture waits, empty, as in a display at a secondhand store.

"I mean I'm guilty because he and I…"

He waits, and when she doesn't elaborate, he says, "You mean you and that kid were having sex?"

It's not the disbelief that rings her ear so much as the disgust, and the phrase "having sex" sounds uncharacteristically puritanical.

"Once."

He hangs the receiver of the telephone back into its bracket on the wall.

"Well, that certainly changes things!" He elbows past her; she stares numbly into the darkened hallway space, tracing his footsteps into the living room then up the stairs.

After a moment, an earthquake tremor vibrates along the wall and up her spine, then she hears great thumps and thuds as if Curt has had a sudden urge to rearrange the furniture.

27

When a police klaxon whips about his ears, Jeff pops upright in
bed with his heart thundering. He stares dumbfounded at the air as
the howling cruiser speeds down their street.

He blinks, confused. His room is bright with the full-blown day.
He's been someplace else, with some girl who's like Susan? What's
she doing? His erection aches. Closing his eyes, he lies back with a
groan and tries to conjure the woman and plunge back into the
dream, wanting to savor whatever they were doing, but the dream is
vapor rising from a highway in July, and the mysterious beauty flees,
taking her setting and props with her.

His chin is slick with drool, and the neck of his t-shirt clammy and
damp; he now recognizes a headache, and the sweet tension of desire
becomes the ache of his bladder. He stares at the ceiling, the Rorschach water-stain. Unicorn head.

What time is it?

Eleven-thirty. His stomach growls. After his mom left for work, he'd gone back to sleep and hasn't eaten since yesterday noon. That weird spaghetti. Lunch room. He's not exactly hungry now, only empty and weak. Friday's taco salad day at Carver, no great loss to miss that…

Thank God Todd doesn't go there. When Susan walked through the cafeteria yesterday, he ducked his head. Had she heard? It'd only been a little over twelve hours since Todd showed the tape, but, man, news travels lightning fast, especially news that brings somebody down.

He should have told her. Instead, he left the cafeteria and went out to the Pegasus side of the building where he sat in the lee of a cold wind with the sun on his face considering how to say it, knowing that he has to before she hears it from someone else.

Chickenshit! He didn't even go back into the building—just took off hiking home, and he spent the afternoon yesterday pacing his room. He plugged away at the portrait all afternoon and last night, thinking some *how* some *way*, this is his only means of showing how much he cares, and when she understands that, can she still hate him? Paige called to say Todd's sorry, that he trashed the tape, that it didn't have anything really bad and it isn't likely anybody was watching. He longed to gobble this whole but knew he was being conned. Still, as he worked on the portrait late into the night, he kept thinking this might blow over, and he can work patiently and persistently on her first line of defense. The portrait—how can she resist this gesture? (And thus its maker?)

Feeling optimistic, he finally went to sleep about three this morning, but when his mom came in to wake him before she left for work, he felt not only exhausted but also hopeless: he couldn't go to school because he'd bet a million dollars that Susan had already heard and she'd either be stone cold silent and never speak to him again or she'd drag him into her office, repeat Tuesday night's speech, only this time she wouldn't be gentle: *You fucking moron, you fool, you stupid twerp, you idiot, get out of my life!!*

He won't lose her now because of her conscience or because it's too risky. No, now she'll hate him; he'll be slime to her.

11:40 A.M. He sighs, flops back, limbs askew. Children, do you know where your mothers are? He wishes it were Saturday and his mom were home. He could holler and she'd bring cold water, an aspirin, maybe a soft-boiled egg on toast and orange juice.

He wishes he had a catheter or that somebody would walk his bladder to the bathroom.

It's weird being home alone, sort-of sick but not really, with the house otherwise empty and the rest of the world out there working or going to school. Missing Algebra II right now. Flunking it, anyway. Hard to concentrate any more with so many things other than school to think about. He's so far behind catching up is impossible.

He's an outcast. People at school are walking about in gaggles, herds, packs, feeling good, jabbering to each other. He'd go except for what he has to face there.

He should get up. His headache and wooziness are probably from not eating.

But what's the point of it? You get up and eat and walk around and then you get hungry then eat and walk around some more then get hungry again. Nothing changes; nothing gets better. Everything's the same then you fall over from a heart attack or a drunk driver crashes into you or you're in a store at the wrong moment and get blown away in a robbery. Until then you just get older and stuck in your stupid life and you look for ways that are like waking sleep to escape it, like his mother's Church of the Geeks.

What's the point of getting up if it only means that you've got the energy to stay awake long enough to hear the news from somebody that Susan has learned about the tape? What's that people say to the widow? *You've got to eat to keep up your strength?* Well, what's the point of keeping up your strength if all your future holds is hearing her curse you?

Suddenly his face rings with rushing blood and his eyes prickle. The walls collapse inward on the bed.

What's the point?

The point is to prevent pissing your pants!

Still, he resists. Gritting his teeth, relishing the ache in his bladder and balls, he stares at the ceiling. What if he does wet the bed? So fucking what? So who gives a shit?

Cursing, he slings his legs over the side and stomps off to the bathroom where his erection melts into the stream of his piss. In the shower, he slumps against one corner of the enclosure and lets the hot spray drill his chest and head; it lifts the ache from the center of his skull as easily as if it had been a hat. When he lathers up his scrotum, something from the dream comes back—he and the mysterious, almost-but-not-quite-identifiable girl in, what? a car? He's lost it, but he grows hard, and he relishes how the lovely warmth of the arousal melts away the foul spell of the morning. Susan's lips, her eyes. He kisses the smoothness inside her thighs.

He lolls about in the memory, but it fast-forwards of its own accord to Klub Video and spoils his mood. Sadness seeps like sand into his calves, and he lets himself slide down the flank of the enclosure until he's hunkered knees under his chin and arms about his shins under the beating rain. He rocks himself. Could he drown here? His mother sometimes spends hours in her tub when she has blue spells. Are they this bad? Does she feel like this? For year after year?

What keeps her going? Does she do it for him? Then if he weren't here, she wouldn't have to suffer for his sake.

The phone's ringing? He turns off the tap. Nope, never is, stupid. He's about to turn the water back on when his deflated stomach rubs its halves together and he almost swoons from hunger.

Dressed in a clean t-shirt, sweat pants and socks, he prepares tomato soup and a cheese sandwich that's toasting when his mother calls. After the bell goes off, he wants to hang up so the sandwich won't get hard as crackers, but she keeps up her pointless chatter—Jesus, she's aggravating sometimes! (He's forgotten that moments earlier he was willing to die to relieve her depressions.) And so to get her off the phone, he says maybe he'll go to supper with her.

Sitting alone at the kitchen table, it's too quiet, like the whole neighborhood has been evacuated. Nuclear war? Toxic spill? His gaze zooms to the dark face of the TV in the living room. He then realizes that he's sitting in his mom's place. The view is away from the windows and through the arch. Drapes over the front windows haven't been opened. So all he sees is a wall with a big upside down U cut into it, an archway that leads into a dark empty room with the furniture there just sad gray humps in the dimness. Jesus, how depressing, Mom! No wonder she goes off the deep end sometimes! He's glad he agreed to maybe go out with her.

He shifts his bowl and plate to his normal place overlooking the back yard. He has neglected her. If he doesn't go to supper, she'll feel rejected. He knows a lot about that particular feeling. He won't be a person who makes others feel it. Maybe by setting a good example, others will follow his example. Maybe there's a kind of invisible machine in the world like a monolithic flywheel that gets its momentum from people's individual acts, and once it gets going, it tends to draw everything into its center by centrifugal force, see? So if the wheel is running off of the good righteous energy of people not rejecting others then other people who are maybe trying to decide to do it or not will be influenced by the wheel's momentum.

Or maybe that's bullshit.

His jaws crunch the toasted bread; slurping soup, he hears his Adam's apple doing chin-ups. It's creepy. Like listening to a cow chew its cud, the stupid pointlessness of it all. He's like the sole survivor. Lonely as Crusoe. What about Friday?

He opens the back door and whistles. There's a jingle and the retriever shoves her large snout through the door and into the house. She stands in the kitchen wagging her tail and barking; the sound exploding in the room shocks his ears, but it also makes him laugh.

"Okay, okay, yes, I know, you're happy to be inside with me, okay? I get it. No more hollering about it, though, okay?"

He straddles the animal with his knees pressed to her flanks and massages her ears and the soft downy fur on her throat while murmuring *Oh such a good dog, such a lonely little bitty puppy, are you happy to be inside?* and feels tears well up.

"You hungry?"

The dog wriggles free and whirls to face him, head up, whimpering. When she tries to barrow her paws onto his thighs, he pushes her off, then he digs a can of dog food from a lower cabinet, opens and spoons half of its contents onto a dinner plate. He lids the can with tin foil and sets it in the refrigerator. He's about to put the plate down on the floor but its size seems incongruous with the unprecedented act of placing it there, so he puts it at his mom's place at the table.

"Come on, girl!" He slaps the seat of his mother's chair, but the dog dances in place, whimpering, looking at him eagerly but with confusion.

"Come on, Tawny, up in the chair!" he coaches her. "Just like those poker-playing mutts, you know?"

The dog paws the seat and one hind leg claws the air helplessly, so Jeff lifts her haunches. He says, "Sit! Sit!" to make her stay seated. She drools on the table, so he moves the plate to the center.

"You can't eat yet! You have to have a bib!"

He snatches a dishtowel from the oven door, quickly folds it corner to corner.

"Okay, hold on, girl! We gotta get your napkin on!" He loops the triangle around the dog's neck and ties the ends. "Now you look just like one of those stupid yuppie retrievers with the red bandannas! Ready to eat hearty?"

He slides the plate back under her nose and she greedily chomps the food. At the other end, he sits and brings a spoonful of soup to his mouth. It's cold. The sandwich is still warm but it's too crunchy.

The dog is already finished. "Jesus, you eat fast! Haven't you ever heard of dinner conversation?"

The dog jumps from the chair and bounds to his side, where she lays her chin on his thigh.

"Go away, you beggar! You've had yours!"

He gets up to microwave his soup, and she follows him back and forth.

"Sit!"

She collapses onto the floor with her chin on her paws.

"I am fascinating, am I not?"

Nobody ever taught this poor stupid dog even simple things like sit. When his dad brought her home years ago Jeff believed she was to be his pet, but that he neither picked it out nor named it is proof his father had himself in mind as the dog's true pal. But then he left the creature here when he went to live in his condo. Tawny! A porn-star's name.

Jeff rinses his dishes and racks them in the dishwasher, but he hand-washes and dries the plate the dog used and puts it back into the cabinet.

"Hey, girl, let's go for a walk."

He puts on shoes, a long-sleeved shirt, and a wind breaker, retrieves the dog's leash from a nail by the back door and leads the dog out the front.

The sky is gray; the crisp wind bites his ears and cuts through the thin fleece of his sweat pants, and he wishes he'd put on undershorts. They walk down Edgefield, the dog tugging so forcefully at the leash that he fears she'll choke herself and he has to heel-toe at an

Olympic pace to keep up. It seems weird to be out walking your dog on a Friday afternoon when everybody's at work or school. Well, not everybody, everybody but people his dad calls the lame and lazy—drop-outs, shopping cart dudes. Mexican teenage girls married to former lo-riders and popping out a niño every year. Redneck Anglo elephants in stretch pants buying seventeen loaves of Wonder bread and lard at Kroger's. He's among them, so therefore he's of them.

He passes the 7-Eleven at Edgefield and 12th that is, he's been told, the site of the original store in the chain, but now it looks like any other 7-Eleven in a shitty neighborhood. If you're here at noon or after school, you'll see black dudes with hundred-dollar hi-tops high-fiving at the video games while *vatos* shop for anything to sniff. At the junior high a block away, weekly mini-riots between black and Chicano gangs bring police to the campus. When school lets out, teachers pace the sidewalks with walkie-talkies, keeping their eyes on vans that regularly cruise the block to dispense drugs from their windows like roach-coaches at work-sites. A shop teacher was knifed there last year by a kid who made the weapon in his class.

God Bless America! he thinks as he and Tawny pass the flagpole in front. Did Susan ever teach at a place like this? He imagines her going down the hall, smiling at students, then in a flurry of images that make him groan and furiously shake his head—being dragged into a restroom, a hand going over her mouth, a knife to her throat, a black guy no two black guys no three black guys....

He blinks back the ugly vision and turns a corner that takes him away from the school. No matter if he's in his room or outside, everything his senses encounter leads back to Susan. And to the horror of having been granted such a precious thing with her only to betray her and dirty it. Slime.

A car honks at Tawny, who, while Jeff is drifting off, decided to walk in the street, and Jeff jerks her back to the curb. They pass little frame houses in need of paint, upright bathtub Madonnas half-buried in the yards. Here mothers still hang their wash out on lines behind the houses but you can see them move about inside, no doubt keeping an eye on the many drying pairs of tiny Wrangler jeans and a hundred diapers. Nearly every house has a rusty auto in the driveway parked at the rear and hiked up on blocks like a big bug wearing boots and no socks.

The gusting wind sends wrappers and old newspapers flat against the waist-high chain link fences that protect the houses. Blowing sand prickles his cheeks. There isn't much traffic on Twelfth, but a police car goes by. Will he be picked up as a truant? Does that happen? Maybe Tawny's good cover, makes him a solid citizen.

It's weird to be doing something so different at such a different time of the day, and also disorienting, like being on a trip and staying in a strange town with relatives he hardly knows. It's weird how one small change led to so many other small changes. Life seems fearful when you imagine it as a series of small steps taken toward something without knowing you're on a path or what will happen: he didn't go to school this morning, so he wound up eating at home so he wound up eating with Tawny so he wound up taking her for a walk so he wound up on Twelfth Street, and so—what next? Get run down by a speeding taxi? Save a toddler in a house fire? Maybe that woman standing on that porch in the black cardigan with her arms crossed watching him and Tawny pass will call out, *Hey, muchacho!* and take him inside for hot chocolate. Then, on the bed, on the sofa. Not wearing panties. (It doesn't occur to Jeff that this spontaneous thought is a healthy sign that Susan's not the only woman who can inspire his lust.)

By the time he puts Tawny back in the yard and has made cocoa, the walk has proved too strenuous for the little sleep he's had. When he sits at the desk, the lift from expending energy turns into a jangly high, and it's like the first day after having the flu. Whatever wan hope sprang from his brisk walk about in the lively panorama of the outside world fades as the walls close in. The headache returns but only as a dull copy of the original. He sips the cocoa. He should study his algebra or his history, but after seeing Susan in the cafeteria, he bolted from school without his books.

From the bottom desk drawer he pulls out her scarf; he sniffs it—her cologne's so faint he almost has to imagine it, and even though he's rinsed out the stains, a pungent residue lingers. He drapes the scarf about his neck with the air of a priest donning a mantle. Sighing, he opens the cover of the large spiral bound pad. When he quit working last night he believed he had a breakthrough, really made fine progress on it. Just before going to bed, he considered ways to present it, all involving delivering it so he won't be present as she unveils it. Seeing it, she's rocked back on her heels, hands blindly groping for the chair arms as she's overpowered by the vision of his working so hard and long in lonely exile. The awe-inspiring genius displayed in it, her beautiful face. She cries, wanting him, realizing at last she shouldn't have sent him away. He couldn't have known his friend would betray him, could he?

He opens the cardboard cover and flips it to the back.

He gasps. During the night his drawing turned to crap. This woman's jaw is way too low and lumpy, and, while one eye is a squished almond, the other is a wobbly marble. The portrait is an insult to Susan's beauty.

"Awww!" he groans. He turns away, tears stinging his eyes. "God!"

This is what it's like to be a mute and be dying to tell somebody something. All he wants is draw a portrait that shows his love shining through. Is it too fucking much to ask?

Should he tear it up? Or try to salvage it?

He cants his head and peers at the portrait from a corner of his eye. He's erased on it so much he'll tear right through if he sets the rubber to it wholesale. This isn't the goddamn Sistine Chapel; he doesn't have half his life to get this right, after all!

He picks up a pencil and tries to feather in a new line above the old one along her jaw but his hand trembles; he's lost his nerve. He looks away, taking the loose ends of the scarf in his fists and jerking with a regular rhythm at his neck, absently, as his thoughts bounce to and fro.

Impossible to fix it. Impossible to toss it and start a new one.

He began it with the best of intentions and hope, full of energy and enthusiasm, and he walked himself right into a corner where he can't go forward or backward. And that corner looks dark as a nightmare: like how he was thinking about the chain of circumstances on his walk, one thing being a little different and you go to the next thing not knowing the path only goes one way. Only now it's not something simple or stupid like getting up one day and eating a different lunch and taking your dog for a walk and winding up in a Mexican woman's bed; no, now it's going to Lakeview and not fitting in and getting kicked out because you stole a credit card and going to Carver and seeing Susan in the halls the second day of school and thinking *God! She is so beautiful is she like a student who flunked or came back or something?* And thinking about her being an older sister, the older sister he's never had but always wanted, no, not like a sister, well, yes, a sister, but one who is willing to….to do sexy stuff sisters don't normally do, then learning she is actually a teacher and following her around, moonstruck, then going to that first meeting of the club, and everything that follows from that—falling, falling, falling in love for the first time, never dreaming there's this beautiful/terrible state of mind and body to inhabit.

Then losing her.

His fate fooled him: what he thought is up is really down. Dominoes, each one collapsing when the one before it goes. The chain of circumstance spirals like a burning kite toward Earth.

Damp splotches darken the thighs of his sweat-pants. He lurches from the chair and tumbles to the bed, falling face-first onto it, where he sobs into his pillow. After awhile, he needs to breathe, so he turns over and wipes his tears with Susan's scarf. He snuffles back his snot.

He breathes deeply to calm himself, but the metaphor of the downward spiral has fixed in his mind: whirlpool in the ocean. She'd be sorry if he were to drown. He can picture her getting the news that he stayed home today and is out walking on 12th Street when there's a house fire and a woman screaming that her babies are still inside, and he plunged into the flames to rescue them, brought them out and saved them, but, not knowing how many there are, went back inside, where he perished. She hears it on the radio, starts bawling, collapses to the floor in the hall at school. Later she gets the letter he started yesterday: *I'll love you forever, Susan.*

He puts himself on Twelfth Street again, this time considering not the house afire but the woman on her porch. Her hair is black, like Susan's. Is that why he thought of going inside her house? And now Susan's embracing him—it seems he didn't die in the fire, she only heard he did and believed she'd lost him, and now she clasps him to her and laughs in his ear and tugs at his belt, sobbing with joy and wanting him inside her.

He slips his hand under his sweat pants and holds his erection firmly, like a rock climber to a safety spike.

He wipes his tears on the shoulder of his shirt. He breathes more easily now. He conjures the way she looked the day he drew her at White Rock, the way she whimpered when he was inside her at Todd's; these images transform his mood like a drug, calm him; desire crowds out sadness and anxiety like a heater in a house keeping the cold outside, and he's grateful for the respite.

He twirls the scarf about in the air with one hand, letting the free end tickle his face. She kissed his chest and neck, happy to see him alive after thinking he is dead. She sat alone in her office sobbing because he is dead, he killed himself because he lost her, well, it's too late to be sorry now! She's sitting there grading exams, the phone rings, and somebody says, *Jeff's dead, killed himself,* and she says, *my God! Why? How?* And the caller says, *People say his heart was broken because some girl dumped him, and so he...*

He what?

Lately since he started driving he considered cruising down a two-lane blacktop and cocking the wheel at the last second when a supertanker comes roaring on. But unless you leave a note, nobody knows why you did it, and it's important for Susan to grieve because he did it over her. Kids up in Plano who offed themselves favored pills and pistols. He has neither. No, wait—probably in his mom's medicine chest there's something, but you don't want to miscalculate and be horribly fucked up for life. Of course, you can be like a convict and use your belt, or a rope.

Or the scarf!

He holds it over his head. His erection has softened but his skin still tingles, so he absently strokes himself with one hand until he's hard again. The scarf is the same as a letter, as good as a letter, if you make a noose out of it.

He drifts off for several minutes, letting erotic images free-float through his mind, dragging the scarf across his flesh, feeling the lovely tension grow and blank everything out. Susan posing while he sketched her, his hands on the backs of her thighs. His hands grew sweaty, his breathing and his pulse jump up a notch, and he's hot, dizzy. He moans. Nipples. Once when they were swimming in Todd's pool Paige's halter came loose and he saw a nipple standing like a pencil eraser; her cousin, from Wichita Falls, she has nice tits, that Saturday he met her with Todd and Chris, Chris talking about a kid doing that thing of cutting off your oxygen when you come...

He sits up on the bed. He knots two opposite corners of the scarf and, holding each side in a hand, yanks them to test the link. He looks about the room, then he stands, holds his sweat pants at his thighs with one hand, waddles to the closet door and swings it open.

It might be done this way—you hook the loop over the corner of the door, press your spine against the door's edge, lift yourself onto your tiptoes, slip the loop under your chin, let your weight sink.

His face blooms red and swollen, so he arches up on his toes to relieve the pressure. It can be controlled by his calves and toes. Whether you want to cut off your air to come bigger or hang yourself, it's all right there in the balls of your feet, just a little up or down.

He couldn't have said at that moment whether he fully intended one or the other. Two seemingly disparate impulses of Eros and Thanatos found themselves a mutually agreeable outlet. When Jeff thinks of Susan he's aroused, and that arousal is sweet and heady, like a fragrance from the legendary Lotus-blossoms, shutting out all else and enveloping him in a rosy glow of heightened sensation; without conscious deliberation, he draws on it, pulls it into form like so much taffy, working and kneading it, letting the images soothe him. His spine scrapes the door when the fast white flower in his scrotum rushes into bloom. His groin bursts inside out, he moans, his hips lurch and his knees shake, so he inches upright to breathe freely, head back against the door, eyes closed, gasping for breath and standing very still as if fearful of waking something asleep in the room.

His knees quiver; he's worried he might collapse and catch his throat in the noose, and he thinks that he'd better lie down. When he opens his eyes, the walls cave in; a gray light washes over the room.

Desire was all he had to keep his sadness out. The portrait lying on the desk is of someone he can't recognize. He sags, chin and throat strapped against the door, sees everything go dim. He thinks *You better unhook yourself!* But it's easier to let go.

～28～

The figure laid across Mary's lap is cold as marble and the ivory sheen of his face is striped red from the passing ambulance. The wail grows distant as it moves on to a crisis somewhere else, and the mother, her robe draped in stone like a wavy stand of stalactites, cradles her son.

In its niche of the sanctuary, the small reproduction of the *Pieta* catches Susan's eye as she kneels at her pew alone in the empty space. Lights from passing cars flare momentarily like a brass choir in the room.

Blessed Mother Mary, my sin is pride. I believed I was too smart to need you. I believed that I could stand off and look and point like a docent, not really a part of it all, Blessed Mother, and now I see the folly of that. I strayed, Blessed Mother, strayed from the Holy Church and from God and your Blessed son, our Lord Jesus Christ. Forgive me, Blessed Mary, please please forgive me! My sins are terrible, and now I see that all my learning is just so many empty words, and my pride and vanity led me to believe that I could do things without hurting myself or others because I was too smart to do something really dumb. And I made a bad confession, I didn't tell all because I was afraid. And I've been so wrong. The story of how our Lord sent Gabriel down to declare that you would bear His Son—oh, I have misunderstood it so many ways! The true meaning was always right before my eyes, but I was too willful and full of pride to acknowledge it, Blessed Virgin Mother, I was full of myself and imagined I could act without regard for the laws of man and God, and now a wonderful young man is dead, and I don't know what to do, Blessed Mother.

"Hail Mary, full of Grace, the Lord is with thee. Blessed are thou amongst women and blessed is the fruit of thy womb, Jesus. Holy Mary, Mother of God, pray for us sinners, now and at the hour of our death, Amen," Susan murmurs to the empty sanctuary. The rear door creaks open, and she turns to see another woman slipping in, sliding into the nearest pew, genuflecting, bowing her head, so Susan lowers her voice to a whisper. "Hail Mary, full of Grace, the Lord is with thee. Blessed art thou amongst women and blessed is the fruit of thy womb, Jesus. Holy Mary, Mother of God, pray for us sinners, now and at the hour of our death, Amen; Hail Mary, full of Grace, the Lord is with thee. Blessed art thou amongst women and blessed is the fruit of thy womb, Jesus. Holy Mary, Mother of God, pray for us sinners now and at the hour of our death, Amen; Hail Mary, full of Grace, the Lord is with thee. Blessed art thou amongst women and blessed is the fruit of thy womb, Jesus," she goes on, and on, as minutes add up to an hour and her knees sink millimeter by millimeter through the padding on the kneeler until her weight is on the aching caps and her thighs are trembling; she goes on until the monotony seeps like a hum into her flesh and transforms her body into a vessel dedicated to this song of supplication; she goes on until she feels hypnotized, dizzy from the chant. She prays to be forgiven; she prays for her mother and father, for their health and safety and above all for their understanding; she prays for Jeff's mother, and she prays for the Blessed Virgin Mother to intercede for Jeff and his soul, that he be granted mercy for the sin of taking his life.

She's aware of a rustle, a movement. She lifts her head, eases up off her knees and onto the pew. The woman who came in earlier is treading up the aisle to the chancel, where she bows, genuflects, lights a candle on the altar.

Susan retrieves a tissue from her jeans pocket and dabs her eyes, softly blows her nose.

Blessed Mother.

Oh how she wishes she could talk to her mother, but it would be too too hard to tell. She needs her mother now, her own personal mother, as well as the one they so flippantly called the BVM. Her mother practiced "the laying on of hands"—her mother took Susan's temperature by draping her hand across Susan's forehead; her mother finished buttoning her blouses or jumpers or zipping her snowsuits by petting her cheek and kissing her nose or mouth or forehead with a loud smack; her mother sat her in her lap and read to her; her mother hugged her good morning and good night. When they went shopping together her mother held her hand; her mother stroked her head when she brushed her hair and braided it; her mother put her arm about Susan's waist if they sat together on the couch when Susan went home holidays during college, and when she was sick, her mother would sit on the bed and hold her hand or stroke her brow; her mother napkined off her mouth for her, wiped her nose, doctored bruises, cuts, abrasions and insect stings with the poultice of kisses and bandages. Naturally, though, by the time she reached high school Susan was shying away from her mother's hands because they reached too deep into her.

Now she longs to be with her, where she can crawl into a lap and feel the arms go around her, her mother's breath on her neck, her voice in Susan's ear. In the church of her mother's arms her guilt or innocence might be irrelevant.

Oh mom I've done such a wicked wicked thing.

When she slips out of the building, traffic on Oak Lawn is heavy as usual for a late Friday night. The front doors and facade of the church are lighted like a state monument, and she scurries quickly as she can away from the floodlighted entry. On the lawn is a large and elaborate crèche: life-sized figures of Mary, Joseph, the Babe, the Wise Men, the Donkey and Camel grouped together as if for a class photo under a sturdy brush arbor built of cedar posts and boughs. In the rotund illumination of the diorama's many footlights Mary's robe is as blue as oceans seen from space.

The parking lot is almost empty. Her car stands alone under a security light in the far corner—the lot was full when she drove in. Standing beside the door fishing for the key, she's overwhelmed by a wash of grief. Let a mugger come, who would care? That poor kid, God, what was he thinking? What was he feeling? It wasn't unreasonable, was it, for her to have been so firm about the impossibility of their carrying on?

She bites the tip of a glove finger to tug the glove off her left hand, roots about in her purse for the key, unlocks the door, slips behind the driver's seat with the glove still clenched between her teeth, puts her bare left hand on the top of the door frame while thinking of her right gloved hand and needing to have it free—and swings the door shut. Even as the door comes in she has a mental flash, a warning—*move your hand!*—but some lassitude or ennui or sorrow slowing her blood holds it in place as the door slams right across her little finger.

She drives with her right hand and her left wrapped in a bloody handkerchief to Holly's apartment in a rabbit-warren complex just East of Central Expressway and off University. There, acres of block-like buildings with wood-shingle roofs set in squares around blue pools compose a haven for singles. She parks and walks up concrete stairs floating in space like ribs joined by wrought-iron spines, nightlights gathering bugs even in December because the first hard freeze has yet to come. The buildings are lighted and busy with noise, opening and shutting doors, voices and music, even though it's after midnight, and Susan is glad she doesn't live here, though who knows what the future will bring, and what is Curt doing or thinking this minute?

"Hey!" Holly, opening the door, looks mussed, a little bleary-eyed. From over her shoulder flickering candlelight halos Holly's yellow hair. "What's wrong?"

"I need to talk to somebody."

"What happened to your hand?"

"I shut the car door on it."

"How foolish! Oh, hon, come on in!"

"Even more foolish because I think I did it on purpose."

Susan enters; a young man is lounging on Holly's cloud-colored cotton sofa. The coffee table holds two empty wine bottles, an ashtray, two glasses. He rises to be polite and Holly introduces them; they nod, Susan not even hearing his name, then Holly says to Susan, "Just give me a sec, will you? There's ice in the freezer for that—"

She leads the young man outside and shuts the door.

Susan sits on the sofa's edge, numb and dumb, as if in a doctor's waiting room. She rocks. The pain in her finger is too great for her to touch this bandage, but it's a welcome relief how it utterly absorbs her attention. Outside, they are discussing her, no doubt; she's being identified to the young man, and Holly is asking to be excused from the young man's company to tend to her friend.

When Holly returns, Susan looks up. She must be weeping, because Holly rushes to the sofa and sits beside her, curls her arm about her shoulders, and Susan collapses against her; she sobs, endlessly, until, hours later it seems, she arrives at a state that feels like waking from a strange and awful dream.

"What's the matter, Suz—gosh! What happened?"

Susan plucks a Kleenex from the end table and blows her nose with one hand.

"I just found out Jeff is dead."

"My God! How awful!"

The news and Holly's response hang in the air as a brief aria in a tragedy, but then Holly's brow wriggles and Susan knows that this tragedy will turn into a sordid tabloid story.

"How? Do you know?"

"Not exactly. The police told me it could be suicide."

"Oh, wow!" Holly whispers.

Holly's "wow!" tells Susan she's in trouble. Susan sighs, leans back; the damp tissue is spongy in her tight grip. She's holding her right arm upright like a post with a bloody wadded bandage on its top. She would love a glass of wine and dimly wonders which glass was Holly's because she could drink from it.

"It gets worse."

"Somebody found out?"

"I guess. The mother is talking about pressing charges. She apparently wants to have me charged with—" she breaks off, her chin quivering. "Sexual assault of a child."

"Oh, my god! Have you called a lawyer?"

"Not yet." Curt may be working on something at home, though; she bolted from the house soon after telling him about her and Jeff. "A detective came and told us that things are still up in the air." "

"Does Curt know about you and Jeff?"

Susan nods.

"Let me make some calls," says Holly. "Let me see if I can find out exactly what's going on and see where you stand on this, okay?"

"Okay," says Susan. "Thanks."

Holly springs up and disappears, and a moment later Susan hears the murmur of her voice coming from another room. She looks at the glasses, lifts one that shows a smudge of lipstick, turns the clean side toward her, and drinks the wine remaining in one swallow. She pours herself a full glass from one bottle, even though she would have sworn both were empty when she came in. Everything seems too bright, surreal.

After taking two more swallows, she lets out her breath and sinks back against the couch, closing her eyes. She thinks *ommmm*. She concentrates on how the blood beating in her injury makes a pain pulse like a metronome: hurt/off, hurt/off, hurt/off. She took a yoga class for a few weeks and now recalls that very slow and very deep breathing can bring calm over you like a lightweight coverlet. She begins in the basement of her body and draws the air up the cellar stairs and down the hall through the first floor and up to the second floor and through her bedroom and up the narrow stairs to the attic where her father has his study and out the skylight that cranks open for ventilation. Then she is a cottonwood seed drifting back through the opened skylight and across his room and down his stairs and through her own bedroom, slowly, slowly, lifted up momentarily on the air currents then dropped, gliding down the staircase and through the kitchen and into the dark hollow of the cinderblock tunnel into the basement where once, a few years after she and her brother no longer bathed together, they inspected each other's parts, and she said, *You've got a bowling alley* and he said *you've got a banana split!*

Weird irrelevance. Except maybe the innocence: how would she have known then that today she could wind up in so much trouble?

She feels nauseated. When she opens her eyes to keep from whirling about on the sofa, she is startled: Holly has come back without Susan's hearing her. She looks different. She's wearing what looks like a man's terrycloth bathrobe, very white and long, with huge lapels and padded shoulders—the kind you see in upscale hotel rooms. On Holly's small frame the shoulders bunch up like folded wings. Her blond hair is wild and unruly and as curly as a cherub's, and her cheeks are ruddy, her mouth a rounded O like a chorister's. In the air is an odd tinkling and whirring sound, musical but tuneless, and Susan thinks it must be coming from wind chimes on somebody's balcony.

But Holly doesn't look happy. "I talked to several people. I'm afraid Jeff is dead, like you say."

"Does anybody know how it happened? I just can't believe he'd kill himself."

"Maybe it was an accident."

"Are people saying that?"

Holly stands at attention, hands clasped. She looks over Susan's shoulder, giving Susan the faint impression that she herself is not present, that Holly is oblivious to her, like the one of those Annunciation Marys hearing wings flutter at her window. Or maybe Holly too is distracted by the tinkling bells.

"Yeah, that's what they're saying," Holly says.

"What kind of accident?"

Holly shrugs as if to say *nobody knows.* After a moment, she says, "What else do you want to know?"

Susan eyes her. Whether from the shock of this experience tonight or from the wine and the wound, she feels off-balance, untrusting of her senses; Holly's form seems to vibrate minutely like something seen above a heated desert highway. Her question has an oddly oracular overtone. To Susan, the everything has an hallucinatory aura that makes her sick to her stomach.

"What can you tell me?"

Holly gives her a smile of pity and compassion. "I can tell you about Curt."

"What about Curt?" Susan's good hand curls into a fist and she steels herself, holding her breath.

"He says he'll stand beside you through the worst of this, but not for an instant longer than he has to. I think he'll be big about it for a while, but only until he's earned the right to be as small as he really wants to be."

Susan swallows, looks at Holly and wonders how she knows this.

"What else?" She feels as if she is visiting a Tarot-reader as a joke but is hoping nonetheless for an accurate forecast. "You think Curt'll stay through the worst of it. What do you think the worst will be?"

Holly stands with her face canted toward the ceiling, attentive. Her curls bob a bit with her motion then settle. The musical tinkling returns. There's a fragrance wafting in the air, spicy, woody, yet also floral - patchouli, maybe. Susan waits, feeling that she's having a dream, a very peculiar dream in which absolutely horrible events are witnessed though a scrim of awesome beauty, like the painting of The Slaughter of the Innocents she saw in Sienna.

Holly's face slowly turns back down; once again Susan receives a beatific smile of compassion. Holly glides to the sofa and settles lightly down upon it, like light down upon it, lightly like down upon it. She takes Susan's hand and presses it between her own, as if Susan is the one who needs anchoring.

"It's better if you just live it out," she says apologetically.

"Better?"

"Easier on you in the long run."

Susan hears that if she were to learn the worst, she would lack the courage to live it out.

⁓29⁓

*A*s Holly hinted, a trauma descended upon a person must be struggled with blindly, hour by hour, with only hope for a glimmer of light ahead. To achieve any measure of peace, the victim summons strength through ignorance of what will be required of her.

We move to a Sunday two years beyond that terrible Friday of Jeff's death—to an office building in Shawnee Mission, Kansas, housing what a contestant on "Wheel of Fortune" would call "a major greeting card company."

Inside we find signifiers of the season: a flocked artificial Christmas tree in the employees' lounge, sprigs of holly and wreaths, and, on office doors, hanging cardboard bells in red and gold. Susan's a card designer and researcher; she pores over slides of paintings and drawings to select images to reproduce for holidays, and today, in mid-December, the necessary lead time for production has her considering not the Nativity but the Crucifixion and Resurrection.

Most work days she wears a dark blue suit, a wool blend, under it a cream-colored blouse fastened at her throat with an slender antique bar pin. Her hair is cut above her ears. She wears no make-up. Her coworkers speculate about her over lunch. She's been here almost a year, but no one knows much about her. She's withdrawn and much too earnest, and she clutches the cards of her life close to her breast—she smiles only when smiled at, never lunches with anyone or mentions weekend plans. One coworker holds that she's a spinster living quietly with her mother; others guess that she's a closet lesbian or a defrocked nun. All would agree there's something dour and, well, not unapproachable, exactly, but *unencouraging* about her. (Of course, they've never seen her chatting merrily in front of a class of bright and spirited students.)

The smokers cluster downstairs all day in the lobby between a grove of dusty potted ficus and a trickling fountain. Susan takes a smoking break as well, but she does not join them: she steps outside no matter the temperature and they watch her pace the concrete apron before the bank of glass doors, the chilly wind ripping at her coat; she's the very picture of a person who is only servicing her addiction and enjoys absolutely nothing about it, including the Fellowship of the Addicted.

What they don't know is that she lives alone in an apartment and spends more than she can comfortably afford on counseling. Her most pressing goal is to glean useful lessons from her experience. Her first therapist, a man, once outlined this interpretation: Nathan profoundly disappointed her; in turn, she grew deeply angry at men. So she kept her distance from Curt and never "invested" in him for fear of being hurt. Naturally, this made her feel something was missing in their relationship—Curt disappointed her too, by not being what Nathan was before he betrayed her, and Curt's failure to be Nathan made her angry both at him and at herself. She shut herself off from her anger and her guilt of not returning Curt's love; shutting herself off made her feel numb, dead. She sought to resurrect herself by getting involved with Jeff (reclaim the past again), as well as punish herself and Curt by derailing their relationship.

Susan bought some of this, but the neatness, the fancy dancing, aroused her suspicion. It was all too *manly* in its directness and presumptions about human purpose. To her, motives tend to be too ambiguous to be accounted for by a narrative of such straightforward logic.

Susan's present therapist, a woman, hints that her first therapist was determined to make everything her fault. In particular, she wants Susan to let go of the idea that she caused Jeff's death. Susan *is* now mostly convinced that Jeff didn't commit suicide, and so, much of the time, she doesn't believe that she is responsible.

That weekend following Jeff's death passed in an agony of horrid anticipation as they awaited the coroner's findings. On Monday, her lawyer, Curt's old fraternity brother, discussed the case with the prosecutor's office and with the coroner, who said he discovered dried semen on the boy's leg. After reconstructing the hanging, the coroner saw that the noose could easily be released by the victim's stretching on tip-toes. "If I really meant to hang myself," he told Susan's lawyer, "I wouldn't give myself that kind of chance to take it back."

He speculated that Jeff's mother had discovered the boy's pants down and pulled them up before the ambulance arrived. He believed the boy died of accidental autoerotic asphyxiation, that he'd been experimenting with heightening his orgasm by temporarily cutting off blood to his brain. He passed out, however, and so he couldn't save himself. The coroner suspected that the mother also removed "a Playboy-type publication" that the boy probably had spread on the bed. In his opinion, she would rather have the world think her son an unhappy suicide than a pervert.

As we know, Jeff wasn't the first boy to have died from this. Susan's lawyer quickly unearthed the case in Houston where parents sued a pornographic magazine because their teenage son used a description of this act as a recipe, as it were, and died.

The cause of Jeff's death was officially listed as "accidental strangulation."

Soon after, rumors spread about the tape, and Jeff's friend and his videotaped record were subpoenaed. Jeff's mother urged the prosecutors to file charges. But since Jeff was 17, the age of consent according to the Texas Penal Code, the prosecutors in the D.A.'s office wouldn't pursue charges of sexual assault (of a minor) or "indecency with child." However, one prosecutor told Susan's lawyer that they were considering a charge of "criminally negligent homocide" (Susan's lawyer actually laughed when he told her this). Shortly thereafter, they heard the D.A.'s office was considering a charge of sexual assault with another "non-consenting" adult under the code's provisions whereby "public servants" and "mental health providers" or "clergymen" were said to be "exploiting the other person's emotional dependency."

One prosecutor suggested they were prepared to pursue on the basis of the tape as evidence. But after Susan's lawyer had viewed it, he insisted it could as easily prove the boy was the initiator and aggressor—the female depicted was for the most part on the receiving end, you could say, and though the disparity in their teacher-student relationship made "consensual" sex a complicated issue, a jury viewing the evidence would be hard pressed to say Susan "exploited" the boy's "emotional dependency."

Susan's lawyer told prosecutors that he would call the coroner to testify as to why he had not ruled it "suicide." If the prosecution were to put the mother on the stand, the defense would then cross-examine and force her to describe exactly what she had done upon discovering her son's body. Jeff's mother backed away, and the prosecutors told Susan's lawyer they would not press charges.

Susan was heart-sick; in her misery she wanted the original charge to stick; she wanted a trial that would prove her guilty; she wanted to have to cower on the witness stand and bear the howls of derision and execration from the righteous. She'd had a taste of that, but it wasn't enough. During the two-day period when she was allowed to return to the school to clean out her office and turn in her keys, she was treated as a pariah who had betrayed her profession, except for those few colleagues who preferred to act as if they knew nothing about why she was leaving, and she knew the students were talking about her behind her back.

She wanted a trial; she longed to have Jeff's mother lurch from her seat in the courtroom and pitch herself at Susan, spit on her, rake her face with her nails.

Curt saw the tape. So did Susan. And so did at least three dozen people in the prosecutor's office, including two judges and one receptionist invited to a screening by a wink from a young lawyer. Susan realized this during conversations with her lawyer, and now it's now only too easy to imagine that many of Jeff's classmates at both Lakeview and Carver have also seen it. Hundreds of strangers have observed her at her most private and vulnerable; hundreds have smirked, jeered, howled, laughed—possibly squirmed with lust—or burned with righteous indignation as she unwittingly performed for a faceless public acts that she could only do after a struggle with her inhibitions and her conscience in private.

When Susan told Curt she wished the prosecutors had found something to charge her with, he exploded. *Jesus Christ! Think of me! Don't you think this is humiliating for me to go to work with my colleagues and my clients and friends knowing you fucked one of your students? What the fuck! do you goddamn think! that's goddamn like! for me, anyway?*

Think of somebody besides your shitty-ass self, bitch!

She did. She thought of Rose Robbins. One of the last things she did before leaving Dallas was to drive to Jeff's house in Oak Cliff and sit parked at the curb on a late winter evening until Jeff's mother arrived home from work. She'd called three times before, but the woman had slammed down the phone the instant she realized who it was.

As Jeff's mother was unlocking her front door, Susan stepped onto the porch and said, "Mrs. Robbins?"

The mother whirled, startled. "You! What do *you* want?"

"I want to—"

"Haven't you done all there is to do? Haven't you! Leave us alone!"

"I'm sorry, I'm so so sorry, Mrs. Robbins, I just want you to—"

"What could you get from me you haven't already taken!? Go away!" She made spastic shooing motions with arms outflung as if trying to disperse a swarm of gnats. She started bawling and leaned with her forehead against the door frame, fists to her ears. Susan stood tearfully behind her, listening as the woman cursed Susan through her sobs. Susan wanted to offer a target for the woman's wrath as part of her penance, but when she saw the mother's devastation and how her unexpected and abrupt appearance chaffed the wound, coming there seemed selfish.

Finally the woman roused herself and worked furiously to unlock the door.

"I know you can't forgive me," Susan said. "I can't forgive myself, either."

"Oh *you!* It's not me you should worry about! You're going to roast in the flames of everlasting Hell! That's what you should worry about!"

How to deal with her humiliation is what Susan and her new therapist work on. At times she is sickened by waves of absurd paranoia when she enters her office building. She imagines that someone has sent the tape to her coworkers, and over the weekend they gathered at someone's house for a barbeque and kegger with her "movie" as the highlight. She walks the halls feeling that everyone knows her criminal history, that people are whispering about her "performance" behind her back. At her most rational, she believes this is delusional, if not obsessive and narcissistic, and she knows she's swept up her in drama the way people are self-centered about their illnesses or failures.

Her humiliation is the drain at the bottom of the pool, always drawing everything toward it, slowly, certainly.

Yet it's a friend, too. She can wear it like a shield that discourages further entry; it renders her quiet (she does not deserve to be heard) when she might choose to reveal herself and connect with someone else; it gives off the faintly repellent aura that contagious diseases do even after those afflicted are officially cured.

Her humiliation is not "the lesson learned," however; it's only a condition she lives with, like a nagging knee injury that never quite heals and causes a slight, but nonetheless noticeable, limp. Her "lesson learned" is neither universal nor absolute, but only contextual, individual, personal. The rules of conduct as a teacher prohibited her from encouraging the boy's sexual interest in her in any way. She violated them by not firmly drawing the line in their relationship, by kissing him when she shouldn't have. Her explanation to herself is that she lacked practice in the manly arts of acting upon decisions. She believes now that the path to gender equality is strewn with many an unseen obstacle, not the least of which is that acting (what her new therapist might call "being empowered") leads to consequences that you don't foresee or intend if you're not used to having results arise swiftly and directly from what you do. Wanting to soothe Jeff's wounds and being stirred by him, she literally reached out when she should have stayed, like her father, remote, aloof, self-absorbed. She was a novice in having a relationship with a man (boy) that gave her the controlling hand, and her very innocence of herself was the source of her guilt.

If she had it to do over again, she would not. She is a sadder but wiser man.

The reserve that her co-workers find so peculiar has its origins in this lesson. When you learn that you're a danger to the world not only because you're the slick highway where accidents happen but also the car careening out of control upon that highway, you become reluctant to venture out.

Given her growing understanding of herself, it seems cruel to abandon her here as she bends over a light board in her office, alone on this Sunday, with little to look forward to except an afternoon of tedious labor followed by a supper eaten alone. To say nothing of how her apartment will be dark and empty when she arrives home, a space where the only human voice will come from the television that she hears, but does not listen to, as she eats.

So we may glide forward another two years, when she'll be working in a large gallery ("a major New York art gallery") and writing reviews of exhibits for an East Village publication. More importantly, she will have married a sculptor she met through her work; he has a five-year-old son from a former marriage and an irritatingly omnipresent ex-wife. Susan will have borne their child, an infant daughter. Susan will be neither as happy as she was in her first days of teaching (or her honeymoon days with Nathan) nor as sad as she was just after Jeff's death, but her contentment with her life will slowly grow.

Thus will she be resurrected. As is mostly true of ordinary lives, this resurrection will not arrive with fanfare and a bolt of lightning, certainly, but it will have discernible, though quiet, origins. In that darkened office in Shawnee Mission, Kansas, on that cold December afternoon, we can locate the moment Susan understood it's possible to rise from the ashes.

The weather's cold, the sky cloudy and promising snow. Wearing jeans and a sweater and a down ski jacket, she comes in to work because she'd rather be in a large empty building alone than in her apartment; working in her office off-hours gives her a safe approximation of intimacy: the security guard for whom she is only one of thousands on a weekday will on a Sunday exchange a word or two about the weather as he holds the elevator door open for her, and on her floor she invariably finds other employees catching up (or avoiding their homes), and as she passes she can trade greetings with these near-strangers who may have one eye on a football game and another on a computer screen.

At her light board now, seated on a stool, she peers at slides, thinking of Easter and its attendant fixtures. Though she avoids imagery of the Crucifixion (too Catholic for the folks in marketing), she's musing about the generic imagery of affirmation, rebirth, spring. An old friend pops to mind—the Annunciation. She hasn't thought of it in some time, but she's been thinking of her childhood and of her parents, and today the two subjects strike a sudden spark across neural spaces: the Annunciation is a child's dramatization of its conception; the characters of the virgin Mother and the omnipotent, omniscient Father represent an infant's innocent (presexual) portrayal of the adults who created him or her.

Having abandoned her thesis, such thoughts are aimless and therefore pleasurable—but are also forbidden, or irrelevant, by the same token. One must push on to "real" work. She considers Botticelli's *Primavera*, but it's as diluted by overuse as Vivaldi's *Four Seasons*.

Woman, why are you weeping?

She slides from the stool, goes to the windows, turns the long rod to tilt the blinds so that the pale outside light turns the dim room gray. Her window faces south and overlooks a subdivision, where a lake and hardwood trees stand in the distance. Wisps of wood smoke rise from chimneys into a sky with a nubbled ceiling; there's little traffic on the snowy residential streets.

Woman, why are you weeping?

Saint Mary Magdalene, she thinks. She was present at the Crucifixion and burial, and when she returned on Easter morning to the tomb with two other women to anoint Jesus, the stone had been removed. Later, as she wept, two angels in white appeared where the body had been. They said, *Woman, why are you weeping?* And when Jesus arrived, those were his words also. Thinking he was the gardener, she explained that the body of Christ was missing; he told her that he was ascending to Heaven and instructed her to tell his disciples.

Later in life, she wandered in the desert? Something about a cave, living in a cave, Susan recalls. Donatello. She goes to her bookshelves and digs out Hartt's *Italian Renaissance Art*, lays the book on her desk, turns on the lamp. After a moment, she has located a large, full-color reproduction of Donatello's Mary Magdalene.

Standing over it, she feels weak and drops back into her desk chair. She saw the sculpture in the Bargello, the lean gaunt woman carved in wood, her cheeks and eyes sunken, clad in what at first appears to be rags but which on closer inspection can be recognized as a robe made of her own unshorn hair. She is a Godiva turned by disenchantment into a crone: her legs are sticks, her feet bare, her arms long and wiry, her hands upraised before her breast, fingertips almost but not quite touching. Hartt's description says, "Emaciated from her long sojourn in the desert, clothed only in the tangled mat of her own hair, this skeletal, even spectral apparition with haggard eyes shrunken cheeks and almost toothless mouth seems the very antithesis of the noble figures created by Florentine masters only a few years before...."

The woman stares toward Susan unblinkingly, her mouth partly open. Her eyes are full of pain and perhaps even bewilderment—hers is not the mystic gaze of one who has seen a great light. She is an ascetic; she has been *unwomaned* by her life—she is breastless, hipless, the tendons in her neck and along her arms prominent. She is all unpadded bone, a soul trapped in a despised human form and struggling desperately to shed it. She suffers.

Woman, why are you weeping?

Susan wants to comfort Mary Magdalene, wants to comfort the aging Donatello who, in a plague-ridden Florence, contemplated her suffering. She shares a kinship with them, a common humanity. They speak to her from across five centuries, and she feels a little less alone.

She goes to a sideboard where a tray stands with her tea fixings (brought here from her Carver office), plugs in her electric pot, and, after a moment, pours hot water into a pottery mug, drops in a bag of Constant Comment.

She holds the hot mug between prayer-cupped palms and bows her head over the spicy vapors. She goes to the window, pulls the cord to the Levellors so that the blinds vanish upward into a compressed stack. The large unshaded window now reveals her room to the world outside, and Susan imagines herself as a figure peering out of the missing wall in a doll house.

Since last she looked, the scene beyond the window has been charmingly scaled down into a toy snow-globe. Swirling flakes drift onto tiny housetops, a shiny dime of lake and the tuft of woods near the glass horizon. This fall of downy snow is contradicted only by the soundless climb of chimney smoke. Out there on the ground, snow angels made by children whisper with the voice of the world, come hither, come hither.